PRAISE FOR

STEEL CROW SAGA

"*Steel Crow Saga* is a vigorously animated novel that shifts from shade to light with the warmth of a beating heart. . . . It's about the emotional experience of confronting one's own colonization or complicity, and untangling the intersecting threads of what people owe one another after inheriting atrocity. But the real joy of *Steel Crow Saga* is in loving the characters so much that you're rooting for all of them despite their conflicting goals."

—*The New York Times Book Review*

"Plenty of magic, wonderful characters, a world that is refreshing and new . . . an epic novel."

—*SFFWorld*

"Pokémon meets *Avatar: The Last Airbender/The Legend of Korra* meets post-Colonial diaspora fantasy."

—*Book Riot*

"*Steel Crow Saga* is the best, most lovingly told, most original epic fantasy I have read in literally years. Instead of the familiar (and by now, often cliché) Fantasy Europe, this is a gloriously etched, meticulously consistent Fantasy Asia, drawing not just on one set of traditions but multiple. It's incredibly diverse, with characters drawn from all parts of the continent, and of the four leads, only one of them can really be considered 'straight.' The characters are meaningful and compelling, and the story surprised me up until the very end."

—Seanan McGuire, *New York Times* bestselling author of the October Daye series and the InCryptid series

"You want action? This book has that. You want magical animal companions? This book has that. You want colourful characters that compliment and clash against each other? You guessed it, this book has that. . . . *Steel Crow Saga* is a book that will appeal to a lot of people. There are lots of high-action scenes, plenty of heart-to-heart moments between characters, and a whole lot of magic."

—*The Fantasy Inn*

"A post-colonial fantasy that draws on Japanese, Chinese, Korean, and Filipino cultures for a multinational tale of political intrigue . . . This Asian-influenced sociopolitical drama explores the complications that ensue after the war, when no one's hands are clean. Characters face the consequences of the choices they made during the conflict and consider whether it's possible to rise above deeply ingrained prejudices and forge alliances with former enemies. Such grave matters are leavened by amusing banter, solid action, and two charming nascent romances of opposites. As tasty as the mushroom adobo that appears in the book both as food and metaphor."

—*Kirkus Reviews* (starred review)

"With a well-realized world and strong characters, many of whom are queer, Krueger's novel will feel as fast-paced and exciting as its animated influences and leave the reader longing for more. Highly recommended for any fantasy fan."

—*Booklist* (starred review)

"A heady look at postcolonial emotions, Asian cultures, and anime influences . . . a well-built magical world of warring factions."

—*Library Journal* (starred review)

"Starts with a bang and never slows down . . . Think Pokémon meets *The Golden Compass,* with plenty of original and frightening twists along the way. . . . Krueger deftly gives each character their own point of view without losing sight of the novel's central theme: We're stronger together than we are alone."

—*BookPage*

"Pokémon combined with *Avatar: The Last Airbender* . . . clever, stylish, and gloriously fun."

—Fonda Lee, author of *Jade City*

"It's only Paul Krueger's second book and already he's writing fantasy like a master. *Steel Crow Saga* is fun, funny, thrilling, heartbreaking, and, above all else, something only Krueger could've written."

—Chuck Wendig, *New York Times* bestselling author of *Wanderers*

"With fierce women, ferocious creatures, and a sophisticated twist on Pokémon meets *Avatar: The Last Airbender, Steel Crow Saga* is the fantasy epic you didn't know you needed, creating a rich new mythology and characters so real you can smell their pipe smoke and adobo."

—Delilah S. Dawson, *New York Times* bestselling author of *Star Wars: Phasma*

"Inventive, action-packed, and set in an Asian-inspired world that feels both fresh and familiar: This is a book I've always wanted but never had until now."

—S. Jae-Jones, *New York Times* bestselling author of *Wintersong* and *Shadowsong*

"You're going to love cheering for these characters as they fight for honor, love, family, and country. This world of steel and souls completely transported me. It's a hexbolt to the heart."

—Kevin Hearne, *New York Times* bestselling author of *A Plague of Giants* and The Iron Druid Chronicles

"A rollicking adventure that wears its heart on its sleeve, and a joyful ode to its anime influences."

—Emily Skrutskie, author of *Hullmetal Girls*

"An incredible voice, an amazing conflict, and a hot mess of emotions . . . Krueger has taken one earth-shattering step and a thousand stories will grow in his footprint."

—Sam Sykes, author of *Seven Blades in Black*

BY PAUL KRUEGER

Last Call at the Nightshade Lounge

Steel Crow Saga

STEEL CROW
SAGA

STEEL CROW
SAGA

PAUL KRUEGER

DEL REY
NEW YORK

2020 Del Rey Trade Paperback Edition

Published in the United States by Del Rey, an imprint of Random House, a division of Penguin Random House LLC, New York.

DEL REY and the HOUSE colophon are registered trademarks of Penguin Random House LLC.

Originally published in hardcover in the United States by Del Rey, an imprint of Random House, a division of Penguin Random House LLC, in 2019.

LIBRARY OF CONGRESS CATALOGING-IN-PUBLICATION DATA
Names: Krueger, Paul, author.
Title: Steel crow saga / Paul Krueger.
Description: New York: Del Rey, [2019]
Identifiers: LCCN 2019014522 (print) | LCCN 2019018073 (ebook) |
ISBN 9780593128237 (ebook) | ISBN 9781984800893 (trade paperback) |
ISBN 9780593156773 (international edition)
Subjects: | GSAFD: Fantasy fiction.
Classification: LCC PS3611.R843 (ebook) | LCC PS3611.R843 S74 2019 (print) |
DDC 813/.6—dc23
LC record available at https://lccn.loc.gov/2019014522

Printed in the United States of America on acid-free paper

randomhousebooks.com

246897531

Book design by Caroline Cunningham
Title and part-title background image: iStock.com/winterbee
Sigil art by Grace P. Fong

To Trung and Alyssa,
who were with me the whole way

STEEL CROW
SAGA

DIMANGAN

Dimangan heard his name and came when he was called.

He stood amid a press of people. Like him, they were all Sanbunas: children of the Sanbu Islands, and specifically of the islands' greatest port, Lisan City. Like him, they boasted beautiful dark-brown skin and hair the blue-black of a raven's breast. Like him, they wore clothes of light, loose-cut linen to protect from the city's unrelenting humidity. But unlike him, they were all moving and flashing him irritated looks, while he stood in their midst like a particularly dumb rock in a stream.

"*Mang!*" the high, loud voice called again: Tala. Small as she was, he couldn't quite pick her out in the crowd just yet, but his sister's voice was unmistakable.

He blinked and stepped back into the moment. "Sorry," he said, tipping his cap to the nearest person and sliding past them. They frowned at him as he flashed his scalp, which he'd shaved to fight the summer heat. He ignored them and hustled along. "Sorry, sorry, sorry . . ."

He jostled his way through the weekend crowd pouring in and out of the shops on either side of the street. Foot traffic was supposed to be confined to the sidewalks, but the people of Lisan City were notoriously blasé about sidewalks. The occupying Tomodanese troops and the colonial governor, the daito, had tried to crack down on this when automobiles and streetcars had first been introduced to Lisan City's roads, back when Dimangan was a kid. But even under occupation, Sanbunas were a stubborn people, and eventually the daito had realized some fights just weren't worth having.

"Hoy! Mang!" Tala called again, and at last he saw her. His little sister was ten: half a lifetime removed from his own age, and as much a surprise to his parents as she'd been to him. But while she barely came up to his waist, she carried herself with the stiffness and seriousness of a woman thrice her age and size. They shared their mother's angular face, but Dimangan could already tell she was going to grow up looking more like their father. She had his broad shoulders, his wide nose, his semi-permanent scowl.

"You're slow today," she said, cuffing him on the thigh when he finally caught up to her. "What's going on with you?"

That was his dear Lala: inconveniently sharp. "Nothing's going on with me," he tried gamely.

"You're a shitty liar," she said. There was no malice to how she said it, but the bluntness still made it sting a little.

"I don't suppose there's any point in trying to get you to mind your language," Dimangan said, sighing.

"You're shitty at changing the subject, too." She turned to scan the thick crowds. "Every time Ina and Ama send us shopping, you practically skip here. Today it feels like a full team of shades wouldn't be able to—"

"Keep your voice down," Dimangan said, casting a wary glance around. Talking about shadepacting wasn't exactly outlawed, but actually doing it was, and the Tomodanese weren't terribly discerning when it came to differentiating suspected treason from the real thing.

"There aren't any steelhounds. I already checked," Tala said, rolling her eyes. "And you're changing the subject again. Does it have to do with Aijie?"

Dimangan froze at the mention of the fruit-seller's son. Like he'd said: inconveniently sharp.

He sighed. There was no point in denying it. "I don't think he's interested in me the way I'm interested in him."

Tala waved his words away. "You have to believe in yourself more, Mang."

He looked away from her, faintly embarrassed. "No," he said carefully. "I mean, I saw him with Liwayway. She was talking with him . . . very closely." When Tala frowned up at him, he added: "As in, lip-to-lip."

Tala's eyes widened. Her expression softened a little, and then she reached up: not to cuff him, but to place her hand in his. She looked up at him thoughtfully, and then said: "He could still like boys, you know."

Dimangan burst out laughing and tugged her along. "Lala."

"It's true!" She looked a bit peevish now. "You can like both! I know kids at school who like both! They like everyone!"

"We're not talking about this now."

"I'm just saying, you haven't even *tried* . . ."

He loved that this was how his little Lala saw the world, that she truly believed getting what you wanted was just a matter of wanting it enough. Soon, Dimangan knew, she would see or experience something that would disabuse her of that notion, probably for good. He and their parents kept her as safe as they could, but with the blue mountain banners of Tomoda flying from every flagpole in the country, a day like that was all but inevitable.

He was grateful they didn't end up encountering Aijie as they went from shop to shop, filling up the two baskets Ina and Ama had sent them out with. Their final stop was the butcher's, where even the stoic Tala came out wincing at the rising price of pork. The Tomodanese, whose culture forbade eating meat, had attempted to outlaw it entirely when they'd completed their conquest of the Sanbu Islands. Steel Lord Kenjiro, a softer man as far as foreign despots went, had ultimately backed down in the face of mass unrest.

But his daughter, Steel Lord Yoshiko, was not so understanding. Rather than ban it outright, she'd instituted a climbing tax on all meat. Already, people Dimangan knew were whispering about black-market butchers, but Dimangan wasn't glad of them. Sanbunas deserved to be Sanbunas out in the open. In her weekly radio addresses, the Steel Lord spoke grandly of the civilization Tomoda was bringing to its subjects, but there was nothing civilized about this.

At the clang of a bell, the thick crowd in the street immediately parted. A black streetcar slithered through the gap left behind: sleek, shiny, with the peaked, gently concave roof that Tomodanese design favored so much. At the front and back of the car were two pairs of conductors, blue-clad Tomodanese with looks of concentration on their faces. They were metalpacting: practicing the Tomodanese art of bonding their souls to pieces of metal via touch. Dimangan wasn't completely clear on how the practice actually worked, but it was how the Tomodanese could move automobiles and streetcars and warships without engines or fuel. How their guns could fire with unerring accuracy. How their blades could sharpen themselves to absurd keenness. Metalpacting was the teeth with which Tomoda had devoured the world.

Normally, passengers would embark and disembark from the streetcar. But through its windows, Dimangan saw only soldiers. They all wore the crisp blue uniforms of the Steel Lord's army, with the narrow silhouettes, high collars, and multiple layers that all made them poorly suited to Sanbu's humid climate. The color of their jackets only accentuated their pale skin all the more, while their coarse black hair peeked out from beneath their tall blue caps. To-modanese soldiers weren't exactly an uncommon sight on the streets of Lisan City these days, but Dimangan drew Tala close to him just the same. In the depths of his gut, something suddenly didn't feel right.

At the very front of the car, he saw a pair who were out of uniform. The first was a woman in a flowing blue silk kimono, elaborately patterned with mountaintops. He couldn't see below her waist, but Dimangan knew that thrust into her kimono's sash would be the ceremonial sword that marked her as the shoto, trusted right hand to the local daito. That meant Dimangan was looking at Kishitani Yumi, one of the most dangerous and feared individuals in the Tomodanese regime. And at the moment, she appeared to be giving a lecture to an audience of one.

As she gestured with a voluminous blue sleeve at the city outside her window, Dimangan keyed in on that audience: a young boy, perhaps Tala's age, who peered curiously out at Lisan City from behind round spectacles. He wore a plain blue kimono, but despite his nondescript dress Dimangan could see deference in Kishitani's posture as she addressed the boy. Whoever he was, this small boy was a big fish.

Someone else moved into view: a tall, severe-looking woman in a lighter-blue kimono with jagged patches of white. Dimangan's eyes widened; that was the uniform of the Kobaruto, the Steel Lord's personal guard. And that meant the boy sitting by the window was—

Tala tugged on his arm. She looked concerned, but not afraid. With a decisiveness that would've made their parents swell with pride, she whispered, "We should go now."

He marshaled his disbelief and nodded, then began to steer her through the crowd and toward the side streets. Home was less than a mile from here, and he was already counting each step.

But as they pushed through, a cry arose not fifteen feet from where they stood. Women and men with green scarves and bandannas over their faces shoved through the crowd toward the shoto's streetcar. Dimangan's eyes widened as he caught sight of one: a woman whose upturned collar had slipped to reveal a bright-red tattoo on the side of her neck.

No. Not a tattoo, Dimangan realized. A pactmark.

"Lala—" he said, trying to pull his sister away, but hers wasn't the only name on the wind.

"*Niyog!*" the woman shouted, and a jet of red light issued from her hand. Onlookers threw themselves out of its way as it solidified into a creature that had once been a spotted sunda cat. But shadepacting—the creation of a bond between the souls of human and animal—had forever altered its form. The cat-shade now stood shoulder-height to its human partner. Huge tufts of golden fur erupted like flames from its four ankles, while a fifth flared from the tip of its thrashing tail. It opened a pair of huge, predatory yellow eyes . . . and then a second pair, just atop the first. Nestled amid the black spots on its long, powerful neck, a red pactmark glowed, identical to its partner's.

The other green-clad Sanbunas called the names of their shades, and their partners materialized: a visayan-shade, with antlers that bristled like speartips. A tarsier-shade, whose pacting had made its simian fists as big and spiky as durians. All told, eight had materialized on either side of the streetcar, and with a cacophony of shouts, growls, and roars, they charged for the soldiers that had begun to pour from every entrance.

The Tomodanese were disciplined fighters. Even caught unawares, they were still quick to fall into formation, shoulder their rifles, and fire. The bullets that hit the shades blew holes in their hides, which immediately crackled with magical energy and patched themselves over. But one lucky shot streaked past the charging shades and caught the woman in her chest. She crumpled to the sidewalk as her cat-shade, Niyog, disappeared in a flash of red light just before it reached the enemy lines.

The world around Dimangan turned to hell as bystanders screamed and fled, shoving and clawing to get as far away from the fighting as they could. He felt like rice in a mill, or meat in a grinder, as his body was pulled in every direction. With each gunshot that rang out, with every scream that accompanied claws and fangs sinking into flesh, the crowd worked up into a greater frenzy.

He gripped Tala's hand tighter and pulled her onward. Whatever happened, he had to get her out of here.

A pair of hands planted themselves between his shoulders and shoved him straight to the ground. *"Lala!"* he screamed as her hand tore free from his. As the first boots stepped across his back and squeezed the breath from his body, he saw a jungle of knees and shins swallow his sister whole. He tried to scream out, tried to reach for her, but he had no air, no strength. His vision swam with panic as he scrambled desperately to get out from under everyone trampling him—

And then the person just in front of him toppled over as a heavy basket of groceries swung hard into their shins. Tala swung it back the other way, screaming at the top of her lungs, and everyone near her parted, like fish around a shark. She grabbed his hand and yanked as hard as she could. "Get up, get up!" she shouted. "Come on, Mang, get up!"

His head was fuzzy from slamming into the pavement, but Dimangan forced himself back to his feet. Slouching low to avoid stray bullets, he and Tala sprinted for their lives. And as they ran—she in front, he behind—they never let go of each other again.

After four blocks, the crowds thinned out enough that they could move with relative freedom and safety. Alarms had gone up all over the neighborhood. No one dared walk in the streets now, as car after car of Tomodanese soldiers sped toward the market square. Dimangan caught the eye of one soldier as her car drove past. She glared down at him with contempt, as if he were no more than a weed she hadn't gotten around to plucking from her garden just yet. The amount of disdain she was able to muster in her expression was staggering, Dimangan thought as her car shrank into the distance.

Then he looked down and saw his sister glaring at the car's taillights with almost the exact same look in her eye.

He tugged at her hand. "Let's get home," he rasped.

She resisted his pull. "Mang," she said. "That boy in the streetcar. The one with the glasses. Who was he?"

Dimangan couldn't say for sure, since the Steel Lord forbade any photographs of the Iron Prince or Princess from being published. But unless the Steel Lord herself had been hiding in that streetcar, there was only one boy in Imperial Tomoda important enough to warrant the personal protection of the legendary Kobaruto.

"Don't worry about that," he said, pulling her along. "We can't be out here anymore."

As they walked the remaining blocks, murmurs followed and preceded them everywhere. Shell-shocked bystanders like them were telling tales to anyone they could, while old men on stoops blustered on about the state of this country.

"'Sthat damnable Erega," one of them said to the friends that had gathered on his porch.

At the mention of that name, Tala stiffened up and stopped walking. Dimangan closed his eyes, exasperated. They didn't have time for this now. He tried to tug at his sister, but she wouldn't be moved.

"Kicking up dust, starting these fights . . . and who gets hurt, neh? If she knows what's good for us, she'll turn herself in and be done with it."

"*Lala,*" Dimangan whispered urgently, "*please don't—*"

"They weren't Erega's troops," she called to the old man.

"*—do that exact thing,*" Dimangan muttered, hanging his head.

The old man, a sun-wrinkled piece of leather if Dimangan had ever seen one, turned to regard her with bemused, patronizing curiosity. "And what would you know about it, batang?" It was a diminutive—affectionate when used by family, but dismissive when it came from the lips of anyone else—and it only succeeded in raising Tala's hackles more.

"I know that Erega's the smartest general in the world, and she wouldn't just attack at midday like that," Tala said. "She's a strategist, and attacking the shoto in an open place with such low numbers isn't strategic. *And,*" she went on, to Dimangan's despair, "she wouldn't start a fight when it might put Sanbunas in danger. She's fighting for freedom for all of us. Even you, you ungrateful—"

"*Forgive us, she's very excited still!*" Dimangan called over her, forcibly steering her back on their way. The old man hurled insults at their backs as they walked on, but Dimangan didn't care about the opinions of the old. As far as he was concerned, it had been their job to fight for his and Tala's freedom, and they'd failed. Better to let the man have his words while he waited to die.

"You should know better," Dimangan hissed, briefly pinching Tala's upper arm tight as a reprimand. "You can't just talk about Erega like that. People are listening." The woman had been Sanbuna gentry, and for a long time she'd been the rumored mastermind of the local resistance. But with the anti-Tomodanese uprisings in Dahal and Shang, she had stepped up her operations and openly identified herself as an enemy of the Mountain Throne. In the Sanbuna sphere of Imperial Tomoda, she was now public enemy number one.

"People need to listen," Tala said. "Erega isn't a rebel; she's a revolutionary. And someday I'm going to pact with a shade of my own and join her."

When Tala had been two or three, Dimangan had tried it himself. He'd read the old texts on shadepacting and tried it in secret with animal after animal. After his fifth or sixth try, he'd realized that he just didn't have the affinity. He'd told himself not to be embarrassed about it; in the old days, boys like him would've had teachers and masters to help him with this, part of the proud tradition of shade-pacting schools that Tomoda had eradicated. He'd made peace with it, even.

But his heart broke a little to hear Tala so set on the same thing. For all his desire to preserve her childhood and innocence, he was starting to think that perhaps it had departed long ago, and he'd just failed to notice.

"Please keep your voice down when you talk that way," he said, as earnestly as he could. "By the time you're a woman grown, maybe we'll already be free. And if we're not . . . please think about the other things you could do to help our people instead, Lala. Let me protect you."

Tala stared up at him for a long moment, serious beyond her mere ten years. And then she smiled—so rare a sight, that was—and shook her head. "No, Mang. You're my kuya, and I love you. But the one who'll do all the protecting here . . . that'll be me."

The fissure in Dimangan's heart cracked open another inch. But then he found his resolve and, like liquid steel, poured it into that gap. In time, he knew, that resolve would cool and harden, and the machine it had welded together would have one purpose: to ensure that Tala would come of age in a nation where she was free, and that she wouldn't have to fight to secure her place in it.

He would come back to this marketplace tomorrow, he promised himself. And at a moment when he was certain the wrong eyes were turned away from him, he would buy himself a green bandanna.

PART ONE

· · ·

SHADE AND STEEL

CHAPTER ONE

LEE

This wasn't Lee Yeon-Ji's first time in a jail cell, but unless the executioner changed their mind, it was looking to be her last.

The kingdom of Shang had never expected much from women like Lee, and she'd never expected a whole lot from Shang, either. All she'd ever wanted was enough room to slip about, pulling the small jobs and scams that had always kept her stomach and her pockets . . . well, not full, but at least more than empty. That'd been easy enough to manage during the Tomodanese occupation, and she figured it should have been even easier now that the Shang kingdom was rebuilding itself. For the most part, she'd even been right.

She just hadn't accounted for the depths to which some people would stoop to be a prick.

She didn't bother getting to her feet as two officers appeared beyond the bars of her cell. They were a tall woman and a short man, in scarlet guard uniforms of fine Shang wool. The tall guard rattled the cell's bars with her baton. "On your—"

"—feet?" Lee said, with a quirk of her eyebrow. It was thin and long and sharp, like the rest of her face, like the rest of her everything. "That was what you were going to say, right? Figured I'd save you some breath, considering you Shang are about to save me a lot of mine."

"Mouth off all you want," said the short guard. "See what kind of mercy that gets you."

"Oh, come on," Lee pouted. "Could you convict and execute a face like this?"

The tall guard sneered. "Get on your feet, or I'll summon my shade and leave it in there with you. You're just a dogfucker. I wouldn't even get in trouble."

There was a time when the slur *dogfucker* would have hurt Lee's feelings. But for any of the thousands of Jeongsonese living in Shang, that particular slur lost its impact by their third birthday. And Lee was a good eighteen years removed from her third birthday; she barely even registered the term now.

So in the face of the woman's threat, Lee just shrugged. "Fuck it. Go ahead. If your shade's a dog, I'd probably find a way to enjoy myself." The thought of actually fucking a dog made her skin crawl. But if these puffed-up Shang were dead set on seeing her as nothing more than a dogfucker, why not play the role to the hilt on her way off the stage?

The woman was unamused by Lee's performance. "You don't want me to do that, girl. She bites." She held up a hand, which was missing its last two fingers.

Lee considered pointing out it was extremely unlikely that the shade had done that, since shades were supposed to contain part of their human partner's soul, and vice versa. But rather than annoy this guard who'd just as soon do the executioner's job for them, she sighed and stood at last. "Lead the way, Officers," she said, and let them take her on one last walk through the Kennel.

The prison hadn't always been called the Kennel. Under Tomodanese control, it had been called Fort Asanuma, after the daito who'd once ruled Jungshao. And before that, in the days of the first Shang kingdom, it had been called the Temple of Justice. Even now, with Tomoda defeated and Shang ascendant once more, it had just been renamed Jungshao Prison. But the locals on both sides of the bars called it the Kennel, and who was Lee to argue with custom?

Besides, in her book there were worse things to be compared to than a dog.

The Kennel's corridors were open air, the cellblocks forming separate buildings within a larger courtyard. This meant her cell got sunlight most days, but today there were only thick gray clouds and a thin, steady drizzle. The rain collected between the slate tiles underfoot, and they sloshed faintly with each step Lee took toward her impending death.

Some of her fellow inmates sat in their cells and stared at their feet as she passed, slouching like beaten circus animals. Others shouted things at her: Obscenities. Jeers about the gibbet that awaited her. Variations on the same four slurs she'd been hearing her whole life. She found it easy to ignore them all. Her stay in the Kennel had been so brief that if she were a man, she wouldn't have even had the time to grow decent stubble.

Right by the front gates of the prison stood a gibbet. On one end of it was a high gallows and a trapdoor; on the other, a polished wooden block whose surface was slick with rain. This was the custom in Shang: that condemned citizens would be allowed to take ownership of their death by choosing how they got to make their exit. Lee just wished Shang custom included options like "drowning yourself in soju" or "death by a thousand naked women."

A few prison guards were there to oversee the execution. A white-robed executioner stood atop the gibbet, leaning on a huge, heavy saber. And waiting at the foot of the stairs was the strikingly handsome Magistrate How, arguably the most powerful man in the newly liberated province of Jungshao. He hadn't been the first enemy Lee had made in her life, but apparently he was going to be the last.

Lee smiled mirthlessly to herself. He'd come to see her off personally. How thoughtful of him.

A squat woman fell into step next to her: Warden Qu. She looked oddly at home in the rain, but perhaps it only seemed that way because of her toadlike appearance. "What will it be, Lee?" she said. "The rope or the blade?"

"Don't suppose you'd let me order off the menu?" Lee said. She kept her tone even, but her traitor heart started to race as she eyed her two choices. It'd been easy to remain cool and detached before now, hiding behind smirks, snark, and silence. But you couldn't exactly smile your way out from under the shadow of a gibbet.

"You're hardly the first guest to make that comment." The warden sighed. She always referred to the inmates as guests, as if they were all friends bunking together at a roadside inn. "Have you made your choice?"

Lee did the math. Escape was impossible. If she made a break for it, they'd either shoot her or sic their shades on her. And it wasn't like she had one of her own to summon; her native Jeongson was a vassal state of Shang, and only Shang-born citizens were allowed to know the secrets of shadepacting. Not that the steelhounds had been better, the bastards. Some of the Jeongsonese had actually welcomed Tomoda when they'd first arrived on Shang's shores, eager to see their oppressors given a taste of their own medicine. But as far as overlords went, the Tomodanese had been more of a lateral move than an upgrade.

She sighed, as if choosing the manner of her death were little more than an annoying household chore. "Sword," she said. "Any chance he can warm it up before he swings it? My neck's cold."

The warden rolled her eyes, then waddled over to the gibbet to let the executioner know. Lee prepared to follow her up the stairs, but the magistrate held up a hand. "A moment," he said in the bouncy tones typical of Shang's public servants.

"You mind, Magistrate?" Lee said. No point in observing pleasantries now. "I'm kind of in the middle of something."

"I just wanted to remind you," said Magistrate How, "that everyone has their betters, and this is what happens when you test them. There's a natural order to things, and Heaven forbids that it be upset."

Lee shrugged. "I'll lodge a complaint when I get there. Get right to the heart of the matter."

Magistrate How, born pale enough, went even paler.

"What?" said Lee. "Can't stomach a friendly chat in the rain?"

All the color had drained from the magistrate's face. Lee could practically see the veins and capillaries in his cheeks. "How dare you!" he shrieked, then slapped her across the face. He didn't have a lot of strength in him, but he had a lot of rings on his fingers, and they stung fiercely when they connected with her cheekbones.

The warden came running. "Magistrate How!" she said. "What—?"

"Don't mind him," Lee said. "The man's just venting his spleen. I'll have me that sword now."

Magistrate How scoffed. "As if I'd ever allow you a clean death," he said, his imperious tones back in full force. "Warden, executioner, you shall hang her!"

The warden shook her head. "Apologies, Magistrate," she said. "The law's clear: We must honor her choice of the sword."

"I am the law," the magistrate said, rounding on her. "I have been appointed by His Most August Personage the Crane Emperor himself. If I say I want her hanged, I will have her hanged." Seeing him carry on, it surprised Lee how much the right kind of sneer could unmake even the handsomest face.

Warden Qu shot an apologetic look Lee's way, then cupped a hand to her mouth. "Bring the rope!"

As the executioner fitted Lee for the noose, the warden read aloud the final rites. There was a promise in there to clean her bones and return them to whatever kin she had left in Danggae, but Lee figured they'd just as soon heave her into a ditch. That was just as well, honestly; the way she and her family had left things, there was a good chance that, on receiving her bones, they would've done the exact same thing.

She sighed. She'd never appreciated how useful the sigh was as a communication tool, and now she was trying to savor the last few she had left in her.

"Do you have any final words?" Warden Qu said.

Lee mulled it over a moment. At last, she settled on what she wanted to say, and opened her mouth to speak. "I—"

"Would anyone mind terribly if I speak for the incipient deceased?" called a new voice. As one, every head turned to see its owner striding up cheerfully through the rain. She was a small woman, wearing a high-collared white coat that was a bit short in the tail but overlong in the sleeves. Her trousers billowed like skirts. Her white trilby hat sloped low onto her forehead, covering her left eye. In fact, nothing she wore appeared to fit her right, except for her shiny new boots. These individual aspects of her appearance were all off-kilter, but somehow they blended into a whole that Lee found surprisingly appealing.

The warden started. "I don't know how you got in here, madam," she said, signaling to the guards. "But you have no business staying."

"In point of fact, this shiny badge here says I have business wherever I so please," the newcomer said. Her hand plunged into the depths of her coat, and from it she withdrew . . . well, a shiny badge, in the distinctive shape of a bronze pentagon.

"I don't care what your badge says!" said Magistrate How. "I am the law here, not some upjumped lapdog of the Snow-Feather Throne, or—"

Lee cracked a genuine smile of recognition, if not disbelief. "An inspector of the Li-Quan."

The Li-Quan. Shang's highest police, who directly enforced the will of the Crane Emperor. There weren't that many Li-Quan these days, since Shang was only just getting back on its feet in the wake of the Peony Revolution, but the few that still existed were able to operate with complete unilateral authority.

Warden Qu pressed her fists knuckle-to-knuckle, then offered them forward with a bow. "Apologies. An agent of the Snow-Feather Throne will of course have our full cooperation."

"I've the fullest confidence of that," said the newcomer cheerfully. "And to you, Lee Yeon-Ji, I apologize for stealing the spotlight during your big moment. I promise, we'll return to the matter of your death shortly. But first, I would like to tell everyone here a story."

"Once upon a time," she began, "there was a young woman named Lee Yeon-Ji. Say," she added in mock surprise, "that sounds an awful lot like your name!"

The magistrate seethed. His cheeks were burning so red, it was a wonder the rain didn't steam off his face. "Can we please move it along . . . Inspector?"

"I'm afraid not," the inspector said gravely, before brightening up and plowing on with her story. "Now, thanks to the marginalized position of the Jeongsonese people in the fabric of Shang society, Lee

Yeon-Ji didn't grow up with many opportunities. She had to do what she could to survive. That meant a little graft and petty thievery, but never anything that drastically disturbed the Crane Emperor's peace. So on one such endeavor, she opted to go into business with a Shang man named Zheng Lok. Is that right?"

Lee had no idea what to expect of this oddball, but every second she was talking was a moment Lee wasn't hanging from a gibbet. "He went by Lefty when I knew him."

The newcomer brightened. "*Lefty*. How folksy. I *love* it. Now, when their business was concluded, Lefty did something very stupid: He attempted to abscond with Lee's half of their ill-gotten gains— a sum of six hundred yuan, if I'm not mistaken."

Lee nodded to let her know that she was not.

"He was quite astute in the way he went about it," said the inspector. "He took great care to leave no trail or word of where he'd gone, and arranged his departure to happen in such a way that Lee wouldn't even notice what had happened until he was already long gone. But that didn't change the fact that what Lefty had done was very, very stupid indeed.

"You see, it didn't matter that Lefty had only left behind the barest of clues that he'd ever been in Lee's life at all. Because Lee took the tiniest shreds of evidence, and from them was able to unerringly track Lefty here to Jungshao. But there was a problem: When she arrived in town, she discovered that her erstwhile comrade Lefty had run afoul of some of the local toughs, who it turned out were involved in a rather lucrative ring of illegal organ-selling and had been looking to . . . expand their inventory."

"But the magistrate oversaw this case personally," Warden Qu said. The man himself looked deeply uncomfortable where he stood. "The evidence presented a clear case for Lee Yeon-Ji's guilt in this despicable criminal enterprise."

"Yes, well, that's our infallible justice system for you," said the inspector airily. "It finds the guilty party each time, and sentences them justly. Why, you could say the only way our justice system would ever fail someone would be if one of our own magistrates were to commit a crime, pin it on a convenient innocent, and then handle the case personally to ensure things went his way. But," she added as her smile suddenly gained an edge, "that wouldn't be possible, would it?"

She took a step up onto the scaffold, toward the magistrate. He yelped a little and visibly shrank from her. "If something like that were to happen," the inspector said with theatrical thoughtfulness, "it would almost certainly attract the attention of . . . well, of the Li-Quan, I suppose. Don't you agree, Magist—oh look, he's running."

Magistrate How had leapt off the scaffolding and immediately taken off at a clumsy dash. "Open the gate!" he shrieked to the attending guards. He didn't seem terribly athletic to begin with, but his ceremonial robes were laden down with rainwater, and that definitely wasn't helping him. "Open the gate and get me away from this corrupt, raving, clearly insane—"

The guards milled around in confusion. The warden sputtered like a cheap Dahali motorbike. Even the executioner seemed to be at a loss for what to do next. Only two people were calm: Lee and the inspector.

Lee nodded to his retreating figure. "Looks like he's getting away."

The inspector's smile was as lopsided as her hat. "I would dispute your observation." She brought her fingers to her mouth and whistled. It was high and piercing, and Lee marveled such a loud noise could come from someone so small. She frowned. What was this woman thinking—that the magistrate would just turn around at the noise and come back like a dog?

But just before the magistrate could make it to the gate, the tiles in front of his feet exploded up from the ground. The warden gave a high-pitched squeal as a spray of dirt and water blew him off his feet. And into sight scurried a rat-shade the size of a large dog, or even a small pony. Its fur looked to be bright white, though at the moment it was matted with brown mud. In the gloom, one eye glinted pink, like a chunk of tourmaline set in its skull. In the other, a plain white eye bore a black pactmark: a square divided into quarters, like a windowpane.

But of course, the real eye-catchers were its large yellow teeth.

"Bring him here, Kou!" the inspector said as calmly as if she were directing laborers hanging a painting. In reply, the rat-shade lunged straight for the screaming magistrate, clamped its jaws around his leg, and scurried back toward the gibbet.

Lee noted that the rat-shade was not particularly delicate about how it dragged the magistrate across the courtyard's stony floor.

"This is an insult!" the magistrate howled. He pointed a narrow finger at the inspector. "I challenge you to gui juedou for my freedom!"

The woman grinned. Lee got the impression she'd been hoping he'd say that. And for a moment, Lee thought she was about to witness an impromptu honor duel.

But then the inspector said, "The rite of gui juedou is forfeit when an agent of the Li-Quan gets involved. But challenge me anyway, and be twice humiliated in the doing. Now do me the courtesy of being quiet, or I shall have Kou ensure your silence myself."

The magistrate shut up.

"Warden Qu," the inspector said, reaching into her coat again. She pulled out a thick envelope and tossed it to the warden. But the throw was clumsy, and the envelope landed in a puddle well short of the warden. The inspector kept her voice smooth and even, but Lee didn't miss the color that crept up to her eartips. "In here, you'll find irrefutable proof that Magistrate How is an organ smuggler and salesman. That should be enough to free Madam Lee."

Qu picked up the envelope, blinking numbly at it. "In a sense, yes," she said faintly. "But there's due process to go through, and a magistrate would need to sign off on it. I could dial up the neighboring magistrate, but it would take at least two days to get release papers to them, and another two days for those papers to return with their signature."

Lee thought about it for a moment, then said, "You don't need their signature to release me," she said. She eyed the inspector carefully, wondering if she had the right measure of the woman. Then she rolled the dice and continued: "You see, I'm an agent of the Li-Quan."

It took half a second for the inspector's surprise to bleed into a mischievous smile.

The warden already looked flustered enough. Now she seemed all but beside herself. "What?" she said, her head snapping up to her prisoner. "No, you're not! You're . . . you're . . ."

"Jeongsonese?" said the inspector. "Very observant of you, Warden. Who better to travel around Shang, conducting, ah, business for the throne, than someone the world will go out of its way to overlook?"

Lee didn't smile, but it was a very near thing.

"The fact is, Lee Yeon-Ji is one of the Li-Quan's finest agents both in spite of and because of her heritage, and the one I'm proud to call my partner. I had her embedded here for a long-term sting operation meant to entrap our illustrious former magistrate over there." The inspector gestured toward How, who was screaming and squirming ineffectually as he tried to escape the rat-shade waiting patiently for a command.

Warden Qu's mouth worked up and down furiously. "I—but this—if this is true, why didn't you say anything?"

"And break my cover?" Lee said. "No. I couldn't. Not until I had How right where we wanted him."

Qu looked both furious and horrified. *"You were about to be hanged."*

"And did I ever look rattled to you?" said Lee.

"Of course she didn't," the inspector said pleasantly. "Because she knew her partner was about to ride in and close this case for good. Now, if you'd be so kind as to send some of your guards to collect my partner's personal effects, we'll be on our way . . ."

Lee shook her head. "Not just yet."

The warden and the inspector both turned to look at her: Qu with exasperation, the newcomer with amusement.

Lee pointed down at Magistrate How, crushed as he was under the weight of a giant rat. "That bastard owes me six hundred yuan."

"You're quite fun," the inspector said once they were alone. Specifically, they were in the back of a car that had been waiting for them outside the gates of the Kennel, with a glass partition between them and the driver. "Quick on your feet, too." She reached into the folds of her coat and produced a large wooden pipe, which she sparked with a slender silver lighter. She leaned back in her seat, sighing smoke. "Your file didn't do you justice."

Lee supposed she was flattered to learn she had a file at all. She sprawled out, luxuriating in her old clothes: a fitted black dress with half sleeves and a surprising number of pockets, and tall, chapped black boots that began where her hem ended. After a few days in ill-fitting prison robes, it was nice to be in something practical again. "I'm just curious," she said. "I like to do things and see what happens."

The lighter flame danced in the inspector's one visible eye. "Like a cat pushing a glass off a table."

"I guess. More of a dog person, myself," said Lee. "So, what can I do for you . . . Princess?"

To her credit, the inspector didn't react, save to snuff out her lighter. "I fear you have the wrong idea of me, Lee. The Li-Quan serves the royal family. We're not part of it."

"The Li-Quan on the whole's not," Lee said, "but you are."

"You saw my shade mere moments ago," the inspector said. "Members of the royal family exclusively pact with white cranes, a class of creature to which Kou could hardly claim kinship."

"I saw him. He was white enough. Every cop I ever met goes out of their way to look respectable. You look like your mother's clothes trunk ate you and shat you back out. But you're not a fashion victim, because you've still got boots that're good for walking and running. To me, that all means you don't mind your authority being questionable, because you've got something other than just your badge to fall back on if you really need."

"Like my badge?"

"Give me an afternoon, an awl, and an old tin can, and I'd come up with a badge," Lee said. "Whatever you're leaning on, it's something you can't forget in your other coat."

The inspector chuckled. "That theory has an awful lot of guesswork."

"If it leads me to the right place," said Lee, "does it really matter?"

"I suppose not." She removed her hat, allowing her hair to fall freely around her face. Lee was struck by how young this girl was.

She herself was barely twenty-one years old, and this girl was perhaps two years behind her. "You have the honor of addressing . . ." She sighed and rolled her right eye, as a stray bang had fallen to cover her left. ". . . Shang Xiulan, Twenty-Eighth Princess, the . . ." She sighed again, and shuddered. ". . . *Lady of Moonlight.*"

Now it was Lee's turn not to react. "Twenty-Eighth Princess" meant she was twenty-eighth in line for the throne, and likely the daughter of one of the less favored Crane Wives. But a lesser princess was still a princess. She guessed a bow was probably in order, so she inclined her head. "Your Majesty," she said. She didn't remember if that was the proper form of address for royals. She'd never really encountered one in the wild before.

"Oh, enough with that," said Xiulan with an irritated wave. "Do you have any idea how hard it would be for me to operate if everyone was bowing and scraping after me everywhere I went? Just call me Xiulan."

"I guess I should," Lee said. She held up a fifty-yuan note to the light, mostly to give her restless hands something to do. "Seeing how we're partners."

Xiulan laughed. "That was a fun little bit of theater, wasn't it? The look on her face . . ."

"Yeah, I hope all the stress gives her an ulcer or something," said Lee. "But that does bring me back to my first question: What does a fancy-pants Daughter of the Crane who can't throw want with a gutter dog like me?"

"I have many ambitions and goals," said Xiulan, bristling slightly. "Throwing things has never been essential to their accomplishment. Simply put: I need to find somebody. Specifically, Iron Prince Jimuro of the former Tomodanese Empire, son of the late Steel Lord Yoshiko and heir to the throne."

Lee raised an eyebrow. "He's still locked up in Sanbu, isn't he? Case closed. Who do I bill?"

"He was. He's due to be moved back to Tomoda, so he can ascend the throne at Hagane and negotiate a future on behalf of his beleaguered and defeated people." Xiulan cocked her head curiously. "How does that make you feel?"

Lee shrugged. "I've got no love for the Tomodanese, but I doubt it'll improve my lot in life much whether his ass polishes the throne or not."

"I, too, harbor some animosity for the Tomodanese," said Xiulan. "But let me then ask: How do you feel about the House of Shang?"

Lee's expression darkened. She eyed her new companion carefully.

Xiulan seemed to understand. "You have my word as a princess that you can speak freely without fear of reprisal or repercussion."

"You don't survive a life like mine if you haven't got a fear of repercussions," Lee said. "But fine, since you asked nicely: You're a bunch of inbred fucks who've beaten down my country so badly it'll never be able to stand on its own again, and kicked my people so much that even if you gave us our country back, we wouldn't know what to do with it anymore. Going from you, to the Tomodanese, and then back to you . . . it's like we're that pipe of yours, getting passed around. You light us on fire, and then you suck everything valuable out of us. Doesn't matter whose lips and lungs are doing the sucking." She thought a moment, then added: ". . . Your Majesty."

Xiulan blinked.

"Well," she said after a second, "I suppose that wasn't . . ." She swallowed. ". . . unwarranted." She took another pull from her pipe. "My father is an old man whose health was sapped by the long war for our freedom. All his eligible successors are quite young. Whomever he chooses as First Princess or Prince would be the chief architect of a reborn Shang. Every one of his children knows this, and they're all vying to be repositioned in first."

"I see," Lee said. "So you think you should be number one, do you? And you want me to help you find Iron Prince Jimuro before he gets to Hagane and ascends?"

Xiulan didn't even shrug the accusation off, and Lee found herself charmed by how unabashed the other woman was. "I would be an excellent ruler. Why do you think I joined a law enforcement agency instead of sitting in a palace all day and having plum cakes gently lowered into my mouth?"

"Probably 'cause you're dead stupid," Lee said. By the time she realized what a daft thing that was to say to a princess, it was already too late.

Xiulan's demeanor remained pleasant, but now a thin layer of frost had formed over it. "Careful, Lee Yeon-Ji," she said, her gaze fixed as she took a long pull from her pipe. "I enjoy you, but proceed with caution."

Lee had mouthed off to magistrates, wardens, and crime bosses aplenty. She'd figured royalty was just like the rest, except they had fancy chairs. But this princess had made her hair stand on end in a way no one else ever had. She shut her trap.

After a moment's silence, Xiulan continued: "A Sanbuna fleet set sail from Lisan City last week, and its flagship was widely reported to be carrying Iron Prince Jimuro aboard. My sister, Second Princess Ruomei, has hired a fleet of her own to meet it on its way and ensure Jimuro never makes it home. Her success would undoubtedly ensure her ascension to the throne, which would be . . ." She pulled a face. "I wouldn't care for such an eventuality, and you wouldn't, either."

It sounded to Lee like Xiulan had come to the wrong place, and she was about to point that out. But then she caught the princess's wording: "widely reported to be carrying." "You don't think he's there."

Just like that, the frost melted. "I think General Erega is far too cunning to play such a delicate matter so broadly," Xiulan said excitedly. She looked like she'd been dying to have someone to talk about this with. "I think all our attention is being carefully diverted elsewhere so the prince can be moved secretly and safely."

Lee frowned. "Why bother with all that?"

"As admirable a figure as the Typhoon General is, her newborn republic is built on quicksand," Xiulan said. "It lacks the long, proud history that makes the Shang dynasty strong. The Li-Quan's informants within the republic tell me all her advisers and underlings are constantly undercutting one another and leaking information to the Sanbuna press. If a foreign power didn't step up to eliminate the Iron Prince, it's likely one of those untrustworthy subordinates might take matters into their own hands. Hence: a covert operation with minimal logistical support . . . but minimal oversight."

"Doesn't sound like much of an operation," Lee sniffed. "More like a big, fat gamble."

"To be fair, I too am, ah, playing the odds here," Xiulan said delicately. "The Li-Quan's information has its limits. But what data points we do possess, I've studied quite closely. I've applied similar scrutiny to General Erega, for that matter. My conclusion: One does not overthrow an entire empire by pursuing the first, most obvious course of action when the eyes of the world are upon you."

Lee frowned a little. That wasn't the most encouraging thing to hear. "I'm guessing you don't want your sister to find him first," she said. "So why not just let General Erega do her thing? She gets the prince to Tomoda, he takes the throne, and your sister doesn't look any better for it."

"I will not put the future of Shang in the hands of the Republic of Sanbu," said Xiulan. "Shang should determine Shang's future, and Shang alone. It's my wish to find and capture Iron Prince Jimuro personally, and present him to my father as a diplomatic puppet. And when he allows me to ascend to the rank of First Princess as my reward, I will be free to, among other things, begin paying restitution to Jeongson and its people."

Lee's eyebrows rose. She'd never been much of a nationalist— a rather natural side effect of never having a nation to call her own. But assuming this wasn't just some birdshit the Shang were shoveling, a lot of opportunities had just opened up.

Still, life had taught her many times over that desperation was never the way to get what you wanted.

"So, what's all this got to do with me, then?" Lee said. "You want me to find him for you? Finding Lefty was one thing, but I knew Lefty. This Iron Prince, I know about as well as I know you."

Xiulan didn't seem daunted by this. "Prior to all this business, you and your confederate Lefty were responsible for the ransacking of Daito Arishima's estate in the province of Guakong, were you not?"

Lee folded her arms over her chest. "Prove it."

"Rest assured that I could if I truly needed to, or I wouldn't have gone to the effort of seeking you out." She puffed again on her pipe.

"A fact of which you may not be aware is that the late Steel Lord took great pains to conceal the appearances of her children, as they were both serving in the Tomodanese military. Photographs of the Iron Prince and Princess were strictly forbidden, save for ones the Li-Quan knows to have been gifted to close friends of the Mountain Throne . . ."

"Like Daito Arishima," Lee finished, catching on.

"Most Tomodanese highborns were good about destroying sensitive documents in anticipation of their capture. But the Li-Quan has located enough files that can be traced back to the Arishima household to conclude that he didn't have time to properly dispose of them."

"Right, got it," Lee said. "You don't know what the guy looks like, and you're looking for the photograph of him I found. That about cover it?"

"You're pleasingly shrewd, Lee Yeon-Ji."

For a second, Lee sized up her options. There was definitely a way to string this slumming princess along. But even as Lee started to form that plan, she hesitated. The earnest hunger on the princess's face was exactly what she looked for in a potential mark. But this woman had also saved her life. And she'd talked about helping out Lee's people, which was more than Lee had ever heard from any other Shang she'd met.

And honestly, that earnestness was its own kind of charming.

"I lost the photo," she said. "Hard to keep ahold of things, with the way I live." Xiulan's entire body slumped with disappointment. "But that doesn't mean I've forgotten what the Iron Prince looks like." The princess perked back up. "If you're looking to go after him, I can help."

Just like that, Xiulan was practically bouncing in her seat again. "Truly excellent news!" she said, before her enthusiasm dimmed a degree. "But I imagine your help, without which I cannot proceed on my mission, will come at a steep cost, yes?"

"A cost ain't steep if it's worth what you get back," said Lee. "Now, that bit you said about helping the Jeongsonese people . . . that's nice and all, but it's a long-term investment. I've never had the luxury of a guaranteed long term, though. I help you do this thing, and what do I get out of it?"

The light in Xiulan's eye changed. Her pipe drooped in her mouth.

"Disappointed, are you?" said Lee. "Hoping I'd be civic-minded and come along on this trip just for the virtue of the cause? You said you read my file, so let me ask: Did it ever say in there that virtue was what kept my stomach full? That patriotism ever kept my head out of the rain?"

Xiulan's shoulders slumped. Lee felt a twinge of sympathy for her, then immediately tamped it down. *Easy, Lee,* she thought. *Don't go soft just because she's got good cheekbones.*

She didn't need Lee's sympathy. She was a princess. She already had everything.

"Name it," Xiulan said after a moment. "What is the price for your help? To the best of my ability, I'll provide it."

Lee didn't have to think about it, but for appearances' sake she pretended to for a few moments before answering.

"I want a fat government salary," she said eventually. "Maybe a nice new dress, the blacker the better."

Xiulan raised an eyebrow, amused. "Is that all?"

Lee shook her head, then leaned forward hungrily. "And I want me a shade."

CHAPTER TWO

TALA

The *Marlin* carved a wake across the ocean like chalk on a slate. The wooden ship bore no sails or engine, or even oars. Instead, just beneath the surface of the waves swam a massive shark-shade, pulling the ship by the thick cables spilling over the *Marlin*'s fore. Every so often, the creature would drift closer to the surface and its human-sized dorsal fin would stab up at the twilight sky before slipping back below the blue.

The *Marlin* was as sturdy a vessel as any in the Sanbuna fleet, though Sergeant Tala had more than a few misgivings about the constant creaking of its floorboards. Unlike the steel ships of Tomoda or the ironclads of Shang and Dahal, the *Marlin* was made in the traditional Sanbuna way: entirely of wood. The ship was a majestic sight, the kind that would have inspired Tala's seafaring ancestors to song and verse. But the wood construction wasn't just about piety for the history of the Sanbu Islands. It was a necessary precaution, given the ship's cargo.

So all Tala could do was grip the wooden railing of the *Marlin* as she glowered at the horizon, and at the shades-forsaken isle that lay somewhere beyond it.

Tala commanded the 13-52-2: the Second Platoon, Fifty-Second

Company, Thirteenth Regiment of the army of the newly liberated
Republic of Sanbu, though at the moment she and her platoon were
technically marines. She was a woman of twenty hard-earned years,
taller than most of the women under her command and shorter than
most of the men. The neat dark-green uniform she wore had become
standard issue only in the last two years of the war; before, the Army
of the Republic had been a piecemeal rebel militia whose "uniform"
had been "as much green shit as you can find."

Though she sometimes missed the old emerald motley she'd worn
as a jungle-runner, she'd appreciated that when the time had come to
take the fight to Tomoda itself, she'd landed on its beaches dressed
as a real soldier. But despite the decisive victory the Garden Revolution's forces had won against the steelhounds on their own blighted
turf, and the snazzy uniform Tala had gotten out of the whole ordeal, the sergeant had left the island of Tomoda with zero desire to
ever return.

Her seaward scowl deepened.

No griping, soldier, she chided herself. *You volunteered.*

She turned her attention back to the deck. A few of her marines
were helping the *Marlin*'s crew struggle to re-secure a huge, heavy
bamboo crate. The crate held the one car that they hadn't had room
for in the hold, so it'd been stuck topside for the whole voyage. Normally, they could've chained it in place, but the no-metal rule meant
they'd had to make do with thick rope.

But that only accounted for four of her command. The majority
of them stood in a circle, clearing a makeshift arena where Private
Minip's shade sparred with Private Kapona.

Kapona was a tall woman with a brawler's swagger and a black-
smith's build. She'd stripped to her waist for this fight, and the dying
sunlight glistened across her bare back. Her opponent, a monkey-
shade, pranced around her. Pacting had gifted it with human size, a
pair of long whiplike tails, and, on the white fur of its inner thigh, a
pactmark—a yellow six-pointed star. When you saw that, it was
easy to figure why Private Minip had named him Sunny.

Kapona swung a fist, but Sunny easily dodged it. His tails threshed
the air excitedly as he darted this way and that. All Kapona's punches
went wild, and Sunny let out a taunting whoop.

"Hoy, Kapona," Private Minip called. "He says he's thrown shits that fight better than you."

Laughter rose from the onlookers. In the privacy of the sidelines, Tala allowed herself a small smile. As their sergeant, she preferred to play the aloof superior whenever possible. But she had to be fair: For Minip, that'd been a pretty good joke.

Kapona's hands curled into fists, but her mouth curled into a smile. "You tell him that he's the one getting thrown next."

Minip rolled his eyes. "Tanga. He can hear you. He's not—"

Kapona gave up a growl and charged, an unstoppable mass of muscle and momentum. She didn't have a shade of her own, but Tala had always assumed that if Kapona ever found the right animal to pact with, it would be a bull.

Once again, Sunny easily leapt out of the way. But this time, instead of turning around to press the attack, Kapona just kept going. Her squadmates threw themselves clear as she plowed straight into Minip, tackling him to the deck.

Safe from the eyes of her platoon, Tala chuckled softly to herself.

Kapona emerged from the tussle with Minip in a headlock. "Call it!" she said. "Call it!"

Minip's round face turned red as he struggled futilely against Kapona. Then he groaned and extended a hand toward Sunny. The shade burst into a cloud of yellow energy, which sucked itself back into Minip's body. Grinning, Kapona let him go, then hauled him to his feet. "You almost had me that time." She patted him on the head.

"You cheated," Minip said sourly.

A shrug rolled through her huge shoulders. "I won. Hoy, Sarge!" she called to Tala. "Pretty good, eh?"

Tala wiped her smile away before she looked up to respond. "Your footwork's still shit, Private."

The onlookers laughed. Once again, Kapona met the dig with a wide grin. "You should take a step into the ring, sir. Show us pups how it's done."

"Yeah," said Private Radnan, a man with a wiry build and a sleepy face. He never lost those half-lidded eyes or that easy smile, even when Tala had seen him carving up oncoming steelhounds with his utility knife. "Take a turn, Sarge. You can fight my shade."

"No, mine," offered up Private Ompaco. It was a tired joke; her shade was a large stingray who, like the other aquatic shades, had no place on deck.

"Sarge has better things to do." A broad, handsome man in a navy officer's uniform emerged from the lower decks. His green coat hung lazily open, rippling in the breeze. He was Captain Maki, known to friend and foe alike as the Hammerhead. It was a nickname well earned: both for his ferocity at sea, and because his shade, Tivron, was a gigantic hammerhead shark whose teeth could puncture a steel hull. "It's her turn down below."

In disciplined unison, the entire 13-52-2 turned toward him and bowed in salute. As a fellow officer, Tala only had to give him a shallow bow. And because he was Maki and she was Tala, she only ever had to do it when there were others watching.

"Guess you'll have to get along without me," Tala called to her troops as she stepped past them. "Try not to light everything on fire while I'm gone." And then her feet deposited her right in front of Maki, to whom she bowed again. "Sir."

Maki rolled his tawny eyes. "Am I ever gonna get you to stop calling me that?"

"Not likely, sir," she said, then smiled a tiny bit. Unless she was by herself, for Tala smiling was mostly something other people did. But Maki and Maki alone had a way of making her behave more like other people. "How is he today?"

"In as fine a fucking mood as ever," he replied. He fiddled with the pommel of his officer's machete, like he always did when he was irritated. He indicated for her to follow him down belowdecks. "The closer he gets to home, the bigger a prick he becomes. He's lucky the voyage was so short. Another day or two, and I'd have popped him on the jaw, right between the bars."

"That's a pretty picture you're painting, sir."

"Idiot should know better," Maki grumbled as the two of them descended the wooden steps. "Talking back to a captain on his own ship . . . the princeling's got a death wish. And if my orders didn't hold me back, I'd grant it."

"You'd have to beat me to it," Tala said darkly. "We're too honest for our own good. Why else would the general sucker us into a mission like this one?" That wasn't strictly true, or even kind of true; it had taken General Erega virtually no effort to convince Tala to volunteer.

"Yeah." Maki sighed as they reached the second deck: the galley, the mess, and the cramped bunks that accommodated both the 13-52-2 and Maki's own crew. He'd invited Tala to share his cabin, but that was a door she didn't want to reopen, in every sense. "Well, at least she put us together on one last job, neh?"

"Neh," Tala grunted. Certainly, she couldn't think of any other person she trusted to sail her safely into Tomodanese waters.

His smile faded. Captain Maki was the kind of man who spent his smiles like they were coin and the world was a card table, so when he got serious, she knew to listen up.

"Tala," he said, "what're you going to do after the war's over?"

Tala eyed a few nearby crewmen and gave him a small shake of her head.

Maki waved it aside. "You think I don't know all the spots on my own ship where I can't be overheard?"

Tala's mouth twisted. Of course she hadn't thought that. She had, however, been thinking about this conversation. Specifically, about how it was one she didn't ever want to have.

"Haven't figured that out just yet," she said after a moment. She hoped her vagueness would end the conversation, but instead it just sparked a light behind Maki's warm brown eyes.

"I get it," he said. "Spend enough time in uniform, and eventually you can't even imagine wearing anything else. Why d'you think I signed up for this mission, same as you?"

Not "same as," Tala thought with a tiny pang of guilt as she listened on. *Because of.*

"But once this mission's done with, that's it for us. You and me, we'll both be decommissioned. And that means we'll both be free to figure out what comes next. What I'm trying to say is, what do you say to making that a group project?"

Inside, she reeled. Somewhere in another life, there was a Tala who had been waiting the whole war for him to ask that question. But that Tala wasn't her, couldn't be her.

So she blinked at him and deadpanned, "You're supposed to get down on one knee when you propose, sir."

Maki laughed. "I know better. All I'm saying is, it's always been one thing or another between us—"

"I seem to remember a whole war," Tala continued to deadpan, while a spike of panic ran through the back of her head.

"—but this time next week, there'll be nothing left but you and me. So why not make a go of it, neh?" He reached for her, though he waited for her tacit permission before he put a hand on her shoulder. And of course, her heart chose that exact moment to flutter.

She wanted to say yes. Shades take her, did she want to say yes.

But with Tala, as long as she lived, there would always be a "but."

"Now's not the time to be thinking about this," Tala said. "Not when we still have a job to do."

Maki had the grace to look only gently crestfallen, but Tala saw his fingers toying with his machete's pommel again. "You're right, of course." He sighed. "Mind on your duty. That's why the general picked you for this." His fingers picked up the pace. "I'm going to go . . . check some of the maps in my cabin."

"Yeah," Tala said. "I know the way."

Maki flashed her a wobbly grin before he turned and left her. Tala watched him go, hating herself. Since she was a marine sergeant and Maki a navy captain, they'd crossed paths a few times in the war. And every time they did, it kicked up a lot of inconvenient questions in her head. She would've been lying to say she hadn't entertained the thought a time or two. But anytime she felt tempted, she thought back to the faces of those she'd lost to Tomoda's bullets and bombs. Her ina, who made the neighborhood's best adobo. Her ama, who always sang while he cleaned the house. And Dimangan.

Always, always him.

That was all it took to remind herself that as long as she lived, her family would always have to come first.

She pointed a finger at the floor next to her. *"Beaky."*

Purple energy erupted from her fingertip and a moment later coalesced into a fully formed shade. Hers had once been a crow, but he was larger than an eagle now, with a proud crest of black feathers atop his head. Their shadepact had painted three interlocking purple rings across his black breast feathers, a mirror of the pactmark emblazoned over Tala's own sternum.

He cocked his head to the side, and she felt his annoyance like it was a chill behind a closed door. As with most shades, Beaky didn't communicate in words, but it was easy enough to suss out his meaning: *What now?*

"Come on," she said. "We're going to go see your favorite person."

His annoyance intensified, but nonetheless Beaky followed her down the next flight of stairs, hopping just behind her the whole way.

The lowest deck was stacked high with wooden crates lashed to the floor to prevent them from sliding. But the real precious cargo was at the very back, sitting on his cot in a cell specially made of wood, like the ship itself, so he couldn't work his country's sorcery on its metal bars.

He was short, and possibly as young as she. His skin was fair, his hair long and black and pulled into a tight round topknot revealing a severe widow's peak. His thin face was adorned with a scraggly mustache and goatee, neither of which suited him well at all. He wore round spectacles and a nondescript blue yukata. Such was the only splendor left for Iron Prince Jimuro, heir to the Mountain Throne of Tomoda.

Until she and her squad went and crowned the bastard, anyway.

"Sergeant," the prince said in flawless Sanbuna. It always grated on Tala how easily he turned her native tongue against her. Her grasp of Tomodanese was nowhere near as firm. "So nice of you to join me. I was just on the verge of getting bored, and we can't have that, now can we?"

Tala regarded him with cold eyes and said nothing. She couldn't trust herself to. The Tomodanese people worshipped this sneering brat as a living god. Extinguishing his holy bloodline would have been a shot in the heart those monsters never could have recovered from, and no one was more deserving of the right to deliver that blow than the people of Sanbu. General Erega was a military genius, the head of their new republic, and a personal hero of Tala's, but it was only out of respect for the woman that Tala had volunteered for this mission, and only out of respect for her orders that the Iron Prince still drew breath.

Her fist clenched tight as her jaw. *We should have delivered you home in pieces.*

She took up her usual position in front of his cell and stood at rigid attention. For the next four hours, this would be her job. Technically, as an officer she could have been exempt from this duty and pawned it off onto one of her marines. But when the general had pulled the 13-52-2 aside to offer them a chance to volunteer for this mission, it'd been Tala who had said yes, leaving her squad no real choice but to go with her. With that knowledge lying heavily across her shoulders, Tala had been determined to put herself through everything her troops went through . . . including time down in the brig.

Next to her, Beaky fell in line, his feathers bristling and wings twitching. His irritation was separate from Tala's own, but feeling his had a way of stoking hers, which stoked his in turn. Beaky liked to be in places where he could stretch his wings. This cramped, dark hold was no place for a bird like him.

"Ah, so it's to be the silent treatment today, then," the Iron Prince continued. "Well, perhaps I can just chalk today up as a loss." She heard him moving around in his cell, though she couldn't see what he was doing. "After all, once we land, we'll still have a three-day drive down to Hagane. Plenty of time for opportunities to catch you when you're feeling more talkative."

Tala fixed her gaze straight ahead, counting the number of bamboo planks it took to form the side of a crate.

"You know, I've been asking the captain about you. Every other soldier always brings some fresh digs at my appearance, or long speeches about why we lost, or a list of relatives they want me to un-kill. But you're the only one who's barely said anything to me."

Tala cursed as his words made her lose count. She started over again: *Two, three, four . . .*

"Forgive me for being self-absorbed, but I find that odd. I mean, here I am: the demonspawn of Tomoda, locked in a cell where you can say whatever you like to me without consequences. Whatever grudges you're dragging behind you, now would be the ideal time to unload them on me. You could really let me have it. And yet, shift after shift, watch after watch . . . you don't."

Tala gritted her teeth. Her shift was four hours. Why couldn't she have gotten a watch where he just slept the whole time?

"Captain Maki tells me you fought like a demon in the rebellion, but it was in ravaging my homeland where you really distinguished yourself." A rhythmic *thunk-thunk-thunk* told her he was dragging his fingers across his cell's bars. "You stormed the beaches at Katagawa, watered the trees at Dokoshima with Tomodanese blood, *and* put the torch to Hagane's beautiful spires? The people of Tomoda will be having nightmares about you for a generation. You and your slave."

A shudder of rage went through Tala's entire body at that last word. It was a common enough slur among the Tomodanese, but it always landed extra hard when lashed across Tala's back.

Her body language had betrayed her, because the prince said, "You object to the term, then? Apologies. What term would you prefer to describe a creature whose will has been overwritten by yours?"

Her grip tightened on her rifle, but by now she had enough self-control to say nothing. Beaky's feathers ruffled, and he loosed a low, annoyed croak.

"That bird was a crow, wasn't it?" the prince said. "Or was he a raven? I can never tell the difference. But they're both remarkably intelligent birds, did you know that? Their minds and emotions are supposed to be nearly as complex as a human's. I'm sure your bird could've outwitted most of the hangers-on in my mother's court. How many years have you spent smothering its will, hm? How long have you been turning its wings and beak and claws against those who were fighting for its freedom?"

A burning spike of rage drove itself through the back of Tala's head. With deliberate, dangerous slowness, she turned around. Beaky croaked, then hopped over to a nearby crate and perched himself atop it. "You monsters never fought for any freedom but your own," she spat. "And the fact that we're giving you yours is a gift you don't deserve."

A sly, easy smile sauntered onto the Iron Prince's face when he saw he'd finally provoked a reaction from her. "You look downright homicidal. Though I suppose that's all part of the job, eh, Sarge?"

She took a step forward. "You don't get to call me that."

That sly smile stretched wider. "You hated me and my people enough to drag yourself from one battlefield to another, each one its own kind of hell. You survived them all, and I've no doubt you and your slave personally ensured that countless countrymen of mine didn't. Who did you lose? Who did you watch throw themselves into the teeth of this war you started to defend so vile a practice? An old comrade from your jungle-running days? A handsome lover from the tiny village you want to return to and rebuild someday? A sad little orphan who—"

"*Everyone,*" Tala snarled with such ferocity that the prince staggered back a step. "My mother. My father. My . . . my brother." Their faces flitted before her eyes again, though none lingered so long as Dimangan's. It was his old face. The one she wanted to remember.

"Everyone I've ever cared about," she went on. "None of them had ever raised so much as a fist against Tomoda, and you killed them anyway. You want to call us savages? We were doing what we needed to do to survive you."

For a second, the prince seemed taken aback by her fury. But then he smirked again. "So you lost your family," he said, singsong. "I couldn't possibly know what that's like."

Tala felt her face twist into something ugly. How dare he compare himself to her? His losses to hers?

The prince seemed determined to try anyway. "Do you know what your people did to my sister when she landed on Lisan to rescue me from my captivity?" he said. "Or what the Shang would've done to my father, if he hadn't taken his own life when they surrounded him? And my mother, may she reign ten thousand years? Divine vessel of the spirits, beating heart of our people? The report I was given said she'd been in the imperial garden, overseeing the safe evacuation of the palace staff, when a pack of slaves tore her to shreds, then lapped her blood off the floor." He pressed himself up against the bars. "But please, tell me how horrible and trying this war's been on—*ah!*"

Beaky surged forward in a puff of feathers. His beak snapped shut just where the prince's finger had been a moment before. Sputtering, the prince staggered back and fell onto his cot. "Restrain that thing at once!"

Tala leaned on her rifle. "According to the only person in the republic who doesn't want you dead, you're needed alive so you can ascend to your throne and negotiate in the peace talks, *Your Brilliance*," she said. "I've seen a woman clear out a redoubt full of steelhounds with one leg, no shade, and an empty gun. If she can do that, you can run a country with nine fingers."

His jaw worked up and down furiously, but nothing resembling coherent language came out—just choked, angry noises. It stoked something viciously satisfying in the back of Tala's head.

She turned back around. "Get some sleep, Your Brilliance. We'll make landfall by—"

The entire ship shuddered. She leaned heavier on her rifle to stop herself from falling, then frowned up at the upper deck. "What the hell was—?"

The ship shuddered again, as if it'd run aground. This impact was far worse; Tala only just managed to stay on her feet.

"What is it?" the prince said, glancing around as if he'd see the source of their troubles lurking just behind a crate. "We've been found out. They're finally coming for me. Who is it? Dahal? Shang? Traitors in your own ranks?"

"Shut it," Tala snapped, and to her surprise the prince complied. Still, that was where her mind had leapt, too. A grand fleet had left Lisan City, purportedly escorting Prince Jimuro home. General Erega was on the same ship, but she'd been confident that her presence alone wouldn't be enough to forestall any assassination attempts. So she'd sent the prince on a small, fast ship sailing to the far north of Tomoda, to travel south overland and arrive just in time for the peace summit to begin. No one was supposed to know this ship even existed.

A familiar, uncomfortable feeling stirred in the back of Tala's head. She shook it off. Now wasn't the time to get bogged down in the past.

"If there's an attack," the Iron Prince said, "I need to get out of this cell." All his former haughtiness was gone. "The whole point of this voyage is to return me home safely. I can't do that if I'm locked in a tiny room aboard a sinking ship."

But they weren't sinking, Tala noted. They'd taken no torpedo fire, and she couldn't smell burning timber. In fact, besides those initial two impacts, she hadn't detected any signs that something was amiss.

"Wait here," she said, then made for the staircase.

"*Wait!*" the prince called after her. "You can't just leave me!"

Tala kept walking.

"I could die in here!"

Tala kept walking.

"*I recognize that probably sounds enticing, but I must insist—!*"

She broke into a run.

At the top of the stairs, she saw crew hurrying toward her. In their midst, Maki rattled off orders, his fingers brown blurs as they drummed on his machete hilt.

She hailed him from the landing. "Sir! Report."

"Don't know anything yet," the captain said. "One of my boys had his shade do a flyby within the hour, and he didn't report any ships. No way anyone could sneak up on us in open water. How's his nibs?"

"Same as before."

Maki smirked ruefully. "I've—"

A shout came from above. Something heavy hitting the deck, perhaps a shade.

And then: gunshots. Lots of them.

Her eyes and Maki's met.

"Get back down there," he hissed. In a smooth, practiced motion, he drew his machete from its sheath. "We have to keep that ungrateful royal shit safe, or we went to all this trouble for nothing."

As he surged topside, Tala lingered for a long moment on the stairwell. If her troops were going into battle, she should be there to lead them.

Reluctantly, she hurled herself back down the stairs, leaping them five at a time.

"We're under attack!" the prince shouted as soon as he saw her.

Beaky cawed in annoyance.

"Save it," she said to her shade. "The bastard's right."

"Do you know who it is?" the prince said.

Tala didn't answer him, but she frowned and worked the bolt on her rifle, so a round chambered itself. Until Dahal had begun funding Sanbu's jungle-runners, ammunition had been precious and expensive. The rebels had survived on superior marksmanship, and Tala had worked hard to make sure she was a good enough shot that every single bullet she spent would end a Tomodanese life. Anything unfriendly that walked through the door would get one right between the eyes.

But the next person to enter the hold didn't come through the door.

A shadow covered the open loading hatch—and then a green-uniformed figure careened through, screaming as loud as his lungs would let him until he was cut short by a hard landing and the snap of bones. It was Private Radnan, bloodied and mangled, his normally sleepy face contorted with pain and terror.

"Private!" She rushed to his side and took a knee. His limbs were bent at the wrong angles, and blood poured out of too many wounds for her to patch. Private Radnan, as fierce a fighter as the 13-52-2 had ever known, was not long for this world. "Report," she said quietly. If she knew who'd done this to him, at least she could make sure his death wasn't in vain.

The fall had taken the wind out of him, but he managed to rasp out: "Shades."

"Shades?" the prince shouted from his cell. "Did he say, 'Shades'?"

"Shut it!" Tala snarled. But even her hatred for the Iron Prince's voice couldn't bring any fire to her chilled blood. Only two countries used shadepacting. One was Shang, a fellow victim of Tomoda's greed that had risen up alongside the Sanbu Islands. And the other was . . . well.

Gingerly, she cradled Private Radnan's head. "Stay with me," she said, stroking his bloody cheek. "Who sent the shades? Was it Shang? Or have we been betrayed?"

Radnan squeezed his eyes shut against whatever pain he was feeling. But he shook his head in an unmistakable no.

"What do you mean, 'no'?" Tala said, fighting to keep calm. "Who's attacking us, Shang or Sanbu?"

Again, Radnan shook his head.

She gritted her teeth. The question was no good when his head wasn't straight. She shifted tactics. "How many hostiles?" she said. A person could only have a single shade. Counting the number of shades on the side of a battle was a good way to get an estimate of enemy strength.

Radnan's ruined fingers flexed themselves to flash the number ten, and then again: twenty.

And then again: thirty.

Tala's eyes went wide. "Shades take me," she muttered. Beaky cawed in alarm.

"What?" the prince chimed in. "What is it?"

Tala ignored him. "Okay, good, Private," she said. She could feel him slipping away. She had to work fast here. "So, thirty enemy shades. At least that many soldiers then, too?"

But Radnan shook his head again, horrified.

"What?" Tala said. "More?" The *Marlin*'s deck wasn't that large. There was no way it could hold that many enemy combatants *and* their shades.

Yet again, Radnan shook his head. Slowly, looking at his own hand like it horrified him, he held up a single finger. And with the meager breath he had left, he forced a single word between his lips:

"*Splintersoul.*"

Tala's skin prickled. She recoiled from her own dying marine. "What did you just—?"

The prince banged on his cell bars. "What does that mean? What does that finger gesture signify to you people? Sergeant, my life could be in danger. As Iron Prince of Tomoda, I hereby order you to answer me, right this instant!"

Tala didn't look at him. She reserved her gaze for the dying man before her. "It means 'one,'" she said quietly as a chill ran through her. "He's saying all these shades are coming from one person."

CHAPTER THREE

LEE

For a long stretch of seconds, there was only silence between Xiulan and Lee.

Lee slouched back in her seat, arms folded. Typical royals. When they wanted something from you, they promised you the moon. But ask them for so much as a pebble to show some good faith, and they'd hem and haw.

Then, with slow thoughtfulness, Xiulan said, "Yes, I suppose you should have a shade."

Lee measured her with a long, appraising stare. "Not the answer I expected."

"Why not?" Xiulan said, with a puff of her pipe. Lee could practically hear the wheels turning in her head. "What better way to symbolize the sincerity of my desire to grant the people of Jeongson greater autonomy than to allow one of their number rights and privileges previously denied her? And when your shade proves invaluable in the apprehension of Iron Prince Jimuro, I'll be able to hold you up as proof of what we can achieve when we empower and enfranchise."

Lee weighed her words for a moment. "That's a long walk to 'yes,'" she said eventually.

"I rather like long walks. Don't you?"

"If they get me where I'm going."

Coyly, Xiulan cocked her head. "And where do you imagine you're going now?"

Lee leaned back in her seat, her lips stretching into a wolfish smile. "Depends on where you're taking me."

Xiulan put her pipe back to her lips and puffed a ring up at the ceiling of their car as it rumbled toward Jungshao.

Lee had spent most of her life bouncing around Shang. She'd done stretches in the countryside here and there, but for the most part she'd stuck to the big cities. Out in the country, the Shang paid her too much attention, their long stares and muttered words inescapable, but city folk generally just treated her with apathy.

Of all the cities she'd been to, though, Jungshao was far from her favorite. She probably wouldn't have gone anywhere near it if she hadn't been on Lefty's trail. The surrounding fields were good for raising sheep, which meant the place always stank like a dead saint's armpit. It had been a wool-and-mutton town once, but when Tomoda arrived they had imprisoned all the people and liberated all the sheep. They'd refitted the mills for cotton instead of wool, and then gotten to planting. Now that it was back in Shang hands, Jungshao had brought wool back into production, and the smell of sheep shit had clogged Lee's nostrils from the moment she'd gotten within ten miles of the place.

When Lee wrinkled her nose at the smell, though, Xiulan just beamed. "That's the smell of civilization."

Lee shook her head. "Not a great endorsement of civilization."

It felt strange, riding into the city like some kind of highborn. The first time she had entered Jungshao's city limits, she stowed away in a train car like a hobo, looking over her shoulder the whole way. Once she'd realized what Lefty had gotten himself into, she'd had to ratchet up her paranoia just to stay alive. Now there was no magistrate snapping at her heels. For once in her life, she told herself as she stepped out of the car, she could just enjoy a place for what it was.

And yet the stench of sheep hit her all the harder. *For a given value of "enjoy,"* she thought.

"If it's a pacting animal we're after, what're we doing here?" Lee said. "We just came from the closest thing Jungshao has to a zoo these days." In the old days, she'd heard the Shang had kept zoos in every big city, so their citizens could marvel at all the beasts from faraway lands. But of course, Tomoda had marched in, broken open every cage, and let the animals run wild and free. The zoos that hadn't been burned and built over still lay abandoned in the wake of the Peony Revolution, waiting to be refilled.

"Ah, but I contend you will seldom find the most interesting or useful partners in a zoo," said Xiulan. "You underestimate the value of more commonplace creatures."

"Right," Lee said. "How about I choose you, then?"

Xiulan flashed that daggerlike smile of hers. "There's nothing common about me, Lee Yeon-Ji." And just like that, the danger was gone, and the batty eccentric was back. "In seriousness, pacting with a human isn't the sort of subject one should joke about. The Sanbunas take it especially seriously. I would keep that in mind, considering the, ah, *polite* company in which you may find yourself as my partner."

Annoyance fluttered through Lee. Did this highborn really think Lee didn't know her taboos? "Right," she said. "Then how's about we get me a white crane instead?"

Xiulan's laugh was high and pleasing. "There truly is no button you won't press, is there?"

Lee shrugged. "Only reason I press a button's if someone's dumb enough to tell me not to."

The princess laughed again. "Come along, then. I suspect you'll be familiar with our intended destination."

Their intended destination ended up being the shrine of Jiaying the Light-Fingered. Of the thousands of saints canonized by Heaven, Jiaying was by far one of the most popular. Lee didn't have much regard for the Canon, but if there were any saint for a woman like her to pray to, it would be Jiaying. She was supposed to be patron to thieves and merchants alike, an overlap that more than one person had smugly pointed out like they were the first to notice it. This particular shrine was more a gathering of merchants than thieves, though in Lee's experience it was hard to find one absent the other.

The shrine itself was relatively modest: a simple three-story pagoda with an unadorned red façade. Far more noteworthy was the open-air market clustered around it. The stalls nearest to the shrine were more permanent, with wooden roofs, painted walls, and bright electric signs. The farther out they went, though, the more temporary the stalls became. On the edges of the market, the stalls were barely more than saggy tarps stretched across sticks jammed into the dirt.

The rain had mostly cleared up, and the market began to fill with people as the merchants tried to make up for the morning's lost sales. The moment the two of them got close enough, Lee was hit by the familiar smells of the place: The crispness of fresh fruit and vegetables. The funk wafting off barrels of fermenting fish. The entrancing aroma of beef on the grill, though the Shang were a soft people who wouldn't know how to season or spice if their lives depended on it.

"You've been here before, haven't you?" Xiulan said as they approached. "Was I correct in my assessment?"

Lee's mouth thinned to a line. She had, when she'd been tracking Lefty. After the sun went down, this was the place to throw dice in Jungshao, and Lefty had never been able to resist a tumble of the bones. During a game, she'd learned, he'd talked a little too loosely about where he'd been, and given the wrong person the idea that if he were to disappear, he wouldn't be missed.

"Might be," she said eventually.

Xiulan patted her on the shoulder. "Rest easy, Lee," she said. "You're a free woman again, and the man who imprisoned you is not."

Lee raised an eyebrow in gentle amusement. "The man who locked me up isn't a free woman?"

"I didn't take you for a stickler on the subject of dangling modifiers."

"Then what did you take me for?"

"The same reason I took a rat and not a crane," Xiulan said, as if that was supposed to make some kind of sense. She grinned down at the demonstrative crackle of white energy playing across her fingertips. "Let's see what we can take for you."

After stagnating in a cell, Lee had already forgotten what it felt like to have so much going on around her. If each of her senses were a cup, every single one of them was filling to the brim, and running over. She chided herself. She'd crawled into busier boroughs than this and been able to keep her wits about her. She couldn't let a mere two weeks in a box dull her edges.

By the end of the hour, Xiulan had dragged her past every single stall in the place. She'd seen fighting roosters, spirited birds that needed to be caged separately to stop them from tearing one another apart. She'd seen lumbering hogs, with their fierce-looking tusks and ridge-backed hides. She'd even seen red-faced monkeys, who had thrown themselves at the bars of their cages and screeched at her as she passed them by. She saw all kinds of dogs, which never failed to make her happy.

And yet each time, she kept walking.

"I understand your reluctance to partner with just any creature," Xiulan said with strained patience as they left behind a merch who was tending goats. "Shadepacting involves entrusting a piece of your deepest essence to another creature, and so it's quite naturally in your best interests to be discerning."

"D'you always wait this long to say 'but,'" Lee said, "or am I just getting special treatment 'cause it's my first day?"

"*Nonetheless,*" said Xiulan, "at some point, practicality must prevail. You have at your fingertips as fine an array of animals as a citizen could hope for, any of which would be the basis for a mighty, fearsome shade. I implore you: Please pick one."

Lee sighed. "You want me to pick the roost—"

"His tail feathers were a marvel to behold!" Xiulan burst, starry-eyed. "And the ferocity in his pecks! He would serve you well."

"And I reckon it doesn't hurt that the rooster's one of the nine animals of Heaven's Menagerie?" Lee said shrewdly.

Xiulan grew somber. "Given the level of skepticism you're bound to face, even in my company, an air of respectability will make you that much more difficult to doubt." Then her glee was back, her one visible eye gleaming like a brown star. "Especially when partnered with so handsome a bird!"

At the sudden display of enthusiasm, Lee felt a tiny surge of affection for the princess. Carefully, she distanced herself from the feeling. *Down, girl,* she thought, and wasn't sure if she was chiding Xiulan or herself.

Maintaining her cool demeanor, she folded her arms. "You pact with him, then."

Xiulan slumped, her white coat making her look like a wilted chrysanthemum. "Would that I could." Her exaggerated motions and wild mood swings made Lee feel like she was taking a stroll with a cartoon. Lee found it, and her, utterly fascinating. "But even you must be aware that a person can only have a single shade."

Lee shrugged. "Sounds like all the more reason for me to be picky, then."

"But you do not—"

"I've had bad partners before," Lee said. "Is it really that surprising I don't want to just up and jump in bed with another one?" A moment after the words had passed through her lips, she remembered that her companion wasn't just some random agent of the Li-Quan, but a fully privileged princess of the Shang family. And even if she hadn't been, she still would've been a Li-Quan agent getting mouthed off to by a gutter dog only a few hours removed from death row.

For just a brief second, she saw a flash of something dangerous in Xiulan's eye. Her stomach tensed, and she planted her feet that much harder into the ground, ready to run if the inspector rescinded her pardon. She didn't know how well she'd be able to outpace that rat-shade of hers, but she wouldn't go back to that cell meekly.

But then that spark in the inspector's eye faded. "You're correct, of course," she said. "I confess, when one grows up in a situation where she becomes accustomed to instant obedience from everyone she meets, it can make more mundane social interactions difficult to navigate. If these options are unsatisfactory, then we can wait. And when you find the proper shade, I give you my word I will assist you to the best of my ability."

At long last, Lee nodded. "Thanks for that." She hesitated a moment, then sighed. "That said . . . the rooster back there did look promising."

It was worth it just to see Xiulan's whole face light up.

"Excellent!" the princess exclaimed. "Once we obtain our newest compatriot, all that will remain is to procure the rest of the materials for the ceremony."

Lee's smile blew like a tire over a tack.

"Ceremony?"

One of the perks of being an agent of the Li-Quan, apparently, was privacy. Lee had spent her whole life in tenement houses and lock-ups, so she'd barely ever been someplace quiet, let alone someplace where there wasn't a person within ten feet of her at all times. Even when she stayed at an inn, she'd usually been in the company of a partner or two.

But once they'd obtained a proper fighting rooster and a few other supplies, Xiulan had herded them to the nearest inn, slapped her badge down on the front desk, and gotten them whisked up to the biggest room—which the stout little innkeeper repeatedly assured them had the thickest door.

"The real best privacy measure is me," he said as he threw open the aforementioned very thick door. In the three seconds before he'd caught a whiff of badge, he'd been surly and distant. But that shiny pentagon had brightened him right up, and he'd kept up a running patter the whole way up the stairs and down the hall. "I pride myself on my discretion, see? All kinds of important people stop by here for . . . important business." He uncomfortably eyed the rooster in its cage for a second, before slapping on a fresh coat of professionalism. "And no matter what, I never tell anybody anything, Inspector, sir."

It didn't escape Lee's notice that though the innkeeper was flawlessly polite, he was also treating this as a two-person conversation. She was well used to it by now, but she always noticed.

"Now," the squat man went on, "I've got a few guests checking in soon, so if you'd just give me a rough idea of how long you'll need the room . . ."

"As long as it takes," Xiulan said with a perky smile, shutting the door in his face. She turned back to Lee, who had the rooster tucked under her arm and was trying not to feel stupid. "He was serious about that door, at least. It should provide us with sufficient solitude."

The room he'd given them was large and sunny, with a wide window covered by thin red drapes. A gaudy red rug was splattered across the wooden floor, its pattern so cluttered it made Lee's eyes cross. Even the wooden bed frame was lacquered in red, the mattress wrapped in red cotton sheets, and the whole damn thing shrouded in fluttering red curtains.

Lee glanced down at her own dusty black dress, then at Xiulan's all-white ensemble. "Don't think we fit in."

Xiulan chuckled, then set down her canvas bag of supplies. Back at the temple of Jiaying the Saint, she'd tried to hand it off to Lee by instinct, but a withering look from Lee had been all it took to set her straight. "The one regard in which we fall short is in our lack of proper ceremonial garb."

Lee had never been to a pacting ceremony, but she had a decent idea of what the Shang considered important. "What would it be? Something drapey and red?"

"Indeed," Xiulan said. "In my haste to procure us a venue, I neglected to—"

She didn't get a chance to finish; Lee had already torn one of the red curtains off the bed frame and draped it around her shoulders. "Oh, get over it," she said when she saw Xiulan's surprised face. "You're rich, aren't you?"

Xiulan sighed, then nodded to an open scrap of floor. "You may kneel, Lee Yeon-Ji."

"Normally when a partner tells me that, we don't have a chicken with us," Lee said, but she knelt. She didn't know what the hell this was all about, but the princess had her curious.

From the bag Xiulan produced nine wooden incense holders, which she placed in an even circle around the spot where Lee knelt. "Traditionally, a pact is sealed on one's thirteenth birthday," she said as she made a second lap to set a stick of incense in each holder. "It's something of a coming-of-age ceremony for family and friends to attend. Do the Jeongsonese have anything analogous?"

"Sure," Lee said as the princess made a third round, singeing each stick of incense with her silver lighter. "One day, Shang decides you're not a kid anymore, and they start hitting you with grown-up punishment. I was ten."

It was a little satisfying to see Xiulan at a loss for words as she finished lighting incense.

"Why are you doing all this again?" Lee said. She was awash in a cloud of scentless gray smoke. "The Sanbunas don't bother with any of this."

"We are not in the Sanbu Republic," Xiulan said, paging through a secondhand copy of *The Nine Truths*. "We're in Shang, and we will seal your pact in the Shang way." She arrived at the page she'd been looking for and began to read: "Lee Yeon-Ji, you have chosen the Path of the Rooster, most loyal of Heaven's Menagerie . . ."

Lee's focus slipped as Xiulan recited from the book—mostly stuff about piety, and fealty, and other kinds of shit that'd never gotten Lee anywhere. But it wasn't the words that kept her attention elsewhere; it was the rooster, who was ferociously pecking at the bars to his cage. The bird looked fierce, sure enough, but he didn't look particularly loyal. Whatever ancient Shang had decided roosters meant loyalty, she decided, had clearly never met a dog.

Xiulan closed *The Nine Truths* and set it down. She nodded to the cage. "You can let that fellow out now."

Carefully, Lee unlatched the cage. The little door swung open, and the rooster stepped out with a rustle of his wings. Lee had to admit, she'd been shallow and mostly chosen him for his plumage. The roosters she'd seen before were usually black or brown, with feathers that seemed to just be there to be plucked. But this bird practically looked as if he'd been painted. His breast feathers were the deep blue of the bottom of a lake, while his impressive cascade of a tail glinted like an emerald in the dark. Their exact hues seemed to warp and shift depending on how the light caught them. Even more than Lee and Xiulan, in the red room he stood out. He began to strut around the circle of incense, neck pumping like a fat little piston with each step.

"Now, then," said Xiulan, eyeing the rooster with some amusement. "You normally would have had months of lessons about the mystical aspects of shadepacting, so we will endeavor to make up for lost time in a stunningly expeditious fashion today. As it was explained to me, shadepacting is very much like lifting a car over your head: simple, but not easy. You simply attune yourself with an animal through physical contact, break off a piece of your essence, and graft it onto that animal. In exchange for accepting this piece of your soul, the animal will ask something of you, which you can neither negotiate nor refuse. The pact is sealed by giving it a name, at which point it becomes summonable and banishable when you invoke that name. Like so: *Kou!*"

A flash of black, and the rat-shade appeared in the room. Its nose and tail both twitched as it acclimated to its new surroundings. But while it didn't seem to be that fazed by the rooster, the same wasn't true in reverse. The bird hissed, puffing up his feathers and brandishing one of its gleaming talons like a knife.

"Little guy doesn't take any shit," Lee observed mildly. "Think I like him already." She weighed the question on her mind, then said *fuck it* and asked it: "So what did you have to promise Kou?"

Lee was beginning to understand that Xiulan could summon up an edge to her smile when she wanted to, and it came out to play when Lee asked that question. Kou cocked his head her way, so his eye with the black windowpane pactmark was staring her down.

"That," Xiulan said carefully, "is a highly personal question."

Lee raised an eyebrow, arched at just the right angle to suggest a playful challenge.

Xiulan's chilliness dissolved into a low, soft laugh. "Another button to push," she sighed. "Kou, return." The rat-shade disappeared as quickly as it had appeared, though that only calmed the rooster down a tiny degree. His neck feathers had ballooned his throat out to twice its normal width. His tail, which had before been shaped like a cresting wave, now pointed straight up and back, like a shark's fin.

Xiulan eyed him. "I don't believe I helped his disposition much with that little demonstration of mine. Apologies. Still, though, look at the spirit on display here. I think you chose well."

Lee considered the rooster. She hadn't felt any particular attachment to him when she'd first spied him in the merch stall, but if she was going to go on a manhunt across the Tomodanese countryside, he was definitely starting to look like a good ally. "Right, enough out of you," she said, reaching over to scoop him up. "Let's get pacted up and get on with—*ow!*"

The moment she reached within a few inches of the rooster, he rounded on her and got in a good peck at the back of her hand. She yanked her bleeding hand away and cursed. She needed light fingers and quick hands to survive. If the Li-Quan couldn't change that about her, then neither would this bird. "Probably a stupid question before I ask it," she said to Xiulan as her future shade hopped out of the circle and onto the bed, "but in all that reading you did to pick up those fancy words you use, did you ever read anything about how to catch a chicken?"

Xiulan shifted her weight from one tiny foot to the other. "There may be a few gaps in my education."

Lee sighed. "Never forget this was your idea," she said before diving out of the incense circle and after the rooster.

She managed to get a good grip on him eventually, though it was hard to stop him from kicking. She ended up having to hold his legs together with one hand as she shoved him under her armpit to keep him from flapping. His head was behind her back somewhere, and he alternated between clucking in protest and pecking in irritation at her dress. "I'm starting to think we haven't got much common ground."

"Pessimism isn't a quality I set stock in," Xiulan said, but Lee could see the misgivings in her face. "And you have your grip. That's important. You need to be touching the creature you pact with. Touch creates a bridge between your souls, and you'll eventually need to cross that bridge to finish the pact."

The rooster still hadn't let up with his squirming. "Yeah, we've never felt closer," Lee grunted. The princess's presence was making her annoyingly self-conscious. She didn't want Xiulan to look at her like some idiot gutter dog who couldn't hack it. "So now I'm just supposed to . . . chip off a bit of my soul, right?" She'd heard much and more about the practice and its significance, but she was starting to realize how little she'd ever heard about how the thing was actually done.

"Ah, yes," Xiulan said. "This will be trickier. Look for the calm place within yourself. That's where you'll find your soul: the most unfettered and pure distillation of who you are. You can close your eyes, if you like; it aids the focus."

Lee wasn't in the habit of closing her eyes. Closing your eyes at the wrong moment was generally the best way to get your purse strings or your throat cut. But Xiulan had a shade and she didn't, so Lee figured she might as well do things the inspector's way.

She squeezed her eyes tight and tried to shut out all her thoughts. But her brain chugged like a train now—after the day she'd had, how could it not? Coming off two straight weeks of quiet, stillness, and impending death, she'd managed to pack so much into the last few hours. The memories were all so squashed together that they were sticking and fusing into one lump, like dumplings in the bottom of a basket.

And the whole time, the dogs-forsaken rooster wouldn't. Stop. Squirming.

But as she began to get a feel for the ways the rooster could move, her grip became more certain. And while meditation wasn't her style, she could feel something warm inside herself, though it felt like it was hovering just out of her mind's reach.

"Good." Xiulan's voice floated into her ears, gentle as incense. "It doesn't surprise me that one so self-possessed as you would be able to attune yourself to your soul energy with such little preparation."

"Living selfish gets you far," Lee muttered. "Now, are you gonna let me concentrate, or what?"

"Apologies," Xiulan whispered. "Pursue that feeling inside you as far as you can. And at its end, a question will await. Answer it in the affirmative, and speak your partner's name."

Lee gritted her teeth to concentrate, and as she plumbed deeper into her trance, she sensed a second warmth drawing nearer. This, she realized, had to be the rooster, who'd grown calm and still in her grip.

Cautiously, she reached out for it . . . or whatever passed for reaching when you were mind-melding with an animal. The presence she sensed was . . . it took her a moment to place the feeling: Curious. Inquisitive. Tranquil.

Hey . . . rooster, Lee said. Her greeting wasn't words, just feelings. But somehow, she had a sense that they'd be understood. *What can I do for you?*

She felt that presence react with pleasant surprise at being asked the question. Lee took that as a good sign. She had to hand it to the Shang: It was a hell of a racket they'd been pulling off, keeping shadepacting off-limits to everyone else. If Lee had known it'd be this easy, she would've tried it years ago.

I want . . . the rooster began.

Bolstered by her early success, Lee prodded him. *Come on now,* she said. *Out with it.*

The rooster took her encouragement well, because Lee felt the connection between them open wider. *I want to bathe in the blood of my enemies beneath the cold and unfeeling moon.*

Lee stopped dead. *Uh, what?*

For too long, the other creatures of the world have not trembled when my shadow falls upon them, the rooster went on. *With your pact, I will at last see them cower—*

Gonna stop you right there, Lee said. *I'm starting to think maybe you and I want different things, little bird.*

. . . Oh, the rooster said to her after a moment. *A shame.*

Before she could suss out what he meant by that, the rooster finally managed to rip himself free of her grasp, slip out from under her armpit, and peck her once in the side. Lee let him go with a shout of pain as her eyes flew open. Immediately her sight was assaulted by red everywhere she looked. But she managed to lock onto the one thing that clearly didn't belong: the angry tornado of feathers running as fast as his pointy legs would carry him.

Xiulan moved to intercept him, but the rooster dipped just below her grasping hands and hopped up onto a chair near the open window. He spread his wings and leapt straight through the gently wafting scarlet curtains, away into freedom.

Lee and Xiulan rushed to the window to see him running along the narrow ridge atop the nearest rooftop. Xiulan started to bring up her hand. *"Ko—"*

"Wait," Lee said, putting an arm out to stop her. "Let's maybe not." And as she said that, the rooster reached the edge of the roof, then hopped clumsily to the next-closest roof with a frantic flap of his wings. He kept running and running, until eventually he darted out of sight.

Silently, Lee watched him go. She was getting the feeling she might've dodged a bullet there, but she was embarrassed by how much her failure stung anyway. In Shang, shades were status. Not everyone had the stuff it took to tame one, and Shang society had forbidden her people from even trying. Having one of her own—and being the first daughter of Jeongson to have one, no less—had been irresistible the moment Lee had let herself believe it was actually possible.

And yet there went the rooster, who seemed to find it a lot more resistible than her.

She tried to mask her disappointment, letting her gaze fall—

—onto her hand, which still lay on Xiulan's arm.

When she glanced up, Xiulan was staring at her hand, too.

She ripped it away, a little too hastily. "Sorry about that," she said. "Wasn't thinking."

Xiulan studied her a long moment, a searching expression on her face. But then she shifted her focus back to the open window and said, "The shortcoming here may not have necessarily been yours. We could have simply chosen the incorrect partner for you to pact with. At some point in our travels, perhaps a more suitable candidate will make itself known to you." She pulled out her pipe and took the time to light it before adding: "But I regret to say we have no more time to search now."

"Made it sound like we didn't have time for this one, either," Lee said. "Why'd you humor me with this one, Your Highness?"

"It's 'Majesty,'" Xiulan said. "And like you, I wished to see what would happen. It's as simple as that, Lee Yeon-Ji."

"Is it really?" Lee said, letting herself drift away from the window.

"I suppose not," said Xiulan. "I'd also thought that since our ship doesn't depart Jungshao port until tomorrow, we had some spare time to fill. That said, perhaps we should part ways for the day. In the morning, you'll meet me at Jungshao Jetty, and together we'll board a ship on which I chartered us passage, the *Wave Falcon*."

"You seem awfully confident I'll be there."

Xiulan shrugged her slim shoulders. "Perhaps I'm not confident. Maybe I once again simply wish to see what will happen. And one way or another," she added meaningfully, "I will. Until sunrise, Inspector Lee." She headed for the door, a bounce in her step.

"Wait, where are you off to?" Lee said.

"I'll secure other lodgings for myself," Xiulan said with a dismissive wave. "Consider tonight's stay a welcome gift from me. I'm certain you'd like the night to relish your newly regained freedom." She lingered in the doorway. ". . . Unless, of course, you had a reason for me to forestall my departure." Her eyebrow raised inquiringly. "Is that the case, Lee?"

Lee briefly entertained the thought before shaking her head. This was some kind of test. There was no way she could actually be making it this easy. "I'm good here."

She expected Xiulan's eye to glint with satisfaction, but to Lee's surprise she saw a twinge of . . . something else. Amusement? Disappointment? It was hard to tell, and in a heartbeat the moment was gone. But while Xiulan was back to smiling, Lee was left with the growing feeling that maybe she hadn't passed the test after all.

"Very well, then," Xiulan said. "Until tomorrow . . . Inspector." And with a swish of her white coat, she disappeared down the hall, leaving the very thick door open behind her.

Lee crossed to it, grumbling the whole way about royals and servants. Over and over, she played the princess's offer in her head, like a movie reel on loop. Except each time she played it, the actress playing Lee Yeon-Ji sounded more and more like a fucking idiot.

She had half a mind to go out for a drink, maybe hire up a girl or a boy to spend the evening with. But instead she slammed the door shut and turned to regard the garishly red and suddenly inviting bed. She meant to just sit down on it, but the moment she let herself relax partway, the rest of her followed suit. She lay back and felt muscles in her back unknot after weeks of holding themselves tense. That morning, she'd woken up at the end of her life. Now she was . . . well, she was a lot of things, the least unlikely of which happened to be "still here."

She glanced up at the ceiling. The one in her cell had been featureless and white, but this one was, to her complete lack of surprise, a deep red. She squeezed her eyes shut and found the darkness there to be preferable by far. And in the darkness of her own head, she whispered to herself the words that were never far from her mind: *Leave them before they leave you.*

She turned it over in her head. Sure, Xiulan was an inspector of the Li-Quan, which meant she had to be at least halfway as good at finding people as Lee was. Hell, she'd found Lee already, hadn't she?

But Lee had spent her whole life living on the periphery of the world's vision. She'd attracted the attention of two powerful, important people in the last month, but that was an aberration. If she disappeared tonight, she knew she could make sure it never happened again.

Then she realized: She was thinking about it. She was taking the time to think out a question that, a few weeks ago, she wouldn't have needed a second to consider.

And that was how Lee Yeon-Ji knew that come tomorrow morning, she would be sailing to Tomoda with Princess Shang Xiulan.

CHAPTER FOUR

TALA

"Thirty slaves to one master? Impossible!" Jimuro said. His shrill uncertainty undercut whatever authority he'd tried to muster in his tone.

Tala kept her back to him, staring down at Private Radnan as he breathed his last. But even though her eyes were on him, her mind was on the word he'd made himself say before he went.

Splintersoul.

"Radnan was an honest man," she said finally, voice heavy as she caught herself switching to past tense. Gently, she reached down and closed his eyes. It lent his face a peaceful expression at odds with the horrible brutality the rest of his body had endured.

Slowly, she rose, fist clenched at her side. Through the loading hatch, she heard the sounds of the battle that was raging topside without her. It was a symphony of roaring shades, Sanbuna war cries, and the staccato report of blazing guns. But even as she listened, she could hear the fire waning. She gritted her teeth as she considered what that could mean.

"I know what you're thinking," the prince said. She turned around to see him leaning up against his cell bars. "You want to hare off and join that fight upstairs. I'll let you know straight off that I forbid it."

Beaky croaked again in a sort of dry, rasping laugh. It was a mirthless sound that echoed even more deeply in Tala's head and heart than it did her ears.

"You 'forbid' me?" Tala said. Only her years of military discipline allowed her to keep her voice from shaking with the rage that boiled in her gut. "I'm not one of your subjects, *Your Brilliance*. I don't take orders from the man who lost the war."

"No," said the prince, unperturbed by her. "But you do take orders from the woman who won it, and hers are to keep me alive. I'm sure you have a burning desire to rush to aid your poor, beleaguered squad, so you can single-handedly save them. Isn't that right?" He didn't wait for an answer. "If you really trained your marines to be any good at their jobs, they should be able to protect this ship without your help."

That brought Tala up short. She couldn't believe it, but the bastard had actually made a fair point.

She scowled at him but stayed put.

The prince smirked as she stood down. "So unless you don't have faith in your own troops, you and your slave will stay right here and guard me with your life."

Her nascent calm shattered.

In a heartbeat her rifle was shouldered, its barrel and a chambered round aimed squarely at the Iron Prince's forehead. He jerked his head back so quickly that his glasses bobbed up, then fell back onto his nose askew.

"*Are you barking?*" he shrieked. "I'm your entire mission! You wouldn't dare!"

But hate pumped through her like venom. She could just put a bullet in him. He more than deserved it. General Erega had stressed he was the only one who could speak for the Tomodanese people, but if these were the things their voice planned on saying . . .

Beaky cawed. Something had him agitated, something that Tala could sense had very little to do with her standoff. Still, the noise was enough to shake her out of her scarlet tunnel vision. Slowly, she lowered her rifle, glaring at the prince as if her gaze alone could stop his heart. "Use that word again in my earshot . . . and I'll shoot off your ear." She turned away from him.

"What word?" the prince sneered at her back. "'Slave'?"

She whirled around. Her hand snapped up like a striking viper, her sidearm gleaming in her grip. The muzzle flashed, and a bullet streaked through the narrow bamboo bars, just past the prince's ear, and buried itself in the wooden wall behind him with a spray of splinters.

He staggered back with a scream and fell flat on his ass. He sputtered madly in Tomodanese, frantically patting his head in search of damage. But good as Tala was with a rifle, she was a proper artist with a sidearm. At this range, she wouldn't have hit him unless she wanted to.

Well, no. She definitely wanted to. But good shooting made a warrior; discipline, a soldier.

"I'm going topside," she said coldly, then turned and stalked toward the door once more. With a flutter of shadowy wings, Beaky fell in just behind her. She felt a pang of guilt at just leaving Private Radnan's body where it lay, but he would have to wait. After all this was over, she and Maki would make sure he was buried at sea with full honors, same as anyone else who fell today on the deck of the *Marlin*.

"Wait!" Prince Jimuro wailed behind her. "I command you, Sergeant, to remain at your rightful post and protect me!"

Tala almost turned around and fired off another shot. She was starting to feel like it would've been worth the gamble, almost. But no. The cylinder only had six shots left in it now. Better to save those for the enemy that lurked topside, rather than the captive prince.

"Captive though I may be," Prince Jimuro cried, "I'm still a foreign dignitary! I have rights and privileges! And by my order, you will not leave this hold unless I—"

The entire *Marlin* rocked hard to port, and the starboard hull wall burst open as if it'd taken a torpedo. Tala swayed and nearly fell as water surged in. But there were no other signs of enemy ordnance: no flames, no sonic concussion, not even explosions.

Besides, the evidence before her eyes spoke for itself.

It was a shade: an orca with a slick black hide blotched in white. It had a heavy bottom jaw and crooked yellow teeth the length of Tala's arm. Huge, jagged chunks of wood protruded from its face like splinters, and its mouth looked large enough to swallow them whole.

The shade had punched a massive hole in the side of the *Marlin*. Already, Tala knew: Maki's ship was doomed.

The orca-shade opened its mouth wide, only to disappear out the breach it had made. It cried in pain as it vanished into the darkness of the water, and Tala was certain Tivron, Maki's shark-shade, was fighting as valiantly to defend the ship as its human partner. But while shark fought whale, the sea continued to pour into the hold like blood from a wound.

She gritted her teeth and ran through the watery onrush. They were only a day's journey from Tomoda. Even with their ship sunk, the 13-52-2 could survive this, if they acted fast.

"Sergeant! Wait!"

She froze at the sound of the prince's voice.

Already the water was nearly mid-shin. In a matter of minutes, the entire hold would be underwater. The Iron Prince of Tomoda was supposed to be a powerful metalpacter, but there was no metal with which he could save himself here. If she left him now, he would die. All the people his nation's lives had destroyed would be avenged in a single stroke. Without him to lead them, Tomoda's people would learn to suffer, the way they had taught the rest of the world.

It would be justice, a voice in the back of her head whispered.

Dimangan's face flitted across her mind's eye again. *Not enough,* she thought with gritted teeth.

"Sergeant!" the Iron Prince shouted. "Sergeant, please! I'll drown!"

Her hand, still heavy with the sidearm it held, shook at her side.

"Sergeant—!"

She sent a spike of will to her waiting shade. "Beaky."

Beaky wheeled around, flying straight for the cell. It only took a single peck to shatter the wooden lock holding the door fast. The cell door swung open as Beaky banked away from it, eager to return to her side. The prince looked at the open door, dumbfounded.

"Run," Tala said. "Before you have to swim."

The pitch of the stairs had already changed underfoot. She found herself bumping into the wall as she climbed. She could only imagine how much more difficult this was making conditions for her marines. She growled to herself and ran faster. She should've been up there to begin with.

"Wait up!" the prince called behind her.

She ignored him. "I don't take orders from you."

"A monster from the depths sinks this ship with a headbutt, and you're worried about chain of command?"

They emerged on the middle deck to find it in disarray but bearing no evidence of a fight. There were no dead bodies, no puddles of blood, not even the gouges in the wood that would've pointed to shades' claws. So it was all hands on deck, then, Tala thought grimly with a glance upward. Next to her, Beaky croaked, and a trickle of fear spread into the stream of emotions she was getting from him.

The prince appeared similarly unsettled by the empty deck before them. "Gun," he said.

"Not likely," Tala said, creeping toward the next staircase. This one, she couldn't afford to take at a run.

"You have two! You can't possibly use them both!"

"And you can't possibly use one."

"My people are metalpacters, able to commune with the very bones of the world," he said, nodding to the shiny metal barrel of her rifle. "That means I can shoot better than you."

Tala scowled, then holstered her sidearm with a showy twirl. "No one can shoot better than me. Shut up and come on."

The searing heat of flame raked across her skin as she crossed the stairway threshold. Everywhere she looked, fires consumed the *Marlin:* on its deck, across its railings, even up in the crow's nest.

The deck was slick with spilled blood, and as far as Tala could tell, all of it was Sanbuna. Mangled marines in equally mangled green uniforms littered the deck. The few remaining survivors fought valiantly alongside their and their comrades' shades, but already the odds looked overwhelmingly against them. She saw Private Ompaco empty shot after shot into a huge green snapping-turtle-shade, only for the bullets to thud harmlessly into its shell with little green sparks of magic. As Ompaco fumbled with her rifle's bolt, a vast white shape unfolded from the night sky: an owl-shade, far larger than

Beaky, which pinned the private to the deck and ended her life with a flash of its beak.

"Spirits take me," Prince Jimuro muttered in Tomodanese, his shrill fear replaced with muted horror. Tala, however, had no room for horror. If she gave horror even the smallest foothold, it would swallow her whole. So she beat back the darkness with the flames of her anger.

Something flashed up on the quarterdeck. There she saw Maki fighting with liquid grace, machete in hand. A tiger-shade bore down on him, but none of its swipes could slip past the steel curtain Maki wove with each flick of his blade. As the beast tried to get around Maki, it presented an open flank to him. It moved so fast that, against most warriors, such exposure wouldn't matter. But Maki was not most warriors, and the shade roared as Maki's machete ran it straight through. As the wound magically closed around the blade, Maki whipped up his sidearm and emptied an entire clip into the beast. On the seventh shot, its body burst into orange energy and dissipated, streaming toward a man on deck in the thick of the fighting.

Something moved in the darkness behind the captain. Tala saw it before he did, and even though the battle howled around her, she called out, *"Sir!"*

Maki whirled around, his machete just catching the owl-shade that had killed Private Ompaco before its talons could sink into his shoulder. As he parried it, he shot Tala a nod of gratitude. *"Nice catch!"* he called to her.

Every shred of Tala yearned to rush up to the quarterdeck and stand with him. But the captain was as good a swordsman as he was a sailor, and she still had a duty to her own troops.

Nearest to her, Private Kapona wrestled on the ground with a snake-shade as thick as Tala was. It had wrapped itself around Kapona's body, and her arm shook with the effort of keeping the creature's snapping jaws away from her face.

Without a moment's hesitation Tala fired a shot and blew the creature's head into ruin.

Magical energy sprayed into the air, then dissipated as the snake-shade's head began to re-form. But that injury was just what Kapona needed to haul the creature off herself, vault to her feet, and throw it over the burning railing with a roar. "Sir!" she said. "We thought you'd jumped ship!" Her gaze slid past Tala to the prince, but she didn't comment on his presence. There was a grim understanding between them that the situation had officially grown dire.

"Who's doing this?" Tala said, scanning the deck for any sign of human hostiles.

But even as Kapona raised her arm to point him out, Tala's gaze fell on him.

Though he knelt, Tala could tell he was tall and skeletal. His black hair hung in a greasy curtain around his face, and the folds of his long purple coat pooled around him on the deck. In the firelight, she could make out a pointed, stubbled chin and bloodshot, hungry eyes. And then she caught sight of the bare torso beneath his coat and gasped.

Every inch of his brown skin was covered in pactmarks.

He knelt over the bloodied, broken body of Private Minip, who thrashed ineffectually against the hand wrapped around his throat. At the sight of one of her troops in danger, instinct jolted through Tala like lightning. She shouldered her rifle and fired a shot straight for his tattooed center mass.

But a blur fell out of the sky, and the bullet slammed into it with a spray of yellow magical sparks. A large wasp-shade crashed to the deck, legs twitching as its entire body curled in around a gaping gunshot wound.

The man looked up from the dying Minip and locked eyes with Tala. And then his eyes, like Kapona's, slid past her to fall squarely on Prince Jimuro.

He already looked gaunt and sunken, but at the sight of the prince he turned into a starving wolf. "Give him to me," he rasped in San-buna. And then, more loudly: "*Give him to me!*" He threw an arm forward, and in a blast of yellow light a white-furred monkey-shade appeared: one with three whiplike tails, and a yellow star on its inner thigh . . .

Kapona's jaw dropped. "That's . . . that's Sunny."

Once again, Tala gritted her teeth and said nothing.

"Well, can't worry about that now," Kapona said, though she looked as though she was worrying quite a lot. She pounded one fist into the other and bellowed, *"Rematch, you hairy fucker!"* before charging headlong to meet him.

"Sergeant," the prince said, "the landing boat is right over there. I must insist we get me off this ship."

But Tala had only just joined this fight. There was no way she was abandoning it.

She pointed to the man. *"Beaky!"* The crow-shade was smaller than most of the others on deck, but Tala liked his odds against any of them. He was an agile flier, a fierce fighter, and more daring than any shade Tala had ever seen. She'd seen him fly into the face of massed Tomodanese guns with only a grenade in his talons, and come out of it with barely a feather out of place.

But when she ordered Beaky to take on this mysterious man, the only response she got from him was a wave of absolute dread.

She turned around in disbelief. Beaky was ornery, but she'd never known him to be unresponsive. Yet here he was, completely frozen in place.

"Beaky," she said again. "We both have to fight if we're going to get through this."

But Beaky was unwavering. Something about that man absolutely terrified him, and the surge of panic he sent through Tala's head told her he wasn't going anywhere.

That's not true, she reminded herself. It was always possible for a shadepacter to override their shade's will. Most didn't; it was widely considered a virtue to build a strong friendship with the creature who was the other half of your soul. And Tala found the idea particularly heinous. Desperation clawed at her, though. This was a dire situation, and she needed to fight . . .

But she caught sight of the prince, with his sneering Tomodanese face. And as badly as she needed to fight, she needed him to be wrong about her.

She threw out a hand. *"Return,"* she muttered, and Beaky turned into a cloud of purple energy before absorbing into her body.

"What just happened?" the prince said. "Why did you send your sl—shade away? And you named him *Beaky*?"

"Your Brilliance," Tala said, working her rifle bolt to chamber another round, "I need you to—"

"*Give him to me!*" The man in the purple coat barreled forward, slavering like a wolf with a sheep in its sights. Shades fell in beside him: the wasp-shade, now healed. A cat-shade, its brindled hide slick with blood. The snapping-turtle-shade, inexorable as a green tide.

And against him, she had two guns, a useless prince, and a shade who couldn't fight.

A soft voice in the back of her head whispered: *That's not all you have.*

She glanced at the few remaining crew and troops continuing the fight. At the sea, whose surface grew steadily closer as its darkness folded around the *Marlin*. At the man in the purple coat and his conquering army.

She exhaled. There was no choice. "*D—*"

In the corner of her vision, the prince moved like a blue blur. Before she even realized what was happening, her sidearm was out of its holster and in the Iron Prince's hands. Its report boomed in her ears as the prince leveled it off to the side and fired it—not at the shades bearing down on them, or even at the man behind them. He'd fired it at the crate lashed to the railing, straining against the ropes.

Tala was a truly superb markswoman, but splitting a rope with a single bullet would have been out of her league even in broad daylight, on a steady deck. Iron Prince Jimuro, however, was no mere marksman. He was Tomodanese, and with metal in hand his people could work terrible miracles.

The rope snapped, and the crate thundered forward, aided by the sharp slant of the deck. The splintersoul threw himself clear just in time, but it bulldozed straight through the cat-shade and wasp-shade, reducing them to colorful bursts of magic. It ground hard against the snapping-turtle-shade, but its momentum shoved the creature into the *Marlin*'s wooden railing. The railing snapped under all that weight and inertia, and turtle and crate disappeared into the depths of the sea.

"*Hoy!*" someone bellowed. Maki stood there, silhouetted by the raging fires behind him. He walked with a limp, and a thin trickle of blood issued from his mouth, but he was still on his feet. He leveled his machete at the splintersoul. "I'm gonna make you pay for what you did to my ship."

The splintersoul regarded him with impatience and contempt.

"You don't have what I want," he rasped. But when he turned back toward Tala and the prince, Maki lunged forward, machete flickering like a tongue of steel flame. The splintersoul roared and sprang just out of the short blade's reach.

"Get him out of here!" Maki shouted as he pressed his attack. He whipped up his pistol, but the man in the purple coat lashed out with a high kick, and Maki's shot echoed off into the night sky.

Tala tried to aim a shot to help him, but he and the splintersoul were too close. And she couldn't ignore the increasing number of shades that were moving to surround them all. "I'm not leaving you!" she shouted as she and the prince fired round after round into the massed ranks of shades.

"We have our orders!" Maki shouted. "If he dies, all this was for nothing!"

"*Yes, what he said!*" the Iron Prince added, firing off a shot that stopped a goat-shade in its tracks. "Two shots left."

"But . . . Maki . . ." Tala said, more to herself than anyone else. The ground felt unsteady beneath her, and not just because the ground at the moment was a sinking ship.

Somehow, he heard her over the din of battle anyway. As he dipped beneath a high kick from the man in the purple coat, he grinned. "Wish you'd started calling me that sooner, Sarge! Now—"

He stopped as the wasp-shade swooped down on him, angling a stinger the size of Tala's forearm. But just before it could hit him, a white blur crashed into it: Sunny. Both shades spilled to the deck as Kapona—shoulders heaving, muscles lined with rivulets of blood and sweat—bulled her way into the fight. *"Come on and fight me, you purple ponce!"*

As she and Maki set upon the splintersoul and his shades, Tala felt herself rooted on the spot. The whole war, she'd led from the front. The people who'd stepped onto the *Marlin* with her had done so because she'd led them there. To leave them now went against every fiber of her being.

"Sergeant!"

Especially if it was for the prince.

She spat out a curse, then turned and ran for the boat. The prince had situated himself in it already, though he'd done nothing to unhitch it from the side of the ship. Tala rolled her eyes. The idiot.

"Hurry!" the prince shouted. "We need—" Then he froze, his eyes wide.

Tala had just enough time to comprehend the shape in the corner of her eye, but not enough time to defend herself as a spider-shade fell upon her from the rigging above. She tried her best to twist out of the way, but there was no mistaking the telltale pain up and down her arm as one of its fangs pierced her shoulder. It stung even harder as it hit bone, and she let out a shuddering gasp as a chill numbness spread beneath her skin like blood in water.

She heard the familiar report of her own revolver. The spider-shade's fang burst into a gaping wound as a bullet tore through the creature's face. It squealed, and its disembodied fang disappeared in a burst of light, only to begin regrowing on the spider-shade's face. Quickly Tala hefted her rifle and brought its butt down between the spider's two sets of eyes, but even though it hit the chitin with a satisfying crunch, she could feel herself putting less force behind the blow than normal. Still, it was the opportunity she needed to run.

The deck pitched hard again, and Tala nearly fell on her face as she sprinted to the boat. She didn't jump the railing so much as throw herself over it, landing hard on the floor of the boat.

"You certainly took your time!" the prince snapped. He tapped the metal hitch above the boat, and it immediately released the ropes suspending their vessel along the side of the *Marlin*. There was an unpleasant lurch as it fell, slapping hard against the roiling surface of the water.

Tala's gut churned as the venomous cold slowly spread up and down her arm. She eyed her wound warily. The prince had shot off the fang before the spider-shade could infect her with too much venom, but apparently some had gotten through. She sucked in an unsteady breath. She just had to hold on until they made landfall.

She turned to yank the motor's ripcord, only to see the prince already at the motor. He gave its surface a gentle stroke, and then it roared to life all by itself before settling back into a gentle purr.

It kicked up a white wake behind it as the tiny boat sped away from the sinking, burning wreck that had once been the good ship *Marlin*.

Tala strained to see the battle as they left it behind. Desperately, her eyes combed the fire for any silhouette of Maki. But all she saw was a swarming mass of shades, and she felt the pit drop out of the bottom of her stomach. If the shades weren't disappearing, then the splintersoul still drew breath. And if he was still alive . . .

That doesn't mean Maki's down, she admonished herself. *Get a grip, soldier.*

"What happened with your—with Beaky back there?" the prince said. His glasses were flecked with seawater. Stray strands of his topknot had come loose, rippling in the wind. The folds of his kimono rippled open. "Why did he freeze?"

Tala, who'd seen the prince freeze up at the sight of that spider-shade, bit back the obvious rejoinder. Now wasn't the time for sniping, she decided. Not when her comrades were fighting and dying behind her.

"I don't know," she said after a moment. "He won't even go near them."

"I find the practice of slavery abhorrent," said the prince, "but I have to wonder: What's the point of having one if it won't even obey you?"

Tala's entire demeanor frosted over. She didn't know whether the chill was genuine, or just the spider venom at work. She remembered her promise to shoot his ear off, but she needed him intact for now. That was the only thing saving him from a reign as Steel Lord Jimuro the Asymmetrical.

Well, she thought with a woozy glance at her now-numb shoulder, that and the onset of fatigue from a wound brimming with spider venom.

"Your Brilliance," she said carefully. "Either we can both fight for our lives . . . or I can give you to him."

The prince shut up again and kept a hand on the motor.

Tala turned back to gaze at the *Marlin* one last time. She'd meant to say a farewell of sorts, but when she looked, she saw a dozen flashes of light: the telltale signs of discorporating shades.

Her jaw dropped open. He'd done it. Somehow, that handsome bastard Maki had done it.

But then she saw someone leap over the side of the ruined hulk.

Someone with a long, rippling purple coat.

A great gray shape breached the water: one Tala knew all too well. She'd seen it pick off Tomodanese patrol boats, and devour any hostiles unlucky enough to get pushed over during a boarding party. It was Tivron, the fearsome hammerhead-shade from which Maki had gotten his nickname.

And now, it had a new master.

The splintersoul landed adroitly on Tivron's back, wrapping his hand around a dorsal fin the size of himself. Tivron dipped back below the surface of the ocean so that only its rider was visible above the chop. They sped for the boat, and Tala knew perfectly well she could never outrun the scourge of the Sanbuna seas.

She blinked, and fresh tears fell down her cheeks. Tivron had been a symbol of hope. Thanks to him, she and her countryfolk had swum safely in the same water that was instant death for the Tomodanese. Now his partner was gone, and Tivron was the enemy.

"With this death, my line ends." For a man staring down the threat of a giant shark with a homicidal maniac surfing on its back, Prince Jimuro spoke with remarkable calm. "An unbroken bloodline stretching back over three thousand years, since the First Spirit itself opened its great mouth and spat Tomoda onto the surface of the world. This is . . . not how I would've liked for it to happen." He hefted her stolen gun experimentally. "Thank you for everything, Sergeant. I know we're more foe than not, but you have a prince's courtesy and gratitude."

She wanted to spit his courtesy and gratitude back in his face. This situation did nothing to change who he was and what he'd done. But she had her orders. She had the weight of her comrades' sacrifices on her shoulders. And she had a fervent desire not to die here, in a boat with a monster, at the hands of an even bigger monster.

And that meant becoming a monster in kind.

"Um, are you going to say something?" Prince Jimuro said. "I just said a lot, and it's customary to at least say something in re—"

She forced herself to stand on the speeding boat and turned to face their pursuer full-on. "Stay back, Your Brilliance," she said. She had finally been pushed to the point where she had nothing left to lose from what she did next. She just had to time it right.

"You'll get no argument from me," the prince said, slipping himself behind her. He looked even paler than usual, though he made an admirable attempt at remaining calm. But all his discipline wasn't enough to stop his hands from shaking as he brandished her gun. When he saw the way her eyes lingered on his trembling hand, he added: "The weapon is steel and I'm a son of Tomoda. When I lend my final shot to you, it will fly straight."

Lending her a bullet from her own gun that he'd stolen, Tala thought ruefully. If that didn't sum up the fucking Tomodanese. "You won't need to shoot."

He frowned warily. "What do you intend to do?"

The splintersoul was almost upon them. If he didn't leap aboard the boat itself, or summon one of his shades onto it, he was surely about to command the shark-shade to open its mouth wide and devour them, bow-to-stern.

But she'd drawn an imaginary line across the surface of the ocean in her head, and just then the shark crossed it.

"*Dimangan!*" she shouted, pointing her finger at the spot of water just behind them. Blue energy spewed from her fingertip in jagged tendrils. Pain ripped through the inside of her skull as something unfolded itself from the deepest corners of her brain. It wasn't like summoning Beaky. It was altogether more probing, like giving birth to a thought made flesh. With a cry, she dropped to one knee.

The shade that formed in midair was twelve feet tall, every inch of him covered in ridges of muscle and skin somehow a soft brown even though he hadn't felt sunlight in years. Shards and spikes of bone studded his body, silver in the moonlight. He faced away from them, so she could see a distinctive pactmark spread across the back of his bald scalp: a pair of blue triangles that lay tip-to-tip, like the wings of a moth.

With ungainly grace, Dimangan landed hard on the flat head of the shark-shade, crouched forward bestially on his spiny forearms. In the back of her head, Tala felt a great tangle of emotions: Confusion, as he took in the fact that he was surfing on a giant shark and facing down a purple-coated stranger. Fury, as he understood this man meant Tala harm.

But drowning them both out was the pain that threatened to split open his and her heads alike.

She gritted her teeth and forced herself to see straight. She had white-knuckled through this before. She could do it again.

The splintersoul's thick eyebrows leapt up his forehead as he realized what he was looking at. *"Abomination,"* he said, horrified.

And Mang rumbled in an inhuman basso: "You don't have to be a jerk about it."

His hand curled into a fist the size of a chicken, and he threw the right cross to end all right crosses. It caught the splintersoul completely off guard, and he flew face-first into the air.

The shark-shade instantly evaporated beneath Dimangan's feet, and he dropped adroitly into the water. He bobbed below the waves, too, but Tala knew better than to worry about him. And sure enough, he resurfaced a moment later right beside the boat. "You okay, Lala?" he said.

Tala barely kept herself collected. She saw Dimangan so rarely, even if he was always there in her head. His face had been twisted into something harsh and ugly by their shadepact, with a heavy jaw and sloped forehead. But thankfully, her moment of weakness had left his eyes intact. They had a way of unlocking a lot of different feelings in her, and she wasn't used to experiencing them without him hanging out in the back of her mind anymore. "No," she said, voice shaking as she fought to control her pain. With each stab of agony, she felt his own as if it were an echo: like her own, but huger and all-encompassing. "But I'm safe now, thanks to you, Mang."

She leaned down and slipped an arm around his massive neck and shoulders, carefully navigating the slick spines of bone there. She'd learned the hard way that it was difficult to hug him normally anymore.

When she glanced up at Jimuro, though, she saw the prince wearing an expression of pure shock, but it was bleeding over into horror. He jerked as far away from Dimangan as he could, then shrank into that corner. *"What the hell is that thing?"*

At last, Dimangan seemed to notice Tala wasn't alone in the boat. His brow furrowed dangerously. "Tomodanese," he growled, his voice as soft as thunder. A fresh knife of pain carved through the back of Tala's head. "Lala, who is this steelhound?"

Any other day of her life, she would've shared the fullness of his ire, and the homicidal spark that flickered just below it. For Dimangan, she would always be ready to pick one more fight, kill one more steelhound, win one more war.

But that wasn't an option now. Couldn't be an option now. The only option she had left was the mission, and that meant explaining some things.

"Mang," she said, gesturing to the prince, "this is Iron Prince Jimuro, heir to the throne of Tomoda." And then she turned to Jimuro and ignored the stabbing between her temples as she said, "Prince Jimuro, this is Dimangan." She hesitated one last time, then finally gave the words voice: "He's my brother."

Both Jimuro and Dimangan erupted with questions and outrage, but Tala couldn't answer any of it. Her head was too fuzzy, her mind too distant. Fatigue had turned her muscles to congee. The pain in her head was sharp and persistent, but the poison was carrying her far, far away from it . . .

There was a blackness darker than the night that surrounded them, and before she could stop it, it swallowed her whole.

PART TWO

. . .

SPLINTERED SOULS

CHAPTER FIVE

LEE

The taste of last night's beer was stale in the back of Lee's throat as she stumbled her way onto the topmost deck of the *Wave Falcon*. She'd never been fond of the stuff on land; it didn't travel nearly as well as whiskey, and Lee never stayed put for long. But the *Wave Falcon* had a large shipment in its hold, part of Shang's long-term strategy to assert control over Tomoda by flooding the island's markets with every commodity it could before Dahal did the same thing. And apparently Lee's new Li-Quan credentials—Xiulan had made her sign a fancy piece of paper and everything—allowed her to commandeer whatever she liked in the pursuit of justice. So Lee figured, what was the point of being a cop if she didn't enjoy the perks?

When Xiulan had first laid out what being her partner meant, Lee had kept cool. But inside, she'd been awed by the possibility it represented. Her whole life, she'd never had the freedom to just *have* what she wanted. Whenever a woman like her felt desire, there'd always been a degree of danger.

In the gray light of morning, however, she was belatedly beginning to appreciate the restraint that danger bred.

Her boots clanked on the ship's steel deck, and the noise only made her head pound worse. Despite her vagrant nature, she liked to be about as put-together as a woman of her station could be. But today her clothes hung sloppily off her frame. Her short hair was matted and messy. She was lucky she hadn't had a chance to get her hands on some makeup before she'd left; on this harsh morning, she was sure smeared makeup would've made her look as dead as she felt.

Well, this is what she gets for partnering with a gutter dog, she thought as she approached the prow of the ship.

Her benefactor was already standing there, arms clasped behind her back. She'd replaced her billowy white trousers with a smartly tailored suit in the same color. Her long, pale coat, however, remained. There was nothing to see but the gray mist, but Xiulan stared out at it as if it were a particularly interesting painting. The sea breeze made the edges of her coat ripple impressively, and Lee wondered if that was precisely why Xiulan was standing there.

As Lee approached, Xiulan casually combed her hair back down over her left eye with her fingers. By the time Lee fell into step beside her, she was a cyclops again. "You had a rough night," the princess said jovially.

"I had a fucking great night," Lee muttered. "I'm having a rough morning. Key difference there."

Xiulan's smile was small but potent, like a drop of chili oil in a bowl of broth. "I was worried you'd miss your first view of Tomoda itself." She didn't look even slightly worried, but Lee figured it didn't bear mentioning.

"Kohoyama, huh?" Lee said, stifling a yeast-flavored yawn. She knew she said the word clumsily. Growing up, she'd managed to duck out of imperial schooling. The Tomodanese leaned heavily on compulsory education to remake the countries they conquered, but even they didn't care if some Jeongsonese girl fell through the cracks. It had made her feel a good deal freer at the time, but it had left her with a limited grasp of how to speak their growling, staccato excuse for a language. Reading it had been a necessity, since their alphabet had been on every sign in the country. But she'd been much better at evading the interest of authorities when they thought she was just some dumb Shang who couldn't understand them.

"That's right," said Xiulan. "In addition to its status as a bustling port, it was a pleasure city for the royal family and their favored companions, where they would vacation in the summers. And the winters. And for the nine major festivals. And . . ."

"You and yours ever have a place like that?" Lee said. She knew it was impudent—and imprudent—to interrupt a member of the royal family, but she was too hung over to be pudent or prudent. "You hear the rumors and all, but I've never gotten within spitting distance of a palace."

Xiulan's smile faltered. "Once, we had many," she said. "One in each of the thirty-three lands of Shang dominion. Now the only one that remains intact is the Palace of Glass. Do you know it?"

Lee shook her head.

"That's not surprising," said Xiulan. "Growing up, we did what we could to avoid publicizing our location to the enemy. If Tomoda had managed to find and eliminate the Shang family, it would've been the end of our kingdom's future."

Lee sighed indulgently. Every so often on their short voyage, Xiulan would get into this kind of lofty talk about her family's place in the natural order of things. It was tiresome, but Lee hadn't gotten quite bold enough to call her on it just yet. Still, she knew herself well enough to know it was probably just a matter of time. "So that's how you spent the war, was it?" Lee said. "Sitting pretty up in a palace, an army of maids with big tits at your beck and call?"

"It was an army of soldiers," Xiulan said evenly, "and their bust-lines varied greatly. We took the Palace of Glass, least of our retreats, and turned it into the seed from which the Peony Revolution would eventually sprout. Someday, though, I would like to go back and enjoy the palace in the manner it was meant to be experienced." Suddenly her manner became brisk. "But I have a lot of work to do until that day comes. And I sincerely doubt Ruomei would give me much time to relax, if she were to be the one to ascend and take the throne."

It was Lee's turn to sour, and not just from the hangover. The past four days, Xiulan had given her a pretty good idea of what the reign of Shang Ruomei might look like. If Xiulan was to be believed—and honestly, Lee wasn't totally sure that was the case just yet—then Ruomei had little desire besides turning Shang into the new Tomoda, when its people had only just caught their breath from fighting the last war. Lee honestly didn't give that many shits about the global order, since it looked bad for her people either way. But lean times had a funny way of being leaner for her people than most.

"What are you hoping to find here, then?" Lee said. "You need me to point out the guy once we find him, but it seems like you're the one who's got all the leads. Not that I'm complaining about getting a free pass out of irons, but why let me roam? What d'you need me for?"

Thoughtfully, Xiulan removed her pipe from her coat and lit it. "Mine was a privileged upbringing," she said eventually. "I can expertly navigate the intricacies of palace intrigue, I'm well versed in all the great classics of Shang's noble culture, and I can paint a fine landscape if I have a free afternoon. The field in which I'm most lacking is perspective: a contrast with my own views, held by a mind I consider to possess sufficient keenness." When she saw Lee frowning at her, she said, "To phrase things in another way: How did you find Lefty? Shang is a massive country, and he very well could've been anywhere. How did you locate him?"

Lee closed her eyes and pictured him. Lefty. There'd been a mistake, if ever she'd met one. But he'd been a handsome mistake. And, Lee thought as his face morphed into someone slighter and younger, with a bang over one eye, she'd always had a weakness for those.

The job had been simple enough: Find a good, upstanding citizen and present themselves to him as landowners looking to reward him for his patriotism during the war. They'd found it in Hong Wei, a dentist who was, by all accounts, the richest man in his small town. She and Lefty had introduced themselves to Hong as siblings who'd inherited a rice farm but needed a silent partner so they could grow the operation even more. They'd toured him through an abandoned farm, the whole time talking up the quality of the soil and the minerals in the water as proof that the place was practically a secret opal mine.

Lee was a born gutter dog who hadn't known a damn thing about farming, but apparently her performance had been convincing enough. Hong Wei had signed over twelve hundred yuan to them in exchange for a generous 15 percent stake in their burgeoning enterprise. She and Lefty didn't mind giving up such a large stake for so little, they'd assured him, because they were just that confident in their little farm's future. The next day, she'd woken up to find her bed empty, the money gone, and the local cops closing in. All because she'd slacked on her one rule, the only law she ever respected.

Leave them before they leave you.

The whole time she'd been trailing Lefty, she'd promised herself that she'd kill him for this. With every whisper that brought her closer to him, she'd treated herself to a new fantasy about how she'd actually do it. And when that trail finally led her to Jungshao, she was just about ready to indulge in all of them at once. But what she'd found instead . . .

The memories of the organ mill welled up in her brain, and vomit welled up in her throat. She threw herself at the nearest railing, leaned over the side, and spewed everything from last night into the dark waves below.

A full minute later, she wiped her mouth on her sleeve, stood up, and answered in a much clearer voice.

"Mostly, I just paid attention," she said. "I knew what kinds of places he liked, and I knew what he liked to do when he was scared. That was all it took to find him, really. People can do a lot of things, Inspector. But if you're really paying attention, they can never surprise you."

Xiulan took a thoughtful puff of her pipe in silence. The smoke of her breath had completely disappeared into the mist before she said, "The palace of Kohoyama is where the royal family was habitually at its most comfortable and relaxed. There, I expect they were the most . . . *themselves,* if that makes sense. I hope between my keen deductive mind and your skills of observation, we'll be able to gain some insight into where the prince might hide himself on his way down to Hagane."

" 'Down'?" said Lee. "Why wouldn't they sail directly to Hagane? Quickest path puts him in danger for the shortest amount of time."

"And it'll be the most watched route by far," Xiulan said, her tone gently chiding. "I thought you were supposed to be a keen judge of character, Inspector Lee."

Lee shrugged it off, though her ears burned a little at their tips. "You said that, not me. So you think they'll land and head south overland."

"With preplanned, secure stops along the way. And at one of those stops," Xiulan said gleefully, "you and I will lie in wait."

Lee grunted while her ears burned hotter. She was annoyed with herself. She wasn't supposed to give two shits what the royals thought. Why was her ego smarting so much? "And between now and then," she said, "we're going to find me a shade."

Xiulan merely nodded, and Lee was struck by how much regality the other woman could inject into such a small gesture. They both stood there for a moment, enjoying the spray on their faces as Xiulan hummed something soft and tuneless.

Pleasant as that moment was, though, Lee eventually felt like she should say something. "You're a princess," she said, tapping her fingers on the cold metal railing. "You should've pacted with a white crane, like the rest of your family."

Xiulan just stood there and smoked.

"Why'd you go and pact with a rat?"

Reflexively, Xiulan frowned. She segued the expression smoothly into a sly grin, but not before Lee noticed the frown.

"For one thing, they're incredibly intelligent creatures, rats," Xiulan said. "They're reliable in a fight. They excel in darkness, they can swim in even the rankest water, and they can climb nearly anything. My sister Ruomei told me they were the scum of the animal kingdom, but I suppose rats are my kind of scum: fearless and inventive." A playful light danced in Xiulan's one visible eye. "Mostly, though, I just think they're cute."

Kohoyama must have been a proud city at its peak, because even under foreign occupation it still looked like nothing Lee had ever seen. It had wide paved streets with neat rows of cars parked along their edges, short buildings with symmetrical façades and gently sloped roofs, and electric lampposts lining all its sidewalks. From the looks of it, it must have been captured without a shot fired, because she saw nary a broken window, bullet hole, or burn mark. In fact, the only real indicators she saw that it had been taken over were the presence of Shang, Sanbuna, and Dahali soldiers, and the flags under

which they marched. Most of Tomoda had been divided into dis-
crete zones of control after the Copper Sage Armistice, but Kohoyama, Xiulan explained, was far too valuable a jewel to leave in
the hands of a single power.

"Easy enough for us to get started," Lee said as they stepped off
the dock and onto dry land. "We go and say hello to the local Shang,
tell them to gas up a ride for us, and be on our merry way?"

Something chilled about Xiulan's bouncy demeanor. "I would
rather as few Shang be aware of our presence as possible," she said.
"Even if they were to learn my true identity, Ruomei commands
more far-reaching authority than I. It would only take a single phone
call for her to realize what I'm up to. We're already looking to face
the might of General Erega's finest. I'd just as soon not add Ruomei
to our list of enemies."

Lee frowned slightly, then shrugged. Streetwise Xiulan wasn't,
but Lee didn't doubt the princess knew her politics. "As you say."

Xiulan tapped some ash from her pipe. "When last I heard, the
palace was in Dahali hands. They're a mercantile society, which
makes their politics more, ah, flexible. For the right price, they'll
grant us access. They may even provide us with a vehicle."

Lee gestured to the lines of cars along the sides of the streets.
"Why not just pick one?" She pointed to a sleek-looking car, shiny
and smooth and black as obsidian. "That one looks like my kind of
ride."

"A Tomodanese-made model," Xiulan said simply. "Appealing
to the eye, but inoperable without their inborn talent of metalpacting."

"And besides that excellent point, Inspector," said someone behind them, "Chetan Parkash doesn't imagine its owner would be too
happy with you."

The two of them turned to see a stocky Dahali man striding up to
them with a rooster's confidence. He was sharp-eyed, with pro-
nounced cheekbones and a long nose. His skin was darker brown
than even the Sanbunas Lee had seen in her day. His beard, long and
black and braided into three separate forks, bounced off his muscu-
lar chest with each step. He wore a military uniform the color of wet

sand, with enough decorations on it to suggest he was someone at least halfway important. But the real eye-catcher was the knife thrust in his sash, with its gilded hilt and jewel-encrusted sheath.

"Afraid I don't know who that is," Lee said, "and I don't really care."

The man smiled, but Lee got the impression the gesture was more an excuse to show his teeth. "If there's anyone whose word you should care about," he said, gently patting his own chest, "it should be Chetan Parkash's." Despite his thick accent, Lee noted that his command of Shang was rather good.

"Well, then why don't you go find Chetan Parkash, and the two of us can have it out, eh?" she said, but Xiulan placed a firm hand on her shoulder.

"At ease, Inspector Lee," she said. "You're speaking to Chetan Parkash."

"What?" Lee said, brow furrowing. "But he said—"

"He's Dahali," said Xiulan. "The personal pronoun is a high privilege for them, afforded only to those who can, ah, afford it." She gave Parkash a shallow but respectful bow. "One which I've no doubt you're well on your way to earning."

"If this one's quarterly earnings are as favorable as last quarter's," he said, pleased. "Very good, Inspector."

Lee squinted at him. "How'd you know we were inspectors?" She figured there was no point in denying that, considering Xiulan's badge was the least of the secrets they had to give up.

"Though the port of Kohoyama is shared among the three flowers of the Garden Revolution, Chetan Parkash counts himself its greatest florist," he said, a twinkle in his eye. "Very little happens in Kohoyama that escapes this one's notice. Certainly, agents of the Li-Quan would attract this one's interest. Particularly ones who charter passage on a merchant ship, rather than going through official channels."

Lee arched an eyebrow, but Xiulan was unflappable. "Your informants served you well," she said lightly. "We're here to investigate confidential matters of personal interest to the Most August Personage of the Crane, and would not wish for our presence to interfere with the goings-on of the local garrison." She opened her coat to reveal her badge pinned to the lining. But just beneath that, Lee saw, she'd left her wallet plainly visible.

Clearly, Parkash noticed it, too. "Of course," he said, motioning for her to close her coat. "This one has the utmost respect for personal servants of the Crane Emperor. Curious as your situation is, in the interest of continuing the warm relationship between your great country and this one's, Chetan Parkash will be happy to assist your investigation in whatever capacity you wish."

Xiulan flashed Lee a grin, but Lee wasn't too sure of this herself. She had a tiny bell somewhere in her gut, and for the entirety of this short conversation, it had been softly ringing.

"We would love to accept such a generous offer," Xiulan said. Lee was struck by the change in her voice. She was prone to using flowery language just as a matter of course, but when she'd used it with the magistrate it had been a weapon, meant to intimate and intimidate. Now her voice pitched higher to turn her words into a shield. This, Lee realized, had to be a skill she'd learned growing up in the court of Shang.

Apparently it worked, because Parkash beamed. "Then allow Chetan Parkash to have you for tea, Inspectors, and you can outline your precise needs."

Tea was starting to sound good to the snarling monster that was Lee's hangover, but Xiulan held up a polite hand. "That won't be necessary," she said. "We merely wish to see the palace. The tea can be a parting gift."

Parkash was quick to adopt an expression of disappointment that Lee didn't quite buy. "Understandable," the man said. "Would you allow this one the honor of driving you there?"

Xiulan beamed. "Nothing would please us more."

Parkash led them to a car already waiting by the edge of the docks. Unlike the sleek Tomodanese cars, this one was clearly of Dahali design. Its roof was high, its nose snubbed, its profile narrow. Lee had heard that the roads in faraway Dahal were similarly narrow and cramped. On the wide-open roads of Tomoda, though, it looked like a toy.

Lee shot a wary look Xiulan's way. She hadn't survived as long as she had by just getting into the first car that opened its door to her, especially when the other passengers weren't supposed to know she was even there in the first place. But once again, Xiulan appeared blissfully unconcerned.

"*Royals,*" she muttered in Jeongsonese, softer than a breath.

A brown-coated soldier stood waiting by the car's door. His uniform was simpler than Parkash's, and the knife in his belt appropriately more plain. When Parkash approached, he banged his right fist against his left shoulder in salute, then bowed to Xiulan and Lee respectfully before opening the door. As she slid into the sunbaked brown leather bench seat, Lee was surprised at how roomy the car's interior was. But the heat trapped inside did little to assuage her hangover.

Lee had grown up in Shang's cities, so cars weren't quite the novelty for her that they would've been for someone from the country. Tomoda had introduced a full fleet of them to Shang, and not long afterward Shang itself had begun mass-producing knockoffs of the Dahali design, with an internal combustion engine. Even before Shang's Peony Revolution had broken out in earnest, both types had been common sights for a city girl like her.

She found the purr of this car's engine beneath her seat oddly soothing. She leaned back and cast an eye out the window. Here and there, she saw Tomodanese people going about their days: cleaning storefronts, walking the streets, standing on corners and chatting as they smoked cigarettes. Sometimes they would look up and stare at the car as it passed them, but for the most part they just went about their business.

It all seemed so bizarrely normal.

Lee had never been to Tomoda before, but she'd had her share of encounters with the Tomodanese. She'd felt the sting of their rifle butts against her face. She'd picked the pockets of the people they'd murdered. She'd listened time and time again on the radio as they chalked up everything they did to ending the barbarism of shade-pacting. Never mind that most of their victims couldn't even pact, whether by ability or by Shang law. To her, people like the Tomodanese had to have crawled out of some red-skied hellscape where the soil was ash and the rain ate at your flesh as it fell on you.

But this city, Kohoyama, seemed like it was just . . . a place. A place with strange-looking buildings and far more cars than she'd ever seen in her life, but a place all the same. The sky wasn't even red.

Parkash spent the drive pointing out buildings and reeling off brief explanations of what they were used for when the royal family was vacationing. And in each case, he made sure to highlight the ways in which Dahali bravery had been instrumental in capturing them, as well as the rest of the city.

"It's an elegant metaphor for the overall shape of the war, don't you think?" said Parkash as he wrapped up another one of his diatribes.

Lee cocked an eyebrow. "What's he mean?" she said to Xiulan.

Parkash studied them in the car's rearview mirror. "Chetan Parkash is surprised an agent of the Li-Quan isn't more informed on the subject of international affairs."

Lee scowled at him. She was getting the sense she'd just asked a dumb question, but the three-bearded bastard didn't get to make her feel dumb about it. "My jurisdiction's a bit more local," she said. "Why don't you dig into it so my limited Shang brain can understand?"

Her sarcasm seemed to delight Parkash more than it irked him. "While the dominions of Shang and the Sanbu Islands both languished under the rule of Tomoda, in the west lay the prosperity of Dahal," he began grandly. "Other nations fell to their metallic menace, but Dahal rose to become a power of equal stature with them, using trade with Tomoda to create innovations envied by even the Mountain Throne of Hagane." He stroked his beard a moment before adding, "Chetan Parkash means no offense to your great nation, of course. This one is simply stating the facts of the historical record."

"Of course," Xiulan said, pulling out her pipe and lighting it. Her eye was at half-mast with barely concealed boredom, though the shadow of her hat meant only Lee could see it. "We wouldn't ever think otherwise."

"When the Tomodanese grew greedy and coveted Dahal's ingenuity and riches, they launched blistering attacks against her border, and gobbled up vast swaths of her land. But while the flat-nosed devils drew first blood, it was Dahal who had the last laugh."

Lee rubbed her very flat nose and scowled more.

"Dahal proved herself ungovernable. Her people formed the Lotus Revolution, elder sister to the Jasmine of Sanbu and the Peony of Shang. And when Tomoda was forced to sink more and more resources and manpower into Dahal, Shang and Sanbu were suddenly presented with an opportunity they hadn't seen in decades." He stroked his beard, and the rings woven into its braids jangled against one another. "Dahal was a seed that lodged in Tomoda's throat, and eventually she sprouted into a garden that choked it to death."

"A story well told," Xiulan said cheerfully, though the lopsided smirk on her face remained.

"This one thanks you. But now, with great sadness," said Parkash, "Chetan Parkash must bring this ride to a close. Your destination looms, Inspectors."

Lee suddenly realized a shadow had fallen over the interior of the car. When she turned to press her nose up against the window, she saw a massive palace, far larger than any daito's mansion Lee had ever seen.

It was taller than it was wide, more like a tower than a proper palace, but despite that simple design it still commanded an air of . . . Lee couldn't think of a better word than *fanciness*. Its walls were gleaming white (*fancy*), its bowed rooftops a bright cobalt blue (*very fancy*), its lawns green and inviting (*oh so fancy*). Like the city, there was nary a scratch on its face. The only things missing were the blue Tomodanese flags that had once surely fluttered from its spires and windows, not the Dahali ones that flew there now.

"So," said Lee as the car came to a stop outside its front gate. "This is where evil goes to get a tan."

"You never struck me as particularly concerned about evil," Xiulan said, getting out of the car and stretching.

Lee shrugged. "Plenty concerned about tans."

"Per the agreement reached in the Copper Sage Armistice, the palace has remained largely untouched and vacated, save for some cursory spoils taken as a well-deserved compensation for Great Da-hal's efforts in securing the peace."

At this, Lee genuinely grinned. Thieving, she understood. "Of course," she said, trying on courtly civility for a change. It didn't fit the best, but Lee looked good in anything.

"There are troops stationed nearby under Chetan Parkash's com-mand," he went on. "If you find them and tell them this one has ordered them to give you a ride anywhere you wish, they will do it. You have the word of Chetan Parkash." He smiled again, teeth gleaming beneath his thick black beard.

"And you have Shang's sincerest thanks for your generosity and discretion," Xiulan said. "We'll have to dine with you before we depart. As a way of showing our gratitude."

"Nothing would make this one happier," said Parkash. "Inspec-tors." He bowed deep one last time, then slipped back into his car.

Lee and Xiulan watched him drive away in silence. Lee's mouth twisted as she stared at those headlights. Soft as a chime on the wind, the bell in her gut was still ringing away.

Xiulan broke the silence first. "Have you ever been in a palace before, Inspector Lee?"

"In Hai-Kwung, a palace was what you called a place where you could hire yourself someone pretty for the night."

"Then I shall take that as a no," said Xiulan. She beamed. "Have heart, Lee. You're in for a treat."

"I don't know." Lee sighed as they started for the door. "The other kind of palace is hard to beat."

CHAPTER SIX

JIMURO

S he still hadn't woken up.

All night long, she'd curled in the middle of the boat, her breaths shallow and her rest fitful. Jimuro had crammed himself into the boat's stern, one hand on the boat's metal motor to keep it running. In his other hand, he held a single bullet: the only remaining round in the gun he'd borrowed from the sergeant. It had no targets now, so instead he held it flat in his palm and coursed his spirit through it, willing it to point due north.

But while he kept an eye on the sea ahead, the true object of his gaze was the gargantuan slave at the bow of the boat, the monster the sergeant had called brother.

His gaze slid from the ridges of Dimangan's back muscles and bones to fall on the unconscious sergeant. Her breathing was still labored, and her face was furrowed with pain. She was mostly still, though occasionally her entire body would spasm. Even as he watched, she did it again, every centimeter of her twitching and convulsing.

The brute cradling her sucked in sharply, though Jimuro wasn't certain exactly how those creatures breathed. Seeing them there, he was struck by how similar the sergeant and her brute looked. Even

accounting for the way barbarism had twisted the slave's form, both
it and its sister were sketched in similar hard lines.

But the more his focus drifted to Sergeant Tala, the brighter outrage sparked in his stomach. She'd been so self-righteous in the brig,
and yet a human slave was a taboo so dire, even people as depraved
as the Sanbunas and Shang considered the practice beneath them.

That outrage curdled into disgust in his gut as he considered the
monstrosity before him—not a monster, for in truth this creature,
Dimangan, was a victim. The true monster lay unconscious in its
lap. Enslaving another creature's spirit was abhorrent enough,
whether that creature was person or beast. But to enslave one's own
flesh and blood . . . He thought of Fumiko, his own sister. She'd died
a terrible death at Sanbu's hands, but in his heart Jimuro knew he
would have wished that same fate on her ten thousand times before
he wished the one the sergeant had inflicted on the thing her brother
had become.

He looked down at the hand holding the bullet and realized he'd
clenched it tight. He shook his head to clear his thoughts, pushed his
glasses back up his nose, and reoriented his makeshift compass. He
considered letting the slave know they were nearing the shores of
Kinzokita, but he stopped himself. They had reached a tacit unspo-
ken agreement, prince and slave.

Neither of them would say anything to each other.

That way, neither of them would have to die.

By the time they finally reached the rocky coast of Kinzokita, it was
full-on morning. The clouds overhead were thick and gray as steel
wool, the way they always were up north. Despite everything, Jimuro's heart swelled. After three long years, he'd finally set eyes on his
beloved country, and soon enough his feet would follow suit. He'd
longed to breathe its air, to eat some genuine udon made from grains
grown in its dirt, to lie awake at night and listen to the gentle call of
the cicadas in its trees. He could feel the spirits of the world wherever he went, but as he beheld the friendly shore, they practically
sang in his veins.

Then he remembered how far away from that life he still was.

And his eyes lingered darkly on the barbarians that had been tasked with bringing him there safely.

Wordlessly, the slave guided their boat into the shallows until the prow ground up against the shore. Jimuro leapt from the boat, the water plastering his kimono's folds against his body. He shivered in the morning chill, his breath visible. But sure enough, beneath the noise of the lapping tide, he could hear Tomoda's unofficial national anthem, the song of the cicada.

He turned around to haul the sergeant out of the boat, only to be confronted with the sight of a musclebound giant nearly four meters tall already holding her in its arms. He gaped up at it.

The slave glared balefully back down. "Out of my way," it rumbled, not giving Jimuro the courtesy of speaking in Tomodanese.

Jimuro wanted to get out of its way, but he found himself rooted on the spot. Though there was little light, Dimangan still managed to cast a shadow over him. Jimuro's whole body felt rigid, as if it were merely a metal vessel into which his spirit had been poured.

Dimangan rolled its eyes, then moved faster than any creature had a right to. It lunged forward, its bone spurs flashing, and then its head was a centimeter from Jimuro's face in less time than it took for the Iron Prince to blink. Jimuro yelped in surprise and fell back onto his bottom, sitting wrist-deep in the shallows and scrambling to get away.

It glared down at him. "If I killed you now, nobody would know. You'd become one of history's unsolved mysteries. Once Tomoda was ground down to dust, you'd become nothing. You would deserve it." It took a slow, ponderous step toward Jimuro and added, "And for me, it would be so easy."

That much was true. The only leverage Jimuro had was the one bullet in his borrowed gun. Against Dimangan, it would do less than nothing. But if Jimuro used it to kill Sergeant Tala, it would sever the magical connection keeping them together. So the question was: If it came down to it, could he get off a shot before the monster ended him?

His eyes fell on the unconscious sergeant bundled in her slave's arms, and the question of *could* suddenly took on a completely different tone in his head.

Dimangan glared down at him a moment longer. It seemed as though it were truly considering the idea. Its muscles bunched and its sharp spurs of bone glinted. Jimuro's prodigious imagination treated him to a dozen vivid visions of what they could do to his own fragile body.

Dimangan's fist clenched tighter. In its contours, Jimuro saw the death he thought he'd cheated.

Suddenly Dimangan's entire form flickered, as if it were a movie on a screen and a bad frame had just run through the projector. It was only for a second, if that long, but it was enough.

The sergeant fell into the shallows right in front of him just as Dimangan reappeared. It looked down at its own empty hands in confusion, then saw its sister lying facedown in the water. *"What did you do?"* it roared, loping forward as Jimuro hastily flipped Tala onto her back.

"Nothing!" Jimuro cried. "Nothing at all!" He pointed to the wound in Sergeant Tala's shoulder. "It was that spider-shade. The one that bit her. Your sister's very strong, but she's been fighting its venom for hours with no food or water. Even she has her limits." When Dimangan looked unconvinced, he snapped: *"If I could do something to hurt you, don't you think I'd have done it before now?"*

That seemed to pierce the creature's doubts like a bullet through bone. When it moved again, it was only to pick its sister back up. "On your way, steelhound," it growled in a voice that made every hair on Jimuro's body stand up. "It's a long walk to Hagane. You'd better get started."

Jimuro gaped. "But you're—your sister was going to—"

Dimangan didn't seem to care what its sister was going to do. It'd stalked out of the surf at last, onto dry land. With its arms full, it could only rely on its smaller legs, which made it move clumsily. But even so, it showed no signs of stopping.

"Wait!" Jimuro called before he could stop himself. Even after three years of imprisonment, he was still a prince born, and used to commanding instant obedience with a word. So he was surprised when the slave didn't even hesitate; it just kept walking, carrying its sister and trailing a single set of massive footprints in the sand.

Though she was months dead, in that moment Jimuro heard Steel

Lord Yoshiko's voice in his ear, as clearly as if she were right next to him. *Leave them to die.*

But they saved me, he protested.

She was ordered *to save you,* rang the voice of the departed Steel Lord. *If it were her choice, she would have let you die. You are the Iron Prince. You are in your own country. The spirits will preserve you. You have no use for savages and slaves.*

She raised some excellent points, he thought as he glared at the retreating forms of the monster and what was left of her brother. What was to stop him from just marching into the nearest town, identifying himself, and finally being shown the respect he was due?

But Sergeant Tala's job isn't to respect you, another voice countered. If the memory of his mother's voice was steel-hard, his sister's was soft and bright as copper. *It's to keep you alive.* He could almost see the mischievous curl of her lips as she added, *How has she done so far?*

He murmured a hurried apology to his mother, and to all his other ancestors watching him. And then he ran to catch up with the Sanbunas.

He had to jog to keep up with Dimangan's long strides. "Wait," he said again.

Dimangan's expression didn't change. Its eyes didn't so much as flicker Jimuro's way. But its next steps were undeniably longer. Rapidly, it was leaving Jimuro behind again.

Jimuro groaned, then broke into a full-on run. "I, Jimuro, Iron Prince of Tomoda and heir to the Steel Throne, divine vessel of the spirits and beating heart of Tomoda's people, command you to halt!"

Dimangan whirled around, and Jimuro nearly fell onto his face trying to stop in time. "I don't have time for you," the creature snarled.

Jimuro did his best to channel his mother. In his mind, she was still the true Steel Lord; he was just a cheap tin replica. But he wouldn't let this slave see that dullness. He had to be true steel, too.

"Where do you think you're going?" he said.

Dimangan glowered at him. "Where do you think? Lala needs me."

Despite his deep-seated fear of this irrational, angry creature, a part of Jimuro's mind registered its use of a nickname. Had it been a family name of the sergeant's? It was so hard to keep track of Sanbuna naming conventions. "Sergeant Tala needs medical help," he said. "Can you provide it to her?"

"You don't know what I can do," Dimangan said, starting to turn again.

"I know your form's only maintaining because on some subconscious level, your sister's willing you to remain while she fights for her life. But you've already seen her start to falter."

"She's stronger than any poison," Dimangan said, though there was the tiniest tinge of doubt hiding somewhere in its tone.

"What if she's not?" Jimuro said. "And if she's still not awake by the time her willpower gives out for good, what happens to her once you disappear?"

Dimangan's eyes narrowed to slits. "Where would you take her?"

Jimuro tried not to show his relief that they'd entered into the negotiation phase. "In addition to our many estates and palaces, my family maintained a separate network of discreet safe houses around the country," he said. "Our spies would use them, as would members of the family who just needed to get away for a while."

"Slaughtering people and enslaving the survivors? That's gotta take a lot out of someone."

Jimuro bristled. Immediately a dozen replies leapt to his lips. That Sanbuna factory workers and manual laborers were paid wages for the work they did for the state. That Tomoda had dragged a screaming, ungrateful Sanbu into the future, and had asked for relatively little in return for its generosity. That the one person who shouldn't be lecturing him about slavery was a willing slave.

His eyes fell to Dimangan's curled fist, larger than Jimuro's own head. As he eyed that powerful arm and those jutting plates of bone, a detailed vision of his future painted itself before the Iron Prince's very eyes.

It was mostly in shades of red.

So instead of all those other replies, he simply said, "General Erega and I have a plan, and the next part involves heading to this safe house. Now, think: Your sister agreed to carry out this plan. With her dying breath, if necessary. You . . . live . . . in her head. Can you honestly tell me she'd want you to walk away from that for her?"

He felt a pang of guilt as the argument dropped from his lips.

Now that he'd pointed it out, there was no way the slave would be able to walk away. Its will was subservient to its sister's, no matter how convincing an illusion of autonomy she'd crafted for it.

Sure enough, Dimangan eventually nodded: just the once, but the once was all Jimuro needed. "How far?"

"A bit," Jimuro admitted. He didn't remember the exact distance. He hadn't been up to this safe house since he was eight years old.

Dimangan grunted, and Jimuro understood: *Lead the way.*

It took them the better part of an hour to make the march inland. As with the voyage, he and Dimangan passed it in silence, while Tala barely stirred as she bounced in her brother's arms.

Jimuro used the silence to address the swirl of questions rampaging through his head. Who was that man who'd single-handedly sunk the *Marlin* and slaughtered every soul aboard? He didn't seem to be affiliated with any one nation, so what had Jimuro done to earn his enmity?

And, he thought as he narrowed his eyes at the sergeant, how had Tala come to be like him?

Her expression was pained, her eyes twitching beneath their lids. Though Dimangan's form had held strong since the walk began, it was only a matter of time before she faltered again. But all Jimuro could think of was that in all of known history, there were only two individuals who'd been able to enslave more than one spirit. The first was a madman who'd been devoured by the sea last night.

And the second was right there in front of him.

Despite everything Jimuro had to consider, with every step they took toward their destination, excitement grew in his chest. He savored the familiar taste of the air, the springy grass beneath his feet. As the landscape transitioned from shore to forest, the cicadas' trilling only grew in intensity.

He closed his eyes as he walked and felt the spirits flow through him. They were everywhere: in the rocks, in the birds above, in the individual blades of grass and in the wind that swayed them. Wherever he went in the world, the spirits there would sing to him. But they never sang so sweetly as they did in Tomoda.

I'm home at last, he thought. *Soon, my work can begin.*

For half a heartbeat, his step faltered.

They crested a hill, and there it was: a small cabin in the middle of a grove of fir trees. It had a gray stone foundation, dark wooden walls, and a thickly thatched roof, steep enough to shrug off the northern snows. The small windows he remembered had a bit of accumulated dust, but they were intact. The door was untouched, too, and it slid open with a simple tap of its rusty iron handle.

The inside was as he remembered it. There were only two rooms, and one of those was the bathroom. Besides the black iron stove in the kitchen area, there was no metal to be found—just wood and stone. It didn't look at all like the sort of place the royal family would have ever deigned to visit.

All things considered, Jimuro couldn't have been happier to be there.

He hadn't realized until just now how much he'd missed being inside a structure of Tomodanese design, furnished in the Tomodanese way. Instead of swinging doors: sensible sliding ones, to save space. Instead of chairs: straw mats and cushions on the floor, so one would never be too far from the earth. Instead of clutter: sparseness, to ensure that the mind was similarly clear. He bowed and muttered a quick prayer of gratitude to the spirit of the house before entering.

It took Dimangan a full minute to carefully squeeze itself through the doorway, limb by limb. When it finally managed its way in, it had to hunch over like an ape just to fit, and even then its huge bald scalp threatened to graze the ceiling. It scowled at the cramped environs. "This is your fancy safe house?" Indoors, its deep voice felt resonant enough to rattle Jimuro's bones.

"I'm sure it's luxury compared with whatever squalor you and your sister lived in as jungle-runners," he sniffed, adjusting his glasses. He tapped the cold stove, and its little door popped open to reveal that it had no fuel stocked. He sighed, then pressed a hand to it and poured his spirit into the iron's emptiness.

The steel is empty, he recited to himself. *The steel is bone, and you are blood.*

In moments, it began to feel warm to his touch, though it would take a while to heat up properly.

He gestured to a straw mat rolled up in the corner. "Lay her down on that pallet."

Irritably, Dimangan nudged the mat flat with its giant foot. Jimuro frowned to himself. From his observation during the sergeant's shifts guarding him, her bird-slave had a similarly bad temper. Was this characteristic of all slaves, or was Sergeant Tala just that callous a master?

He shifted his grip up on the iron stove as it got hotter. He was channeling his spirit into the round belly of the device, and that was where most of the heat flowed, but magic couldn't circumvent the laws of thermodynamics and convection. In another minute or so it would be entirely too hot for him to hold, but by then it would have enough built-up residual heat to last a few hours.

The slave knelt by its sister's side, stroking her hair with a tenderness that took Jimuro aback. But then its image flickered again. When it popped back into existence, its entire body shook with frustration for a moment. Not tearing its gaze away from its sister, it asked: "What now?"

"What do you mean, 'what now'?"

With ponderous, dangerous slowness, the slave turned to regard Jimuro. "You brought us to this rathole," it said, gesturing to a cabin that Jimuro was only just realizing would not withstand a sufficiently angry Dimangan. "What was the next part of your plan?"

"Bringing you here *was* the plan," Jimuro said, determined not to show this creature fear. "*Somewhere safe and warm,*" he added, raising his voice to be heard over Dimangan's vocal annoyance, "where we can stabilize her condition. The rest of it will come to me. I just need time to think."

Dimangan growled, then sat down heavily enough to make the whole house shake. "How can you think in a place like this?"

This wretched, sullen creature didn't deserve the gift of a prince's honesty. But when Jimuro opened his mouth, it was to give that gift just the same.

The first time Jimuro had laid his eyes on the Kinzokita estate, he was in the passenger seat of a car. His family had been wintering at the palace at Kohoyama, a full day's drive south and to the west. Lord Kurihara was back from the front in Shang, and for his valor had been rewarded with a stay at the palace as the royal family's honored guest. It'd been fun for Jimuro's parents, who were quite close with Lord Daisuke and Lady Kaguya. It'd been fun for Fumiko, who loved to tease her friend Kurihara Keiko about the crush Keiko supposedly harbored on him. But Jimuro had mostly stayed in his room, studiously drawing the snowfall outside while his friend Kohaku warmed her paws near the heater.

He'd been asleep in his bed, Kohaku curled up at his feet, when he'd been shaken awake. He'd expected it to be a servant, getting him up for the day, or maybe Fumiko, wanting to sneak out and explore the grounds at night. But when he'd opened his eyes, he'd found himself staring into the face of the reigning Steel Lord, divine vessel of the spirits, beating heart of the Tomodanese people, and the most powerful woman in the world.

But saying all that got cumbersome, so he'd given her a nickname.

"Mother?" he'd said. Even though he knew light and sound had no bearing on each other, his voice had sounded smaller in the dark, somehow.

Not hers, though. "Get dressed," she'd said. Her voice was customarily hard, but the thumb she ran along his cheekbone was gentle. "We're going somewhere." She'd risen to her full height and swept out of the room without another word. She knew she didn't need it. Jimuro would follow and obey.

Despite Captain Sakura's agitated insistence, the Steel Lord refused the company of even a single member of her royal guard, the Kobaruto. Rather than the sleek, futuristic car that was the chosen transport of the royal family, she'd commandeered an unremarkable staff car. "I miss being my own driver," she'd said as they pulled away. The whole car hummed as she infused its metal with her spirit and willed it to go. "When I was Iron Princess, I'd take one of these out and drive it for kilometers before I turned around."

Jimuro's eyes, still heavy with sleep, had gone wide at the thought of his mother as a joyriding princess. "Where are we turning around?"

"A secret place," she'd said.

His little eyes had grown even wider. "A secret place?"

For just a moment, his mother had shown him the barest hint of a grin, brief as sun flashing off steel. "Yes," she'd said softly. "And my favorite one in the whole world."

When they'd finally arrived after a full day of driving, Jimuro had been tired and irritable. His mother had entered eagerly, removing her rings and necklace as soon as she crossed the threshold. She stowed them amid other jewelry in a box hidden beneath a front-hall floorboard before changing into plain clothes. But Jimuro had failed to see the charm of this nondescript cottage in the middle of nowhere, surrounded by snow-laden trees. The night did little to dispel that first impression; he'd spent it shivering next to a fire his mother had built herself. In the morning, he'd had to wait while she painstakingly prepared them rice, soup, and natto herself. And once they'd finally, finally eaten, she'd told him to get his coat on so he could go out and chop wood.

That was when he'd put his foot down. "I'm the Iron Prince," he'd said, nose pointed skyward. "I'm the future of Tomoda. I don't do these things."

He'd steeled himself for his mother's disapproval. But she'd reacted with something much more unsettling: a genuine smile. Perhaps in other families, that would've been a sign of approval. But young as he'd been, Jimuro had known then that he'd just walked into a trap.

"Tomoda does these things," she'd said. "Every day, while you enjoy sweets, and run around causing trouble with your sister, the people you serve are up with the sun, working with their own hands."

He'd frowned. He'd grown up in Hagane, a glittering jewel of progress. The food there came from stores and restaurants. The streets were lined with cars. The heat came from natural gas, the light from electricity.

His mother had listened patiently as he went on about this. And then she'd calmly asked him the question that he'd known would doom him the moment he heard it: "And where do you think all that comes from?"

He'd sat there, stunned by his inability to answer such a simple question. After a moment, his mother took mercy on him.

"To me, this place is the greatest treasure the Steel Lord has," she said.

"Not the Mountain Throne?"

"No," his mother said, shaking her head. "Not the Mountain Throne."

"Not the sword of Steel Lord Setsuko?" She'd been the first Steel Lord, and Jimuro had treated himself to more than one daydream of what he would do with its bright blade.

His mother snorted. "No, not the sword, either. This place."

Jimuro frowned. How could this dump possibly be better than that sword?

His mother seemed to sense the question. "I appreciate this place because here, I'm not the Steel Lord," she said, stroking his cheekbone with her thumb. "Here, I can regain sight of how things are for the people I serve."

Jimuro had blinked. There was that word again. "Serve?"

"Serve," his mother repeated sternly. "The petty chiefs of the Sanbu Islands. The gluttonous Crane Emperors of Shang. The greedy merchant-lords of Dahal. Those people do what's best for themselves and pray that their people will follow. But the Steel Lord is a servant with a thousand masters. My life is dedicated to putting all their needs before my own."

He'd stared up at her, eyes wide as the weight of all this sank into his head. But she'd just smiled again, and knelt down so that they were eye level.

"And someday, my sweet son," she'd added as she ran a finger along his cheek, "yours will be, too."

After Jimuro finished his story, Dimangan sat there, rocking back and forth as it chewed on the prince's tale. But then its huge shoulders shook. A low rumble rose in his throat. Jimuro's eyes darted to the prone sergeant, thinking her condition must have been deteriorating. But her breathing was still steady, if labored and shallow.

And then Prince Jimuro realized.

The slave was laughing at him.

He felt a rust settle all over his body. "What is it that you find so funny?" he said in controlled, careful tones.

"That's what you think your subjects live like?" Dimangan said, shoulders still shaking with unkind laughter. "You chopped some wood, man. How horrible for you."

Jimuro's face twisted into a snarl. "The Steel Lord wanted to impart to me the virtues of wisdom and humility—"

"If that bitch wanted you to know what it feels like to be a subject of Tomoda, she should've thrown you into an iron mine and never let you out," said Dimangan. "She should've rounded up your friends in the town square and executed them in front of you, just because rumors said they had relatives in the resistance. That's your *civilization.*" It practically spat the last word.

Jimuro was acutely aware of the danger he was in, but his hackles rose all the same. "*She was the Steel Lord of Tomoda!*" he roared. "She was my mother! What she and her servants did, they did for the good of the empire, and I will not allow you to talk about her in that—"

But his rage had taken him too close to Dimangan, and so he was helpless when a massive hand shot out and wrapped two fingers around his throat. Effortlessly, Dimangan lifted him into the air, Jimuro's legs kicking futilely.

"Give me a reason, steelhound," it said, its voice low and thin. "Don't doubt I'll do it."

Desperation for breath drove Jimuro to flail his limbs, even as his strength bled from them. His glasses fell askew on his face, but this close even his damaged eyes could clearly see the face of the thing that would end him. If Dimangan was a slave to Tala's subconscious will, was this what Tala really wanted to do to him? He'd gone out of his way to save her, but had he just entrusted his life to someone all too happy to just take it?

"Hoy," said a soft voice. "Mang."

Immediately the slave's giant head whipped around. "Lala," it breathed, dropping Jimuro to the floor. Jimuro scrambled to his feet, doing his best to maintain his dignity while gasping greedily for air.

He had all manner of choice words for the slave, but by the time he'd regained his senses (and his breath), he saw her sitting up, propped up by her brother's huge hand. It looked down at her with deep concern, all its previous malice gone.

"Report," she said groggily. Despite the golden-brown of her skin, she looked deathly pale. Her lips were chapped and dry, her hair limp with sweat. Her eyes, when she could keep them open, were unfocused—a worrying departure from their normal hawklike sharpness.

"I brought you to my safe house, but this creature tried—" Jimuro began, but he saw Dimangan had spoken at the same time. The two abruptly stopped.

"Like I was saying," Jimuro went on, "I was in the process of figuring out how best to treat your—"

But once again, Dimangan had spoken up, then stopped when he did. Jimuro glared death at the slave, and the slave returned the look with interest.

"Mang," Tala rasped.

"*No,*" Jimuro said, cutting across Dimangan. "I am the Iron Prince of Tomoda. Three years a prisoner of Sanbu have not changed that, and now I have been returned to my country. *When I open my mouth here, all others close.*"

Tala simply stared at him, as if she couldn't quite believe what she'd just heard. Dimangan was far more expressive; it looked as if it wanted nothing more than to pulp Jimuro's entire head with its fists.

But neither of them said a thing.

"You're in the first royal safe house at Kinzokita, per phase one of Operation: Grand Tour," said Jimuro. "But while I was able to get us here, we can't go any farther while you have that venom in your system."

"I've had worse," the sergeant said, wincing. She tried to stand, but Dimangan put a firm hand on her shoulder and shook its head.

"I don't care what you've had," said Jimuro. "Thanks to that visit from our plum-colored friend, you've become the entirety of my security detail. I'm not going anywhere unless I know you can run and fight."

Tala glared at him now. It occurred to him that he perhaps shouldn't have been so blasé about the deaths of her comrades, but he set the thought aside. He'd have plenty of time to make amends. The generosity of a Steel Lord paid rich dividends.

"We don't have time to wait for me to heal up," she said. Her voice sounded more ragged with every word she squeezed out. Nonetheless, she was right. He had to get back to Hagane. His people were counting on him. Each moment he delayed was a moment when he was letting every single citizen of Tomoda down.

Jimuro fidgeted irritably with his glasses as he racked his brain. From here, they were supposed to have driven south to Hagane in the cars that had been stowed in the hold of the *Marlin*. That had also been where their other key supplies had been: Munitions. Rations. Money. And of course, medical kits.

"We don't have enough resources here," he said eventually. "There's a town five kilometers away. I could walk that in an hour. Once I'm there, I could get medicine." Tomoda had its own native spiders: bright-yellow creatures with pointy, banded legs. The spider-shade that had attacked the sergeant didn't have the same coloring, but it was the only antivenin he was likely to find without breaking into a hospital.

Sergeant Tala's face hardened.

"And not just antivenin," Jimuro continued, as if he hadn't noticed. "We need food. You need new clothing. We'll need weapons. Money. Even a car. I just need to know: Do you trust me?"

"*No,*" Tala and Dimangan chorused, at once.

Jimuro sighed. He should have expected as much from these shortsighted savages. He'd already lost a war he'd barely even fought in, yet they insisted on putting him on trial just the same.

"Well, I suggest you reconsider your position, Sergeant," he said, his glasses flashing. "Because at this point, your only other option is to die."

CHAPTER SEVEN

LEE

When Lee thought of royalty, she thought of the photos of the Shang family palaces she'd seen in the newspapers. The floors were tiles of polished stone. Their walls and furniture were made of shiny, lacquered wood. If Lee were ever to set foot in a place like that, she'd often thought, she would've taken a hammer and chisel and made off with as many fixtures as she could.

But the palace at Kohoyama was a study in sparseness and restraint. For a place built by a people so obsessed with metal, Lee was surprised by how little of it she saw in evidence. The floors were simple polished wood, as were the elegant frames of the walls and doorways. The light fixtures were made of metal, though, and the lightbulbs in them looked sleek, like they'd been made in a year Shang hadn't experienced yet. The ceilings were wide, tall, and inviting, in a way that made her feel as if she were already thinking more clearly beneath them. The strangest thing she noticed, though, was that the doors appeared to be made of . . .

"Paper?" Lee said, wrinkling her nose. She prodded at a nearby doorway, pushing right up to the brink of tearing it before she relented. She frowned at it. "What's a paper door supposed to keep out?"

"Nothing," said Xiulan. "That's what household guards were for. Remember, this was a palace, not a fortress. It was a place of quiet contemplation and pleasure."

Lee's frown deepened. "Not really seeing the overlap there." She slid a door open to reveal a wide room with an almost completely bare floor. There were low wooden chairs and tables, but they were so spread out that to Lee's eyes they looked like islands. "Wood, wood, more wood. I thought the steelhounds were nuts about . . . well, steel."

"They are," Xiulan said. "The stuff is quite scarce on Tomoda. In fact, I wouldn't be surprised if I were to learn that its scarcity was why it became sacred to them in the first place. Even in matters of faith, you can always depend on the constants of supply and demand."

Lee smiled and just let her talk when she got like this. Xiulan had never met a three-word thought she didn't want to turn into a ten-word sentence, but in the short time they'd known each other Lee had grown fond of her partner's circular way of talking.

"Besides," Xiulan continued, "metal is closer at hand than you realize." She flipped a switch on the wall, and the lights up and down the hallway flickered on. "The walls are full of metal wires and ducts, to give this palace light in the darkness and heat in the cold. Metal pipes snake their way beneath these floors, to bring them hot and cold water at their whim. This palace's face may not be made of metal, but her skeleton is. And in my mind," she added with a mischievous glance Lee's way, "it's the bones that make something truly beautiful."

Lee raised her eyebrow and smirked. She thought she saw the specter of an identical smirk on Xiulan's face, but then the princess turned away from her and used her pipe to point down the newly lit corridor. "Onward."

Though Lee wanted to poke around some more, Xiulan seemed to have a very specific room in mind that the two of them needed to visit.

But she didn't know where the room was, so they ended up poking around anyway.

In the kitchen, they came upon a wide array of metal pots and pans for cooking, as well as knives, chopsticks, and any other accoutrements a royal chef might need. But Lee noticed something strange right away: In place of cooktops, there were only flat slabs of steel. It took her a second to understand: The Tomodanese didn't need gas flames when they could just metalpact heat directly into their pots and pans.

"I suppose it was too much to hope that we might find something of note in the kitchen," Xiulan said, sighing as she cast an eye over the neglected gear and countertops. "I'd hoped we might at least ascertain some insight into what the Iron Prince enjoys at mealtimes."

"Which we were absolutely going to find in a kitchen he probably never went inside, in a palace he hasn't been to in at least four years, and that's most definitely been picked clean by every soldier that got here before us," Lee said.

Xiulan tried to look annoyed instead of amused, but Lee knew better.

It took them another hour of careful exploration to find the room they actually wanted: Prince Jimuro's. It was located on the second-highest floor of the tower, where the walls weren't enough to keep out the sound of the howling wind outside. Lee felt a jolt of unease. For some reason, it hadn't occurred to her while she was climbing all the steps to get here, but now that she was up here, she realized this was the highest up she'd ever been in her entire life.

Xiulan beamed at her as if she could read Lee's mind. "I told you life in the Li-Quan would take you far, didn't I?"

"I don't remember you telling me anything like that," Lee said.

The inspector chuckled softly. "It was last night."

It had been hours, but Lee's temples still throbbed gently whenever she looked at bright lights. "What else did we talk about last night?"

As she slid the bedroom door open, Xiulan's smile was small and sly as a baby fox's. "A variety of things."

Lee was disappointed to see that there was nothing particularly interesting or valuable up here, either. At first, she would've said that the place had been cleaned out by the Dahali who conquered it, but it took only a moment's glance to realize that wasn't the case. There were no telltale signs of breakage, nothing overturned, nothing chipped off the wall. The place still felt sparse, but purposely so. It didn't feel like any piece of it was missing.

Prince Jimuro's room was just as orderly as the rest of the house, but here Lee got the feeling this wasn't its natural state. The bed was immaculately made, and a fine rug was neatly centered in the middle of the floor, but the bookshelf told a different story. The volumes there were crammed in haphazardly, with no discernible order or system. Some were shelved sideways, some lay horizontally atop rows of other books, and a couple looked as if they'd been read so often that their spines needed repair. Those ones, Lee noticed, were the ones positioned closest to the bed.

"What do you think, Inspector Lee?" said Xiulan. "Demonstrate to me that observational acumen that carried you unerringly down Lefty's path."

Lee bristled slightly at being commanded to dance like some pet. But the truth was, she kind of liked getting a chance to show this highborn what she could do. "The bed's made. The rug's centered. The art on the wall's specially hung so it doesn't spend all day in the sun and it won't fade. Everything here's been arranged *just so* . . . and then, there's this bookshelf."

Xiulan had the pleased expression of a teacher who'd just heard the answer she was hoping for. "Good," she said.

"This thing is just plunked right down here, next to the bed," Lee continued. "The feng shui doesn't make any sense at all. And what's more: It's dustier than everything else in the room."

"Very good," Xiulan said.

"So the servants were cleaning this room right up until the palace was taken," said Lee. "But they weren't cleaning that bookshelf there, weren't straightening it up. If I had to guess? Probably because someone told them not to, and they were the kind of boring people who listened." She patted the bookshelf, dislodging a fair amount of dust. "Anything you want to know about the princeling, this shelf here's your best bet."

"Sterling detective work," said Xiulan. "Now if you'd be so kind as to take the top shelf, while I start at the bottom . . ."

They flipped through the prince's personal library, book by book. Xiulan was very deliberate in her search, eyeing particular pages that had been dog-eared or looked particularly well worn. Lee, on the other hand, just held each book open and gave it a good shake. When nothing interesting fell out, she tossed it into the pile that was rapidly accumulating atop what had once been the prince's bed. She eyed it scornfully, even as she polluted it further. Dusty and neglected as it was, that bed was still a damn sight better than anyplace she'd ever laid her head in her life.

She reached for a green-bound volume next and was surprised to see that its pages looked to be adorned with only drawings. The page she'd opened to, in particular, showed a surprisingly lifelike dog with short, pointed ears and a curled-up tail. The dog was mostly gold, but its legs were black up to the knees, so that either it had just trampled through a mud puddle or it was wearing boots.

She noticed a smudge in the corner, which had been turned somewhat convincingly into a cherry tree. "It's not printed on," she muttered. "Guess he must've drawn it." She had to admit, the Iron Prince wasn't bad. She guessed if one was going to lead a life of idle leisure, drawing was as good a way as any to fill the time.

Something clicked in her head. She glanced up at the wall, where there hung a painting of a ship sailing against the sun. She studied the brushstrokes on it for a moment before saying, "He painted that."

Xiulan turned to examine the painting. "What makes you say that?"

Lee held up the sketchbook, then flipped through its other pages. Sure enough, each of them had a different drawing or painting on it. Sometimes they were people, sometimes they were landscapes, and sometimes they were the dog with the muddy feet. The style evolved here and there, as the prince played around with new techniques, but all the art had undeniably been wrought by the same hand.

Xiulan glanced from the painting to the sketchbook, then back to the painting. "Most interesting," she said politely. "But I'm reluctant to believe that our quarry would have embedded the geographic coordinates of a secret royal family hideout in his personal doodles."

Lee shrugged, a little stung. "All right, then." She tossed the sketchbook onto the bed with the others.

Xiulan seemed to realize she'd misstepped, because she sighed and put down the book in her hands. "You have my sincerest apologies for my dismissiveness," she said. "I'm merely frustrated at the lack of workable evidence here. I shouldn't have directed that frustration toward you."

Lee grunted. "That's a long walk to 'I'm sorry.'"

"Our beautiful language has gifted us with such a multitude of words," Xiulan said. "What better way to glorify them than with their use?" But she sighed. "I don't believe this line of investigation will bear the fruit I'd hoped. We should go."

As they headed downstairs to begin their trek back, Xiulan was uncharacteristically silent. She'd practically bounded up the steps earlier, but now she trudged down them.

Lee let it pass for a flight or two, but eventually the other woman's disappointment got to a point where it became intrusively palpable. She had to say something. "What, did you think we were going to find some magic compass with THIS WAY TO THE PRINCE written on it?"

Xiulan sighed ruefully. "I'm not sure what I expected to find here, Lee," she said. "I thought being in his space, where he was at his most comfortable and genuine, I'd be able to step into the shoes of the Iron Prince himself and deduce what his next move would be. Wishful thinking, I know."

Lee barked with laughter. "What? A neat, tidy mystery to solve, like a Bai Junjie novel?"

Xiulan glanced back over her shoulder, though it was with the eye covered by her loose bang. "Reading those books as a child is what made me want to become a detective," she said simply.

Lee put up her hands: *Hey, it's all good with me.*

Xiulan seemed satisfied with this. "You're familiar with the canon of Bai Junjie?"

"Never read them, exactly," Lee said. "But we had a radio, and they'd do these plays based on the books, so mom would let us listen to them during dinner. They had some other show on after, about a woman who flies around in this machine of hers and punches Tomodanese soldiers a lot. We'd always beg mom to let us stay up past bedtime to listen to it."

"I take it such negotiating tactics were unsuccessful."

Lee snorted. "Shang or Jeongsonese, queen or beggar, a mom's a mom."

"Yours was a beggar, I imagine?" Xiulan said.

Lee bristled at Xiulan jumping so quickly to that conclusion, but stopped herself from saying anything. She supposed there'd been a reason she'd used that word herself.

"Sometimes the begging was with a hat while she sang on the street," Lee said. "Sometimes it was cleaning houses and hoping she'd actually get paid what they promised her. I didn't settle on an illustrious career of petty thieving because I was a bored rich girl."

Xiulan hesitated on the stairs—only for half a heartbeat, but long enough for Lee to notice.

"What we've done to the children of Jeongson is unconscionable," Xiulan said carefully. "I want you to know that I never—I've always believed—"

Lee sighed. "Save it."

Xiulan whirled around. "No," she said, and Lee was taken aback by the earnestness shining in her eye. She was already young, but it made her look even younger. "I need you to know I'm not like the others, Lee."

"Right, so now I know," Lee said simply. "You feel better yet?"

Xiulan frowned. "I'm trying to say I want to help you. Is this how you treat all your allies?"

"I'm just saying I've heard it before," Lee said with a shrug. "Normally from shopkeeps as they handed me stale bao. They'd give me a whole spiel, then walk away whistling and skipping because they'd done their good deed for the day. They acted like it was gonna make the bao taste better, when really I just wanted some gochujang."

Hurt glinted in Xiulan's eye, but Lee didn't show her a shred of sympathy. Her partner was a princess. She didn't need a backpat, least of all from Lee.

They climbed down the rest of the way in silence.

It wasn't until they reached the ground floor again that Xiulan spoke. "Commandeering a vehicle from the Dahali shouldn't be too difficult," she said bracingly. "But before that, I could stand to eat."

Lee's own poor gut cried out for something oozing with grease and salt. "Speaking my language, Princess."

"I've been given to understand Kohoyama is host to some of Tomoda's finest establishments. Do you enjoy soba?"

"What's the point?" Lee said ruefully. "These steelhounds don't eat meat. If you ask me, a meal's not a meal unless something had to die for it."

They crossed the threshold into the afternoon sun. "You would be surprised what culinary miracles can be worked in the absence of meat," Xiulan said. "I happen to be in possession of an excellent recipe for mapo tofu . . ."

She trailed off mid-sentence.

Walking straight into a line of brandished Dahali rifles had that effect on people.

Lee regarded the row of gleaming gun barrels, and the brown-jacketed soldiers holding them. They were all men with long black beards. Mixed in with them were uniformed women with flowing dark hair who bore no weapons at all. But they didn't appear to need them; their hands all crackled with white auras of magical energy.

Lee sighed, then regarded the triumphant Chetan Parkash, who stood at their head. "Were you out here the whole time?"

"Chetan Parkash saw no harm in letting you wander while waiting for confirmation of your identities," Parkash said mildly.

Xiulan paled, then recomposed herself. "I understand," she said. "We asked too much of you, proud merchants that you are, without paying what was due you. Allow me to retrieve my billfold and—"

"You will do no such thing," Parkash said, and Xiulan froze halfway through reaching into her coat. Reluctantly, the princess put her hand down at her side.

That seemed to satisfy Parkash. "Chetan Parkash apologizes for the imposition on whatever plans you had," he said. "But nonetheless, this one wishes for you to know that it's an honor to meet you, Your Majesty." He bowed deeply.

Xiulan paled further. Lee, however, was feeling fairly bold. "If she is who you say she is," she said, pointing to the shouldered rifles, "you wouldn't dare fire those things. The Crane Emperor would have each of your nuts in its own gold-plated vise."

"That's true," Parkash said. "This one admits, they were largely for show."

Lee sighed, then nodded to the nearest woman in his contingent. "But the glow-hands aren't for show, are they?"

There was genuine regret in Parkash's smile. "This one is afraid not."

"*Ko—*" Xiulan began, but a white bolt of energy hit her squarely in the chest. Her eye rolled back in her head, her entire body convulsed, and then she crumpled to the ground like a puppet with cut strings.

Lee wasn't the type to shout in horror or anger when things went tits-up for one of her partners. She was the type to make a break for it, then thank the dogs later that she'd been quick on her feet.

But at the sight of Xiulan falling, fury stirred in her chest. A roar of outrage began to grow in her throat. It would have crescendoed into something terrible, she knew, but it was cut short when another white bolt struck her in the gut and folded her in half.

There was pain. The dogs take her, there was pain rippling across every inch of her body.

But, Lee Yeon-Ji thought as she slipped her way out of the world, it still hurt less than her hangover.

CHAPTER EIGHT

TALA

*E*ven through the ringing of her ears, she could hear his screams.
Moments before, they'd been a family at their table, eating dinner. Ama had put a massive banana leaf on the table, then piled it high with the rice and pork he'd cooked for them. The pork had been special, illegally obtained at an underground market. And at Ina's nod, they'd all reached for it the proper Sanbuna way: with their bare hands.

She was a small girl of ten, eagerly shoveling food into her mouth with tiny hands. Ina chided her for tempting fate and making herself sick. Ama chided her for not properly enjoying the food he'd spent so long on. Mang pounded the table excitedly, cheering that she was on track to break her old record.

When she swallowed a mouthful, she tried to steer the subject toward an assassination attempt by the rebels she and Mang had witnessed in the market that day. Rumors all over Lisan City had it that the Iron Prince himself had been there, but she was proud to say she had better than rumors; she'd seen the boy with her own eyes.

But her excitement was met with stony worry from her parents, and Mang shot her a warning look not to prod the subject further.

She scowled into her rice. They were living in exciting times. Revolution was in the air. Even a child like Tala could smell it, not to mention the more tempting scent of freedom that wafted in its wake. She knew she'd grouse to Mang about it later, but for now she remained fixated on the question: Why was the rest of her family so intent on ignoring what was inescapably obvious to her?

And then the world was fire and thunder.

She didn't remember the bomb hitting, just waking up covered in soot and blood. She had ash in her mouth, ringing in her ears, and tears in her eyes, even though she didn't totally understand what had just happened. But even for one so young as her, it took only moments to put the pieces together.

Her family's modest home was in ruins, blasted down to its concrete walls. Nothing glass or wood was whole.

Neither was anything of flesh and blood.

In the ruins of their dining room, it wasn't hard for Tala to identify her parents. Their skin had been blackened with flame, their bones shredded by shrapnel. But she couldn't freeze up at the sight. Not when the air was thick with Dimangan's screams.

He looked as if he'd nearly been cut in two by the blast. His shiny scalp had been burned into an angry red mess of seared flesh. His own guts were spread all around him, sauced in blood. He tried to move himself, but it was no use. Nothing pinned him in place, but he wasn't going anywhere.

Everything Tala had eaten climbed back to her throat and hovered there, ready. Any one thing she saw would've been enough to shut her down completely. But all at once, she didn't even have room to feel things. She had been spared. The only one of her family left alive.

Except for Dimangan.

She looked down at her shaking, bloodstained hands. She had so many questions. So many fears. But right now, what she really had were things to do.

She laid her hands on Mang's twitching, ruined body, and he didn't flinch back from her touch. His eyes met hers, and they were wide with horror and agony.

"Sanbuna lore has countless monsters," he had told her once. "But the worst of them wears a human face."

In that moment, splintersoul legends flashed through her head: Of Tikat, who tried to drown the world in night by pacting herself with the sun. Of Hui the Maw, whose shades devoured whole cities until the Tiger Emperor's armies finally ended him. One after another they came to her, until she had a dozen splintersoul stories floating around her in a cloud.

And then her mind began to pen a thirteenth.

She had to speak up to hear her own voice through the ringing in her ears. Tears continued to flow from the corners of her eyes, but she knew her jaw was set, her sight steely and clear.

"Tell me what to do."

Dimangan looked up at her, uncomprehending for a moment.

Then, dawning horror. He shook his head, as far as it would go.

Tala tightened her grip. She was set on this path now, and that determination was the only thing keeping back the fires of her grief. In a stroke, Mang had become the only person she had left in the world, and she couldn't lose him. "Please," she said.

Mang stared a long while. Her pulse quickened. Had he died just the same? Had she waited too long?

But then at last, her brother's mangled lips parted. He began to whisper instructions.

As she closed her eyes and concentrated, something changed about the tears carving through the grime on her cheeks. She was only a girl of ten, but already she recognized them. They were the tears she cried when she was about to do something unforgivable.

She didn't need to hear the question that he was going to ask of her when they met in the center of the bridge that spanned from soul to soul.

She already knew what her answer would be.

A rumble broke through her dream. *"Lala."*

Tala's eyes snapped open. When her sight returned, the throbbing all up and down her body came with it. She wasn't sure what kind of poison that spider-shade had been packing, but even a small dose had been potent enough to almost completely disable her. She couldn't feel her hands and toes anymore, could barely feel the limbs to which they were attached. And yet despite that, the special pain she felt only with Mang remained, clear and sharp as the trumpet at reveille.

She tried to breathe deep, but her lungs felt as if they were in a vise that had cut their volume in half. If she'd taken any more punishment, she had no doubt she would be dead by now.

That said, she also had very little doubt she'd be dead soon enough, anyway.

Dimangan could sense the specifics of the fear nestled in her head and heart. "He's still not back," he muttered. His tone made it clear exactly how likely he found it that the Iron Prince would actually return.

Words were hard for Tala to form. She was grateful that their pact meant she didn't need them. Stiffly, she nodded, while she sent Dimangan a wave of resigned cynicism: Of course he'd come back. He had to. He was too much of a coward to try surviving on his own.

"In Sanbu, maybe," Mang said. "He's in his own country now, as he was quick to remind us. No place a person feels more comfortable, and comfortable people aren't careful people."

Tala closed her eyes again and leaned back. She understood Mang's reticence. He'd lost more to Tomoda than anyone else she knew. And she herself could hardly think to trust Iron Prince Jimuro, living face of the enemy. But the truth was, the prince had been right when he'd stared down at her over the rim of his glasses and told her what was what. For better or worse, he was her only hope now.

She'd obviously known him to be royalty, but that moment had been the first time she'd truly appreciated the fact that he was going to be a king. As he'd issued that ultimatum to her, she'd glimpsed whatever dented steel lay at the heart of the soft, shrinking young man she'd been guarding. She still didn't trust him, but with that demonstration she at least believed that if he were inclined to honor his word, he might actually be able to pull it off. If she couldn't trust him to do the right thing for the right reasons, she could at least trust him to do it for the wrong ones.

"Stop thinking about him," Mang muttered. "I just got his stupid voice out of my head."

Tala closed her eyes again, and tried to shift her thoughts as a courtesy to Mang. It was hard for her to think about anything but the question of whether or not she'd live through this, and that all hinged on Prince Jimuro now.

But then, with a flash of violet, she remembered how she'd come to be here in the first place.

Dimangan's entire body stiffened up as the thought leaked into his own mind. "Who was he?"

Tala groaned and shook her head. How the hell was she supposed to know? That man, the splintersoul, was hardly the first blood-thirsty lunatic who'd tried to kill her.

"No," Mang said with admirable evenness. She knew the pain he was in. How did he always sound so calm? "But he is the most . . . interesting." His mouth creased into a thoughtful frown. "You can't tell me you don't think it's weird, Lala. You were the only person in the world with two shades. The only real splintersoul. And then this guy shows up and he's got a whole army?"

Tala grunted. Seeing Sunny and Tivron turned against her had told her exactly how the man had recruited. Under that coat of his, she'd seen a body flecked with pactmarks and scars. And it wasn't hard to imagine the dead Shang and Sanbunas he'd left behind in the process of collecting.

"That was why I thought you might have some insight," Mang said. "You're the only one to—"

His form flickered. Tala sucked in a shallow breath, and her chest burned. When he re-formed, he wore a stricken expression on his huge face. "Lala," he said. "You're—"

He faded again, and the world faded with him. A surge of panic ran through her as she felt her throat closing up, her breath growing shallow as a saucer, her vision blackening around its edges.

Dimangan appeared one more time. She could barely feel his hands envelop her shoulders, could only just tell he was shaking her as gently as his deadly strength would allow. His lips were moving, and she could feel his breath on her face, but the words bounced off her ears like bullets off a tank.

At last, her will gave out. She felt the connection inside retract it-self as he disappeared in a burst of bright-blue light. Her body fell back to the floor. The soul-pain bled out of her, but even that relief only underscored how alone she was now. Alone, and dying.

She breathed.

The world darkened.

She breathed.

The last sounds in her ears died.

She breathed.

The last tension drained from her body.

She breathed.

Her eyes closed.

And she hoped she would breathe again.

The national dish of the Sanbu Islands was adobo: meat, either chicken or pork, stewed in a combination of soy sauce, garlic, pepper, and sugarcane vinegar. It was often joked to be the one thing the ten Sanbu Islands had in common, but even that wasn't true. Recipes varied from island to island, city to city, even family member to family member. There was only one thing all Sanbunas could actually agree on when it came to adobo: Their ina's was best.

On other islands, Sanbunas added things like sugar, fried onions, or even coconut milk to their adobo. But Tala's ina was a purist, and insisted that anyone who needed the sweetness to temper the sharp sauce might as well be eating bland Tomodanese food. For her, all adobo needed were those four ingredients: vinegar, soy sauce, garlic, pepper. When she cooked it, the whole house was filled with an aroma so hearty, even breathing it in felt fattening.

It was that smell that brought Tala back to life.

She sat up before she remembered she couldn't move anymore. Her throat was so dry that even breathing hurt, but at least she was breathing deep again. Her muscles screamed in protest with every twitch and motion, but when she willed them to move they obeyed. And while the light stabbed at her eyes, they saw as clearly as ever.

She blinked. Iron Prince Jimuro stood at the stove, working the contents of a wide, shallow pan with a pair of long metal chopsticks. He wore a different kimono than the one he'd washed up in, and his tight topknot had been undone, revealing a curtain of hair longer than her own that framed his cheekbones just so. She inhaled again and didn't know what surprised her more: the smell of adobo here in Tomoda, or her still being alive to smell it.

She studied Prince Jimuro as he calmly went about cooking the adobo. Though she'd mostly seen him in various states of sullenness and panic, here she saw him unhurried and possibly even enjoying himself. It wasn't like he was whistling while he worked, but there was a calm satisfaction about him that lent certainty and confidence to his movements.

Then he looked up, saw her, and dropped his chopsticks with a squawk. "Sergeant!" he said, then forced himself to calm down. "You're awake."

"Barely," Tala said. She rubbed her temples and felt how clumsy her arms and fingers still were. Briefly, fear gripped her: Had the venom's damage been permanent? Was this how she would always feel from now on? But she pushed it from her mind. She had other things to worry about. "Report."

Prince Jimuro only seemed slightly put off by her brusque demeanor, but she wasn't about to make apologies for it. He seemed to understand that, because rather than demand one, he reported.

"You've been asleep for the better part of a day and a night," he said. "By the time I returned and got the antivenin into you, you were more dead than alive."

She groaned. Now that the thrill of surviving was done with, her body had started cashing in on the debt of pains and sores she'd racked up. It was enough to make her think maybe dying wouldn't have been the worst thing. She eyed a ceramic kettle on the stove, next to a bubbling rice pot. "Coffee," she croaked.

"Ah. Yes." Prince Jimuro produced a simple white ceramic cup, then from the kettle poured a thin stream of pale green tea. A woody scent cut into the overpowering adobo smell, subtle but undeniably present.

"That looks like the opposite of coffee," Tala said as the prince brought it over.

"You're the better for it," he said, pulling a face as he handed it to her.

Tala frowned down into the cup's translucent green contents, at the bits of leaf floating at the bottom. "This some kind of Tomodanese medicine tea?"

"Hardly," Prince Jimuro said. "Just my mother's favorite."

That got Tala to raise an eyebrow—a gesture that, like every other, hurt something fierce. Tea was no kind of acceptable substitute for coffee, and she doubted the tepid leaf water in her cup would give her any sensation except that of a mouthful of mulch. Still, she had to admit: The idea of sampling her hated enemy's favorite leaves did make her curious . . .

When she sipped, a peaty, bitter taste hit her tongue. But she couldn't deny that her shoulders and her stomach felt lighter.

She took another sip. It was no coffee, but it would do.

At least until she got some coffee.

That was the moment it truly sank in for her: She was in Tomoda now. Last time, it'd been with supply trains and full complements of rations. But now she was full-on behind enemy lines and in survivalist mode. As far as she knew, the Tomodanese didn't even drink coffee.

Shades take her. She was staring down a three-day drive with the Iron Prince of Tomoda and no coffee.

She nodded to the pan he held. "Adobo?"

"I'm sure it must be quite the surprise for you," Prince Jimuro said, more than a little proud of himself. "I developed a taste for your native dishes over the course of my long captivity. When she wasn't on the front, Erega would often take her meals with me and discuss matters of state."

That made Tala do a proper double take, which she immediately regretted. "She what?"

Prince Jimuro shot her a look over the top rim of his glasses. With his hair down, his expression felt less severe and more thoughtful. "Being a head of state is a lonely thing, Sergeant."

Tala thought back to the war, after she'd earned her stripes. It'd been an impromptu thing in the heat of battle, born less out of her suitability and more out of the fact that she was the only one of the 13-52-2 to step up. At the time, she'd done it because her squad had needed someone to lead it. But afterward, her troops had treated her differently. They still joked with her, but now there was a slight tension in the way they addressed her. It'd been isolating. Eventually, it'd even made her lonely. It was part of what had made Maki such a good person to talk to. He was the only other one on the ship who'd understood.

Ice ran through her veins at the thought of him. Of Privates Kapona, and Minip, and Radnan, and all the rest. Each absence was another twist of the knife, as was the realization that she was truly the only one left.

She closed her eyes and tried to remember their faces. For now, the details were sharp, but she knew they would fade with time. She only vaguely remembered what her own parents looked like anymore. But she would hold on to the memories of every soul dead aboard the *Marlin* for as long as she could.

When she opened her eyes, a steaming bowl of adobo and white rice sat in her lap, a pair of wooden chopsticks resting on the bowl's rim. But Tala stopped short of tearing into it when she eyed the strange round shapes in the bowl, lapping up all its rich brown sauce.

She prodded one, and then looked back up at the prince. "This isn't adobo."

"Mushroom adobo is adobo," said Prince Jimuro. "All of your national dish's rich flavor, none of the senseless slaughter, and a certain Tomodanese umami as a bonus." He turned from her and went back to tending the stove before she could issue a rebuttal.

Tala set aside her tea and picked up the bowl. It smelled enough like adobo. She wasn't used to eating adobo with chopsticks, but they picked up the mushroom caps easily enough. She popped one into her mouth and chewed. There was that burst of salty and sour and herbal tastes she'd grown up on, but the tender mushrooms added an earthy dimension she'd never tasted in adobo before. Her whole body shuddered from the familiar flavor of it, and for just a moment she felt ten again, transported right back to her home in Lisan City.

Something seared across the back of her head, and her rapture burst like a balloon.

Prince Jimuro looked down at her expectantly. "Well?" he said. "Does it measure up?"

Carefully, she fed herself a glob of sauce-stained rice. "It's fine," she said quietly. "We need to hit the road today."

"Not necessarily," Prince Jimuro said carefully. For a moment, something resembling apprehension shone in his eyes. But then with an unexpected gruffness, he added: "As I said before, I need a body-guard that can run and fight. As of this moment, you're in the shape to do neither."

"I'm touched by your concern for my well-being, Your Brilliance," Tala deadpanned. "But the longer we stay here, the more danger you're in." This felt better. Just a moment ago, they'd veered danger-ously close to banter. This, at least, was an argument.

"Nobody knows I'm here," said the prince. "Nobody even knows I'm in the country yet."

"No one was supposed to know you were on the *Marlin,*" Tala said darkly.

A shadow cast itself over Prince Jimuro's expression. "He's dead and gone, though." Tala didn't miss the quiet note of pleading in his voice. She shared his desperation to be shut of the splintersoul, but she couldn't share his certainty.

"Even if he is, we don't know who sent him or why he was after you," she said.

"I've never seen him before in my life," the prince said, "but he seemed so intent on getting to me. What in the world do you think I did to earn such contempt?"

Knowing you, Tala thought, *probably talked to him.*

"Very well," the prince went on. "I suppose you're right; we should leave as soon as you've eaten. You can use the drive to re-cover more of your strength. I managed to get us a bit more food, as well as some new clothes for traveling. You'll need them; you al-ready look enough like an outlander."

Tala slurped down the last of her adobo. The mushrooms had long disappeared, but she honestly liked the sauce and rice more than she liked the actual adobo itself. She put the bowl down and experimentally flexed her arms. They still felt weak, but even a bit of food in her belly improved the feeling immensely. In a few weeks, she'd be back at full strength and this whole ordeal would be long behind her.

"How'd you pay for it?" she said.

"Hm?"

"Food. Antivenin. Clothes. Our money sank with the *Marlin,* so how'd you pay for it all?"

Before he could stop himself, the prince's eyes flitted to the floor by the front hallway, near where Tala's gun lay atop the neatly folded top half of her uniform. "Don't concern yourself with that."

Tala frowned. She didn't care much about the Tomodanese people at all. She didn't even care that her gun had been used as a tool to rob them. But the tiny embers of goodwill she'd begun to feel for the prince snuffed themselves out. Whoever those people in town had been, they'd been the prince's own subjects. She'd expected that kind of callousness from the Tomodanese, but for the first time in her life a small part of her wouldn't have minded being proven wrong.

Unsteadily, she stood. She groped for the wall to brace herself, but found after a few steps she didn't need it. Every inch of her felt like a wrung-out towel, but if she could stand, she could walk. If she could walk, she could run.

And if she could run, she could fight.

She'd been stripped of her boots, shirt, and jacket, but she still had her pants and undershirt. She eyed the door. "I'm going for a walk."

"Not dressed like that, you aren't," said the prince.

"I'm not going far," Tala muttered. "I just need fresh air. Wait for me."

Though it was the height of summer, she was surprised by how cool and crisp it was outside when she shut the door behind her. The sun was not yet at its peak, and the air was thicker with cicada song than it was with humidity. She breathed deep, and though the air was Tomodanese, it was still sweeter on her tongue than the staleness of the prince's cabin.

She found herself in a clearing, surrounded by tall spruce trees that kept the cabin permanently shrouded in shadow. A narrow dirt road led into the wood, and right at its mouth was parked a simple black car. Unlike the cars that they'd packed into the *Marlin*'s hold back in Sanbu, this one was of Tomodanese make and would only move through metalpacting. If Tala went with the prince now, she wouldn't be able to drive.

She glanced back at the house, then pointed. *"Beaky."* And after a moment to brace herself for the pain: *"Dimangan."*

A purple flash issued from one hand and a blue one from the other as her two shades emerged. Whether they were manifested or not, the two of them couldn't communicate directly with each other the way each could with Tala. But she could sense what each of them was feeling, as if she were standing in the cross breeze from two drafty rooms. Each shade regarded the other coolly—Mang because he considered the bird's surliness to be unpleasant, and Beaky because . . . well, because he was an unpleasantly surly bird.

Beaky cawed and stretched his wings, then took to the air. Tala mentally cautioned him not to fly too high, lest an obvious shade attract attention here in Tomoda.

The response she got back amounted to *Yeah, yeah,* as he flew higher and higher in a lazy spiral.

Mang hunched before her on his haunches. "Lala. Shades take me, you're alive." Gingerly, he wrapped his arms around her and pulled her close. She angled herself carefully to avoid the sharp bone growths bursting from his broad chest. "I mean, I knew you were, because I could still feel myself in there, but I didn't know if you'd—if I'd ever—"

"At ease," Tala said, patting him. Her head throbbed with the effort of keeping him manifested.

"So how'd you do it?" he said. "How'd you wake up so fast?"

Tala nodded to the car behind him. "The prince came back."

Mang withdrew from their embrace and looked at the car in quiet disbelief. Or at least, it was quiet on the outside. Thanks to their empathic link, the disbelief inside him was anything but quiet to Tala.

"What does he want from you in return?" he said eventually.

"Just to honor my orders," Tala said. "Escort him to Hagane. Make sure he gets seated safely on the throne. After he gets crowned the Steel Lord, he stops being my problem."

"Our problem," Mang rumbled.

The sudden spike of annoyance she felt from him caught her wrong-footed, and with it came a sudden sharpness to the pain that made both of them wince.

"Right, sorry," she said carefully. "It's our problem, not just mine." But even with her apology, the current of tension flowing off him didn't abate. She exhaled. "What?"

"When you saved me—"

A generous term for it, she thought.

"—you tied our souls together. And then you went off to fight in a war. It put us both in danger every day, and most of the time you couldn't even use me to keep you safe. But I made my peace with that, because that was a war that needed fighting, and nothing was gonna stop you from fighting that."

"You're not telling me anything I don't know."

"The war was over, Lala," Mang said, his impatience now as naked as he was. "It was over, and then you volunteered for another tour of duty, and for what? *For him?*" He gestured to the house. "He's the face of the enemy. The one who most deserves to hang for Tomoda's crimes. And you jumped at the chance to protect him—"

"I didn't jump at—" Tala tried to say, but Mang plowed right over her, his anger bringing a fresh wave of agony that almost dropped her to her knees.

"—and you did it without even trying to consult me," Mang finished.

Tala's mouth opened, but no words came out.

Dimangan leveled a simmering stare at her and sat further back on his haunches.

"I didn't have a chance," she said. "Erega asked for volunteers. I couldn't just sneak away and ask you."

"Then you should've said no," Mang growled. "This mission wasn't just your choice. Your life is the only thing sustaining both of us, and you almost spent it trying to protect a steelhound. Have you forgotten what they took from us?"

"Of course I haven't," Tala snapped. Normally, she tried to be patient with Mang. Their need to keep him secret meant he could come out so rarely. But the spider-shade's venom had sapped her

patience along with her strength. "Why do you think I threw myself into that war?"

"Because you promised that bird—"

"Because I promised *you.*" Tala cut across him even as more intense pain crackled between them. "I wanted to make every last one of those monsters pay. I wanted to make them regret leaving me alive."

"But you'll lay your life down to protect their king."

"To honor the sacrifice of my squad!" Tala said. "If I don't get the Iron Prince to Hagane—"

"—they'll have died for nothing?" Mang said. "Because they weren't dead when you signed up."

Tala froze.

"No," Mang rumbled on. "That's just what you're going to tell yourself every time you drag us both into another fight. But you just like fighting, because you're terrified there won't be anything left over once you let it go. You'll fight the steelhounds whenever you can, but if it comes down to it, you'll fight alongside them, as long as it means you get to fight. And don't bother lying to me, Lala. I live in your head."

Tala reeled as if he'd just slapped her. Honestly, a slap from him might've hurt less. "That's not true," she said. "You just know that's what I'm afraid of, and you're saying it to hurt me."

"Fine," said Dimangan. "Then walk away from this fight with me, right now. Leave that monster inside to die. You've saved his life, he's saved yours. You don't owe him any more. So walk away from him. We're partners, right?"

"Of course!" Tala said indignantly.

Mang sat back defiantly on his haunches. "Then do what I want, for once."

Tala's eyes met her brother's, the one part of him she hadn't managed to ruin. He wasn't wrong: She'd let Jimuro out of his cell, but then he'd shot the spider-shade. She'd gotten him off the boat, and he'd cured her poison. By any metric, the two of them were square. It would be a trek to get to the nearest Sanbu-controlled zone, but she didn't have to fear for her safety with both Beaky and Mang at her back. She could survive. It was what she did best.

"I can't," she said eventually.

He shook his head. "You can do anything if you love someone enough."

But though her bare feet tensed against the grass beneath them, they didn't move.

Mang's eyes narrowed. "Put me back," he said at last. "And don't call on me. Whatever you have left to say, I don't want to hear it."

"Mang—"

His eyes narrowed further. "There's no point in a conversation when only one side's listening."

And then he turned his back on her, leaving her to stare at the blue pactmark stretched across his scalp.

Bitterly, she reached a hand toward him. She wanted to lay it on his back, to tell him she was ready to listen, that she couldn't do this without him.

But then she swallowed it and willed him to return instead.

The blue light faded, and her focus sharpened as the pain receded. She stared at the huge, deep footprints he'd pressed into the grass before they, too, began to fade as the wind shook the blades loose.

She cast her eyes skyward, to the shadow swirling overhead with the sun on his back. "What do you think?" she said.

She got back a combination of wariness and weariness. Tala translated it to mean: *Just try not to die.*

She laughed mirthlessly. "I'll keep that in mind," she said, then willed Beaky to return, too.

When she slid the door to the cabin open, Prince Jimuro had changed into a slim-cut suit: black pants, a bright-blue jacket, and a blood-colored tie. But the most striking difference in his appearance was that he'd shaved off his thin beard. With it, he'd shaved a good five years off his age. She'd known the two of them were of an age, but now that he had a clean face she could actually believe it.

She frowned at his garish attire. "You look like a blueberry."

"Just because I'm incognito doesn't mean I can't be myself." Prince Jimuro sniffed.

She stared at him. "That's literally what it means."

He appeared unbothered by the remark. "Blue is the color of the

Tomodanese sea and the Tomodanese sky, and it is the color of the To-modanese. Therefore, it's my color, as well."

". . . You do know we have blue skies and seas, too, right? Every-one does."

"*In any case,*" the Iron Prince continued loudly, "your outfit's over there." He indicated a gray suit lying draped across the pallet she'd slept on. She frowned at it. It didn't seem right to her, march-ing back into battle without some proper Sanbuna green on her back.

When she noticed the prince studying her, she stalked past him and toward her new outfit. "Is everything all right, Sergeant?" he called after her.

"It's fine," she replied, limping for the pallet. Her usual strength wasn't back, but she could pretend. "Go outside and give me three minutes. Then we hit the road."

PART THREE

· · ·

SINGING CICADAS

CHAPTER NINE

XIULAN

Xiulan had read once that all the world's known disciplines of magic were fruits hanging from different branches of the human soul. In Shang and Sanbu, the solemn and sacred art of shadepacting had emerged. Scholars disagreed as to which of the two nations had been its true creator (though among *reputable* scholars, Xiulan noted, the consensus was solidly in Shang's favor). On the island of Tomoda, the people had worshipped metal, and in doing so learned to attune their souls to it so they could bend it to their will. It differed from shadepacting, and yet like that art involved channeling one's soul into an external vessel. But to the west, in the vast and wealthy land of Dahal, the people had turned their focus inward.

In the hours and days of her childhood Xiulan had spent in the royal libraries, she'd read accounts of the Dahali enhancing themselves to briefly run faster, lift more, and even sharpen their senses to levels a dog might envy. But most notorious was their ability to project their own soul energy into others. Per Xiulan's reading, it was an ability only taught to the women of Dahal, in the interests of limiting such a potent ability's prevalence. But potent it was, indeed. An injured friend could count on a Dahali hexbolt to make them whole again. An enemy, on the other hand, could count on one to disrupt all their body's basic functions from the inside out, rendering them unconscious in the most painful way possible.

So that was how her afternoon was going.

She lay on a bed in a large cell with a wooden floor and bright lights hanging overhead. The window along the wall let in sunlight, but revealed far too long a drop to be a viable escape route. The heavy sliding door was made of pure steel, clearly meant to be opened with steelpacting. But in the absence of Tomodanese occupants, the room had been transformed into a prison cell.

The bed was soft and comfortable but did little to combat the lingering ill effects of being on the wrong end of a hexbolt. She wasn't in pain anymore, but fatigue had replaced her pain. Her entire body had seized up before she'd lost consciousness, and now all her muscles felt spent. Even her tongue in her mouth felt heavy and clumsy, resting limply against the inside of her cheek.

The room itself was in a mansion that had once belonged to the Kurihara Clan. Now, though, Kurihara Daisuke was in prison awaiting trial for his myriad war crimes, and his home had been temporarily deeded to the occupying Dahali forces. The Kurihara Clan, as Xiulan understood, had been one of the more powerful and wealthy families in Tomodanese society. Though their status was on the wane, even this prison cell in their home was fairly luxurious.

But as the great detective Bai Junjie had once observed during his captivity at the hands of his Tomodanese archenemy, Professor Sakini: A gilded cage was a cage still.

"Funny, how life seems to keep bringing me back here," Lee said from the floor, where she sat. The low stance of Tomodanese furniture meant they weren't half as far apart as they'd have been on raised, Shang-style beds.

"I'm thrilled to hear you can find some levity in our predicament," Xiulan snapped.

"That's what you pay me for, right? To find stuff?"

Xiulan sat up and rounded on her, though her body's general fatigue made her whole upper torso feel like a weight, awkwardly balanced on her hips. "How can you be so blasé about everything that's happened?" They were all of a day into her grand mission to win the unattainable Snow-Feather Throne, and everything had already fallen apart. What had she done to arouse Dahal's ire so? Why were they so insistent on standing in her way? And how could she think her way out of this cell?

Lee, who had her hands cupped behind her head, just barely turned to meet her gaze. "Because you're worried, I'm not, and we're both still here anyway."

Xiulan glared at her, any number of stinging rejoinders heavy on her tongue. But before she could say any of them, she was interrupted by the creak of the door sliding open at the far end of the room.

Chetan Parkash strode into the room. In his wake trotted a small dog with a golden-and-brown coat, pointed, catlike ears, and a tightly curled tail that wagged excitedly. At the sight of it, Xiulan noticed Lee perk up, but she had other things to concern herself with at the moment.

"This is an outrage, Commander Parkash!" she said at once, getting to her feet. "We are agents of the Snow-Feather Throne in good standing, and once I've returned to Shang I intend to speak at length with the royal family about the treatment I've received at the hands of our Dahali allies!"

She'd hoped he would be at least a little cowed by her threats, but he took them unflinchingly. "There's no need to continue the charade, Your Majesty," said Chetan Parkash. "This one has already confirmed your identity with Second Princess Ruomei, who posted the bounty for your arrest and safe return."

At the sound of that name, Xiulan's building bluster left her entirely: not leaking out so much as escaping her en masse and leaving something hollow and deflated behind.

Ruomei.

Again.

But how? Xiulan wondered. Her mind whirred. How could Ruomei have possibly known where she was? If she herself was fixated on General Erega's announced plan for moving the Iron Prince, how could she have also planned so effectively to check Xiulan's progress? Or had she not known what Xiulan was up to, and just placed the bounty in case?

She slumped back onto the bed. It never failed. *Stupid White Rat,* she chided herself, *thinking you could fly like the hawk. Stupid, stupid, stupid* . . .

"For what it's worth," Parkash said, "Chetan Parkash wouldn't normally imagine interfering with a Li-Quan investigation, no matter its subject. This one's time fighting in the Garden Coalition has left him with a profound and sincere respect for the people of Shang."

"But a greater respect for half a million jian, I bet," Lee said from the floor.

Parkash's beetle-black eyes glinted apologetically. "A hundred thousand."

Xiulan wished she could sink even lower into the bed. She was a princess of Shang. She should've commanded a far more generous price.

"What if we give you half a million to let us go?" Lee volunteered.

At that, Xiulan sat up slightly. "Do you have in your possession such levels of currency, Inspector Lee?"

"Not unless you give me a raise," Lee said cheerfully. "But you've got it, don't you?"

Xiulan frowned, but turned back to Chetan Parkash nonetheless. "I suppose my associate raises a point. You're a businessman, aren't you, Commander Parkash?"

"The Dahali have a mother language, pleasant to the tongue and ear alike," said Parkash. "But our father language is commerce. Which is why Chetan Parkash won't entertain any offer you tender, unfortunately. This one's choices are between a guaranteed reward from an empowered princess, or a promised one from a princess who will tell Chetan Parkash whatever she thinks will get her out of her cell."

It had been a long shot, but his words still made her feel stupid for having offered at all. She'd gotten as far as she had in life by believing in herself. By believing that no matter what adversary she faced, she would always be better. It didn't matter how much smarter she was, or how much better letting her go free would be for Dahal in the long run. If given a choice between Ruomei or herself, people would always listen to Ruomei. Xiulan had the facts on her side, but people *liked* Ruomei. There was nothing quite so frustrating as being reminded of which of those carried more weight.

"So you didn't come to bargain," Xiulan said, barely able to keep the bitterness from her voice. "To what pleasure do I owe this visit, then?"

"To see that you are well accommodated before the handoff," Parkash said. He reached into his pocket and produced a small object: her pipe. "And to provide the comfort of the familiar, Your Majesty."

He approached to give the pipe to her, and Lee stirred at last, like a guard dog. Parkash stopped, eyeing her warily. But the dog at his side trotted right past, rushing up to Lee and shoving its nose right into her own. Lee sighed, then scooted aside and scratched behind the dog's ears as it continued to explore the interesting subject of her face.

Parkash stepped past her and offered the pipe to Xiulan. With her hair covering half her face, she had to sit up to actually look at it, and by extension him. She knew the gift was kindly meant, but it was hard not to feel she was being patronized. She took the pipe anyway, slipping it between her teeth. "My lighter?" she said.

Parkash shook his head and instead pulled out a box of matches. Xiulan scowled, but nodded. He struck one for her, lit the bowl, then handed her the entire box.

"Food will be brought to you shortly," he said. "Until a Shang delegation arrives to collect you and pay this one's fee, every measure will be taken to ensure your comfort."

"What about mine?" Lee said, and Xiulan winced at what was surely coming next.

Parkash didn't disappoint her. "Chetan Parkash was given no instructions regarding you. It's only thanks to Her Majesty's presence that you're still alive. It's this one's understanding that Shang society would not miss the loss of a Jeongsonese drifter."

Color rose in Xiulan's entire face. "That woman is an agent of the Li-Quan," she said, anger sharpening each syllable. "She should be treated with every ounce of respect with which you treat me."

Parkash shrugged. "As you say, Your Majesty." And then he and the dog turned and left, while Xiulan seethed behind him.

The door slid shut again, and Xiulan leapt to her feet. "That complete and utter bitch," she muttered, taking an angry drag from her pipe. She began to pace back and forth.

"Guess this isn't going to improve things between you two," Lee said.

The sound of her laughter normally charmed Xiulan, but now it set her teeth on edge. She rounded on Lee. *"Don't you dare laugh at me."*

But Lee just laughed again, now with disbelief. "Hell of a tone there, Princess," she said. "What got into—?"

Rage overcame Xiulan before Lee could say any more. Her grip tightened, and she hurled her pipe with all the strength she could muster, right at Lee's grinning face.

It flew clumsily as a baby bird, tumbling end over end and clattering uselessly to the floor a few feet short of Lee.

In a flash Lee was on her feet, the gap between them reduced to nothing. Xiulan's throwing hand was still outstretched, and with one easy movement Lee twisted it behind her back, causing Xiulan's whole side to erupt in pain. "Lee, I—*ah!*"

Lee pressed a little, and a fresh wave of pain made Xiulan collapse onto her knees. As she struggled, she was suddenly aware of a pair of lips hovering beside her ear.

"Try it again," Lee said, "and you'll have to learn how to light that pipe of yours with one hand. Good?"

Xiulan struggled for just a second more, then deflated again and gave a dull nod of defeat. At last, the pain abated as Lee let her go. By the time Xiulan managed to pick herself up from the floor, her partner had already lain back down.

Xiulan collected her pipe from the floor, slipped it back into her pocket, then carefully sat down next to her reclining partner. "How did you do that to me?"

"Wasn't a big girl," Lee said, not opening her eyes. "Coming up, that made people think I was someone to be fucked with. Only reason I'm still alive is because I got good at proving them wrong."

Xiulan took this in quietly. She stared at her own shaking hands. Now that the moment had passed, she couldn't believe she'd just lost her control so thoroughly. Looking back on her attempt to hurt Lee, it almost felt like an out-of-body experience.

Except it hadn't been. It had all been her, and that made her sick to her stomach.

She turned her gaze away from her partner. "I apologize, Lee," she said. "You deserve better than the partner I was to you just now. You deserve a better princess."

There was a heartbreaking nonchalance to Lee's tone as she replied, "No skin off my nose. 'Snot like there's ever been a point in my life when I could count on people like you."

Xiulan blinked. "That's not fair," she said quietly.

"I noticed," Lee said.

Xiulan continued to stare at her hands. Their shaking abated, but she still felt her heart thundering against her ribs.

"It doesn't matter how hard I work," she said eventually. "Or how careful I am. How meticulously I plan. No matter what, my endeavors are always doomed to failure. Do you know, Lee, how frustrating it is to work diligently for something—to do everything right—and have it denied you all the same? Do you—"

"Yes," Lee said flatly.

Xiulan's mouth snapped shut—first from outrage that someone would dare talk over her, then from guilt as she realized how stupid she sounded right now.

Lee sighed. "But let's pretend I don't. What were you going to say?"

Xiulan clenched and unclenched her fists. "My sisters and brothers had a nickname for me," she said.

"Yeah, Lady of Moonlight," Lee said. "You told me."

"No," said Xiulan. "That's the title my father gave me. It was supposed to be a tribute to keep Lord Yao happy, so he wouldn't defect to Tomoda or something. My siblings called me something else: White Rat."

"White Rat, eh?" Lee said, as if she were tasting it.

Xiulan nodded. "I thought it was nice, at first. Rats are smart and cute. I liked to believe I displayed similar characteristics. But one day, my brother Qingkai told me why I'd really earned the soubriquet. He said that white rats were the easiest for hawks to see, and catch, and eat. He told me that white rats were rats that were born unlucky. That's who you have as a partner, Inspector Lee: a white rat. My sisters and brothers have spent the entirety of their lives muttering that name and laughing at me. So when you laughed . . .

when I heard you laugh at *me* . . ." She trailed off, too embarrassed to finish.

Lee seemed to mull this over for a moment. "White Rat," she said again. She measured Xiulan with a look. "Looks like you leaned into it."

"With Kou?" Xiulan sighed. "I first acquired him as my own little show of defiance. I never intended to pact with him. But much like yourself, my soul ended up being rather selective about the company it chose to keep."

Lee nodded and said nothing.

When Xiulan had first become aware of Lee's case in the course of her investigation into the looting of Daito Arishima's home, she'd imagined at length what this mysterious Jeongsonese criminal mastermind would be like. In her mind, she'd expected a refined, upper-class criminal, like the antagonist in the third Bai Junjie novel, *White Diamond in a Black Glove*. Bai had faced down a dashing gentleman thief (he called himself an acquirer or fingersmith) who moved among high society, sending advance warning to his marks about what valuables he intended to steal, making it all the more spectacular when he managed to pull off his heists anyway.

But Lee Yeon-Ji wasn't like that at all. She had no euphemisms for what she did, nor apologies for doing it. In almost no time at all, she'd become incredibly comfortable mouthing off to Xiulan in a way that would've gotten her mauled by a shade if she'd done it to anyone else in the family. What Lee Yeon-Ji was, was a challenge. She existed, she would keep existing, and the challenge you faced was that you just had to deal with it.

Their journey had been short, but Xiulan had enjoyed it so much more than she would have time with a gentleman thief.

"If I guess which of your twenty-seven sisters and brothers gave you that name," Lee said eventually, "would you give me half a million jian?"

"Thirty-three," Xiulan said. "Fourteen sisters, nineteen brothers, from nine different wives."

"Nine women," Lee said with a low whistle. "My record's only three at once, myself. Your father's gotta be one hell of a man."

A disgusted laugh erupted from Xiulan. "You can't just joke about my father . . ." She faltered. ". . . you know . . ."

"Just trying to pay him a compliment. Not often I do that to men," Lee said. But she sank back in thought. "Why'd Ruomei put a price on you?"

"She knows of my desires to supplant her as the favorite," Xiulan said. "And she's the only sibling who doesn't underestimate me. Why do you imagine she's worked so hard to keep me down?"

"Didn't you say she was off with a fleet, trying to stop the prince from getting here directly?" said Lee. "Why's she care if you take a little joyride up north?"

"She doesn't like to leave things to chance, my dear sister," Xiulan said. She reached for her pipe, suddenly self-conscious of its absence. She'd picked it up as an affectation to mirror Bai Junjie. But over the past year or so, she'd come to genuinely enjoy the pipe, and found it soothing when she was in thought.

"Looking for this?" Lee said.

Xiulan looked up and saw Lee with the pipe dangling jauntily from her lips. She bit back a smile. "Give me that back, please."

"Why're you really doing this?" Lee said. Her tone wasn't demanding, but it also left the impression she wouldn't accept evasion. "Not just this whole thing about finding the princeling. Why'd you go and join the Li-Quan in the first place? What's any of this about?"

Xiulan froze. The truth of the matter was painfully embarrassing. What, was she supposed to just look this hardened criminal in the eye and tell her—

"I wanted to have adventures like Bai Junjie," she said, surprised at her own bluntness. "And I wanted to prove myself. And I wanted an effective way of antagonizing my sister while I set about saving the country from the prospect of living under her rule. This endeavor— what is the expression?—*checked a lot of boxes for me.*"

Lee raised an eyebrow. "So you snatched me out of the jaws of the justice system because you're a bookworm who's mad at her sister?"

Xiulan was a princess, one of the most powerful in the world. And she knew for a fact she had perhaps the most brilliant mind of which any branch of her large, extensive family could boast. But something about the way Lee looked at her just made her feel small and stupid.

She had no choice but to hang her head. "I sincerely wish to help the Jeongsonese," she said. "But . . . yes. If you put it in those words, they would not equate to something inaccurate."

She expected Lee to rail at her for doing something so patently stupid. No, that wasn't right. Lee wouldn't even bother. She'd just turn back around in disgust, leaving Xiulan alone to marinate in her own shame.

But to Xiulan's surprise, Lee did neither. She threw her head back and cackled with delight.

Xiulan's whole body stiffened. *"Have we not already established where we fall on the matter of laughing at me—?"* But even as she said it, she could already hear the difference in Lee's tone. The other woman sounded . . . impressed?

"You did *all this* just to get even with your sister?" Lee repeated.

"There was some notion of serving the people of Shang," Xiulan groused, but Lee had pulled herself upright, so she was sitting next to Xiulan now. The pipe in her lips didn't look like an affectation or a costume, the way Xiulan feared it might have looked on her own person. There was something effortless and natural about the way Lee's gently curving lips rested against the pipe's polished wooden button. It was as if the pipe, handsomely carved piece that it was, had been made for her.

"I like audacity," Lee said simply. "When you're on the worst kind of job, audacity's the only thing that'll get you through it: being willing to do something so stupid, there's no way anyone could see it coming.

"But." She stood and stretched. "I've had it with partners who don't play me straight. I got plenty of that with Lefty, and all the girls and boys who came before him. So if I'm helping you out from now on, it's because I know where we're headed, why we're headed there, and what we're getting up to once we arrive. You got that . . . White Rat?"

And then she extended a hand.

Furtively, Xiulan took it. "Gutter Dog."

Gruffly, but not unkindly, Lee pulled her to her feet.

And quite suddenly, Xiulan and her partner found themselves face-to-face.

Xiulan's breath caught in her throat. Her chest tightened. And she was painfully aware of how suddenly damp her palm had just gotten, clasped to Lee's own.

She couldn't tell which of them let go first. She just felt her hand fall to her side, where she carefully wiped it on her coat.

Lee coughed, then took the pipe out of her mouth and wiped its button on the dark folds of her dress. She offered it to Xiulan. "Guess you'll be wanting this back."

Xiulan took it. She inhaled, hoping to catch the last embers of her leaf, but the bowl had already been cashed. Only somewhat disappointed, she slipped it back into her coat pocket. "Thank you."

Lee nodded. "Right," she said, stretching again and stepping back from the door. "Get us out of here, then."

Xiulan blinked. "I beg your pardon?"

"You heard me," Lee said, then waggled Xiulan's pipe in front of her face.

Xiulan's eye went wide. She patted the pocket in which she'd just placed it, but sure enough, it was empty. She gaped at Lee in disbelief. "*Again?* How did you—?"

"Me stealing things is like you talking, Princess." A mischievous grin broke across her face. "I do it all the time, and most people wish I'd stop already."

Xiulan barely smirked. She folded her arms. "I admire you and your wit, Lee, but you're being very childish right now."

"Use that fancy detective brain of yours," Lee said. "Where are we?"

"In a cell," Xiulan said impatiently, then reconsidered. "Well. A bedroom."

"Right. So that door there: It's made of metal, because it's meant to be opened with metalpacting."

"Whatever point you're driving at eludes me," Xiulan said with a tiny flare of impatience.

"I'm saying, we're not in a prison cell," Lee said. "We're in a bedroom. Maybe they're using it like a prison, but it's not built like one."

The simple obviousness of it hit Xiulan like a runaway car. Slowly, she turned to stare at the shiny steel door . . . and then at the wall to which it was joined.

She felt another surge of awed affection for her partner. Xiulan regarded herself as intelligent, but the woman was *wise*.

"Of course," she whispered. "The door may be held fast, but the walls won't be reinforced." She pointed. *"Kou!"*

She remembered how Kou used to be: a tiny white ball, curled up on her pillow every night. A friendly pair of paws nudging her awake in the morning. A small lump of warmth in the folds of her daxishuan, smuggled in to keep her company through yet another long, boring state dinner.

Kou couldn't fit into her gowns anymore. But running her fingers through his snowy fur, the warmth was still there, familiar and strong. He looked up at her with bright-pink eyes, and the shape of the feelings he sent to her asked the question, *What can I do?*

She nodded to the wall section above the door and thought back, *What you do best.*

Through the thick door, she could hear the dog barking. Xiulan didn't know how long it had been at it, but by now there was doubtlessly someone coming. They had to move fast. Fortunately, Kou felt her urgency. With a burst of agility, he scrabbled up the smooth surface of the door and set about gnawing at the wooden wall above. It easily gave way to his curved yellow teeth, pulpy and soft as the flesh of an orange.

Lee fell in beside her, looking up at the shade with admiration. "Way to use your head, Princess." She offered up the pipe.

And instead of taking it again, Xiulan pulled her close, closed her eyes, and slipped her lips over Lee's in a kiss. Her heart hammered with—fear? Panic? The self-loathing that could only come from knowing you were doing something incredibly stupid and willfully ignoring every opportunity to abort?

You've been gifted with an exceptional brain, Xiulan, she thought as she let go and stepped back with an anxious lick of her lips. *There's plenty of room for all three.*

Still feeling the taste of Lee on her lips and tongue, she realized she'd quite forgotten to breathe. "Inspector Lee—"

Lee stepped back, flushing the color of a strawberry. "Time and place, Princess. Escape now, feelings later." She turned her attention back to Kou, who was still digging away at the space above the door. But she was smiling.

Xiulan found it impossible not to do the same.

CHAPTER TEN

TALA

An hour into their drive to Tajiri, Prince Jimuro finally turned down the radio and said, "Sergeant, I have questions."

He'd punctured the conversational mode with which Tala had grown most comfortable when it came to Prince Jimuro: complete silence. She'd gained some respect for the man after he successfully saved her life, and Mang's along with it. *Twice,* she reminded herself, thinking of the spider-shade on the deck. Then she thought of him severing that rope and taking out those three shades with a runaway car, and had to admit that maybe he was pulling his weight. But she hadn't forgotten who or what he was, and it didn't make her inclined to listen to him.

All around them, the Tomodanese countryside blurred past. For a nation so invested in its own industry, it surprised Tala to see how much greenery there was. But through the thick, verdant trees and tall, swaying grass, someone had gouged out a wide gash of open land, then paved it over in black-gray asphalt. According to the prince, such highways crisscrossed all over the island, to bring its people closer together. It was a far cry from the packed dirt roads she saw on pretty much every island of Sanbu except for Lisan.

She eyed him sidelong. "Do you?" Despite her discipline, she fidgeted in her seat. The Tomodanese clothes draped differently across her figure, and it was taking some getting used to. The prince had chosen for her a slim gray suit, a white shirt, and a black tie, with a wide-brimmed gray fedora pulled down to shade her face so she could hide her Sanbuna coloring. Of her old uniform, only her weathered boots remained, bouncing on the dashboard where she'd propped them.

"Indeed." The prince sat at the iron wheel, while his feet lay bare on the metal floor of the driver's seat. At first, Tala had been disappointed in the effect of metalpacting; it wasn't nearly as dramatic as summoning a shade. But then again, she supposed with another glance out the window at the blurry green expanse, they were moving, weren't they?

It wasn't the first time Tala had seen the trick done. The massive Tomodanese warships that had been the scourge of the sea were powered by dozens, even hundreds of Tomodanese sailors all metalpacting in concert. But it was the first time she'd seen it done so up close, and part of why she forced herself to look out the window was to stop herself from staring.

"Well," Tala said, "are you going to ask me any?"

"I was considering how best to word them," Prince Jimuro said. "You have something of a temper, you know."

She cocked an eyebrow his way. If he thought this was a temper, he didn't have the measure of her at all.

"Very well," he said. "As I understood it, the way your magic is supposed to work, those of you capable of manifesting a . . . *shade* . . . are only capable of manifesting one. The man in purple was able to defy this hard-and-fast rule. And so, for that matter," he added, "are you."

Tala crossed her arms over her chest as the prince's lips moved, but Mang's voice came out. She wasn't going to make it easy for him.

"I suppose my question, simply put, is: How?"

Her mouth thinned. "What makes you think I know?"

"Surely you must. If not you, then whom?"

Tala didn't answer; just returned her attention out the window, where it belonged.

They drove on for another minute before the prince tried to pick at it again. "I ask because if that man should return—and given how intent he was on ending my life, it wouldn't surprise me—insight will be our most effective survival tool."

Tala frowned. Since her fight with Mang earlier this morning, she'd been doing everything she could not to think of the other splintersoul. She'd thought she was the only one like herself, and she'd been much happier believing that.

"Nothing, then?" the prince said. "Nothing to contribute at all?" She could feel him struggling to be polite about it, and somehow that just made him even more aggravating.

She shook her head. "We don't need to know how men like him are made." She patted the gun hanging from the shoulder holster in her suit jacket. "Not when we know how to unmake them."

Prince Jimuro opened his mouth to say something else, but suddenly his entire body went rigid. The car screeched to a halt so suddenly, Tala's seat belt nearly folded her in half at the waist.

"What the—?" she began, but before she even finished the question she saw for herself what had made them stop.

A bright-red car with the white crane of Shang splashed across its door had pulled across the road, barring their path. Two red-jacketed soldiers slouched against the car like delinquents. A third sat behind the wheel, looking bored. And a fourth stood slightly in front of the car, legs planted and shoulders squared.

"Come out with your valuables," he called in clumsy Tomodanese. "Do now, or we shoot."

"What do you think?" Jimuro hissed to her. "Have we been betrayed?"

For a moment, Tala considered it . . . but no, that was impossible. There was no way anyone could've known they'd survived the shipwreck, if they'd even known there was a ship to wreck.

"I don't think so," she said. "They're probably just soldiers."

"'Soldiers'?" he growled. "They're highwaymen with matching coats. They probably extort money out of every single law-abiding citizen of Tomoda that passes through." Jerkily, he resettled his cobalt-colored blazer on his shoulders and glared at the Shang soldiers over the top rim of the steering wheel. "What these monsters have done to my country . . ."

Tala eyed the clothes the two of them wore, the car they sat in, and bristled. It wasn't that she wasn't concerned about the Shang in the road, but this was rich to hear from the prince when everything around them had been stolen from the Tomodanese people by their own ruler.

The air split as the Shang leader rolled his eyes, pulled a narrow-barreled pistol from his belt, and fired a round skyward. "I was meaning it," he called, then leveled the gun at their windshield.

Tala shot Prince Jimuro a look. She frowned. "Stay behind me," she said, and popped her door open.

As she got out, she ran the math in her head. If she left her car door open, it would serve as suitable cover in a prolonged firefight. The pistol in her coat had two rounds, and she was a good enough shot that she could make both of them count before anyone made things messy by summoning a shade. If she kept this to bullets, she'd only have to kill a few of them. If she summoned a shade of her own, she'd have no choice but to kill them all.

That said, what she really wanted was to end this without firing a shot at all. Her Tomodanese was more passable than these soldiers', so hopefully if she kept her distance she would be able to maintain the ruse that she was as native as Prince Jimuro.

She thought of the ways Jimuro formed his words, of the guttural tone she would have to use to sound like a proper native speaker. And when she thought she had a grip on the accent, she opened her mouth and said, "We don't want any—"

The car rocketed away from her and toward the blockade, its open door flapping like a broken wing.

The Shang officer's eyes bugged out as the car careened toward him. He fired a shot, but it went wild as he reeled from the fresh gunshot wound that had just blossomed across his chest. Tala whipped her gun over to the next-closest target, her soldier's instincts keeping her panic at bay. Normally, panic would have had no place on her battlefield, but she wasn't fighting alongside the fire-forged vets of the 13-52-2. She was fighting with a mad prince who seemed even more determined to kill himself than the rest of the world was.

Before the officer had a chance to fall, the black car rammed into him and flipped him right over its roof. The other soldiers scattered with a shout, but the Shang car couldn't move in time. It crumpled like a can and screeched as Jimuro's car dragged it across the face of the road.

"*Your Bril*—" Tala shouted before she caught herself. She took aim at the remaining soldiers as they broke for the tree line, only for her gun to click empty. Of course. She gritted her teeth and growled as she stared at the retreating blotches of red in the foliage. Instinct told her that they'd seen too much, and that she had no choice now but to pursue them with Beaky and make sure they didn't get a chance to report any of it. But her sense of duty stayed her as she turned to eye the dented wreck of their car. She had to make sure the idiot prince hadn't just rendered their entire mission moot.

The driver's-side door of their car flung itself open, and Prince Jimuro climbed out. He wobbled unsteadily on his feet but otherwise looked no worse for the wear. "*Lowlifes!*" he bellowed at the trees. "*Barbarians! Slavers! Come back here, you cowards, so I can send you to whatever*—"

Without even skipping a beat, Tala stomped the distance between them and belted him right in the face, sending him spilling to the ground. Before he had a chance to sputter his outrage, she stood over him, pinning him by the chest with her boot. "What the hell were you thinking?" she roared.

"That someone needed to do something!" Prince Jimuro shouted, shoving her foot off him and sitting up.

"Not *that*!" Tala said, gesturing to the twisted, bichromatic lump of metal that was the wrecked cars. "What was in your head, soldier? What were you thinking right then, except that you wanted to play hero, and you didn't give a shit what happened next?"

"I was thinking," snarled the prince, "that these monsters have been a parasite on the people I'm supposed to protect and serve. Someone has to stand up for the people of Tomoda."

"*The people of Tomoda . . . !*" Tala roared, then fell silent.

"What?" Jimuro said. "What is it? Are you going to tell me my people deserve bandits on their streets? Bombs falling from their skies? Empty pockets and salted fields?"

"Yes," Tala said, though her thoughts betrayed her.

He threw his arms up in fury. "Then why are you even putting yourself through this, Sergeant?"

"Because unlike you steelhounds, I have honor," Tala snarled. "This was unacceptable. I have a mission to complete, and we can't fulfill it by gambling with your life. It's too . . ." She hesitated. "Valuable."

The prince's jaw set. "A king should fight for his people. If I don't fight for mine, then my life isn't worth a fraction of the price you claim."

It made Tala want to tear her hair out. How was it possible for someone to be so right and so wrong at the same time?

She brushed past him. "Arguing further is pointless. We have to make it to the next checkpoint before sundown. Is the car drivable?"

"If we could disentangle it from the other vehicle, I suppose."

No thanks to you, she thought. "Can't you use your . . . whatever you people do?"

"Not if you want me to have the energy to drive us the rest of the way," the prince said. "To separate these two, we merely need brute force." He eyed her meaningfully, and a ripple of pain across the back of her head only underlined it.

She shook her head as it filled with memories of her last discussion with Mang. "That's not happening, Your Brilliance." She dropped her gun, pulling another pistol off one of the dead Shang soldiers. She hefted the weapon experimentally. It felt flimsy compared with what she was used to, and she had no idea how long it would take her to get used to the sights, but it would have to do.

Then she began stomping down the road. "We're walking."

"Don't be ridiculous!" the prince called behind her. His voice got smaller with each furious step she took. "Summon him this instant and—"

Tala didn't even bother turning around. "*We're. Walking.*"

She heard annoyed growling behind her, followed by muttered

cursing, and then the rapid footsteps as he sprinted to catch up to her. "We're still several kilometers from Tajiri, you know."

Tala said nothing. She was a soldier, and no stranger to marching.

"To say nothing of the fact that we'll be exposed to all manner of danger on this road."

Tala said nothing. She was a soldier, and danger was an old, if uneasy, friend.

"We assumed we'd be driving to Tajiri, and we don't have any rations to fuel us the rest of the way."

That put a stop to her resolve. Tala was capable of immense fortitude, but all that could be easily short-circuited if food were taken out of the equation.

"You should've thought of that before you weaponized our ride," she said after a long moment.

"I was using the weapon I had," the prince said. "And now you need to use yours. Summon Dimangan back and make him disentangle our car so we can be on our way."

"It doesn't work that way," Tala said. But it did, a dark little voice reminded her. She would only need to apply a little psychic pressure, and Mang would do whatever she wanted.

The prince was thinking along similar lines. "Of course it does," he said. "You say something, he does it. Like a good, obedient sla—"

A furious chill spread through her. She stopped in her tracks. "I told you what I would do to you if you used that word again."

The prince pivoted back to face her. "You know my beliefs. Surely, you're wise enough to realize no feat of rhetoric from you is likely to change them."

"Your beliefs," Tala snapped, "are shit. You don't know anything about shadepacting, and you don't know about Mang. We argued this morning, before we left Kinzokita, and he told me not to summon him anymore."

"Why should I care what he wants?" Jimuro bristled.

"Because he wanted me to leave you to die and I wouldn't," Tala said.

For just a moment, he was stunned.

But then the color rose in the Iron Prince's cheeks. "Well, I don't know how your, your . . . *conjuring* is supposed to work!" he said.

"I just know what I see: You say something, they do it. So bring out your slave and say, *Fix our car,* so he can do it."

Tala's cool didn't melt so much as instantly evaporate. Before she knew what she was doing, her fist hurtled straight for the prince's head again.

Surprise crossed his face, but he was ready for her this time. He turned her blow aside with his forearm, then slammed his knee right into her stomach. She tried to angle away from the hit, but she wasn't fast enough. She staggered back a step, clutching at her midsection and fighting to keep her breath under control. She cursed at the way the spider venom had left her with lingering weakness. Any other day, this fight would've been over by now.

Prince Jimuro pivoted into a kick, but Tala jerked away from him just in time to avoid it. She understood right away: He was compensating for his shorter height by using his legs to close the gap. She bulled toward him, arms up to block his next kick. She took one step inside his guard before her hand shot out. He tried to twist away from the punch, but it wasn't a punch at all. She'd grabbed his tie, and with a hard yank she pulled his chin right into her waiting fist.

They heaped blow after blow onto each other, anger and hate weighting Tala's like a set of brass knuckles. Each punch she landed brought her a sweet, stinging satisfaction, and each one she took only hardened her resolve to be the last one standing. The prince was a surprisingly capable fighter; he'd probably been trained by Tomoda's best, and he didn't show any of the shyness Tala usually saw from people who'd only ever thrown a punch in the safety of a gym.

But she was Sanbuna. He was Tomodanese. She'd been in this fight dozens of times before. Maybe even hundreds. And she hadn't lost it yet.

She threw a punch he wasn't nearly fast enough to avoid. But rather than fold from the impact, she felt his grip lock around her entire arm, and the unmistakable feeling of her feet leaving the ground. Gracefully, the prince moved with Tala's own momentum and threw her over his head before flopping her onto the pavement like a pancake.

Tala's entire body flared with sudden pain. She'd hit the back of her head, and the impact had sanded all the sharp edges off her thinking. She was aware of the dull roar coming from both of her shades demanding to be let out, but she pushed them aside. This was her fight.

The prince's shadow fell over her. "Yield," he gasped. "You—"

Tala pushed through all the aches and pains, windmilling her legs to catch the prince behind his knees. It took him right off his feet, and he landed hard on his back next to her.

For a long time, they both lay in the middle of the road, wheezing in and out of time with each other.

"You know," he rasped eventually, "how to hit."

Though he couldn't see her, Tala nodded. "You know," she panted, "how to," she panted again, "take one."

"If," he said, "I sit up again, will you strike me?"

The temptation flitted across Tala's mind, brief as a daydream. "Not," she said, "this time."

She heard him groan as he forced himself upright. His glasses were askew, his tie out of place, his topknot coming apart, and his bright-blue jacket streaked with dirt. He tottered to his feet, then offered a hand down to her.

She took it and he pulled her up, her arm and stomach muscles protesting the whole way. Without adrenaline to soften the blows, she was now starting to appreciate just how hard the prince could hit when he wanted to. Absently, she began to readjust her own outfit. Her coat sleeve was torn, her fedora rumpled, and she had a large bootprint stamped across her shirt and tie alike.

The prince observed her for a moment before he tsked and said, "Give me that." Without waiting for an answer from her, he reached over and began re-knotting her tie.

She chafed at his casual touch. And he seemed to notice, because he froze mid-action, staring cagily at her.

She sighed. "Get on with it."

When he finished, he yanked off his hair tie, letting his black hair fall to his chin. With practiced ease, he began to retie his topknot. "I'm sorry," he said. "About the car."

Tala grunted as she fiddled with her bootlaces. They weren't even slightly out of place, but shame was making it hard for her to meet the prince's eyes. She shouldn't have lost control like that.

"The throne was always . . . abstract to me," Prince Jimuro continued. "Its attendant duties, abstract as well. But now that I've been returned home, I keep turning over in my head the sheer scope of my responsibilities. You have to understand: I was supposed to have the rest of my mother's lifetime to prepare for this. However else you may feel about me, surely you can at least understand that."

Tala just nodded.

"So when those Shang bandits appeared on the road, all I could think was that they were only in my country because I'd failed as a ruler. I thought with every masu they stole from my people, I failed that much more. I . . . had to do something."

Tala nodded again, but apparently that wasn't good enough this time.

"Don't make me feel like I'm back in my cell, Sergeant," he said. "Say something . . . please."

What was she even supposed to say to that? To him, this was all about thrones and kingdoms: all well above Tala's pay grade. She was just a soldier, and not even a particularly important one.

But even as she thought that, Maki's face swam through her vision for just a moment, fleeting as a dream. By the time she blinked, he was gone again.

She sucked in a breath. "You're trying to do a job to honor the memory of the people you've lost," she said haltingly. Each word tasted vaguely poisonous on her tongue, but something in her gut told her she had to make an effort. "I'm just a grunt, Your Brilliance, but I get that."

He took off his glasses and polished them with the end of his tie. She found it striking, how odd the sight was to her. She knew they were an artificial addition to his face, but that didn't change the fact that he looked incomplete without them.

"Something you've gotta remember about me, though," Tala said, "is that I carry my lost ones with me everywhere I go, and I don't mean in my heart."

He sighed. "Listen, Sergeant—"

"No, you listen," she said, her voice regaining some power. "What I did to Mang? That's not something that's supposed to happen. I can't just dial him up like he's delivery. When I summon him, it's . . ."

Her voice dropped away. "Imagine the day your mother died, Your Brilliance."

His expression darkened. "I don't have to."

Her eyes burned as they met his. "Take that pain. Turn it into a knife, the sharpest you can. Then stab yourself a hundred times with your right hand . . . while with your left you stab your sister a thousand." Her fists trembled at her sides. "That's what I put him through every time I summon him. That's what he lives with because one day I was a scared little girl who'd lost everything. To *your* people."

The prince's mouth hung open, as if he couldn't believe what he was hearing. Honestly, Tala couldn't believe she was telling him any of it, but she could hardly stop the momentum now.

"So," she said, "let me make one thing clear: I have a friend named Beaky. I have a brother named Dimangan. I don't. Have. Slaves."

Prince Jimuro stared at her as if something had short-circuited inside him. Tala had a vague feeling that now wasn't the time to push this, but they'd just beaten the shit out of each other. When would she have a better time?

"So long as you understand," he said eventually, "that I am not my mother, or my grandfather. I'm my own man, and I have better uses for my throne than to rebuild the world order as it was. Do we have that understanding?"

She didn't know what trick he was doing with his voice to make her believe what he was saying, but somehow she did. At long last, she nodded.

With visible relief, Jimuro cleared his throat. "I offer my fullest apologies. You've sacrificed so much to get me this far, even though—and I know you tried to be subtle about it—I'm fairly certain you don't like me all that much."

And then he smiled uncertainly.

A bubble of ire swelled in the back of her head . . . and then popped.

She didn't return the smile, but she did favor him with a single dry chuckle. "Heh."

Apparently, it was good enough for Prince Jimuro. "Well," he sighed, "thanks to me, it appears we have a bit of a stroll ahead of us."

Tala nodded, then stood. She took her fedora off her head and massaged the dents out of it. "At least we're out of cars for you to wreck."

The walk to Tajiri was a grueling five hours. By the time they reached town, it was well after sundown. Not that it really mattered once they staggered across the city limits; the streets were so thickly crowded with streetlamps that, unless she looked directly up at the blank dark sky, she never would've known it was night.

As an inland city, Tajiri hadn't been a staging ground for the Garden Revolution's invasion of Tomoda. But since the Copper Sages had surrendered in the Steel Lord's stead, all three conquering nations had encroached farther and farther, eager to get at the riches of Tomoda that they hadn't already bombed straight to hell. And from the red banners and white crane sigils that fluttered in every which direction, it seemed readily apparent to Tala that Tajiri had become Shang turf.

They were already tired, but Jimuro was actually in relatively good spirits, all things considered. He'd kept up commentary on the kinds of plants and animals they saw on the side of the road, explained the ingenuity of the Tomodanese highway system, and even sung snatches of songs when the mood struck him. When silence fell between them, it was no longer a tense, unstable thing, but almost comfortable . . . or at least tolerable.

But the moment he laid eyes on the Shang banners, the prince's entire expression darkened. "Barbarians," he said, glaring up at a banner fluttering from a windowsill.

Tala threw a wary look at a nearby trio of soldiers in red longcoats, who chattered away in Shang while crowds of Tomodanese citizens flowed around them. A large snake-shade circled them lazily, encouraging passersby to keep their distance.

"Keep your voice down," Tala muttered, hurrying him along.

Tala wasn't without her own misgivings about Shang. They'd

been stalwart allies during the war itself—even adjusting for each country's propaganda campaigns, they'd sacrificed the most bodies to the cause. But when General Erega had briefed the 13-52-2 on its escort mission, it had been the threat of Shang that she'd specifically highlighted. Shang had almost ten times the population of the Sanbu Republic, and a commensurately bottomless thirst for resources. That was one of the main reasons escorting Jimuro back safely was so important, the general had said: Without a strong Tomoda to act as a counterweight, there would be nothing to stop Shang from swallowing Sanbu whole if it ever got it in its head to try.

"Do you see that?" Prince Jimuro said, pointing to a bright metal streetlamp as they passed it. "Tajiri is the greatest oil refinery in the civilized world. My grandfather, Steel Lord Kenjiro, saw fit to order that it be lit even better than our own fair city of Hagane, so the world could see the shining light of our progress."

Tala rolled her eyes under the cover of her fedora's wide brim.

"Of course," the prince said, tone darkening again, "that explains perfectly well why the Shang were so eager to snap it up. I imagine I'll be negotiating a lot of our reserves over to them just to keep them from putting it to the torch. As I said, Tala: *barbarians.*"

"And as *I* said: Keep your voice down. Where's the safe house?"

"We have a bit more to go." Prince Jimuro sighed. "But fear not; I remember the way."

They walked past a well-lit booth offering deep-fried vegetables. The smell of frying oil filled Tala's nose. "Would it have killed you to give us even one contact person?"

"Erega said we couldn't rely on them. We don't know how much of my family's intelligence network was compromised when the empire fell."

The way Prince Jimuro casually threw out the general's name struck Tala. She remembered what he'd said that morning in the cabin: *Being a head of state is a lonely thing, Sergeant.*

"What was she like?" Tala said, unable to keep the reverence from creeping in around the edges of her voice. Before she'd been the leader of the Republic, before she'd been a general, Erega had already been a figure of awe. Dahal had been the first country to fall into open revolt against Tomodanese rule, but Erega had been leading and funding Sanbuna resistance efforts all over the archipelago for years before. She'd even paid for long-term care for any of her fighters that were wounded in action. When someone was deemed "a one-woman army," it was generally praise for her fighting ability. But while Erega had proved a capable warrior in her own right, she'd also provided the leadership and logistical support to make herself truly worthy of the phrase.

"The first time we came face-to-face, I was . . . defiant," Prince Jimuro said mildly, because he was the sort of person who could be mild about mouthing off to General Erega herself. "I'd read all the stories, listened to all the newsreels . . . she even appeared in a few of our movies, did you know that? We found just about the ugliest actress in all of Tomoda to play her . . ."

Tala scowled.

"Ah, yes," Prince Jimuro said, coughing and readjusting his glasses. "The point is, I was prepared to make my brave last stand against a snarling, one-eyed demon who'd engineered sorrow after sorrow for my people. I was . . . well, how would you put it?"

"Scared shitless," said Tala.

"I'm not inclined to use such vulgar terms, myself," Prince Jimuro said, "but you're not incorrect." He looked as if he was about to continue, but his expression changed. "What's the matter?"

"What?" said Tala, looking around. "What is it?"

"You're frowning."

"Where are your eyes? I'm always frowning."

"No," Prince Jimuro said. "I'm adjusting for your normal levels of surliness. What is it? What did I say?"

Tala's mouth tightened. She hadn't realized it until Prince Jimuro had pointed it out to her, but what he'd said just now had reminded her of the only other person in her life who bothered to chide her for her coarse vocabulary.

Prince Jimuro sighed. "That's fine. I suppose I should've known better than to hope for a straight answer to a simple—"

"It's Mang," Tala said bluntly.

The prince did an admirable job of keeping his composure, but she could see through it. She knew he was bursting with questions, or at the very least snark. She was almost impressed when he managed to tamp it all down and ask a relatively subdued, "Why did you fight about me?"

"Why do you think?" Tala said. "He doesn't want to devote his life to protecting the enemy."

Prince Jimuro turned frosty. "We're not enemies, Sergeant," he said with aggressive overenunciation. "The war's over."

"You're always going to be . . . his enemy, Your Brilliance," Tala said. "It was one of your family's bombs that dropped on our house, part of Tomoda's revenge for . . ." She stopped just short of telling him that the bomb had fallen on the same day jungle-runners had tried to assassinate a boy who looked an awful lot like he did. That wouldn't help anything now. So instead she just cleared her throat and continued: "It was your family's soldiers trying to kill us, these past few years."

Thankfully, Prince Jimuro didn't notice her pause. "It was a *war*," he hissed, indignant as a wet cat. "And now it's over."

Tala squeezed her eyes shut in annoyance. She'd thought she'd already gotten through to him on the road earlier. How could she make him understand?

"When you shadepact with a creature, you're taking responsibility for its life," she said. "The moment you say its name, every decision you make has to be made for two, not one. The legends say a great sage taught the Sanbuna people that at the dawn of time, sailing into the islands from the far southern sea."

"I seem to recall a Shang legend of a wise man from the northern steppes, who taught their people shadepacting first. From the back of a golden-furred deer, if memory serves."

"I don't give a shit about the legends," she said, ignoring the way the prince winced at her language. "I'm telling you how it is: When you shadepact, you don't live for just you anymore."

"But he thinks you are anyway?"

Tala frowned again: not at his question, but at the fact that the more she considered it, the more she found herself wondering if Mang really did have a point. It was hard for her to concentrate: She was tired from the day's march, and the rising whine of car engines cut into her thoughts.

Fuck it, she thought. She had to know. "Why'd you come back for me, Your Brilliance?"

It was the prince's turn to frown. "I would've thought that obvious."

Tala stopped walking and turned to face him full-on. "If I'm asking, it's not."

"You've fought hard and well to protect my life against the impossible, all while despising the fact that we breathe the same air," he said. "You take your duty seriously, and I can't have made it pleasant for you. So yes, Sergeant, I thought your life was worth saving."

Tala found herself flat-footed. She'd expected something strictly pragmatic: that he needed a good bodyguard, or at least that he'd wanted some company on the road. Honesty was just about the last thing she expected from the prince, especially if it was an honesty that painted her in anything approaching a good light.

She opened her mouth to answer, but she was cut off by a bright-red truck trundling past. A pair of riders preceded it on motorcycles, while two cars followed closely behind, full of Shang soldiers. In comparison with the quiet pact-powered Tomodanese cars, these vehicles were all clumsy, nasty beasts, their engines belching noise and black smoke in equal amounts.

Tala saw the citizens on the streets eye the motorcade warily as it passed. With a start, she was catapulted back in her memory, to a day ten years ago when she stood in a Lisan City street market. A black steel streetcar was carving its way through, while on either side Sanbuna people looked on. And all of them, including Mang, wore the exact same expression as the Tomodanese wore now.

She rejected the comparison. She found herself vaguely offended that she had even drawn it, since there was a night and a day's difference between a people who'd been occupied and a people who were in the process of paying for their crimes.

And yet . . .

Prince Jimuro gritted his teeth as the second car passed. "That truck is built for the transportation of loot," he said. "And the Shang are driving it up the most crowded thoroughfare in the city." He

pointed over the rearmost car, at the truck's rear door. "They're pa-
rading their plunder in front of the people from whom they stole it."
He spat. "Disgusting."

"Watch yourself," Tala said, snatching his wrist and yanking his
hand down, but it was too late. The car's taillights flashed red as it
came to a stop.

All Tala's senses flared to life. Even fatigued and venom-racked,
she was still made for walking into fights and walking back out
again. "Stay behind me, Your Brilliance," she said. "And actually do
it this time."

She reached into her coat and wrapped her hand around the butt
of her new Shang pistol. While she wished she'd had more time to
acclimate herself to the weapon, she was just going to have to trust
that when it came to a fight, a gun was a gun.

But then she saw that a black car had pulled into the intersection,
cutting off the motorcade. Its doors flew open, and women and men
piled out. Some wore suits, some wore kimonos, but all wore elaborate metal masks of some kind on their faces.

And all of them had weapons.

A stout masked man held a shotgun at his hip and blew one of the
motorcycle riders off her saddle before she could react. Another, a
tall and rail-thin woman, darted for the other motorcycle rider, carrying no weapon but a long sword in its sheath. As the rider shouted
and brought up his pistol, her blade flashed, and both the rider's
hand and head fell to the ground, neatly separated from the rest of
his body in a spray of blood.

While most citizens turned and ran, Tala's sharp eyes caught a few
in the crowd that were staying put. In fact, they were donning masks,
too. Up close, she could see they were all the same shape: like an
insect, with splayed wings over their wearers' eyes.

"Cicadas?" Prince Jimuro muttered, and Tala's whole gut jolted.
She knew who they were dealing with. She'd been briefed on them
during mission prep.

"We have to get out of here right now," she said tersely. She
grabbed his wrist again and yanked him back the other way, but her
heart sank to see more Shang soldiers already en route.

As more gunshots erupted from the motorcade, a short masked

man in a black wave-patterned kimono clambered up onto the hood of the black car, a megaphone in his hand. *"Citizens of Tajiri!"* he bellowed, his voice ringing out over the entire street. *"Children of Tomoda! Tonight, we take back what is rightfully yours!"*

Tala yanked at the Iron Prince, but he was rooted on the spot. He looked transfixed by the sound of the speaker's voice. *"Your Brilliance—!"* she hissed.

"While the Copper Sages cower in Hagane, we will fight for you all!" the speaker roared. Most of the everyday citizens had deserted, and his cohorts were engaging the Shang troops, but he spoke as if there were a rapt audience before him.

"We will fight for your future!" he went on. *"We are the Steel Cicadas, and we will fight for Tomoda!"*

CHAPTER ELEVEN

LEE

Even with the boost Lee gave Xiulan, the princess was still barely tall enough to haul herself up into the hole that Kou had gouged into the wall. "Would it have killed you to eat your vegetables growing up?"

"That sort of attitude will get you nowhere, Inspector Lee," Xiulan grunted as her weight finally left Lee's cupped hands.

Lee gestured to the top of her head. "It got me up here."

She caught only a fleeting glimpse of the princess's smile before Xiulan disappeared from sight completely. And then she stood there and waited to see if the door would open.

Of course it will, she thought. After everything they'd been through so far, why would the princess leave her behind now?

You have one rule, she reminded herself.

Lee frowned and pushed the thought away. *That's my rule, not hers.*

Her finger wandered to her lips, which still tingled from Xiulan's touch. It didn't change much for her, honestly; of the many women and men Lee had teamed up with in her life of petty crime, she'd ended up in bed with most of them. And while Lee had been disappointed by partners like Lefty who hadn't respected honor among thieves, Xiulan was a royal. That meant Lee already knew she couldn't trust her.

But it was hard not to lose herself a bit in the fantasy of reliving that kiss. There'd been something electric there, and not just the sheer surprise of it. Though, thinking back to the hotel in Jungshao, to the princess's question . . . was it really a surprise?

Look at me, she said to herself with a sigh. She was a woman whose palms could be dry and steady as they lifted a wallet from a copper's tight-sealed pocket, but now they shook with a treacherous sort of excitement.

She frowned down at her fingers. "Cut it out," she muttered.

The lock gave way with a *clunk.* Lee grabbed the door's edge and pushed. As the door sank into the wall, she saw Xiulan just on the other side of it, pulling right along with her. And then the door was completely gone, and the two women stood face-to-face.

Their eyes met.

Xiulan's lips parted ever so slightly.

Lee swallowed. *Don't do this,* she thought. *You always do this, and it always goes bad in the end.*

So instead she offered up a gruff, "Nice one, Princess," and slipped past her to the unconscious Dahali guard on the floor. It looked like Kou had chewed him up, but he would live. With experienced skill, her fingers roamed his uniform, picking out his spending money and the rings on his fingers. For good measure, she took the knife from his belt. It was relatively plain compared with Parkash's, but Lee didn't care about that. All she cared was that the blade was sharp. She wasn't much for killing, but knives were good for more than that.

Xiulan eyed her with vague disapproval. Lee shrugged and slipped the knife into her belt anyway. "Gotta eat," she said.

Neither of them had been black-bagged as they'd been escorted back to Kurihara manor. That meant that Lee had gotten a good eyeful of the place during their frog-march from the front door to their ad hoc cell. Thief that she was, it was a matter of course that she'd have kept an eye on the exits, but she was pleased to see Xiulan immediately head left, toward the one Lee herself had marked as the best way out.

Xiulan seemed to notice her approval, and grinned. "I *am* a detective, you know."

"Like you'd ever let me forget," Lee said, sighing. "Come on, then. We might even be able to get out clean, as long as we keep—"

From behind them came a high, sharp bark.

And then another. And another. And another.

Lee turned to see the dog there, the one that had come in with Chetan Parkash. She'd never seen it before today, but something looked vaguely familiar about it.

Xiulan appeared at her side. "Go away," she hissed at it. "We don't have time for you."

But as she eyed that dog, something snagged in Lee's head. She couldn't quite place it, but she knew by now that her instincts were there for a reason. So instead of running from the dog, she took a careful step toward it.

"Inspector Lee," Xiulan whispered. "What are you—?"

"Go with me on this," Lee said, holding up a hand. "Um. Your Majesty." She knelt down before the dog and carefully offered out a hand for it to smell. Furtively, it stepped forward and nosed her fingers, leaving a wet trail across them.

And then it pressed its face into her hand, licking at her palm eagerly.

Lee's heart just about burst. "There you go," she whispered. "Good . . ." She took a quick glance. ". . . girl."

"Inspector Lee," Xiulan said. "Is this really the time and place for this?"

Casually, Lee glanced back over her shoulder. "You hear her barking?"

That brought Xiulan up short.

Lee weighed the situation, then scooped the dog up into her arms and stood. The creature's fur was short and soft and warm, and it made Lee painfully aware of how long it had been since she'd petted a dog.

"All right," she said as Xiulan gaped at the happy dog bundled in her arms. "Now we can go."

Normally, Lee was cool in a bad situation, which this definitely was. But she was able to do that because no matter what else was going on, she could keep her eyes on the prize, whether that was a purse of jian, a priceless sculpture, or a hasty exit. This time, though, her focus was muddied: by the warm, wriggling dog in her arms, and by the tingling on her lips. The dog, Lee managed by gripping her tighter to keep her still.

The tingling, on the other hand, proved remarkably persistent.

Ease off, she thought as she ran. *You're the one who said to worry about it later.*

But she couldn't help it. She'd kissed sailors, cutthroats, sweet boys, stablehands, soldiers, whores, and barkeeps, but she'd never kissed a princess. And she'd certainly never been kissed by one.

When they got down the stairs, the dog started barking again. Lee stopped to let her down, but she just shuffled her forepaws excitedly and barked away.

"You know the Dahali word for 'shut it'?" Lee said.

"My knowledge of their language is strictly academic," Xiulan said. "I wouldn't know idiomatic—"

"That's a long walk to 'no,'" Lee said. Not sure what else to do, she reached for the closest thing she could think of in Tomodanese. *"Quiet."* She said it like her mom had taught her: with authority, so she'd listen, but not loudly, so she wouldn't think Lee was barking back.

And to Lee's surprise, the dog's snout snapped shut as her pointy ears perked right up.

Xiulan stared. "Inspector Lee," she said quietly, "how did you know how to do that?"

"Didn't," Lee said. "I just know dogs."

"Sit, girl!" Xiulan tried, but her voice was too high, her words too fast. The dog cocked her head rather than obey, then started barking again.

"Quiet," Lee said again, in Tomodanese. Then: "Sit."

The dog sat on her dark-brown haunches, looking up at Lee expectantly . . . and quietly. Lee grinned, then made to scoop her up again, but Xiulan stepped into her path.

"I'm sorry, Lee," she said, her voice inflected with the textures that made it sound genuine. "We can't."

"I'm telling you, Princess," Lee said, "I've got a feeling about this dog."

But Xiulan just frowned, eye shining with regret.

Lee sighed. "Stay," she said to the dog, then turned to resume their escape.

"You have . . . quite the affinity for dogs," Xiulan observed as they sped along. Behind them, the dog sat at attention, her eyes fixed on them, ears flat. A small whine rose from her and dragged across Lee's heartstrings like a key across a car door.

"You get a lot of them where I come from," Lee said, unable to keep some edge out of her voice. "Spend enough time around them, and you pick up how to talk to them eventually, same as a person. Now shut it, Your Majesty, before your barking's what gets us caught."

As they crept through the mansion, Lee was struck by the contrast between this place and the royal palace they'd just come from. There was no artful sparseness here; the halls and rooms were crammed with art and decoration that all seemed shiny enough on its own, but in concert just made the whole place seem busy. From the looks of things, Lord Kurihara hadn't had any vision or taste; he'd just wanted expensive things for the sake of having them.

Those types were Lee's favorite pockets to pick.

She eyed all the metal in evidence: The art. The appliances. The little knickknacks cluttering up every tabletop. She couldn't believe the Dahali hadn't cleared them all out yet, but she supposed Chetan Parkash probably liked living like a highborn.

Xiulan seemed to follow her eye. "Lee," she said.

Lee frowned. "Gotta eat," she repeated, but she moved on anyway.

They skulked through the house, taking the sequence of side rooms and servants' corridors that would lead directly to the parking lot they'd come from. Lee had seen whole neat rows of cars there, open for the taking. Their patience was its own reward: It allowed them to get the drop on guard after guard, letting Kou make short work of them. One fortunate thing about Kurihara manor was that it seemed to have no shortage of closet space, though Lee supposed the cleaning crew would be in for a hell of a surprise.

"Why haven't we encountered more resistance?" Xiulan said as they stuffed another guard into a bathroom and shut the door. "Not that I have cause to complain, of course . . ."

Lee had been wondering that, herself. "Near I can tell, it's probably your fault," she said. "You're a princess. They can't just be sticking you in their ratty—er, *dirty* brig while they figure out what to do with you. If word ever got back to your dear old dad, he'd have Chetan Parkash's balls in a bowl of broth before sundown."

"Earlier, you'd suggested individual gold-plated vises. That's quite the downgrade."

"So we get the royal treatment," Lee went on. "Minimum security. Besides, they probably thought once you were caught, you'd just sit in the cell and wait, like a good little princess."

Xiulan laughed ruefully. "They weren't inaccurate, were they?"

"You said it, not me."

By staying low and sticking to the shadows, they were able to reach the side entrance. They only ran into a few more guards, each of whom they ably dispatched as before: Xiulan with strategic summonings of Kou, and Lee with a swift punch in the jaw. Lee wasn't used to leaving behind a trail like this. Breaking-and-entering wasn't even really her style, for that matter, unless she knew the place was empty. Xiulan seemed to think of her as some kind of all-purpose criminal mastermind, but her résumé didn't have much more besides pickpocketing and the occasional con job.

Still, she had to admit, when it came to being a master thief and spy, she was doing pretty great so far.

They took up positions on either side of the door, which had a friendly-looking square window. Night had fallen outside, but the moonlight swathed the entire parking lot in a silver glow. It glinted off the domed roofs of the cars, making them glint like beetles neatly arranged in a collector's case.

"Nearest I can figure," Lee said, "our best chance is to make a break for the nearest car, hope for the best, and try not to die."

Xiulan eyed the ground outside appraisingly. "Do you know the mechanisms of a car door lock?"

Lee held up her borrowed knife.

Xiulan shook her head. "I'm acquainted, at least on a theoretical level, with their inner workings."

"Think you could hot-wire one, too?"

Xiulan's eye shone with reluctance. "Theoretically."

Lee grimaced. *Theoretically* wouldn't have ever passed muster with any self-respecting crew on a job like this. But she guessed they didn't have a choice. "You think you can do it, you make the run."

"What will you do?"

Lee glanced at the knife again. "Make sure we're not followed."

Xiulan nodded, absorbing this. Then she hung her head and started laughing.

"What?" Lee said warily.

"It's just . . ." Xiulan let out another laugh, tinged with disbelief. "We arrived in Tomoda *this morning*."

The absurd truth of it hit Lee like a policeman's baton, and suddenly she couldn't help but laugh, herself. "Guess we've had ourselves quite a day, haven't we?"

"I'm rather averse to living a boring life." The princess sighed. "Shall we count to three, then?"

Lee cracked the door. "Three."

They burst outside, skimming low to the ground. Xiulan peeled off left to break open a car, while Lee banked hard right. She tossed the knife to herself, caught it backhanded, and casually jabbed it into the first tire she saw. It let out a surprisingly loud hiss, but only for a few seconds. By the time it subsided, Lee had already moved on to the next car.

The tension in her rose with each tire she stabbed. The longer they stayed out in the open like this, the more likely someone would happen on them by accident, or discover one of the bodies they'd left behind and raise the alarm. But every time she glanced over at the car they'd chosen for escape, Xiulan still knelt at the door, fiddling with it.

As she finished up the third row of tires, she heard a click far behind her. Her skin came alive with electric tingles, as she expected to come face-to-face with the barrel of a Dahali gun. But when she turned, she saw that it was just the car door, which now stood slightly ajar. Xiulan had stuffed herself into the car, and stuck one hand out to urgently beckon Lee to follow.

"Were you successful?" Xiulan said as Lee threw herself into the backseat.

"They'll have a hell of a time chasing us," Lee said. "But I made me a fair bit of noise, so we'll probably be hearing alarms . . ." She paused, listening.

"What is it?" Xiulan said.

"Nothing," said Lee. "Normally it's just that with my luck, the alarms wait until I'm talking about them to actually—"

The air filled with rising sirens.

Lee hung her head. "Tell me you've got that hot-wired."

"As of yet, it's been reluctant to yield to me its—"

"Long walk to 'no,' then," Lee barked.

"Why do you always say that?" Xiulan shouted back.

From outside the car came angry shouts in Dahali and the telltale tromp of boots. In the car's rearview mirror, she saw troops falling in, hands aglow.

"What happens if a hexbolt hits this car?" Lee said.

"Theoretically, anything," Xiulan said as she fiddled with a tangle of wires. "I know little of Dahali sorcery, save that it involves the direct channeling of soul energy."

"More theories."

Xiulan grunted. "I take it we're about to be treated to a practical lesson?"

"Only if you don't hurry the fuck up, Your Majesty."

"It's an honorific, you know," Xiulan grumbled through clenched teeth. "Why do you only call me that when we're—"

A bolt of white light slammed into the rear window. Cracks spiderwebbed through the glass. More filled the air around them, as if their car were caught in the epicenter of a gigantic firework. The entire vehicle groaned and swayed with every impact.

"*Damn it!*" Xiulan threw the wires down. "All the books in the world will never convey the technical realities of a procedure."

Lee ducked as another hexbolt deepened every crack in the rear window. "If you spent as much time hot-wiring as you did saying all those big words, we'd be out of here by now!"

"Lee, you aren't listening: *I can't do it,*" Xiulan said. But it wasn't her words that gave Lee pause; it was her tone. Rather than the heights of hysteria, she was speaking in the flat, even tones of despair. "Ruomei was right: I'm the White Rat, and we're clutched in the talons of the hawk."

Lee bit the insides of her cheeks. The hexbolts outside had stopped, which meant only one thing: The Dahali were closing in on foot. They'd played all their big surprises to get out of their cell this time. If they got caught again, there was no way Parkash would give them even an inch of wiggle room.

She inhaled. "Shang Xiulan," she said. "If you don't prove me wrong about how worthless you inbred excuse of a royal class are by hot-wiring this fucking car, you're not getting another damn kiss out of me."

Xiulan's head whipped around like she'd been slapped by an invisible palm. With a growl, she grabbed two wires and forcibly twisted them together.

And the engine in the rear of the car roared to life, before settling into a low purr.

Xiulan's eye snapped wide in disbelief.

Lee kicked the back of the driver's seat. "*Go!*"

Xiulan swiveled around, then slammed a booted foot onto the gas pedal. The entire car surged forward so suddenly, Lee had to throw her arms out to stop herself from breaking her nose on the seat in front of her.

She swerved wildly to avoid a charging Dahali soldier. "Was that worth a kiss, Inspector Lee?" Xiulan said.

"Get us out of this one alive, Princess, and kissing's the least of what I'll do to you."

She turned back to laugh at the sight of their pursuers trying to chase them with flat tires.

But instead, she only saw a four-legged silhouette sprinting through the headlights.

She knew what was about to happen just before it did.

A hexbolt slammed into the dog as she ran, cutting her off mid-bark. She fell right to the ground with a sharp whine Lee could hear over the din of battle.

Lee threw herself at the driver's seat. "Turn us around."

"Have you taken leave of your senses, Inspector Lee?" Xiulan said. "We need to—"

"Either you turn us around, or I'm throwing myself out that door and going back myself."

Xiulan gaped. "For a *dog*?" But then she exhaled and threw the car into a sharp power-slide with a yank of the hand brake.

With the headlights now facing their pursuers, Lee could see their ranks swelling. If they so much as stopped, their car would be overwhelmed by bodies and hexbolts alike.

"Speed up," Lee said.

"What do you intend to do?" Xiulan said.

Lee sighed. "Something fucking stupid."

Xiulan sped up.

Some soldiers fled while others stood their ground and unleashed a deluge of hexbolts. One took the left side mirror clean off, while another splatted right into their windshield, turning it almost opaque white with microfissures. Xiulan cursed and swerved, but Lee shouted, "Close your eyes!" She hoped Xiulan obeyed, because she hurled her borrowed knife straight at the cracked windshield, and the entire pane shattered. Sharp, glittering shards of glass flew back into the car, and Lee turned just in time to avoid a mouthful of them.

Then she threw her door open.

The wind roared against the opening, and she had to brace her feet against the seat so she could keep the door open with her hands. Struggling mightily against the weight of it, she leaned her head out to get a glimpse of the dog. They were coming up on her any second now.

Something white-hot rushed past her cheek, slamming into the door a mere inch from her hand. The entire car door bent too far on its hinge. Lee let go as the entire thing peeled right off the side of their newly minted jalopy and skidded into their wake.

Another one screamed past her, singeing some of her short hair as it flew wildly in the wind. She ignored it, though she couldn't stop her memory from reminding her what a direct hit would feel like . . . especially at this speed. But she refused to let that distract her for the next three . . . two . . . one—

Less deft hands than hers would've shattered their fingers on the asphalt, or missed their target entirely. But fingers were all Lee ever had, and in that split second she wrapped them around the prone dog, then yanked herself back into the wreck of a car they were driving. The creature shivered in her arms, barely alive.

"I hope you're satisfied!" Xiulan shouted, then threw the hand brake again. Shouts rose outside the car as it went into another controlled slide, drifting around the narrow bend between rows of parked, disabled cars. The car, top-heavy and vertical as it was, teetered for a moment on only two wheels before settling back down hard on all four. And then they were off into the night, hexbolts in their wake, but thankfully no cars.

Which left the poor dog in Lee's lap.

"We have to help her," Lee said. She stroked the dog's flank, and the animal whined in response.

"Where would we go?" Xiulan said. "The Tomodanese hold animal spirits equal to human ones, but they'd never help two humans like us. And if the Dahali are willing to ship me back to Shang, then surely our own troops would be doubly so."

"We can't just let her die!" Lee shouted. That wasn't good. She was losing her cool, really losing it. People who did that were never long for Lee's world.

"We have no recourse," Xiulan said. She sighed. "Why do you even want to save this dog so badly?"

Lee didn't answer. She rocked in her seat, and rocked the dog with her. She didn't know what else to do. Her mind whirred as she tried to think up a way to save this one. But she only knew thieving. She didn't know anything about science, and she didn't know anything about . . .

About . . .

She sat upright. The dog whined again.

Lee caught Xiulan's eye in the rearview mirror. And with all the gravel she could muster, she said, "Teach me how to shadepact again. Right now."

"We don't have anything we need," Xiulan said. "The incense, the cloths, *The Nine Truths* . . ."

"*That's how the Shang do it,*" Lee snapped. "Do I look Shang to you?"

Xiulan's mouth creased. Bitterness flooded every bit of Lee's being. Her partner was picking one hell of a time to remember she was a royal.

But then Xiulan's voice grew very soft. "It might not work." Lee had to strain to hear her over the roar of the whipping wind. "But I'll help you try. Lay your hands on her."

Carefully, Lee obeyed, letting the dog's shallow breaths bounce her palms up and down.

"Good," Xiulan said. "That's the first step in creating a bridge between her soul and yours. Once you do that, it's imperative that you maintain that connection. Without it, your bond will falter and fail, and she will die."

"I remember that bit," Lee said, a bit more testily than she'd meant. "What do I do now?" She'd been given the steps before, but the more she grasped at the memories, the more easily they eluded her.

Xiulan hesitated a moment before answering. "What comes next is much more intuitive," she said. "We're speaking of souls—a component of yourself you will never find on an anatomy chart, but which is nonetheless essential to your existence. It's like . . ." She thought. "Close your eyes."

"That didn't help last time," Lee said. Closing her eyes was the last thing she wanted to do. Hell, she barely even wanted to blink. She felt an overpowering need to keep eyes on this dog, because one blink was all it might take for the dog to stop fighting and give in.

"It will help you focus on my incredibly calming voice," Xiulan snapped. "Now do it."

Lee spared one last worried look into the dog's increasingly misty eyes. And then, hesitantly, she shut them. She tried to reach for that calm place inside herself again, but it was nowhere to be found. It had been impossible to find when all she had to deal with was the world's scariest rooster under her arm. Now she was fresh out of another prison cell, in a speeding wreck of a stolen car, and cradling a dog at death's door. How were closed eyes and a couple of deep breaths supposed to make her just up and forget all that?

The harder she worked to achieve calm, the more that calm eluded her. Every time she created a gap in her thoughts for emptiness and silence to go, instead more thoughts would just flood in. And in her hand, she felt the dog's breaths growing shallower and shallower.

"You're not trying hard enough," Xiulan said. "Your mind must be in order so you can focus. Find that focus, or she'll die."

"The dogs take you, I'm focusing!" Lee shouted, but she felt hopelessness creeping in. This was pointless. Hers wasn't an orderly mind; if anything, order made her uneasy. It reminded her of shiny Tomodanese jackboots, and the Shang boots that had tromped over Jeongson's soil before them. She'd spent her life running away from order. It'd never meant "calm" for her. No, she'd always found her peace in—

The memories flashed through her head: The woman on her deathbed, her children crowded around her. The welcome that fled the house with her passing. The young girl who fled with it.

Lee's grip tightened on the dog. *No,* she told herself. *Don't go there.*

The memories shifted: Pulling her first big job with Lightning-Finger Liao. Coming back from a successful boost with Tungmei, and heady from the thrill as they sank into bed together. She and Lefty, up late in a ratty tenement room, plotting out the particulars of their con job by candlelight and exploring each other's bodies in the dark.

Xiulan's lips on hers in the cell, as her own heart pounded in her ears.

And then, something new: running through a garden, alongside a young boy with a blue jinbei and glasses, his long hair streaming behind him as he laughed in the sunshine.

That was what she felt within the dog in her lap. What resonated in her own soul. Not order. Not discipline.

Love.

Her fear for this dog didn't subside, but the panic did. The moment Lee let go of the urgency she felt to save it by any means necessary, her thinking sharpened itself. She didn't just feel the dog's shallow breaths against her palm anymore; she felt every pulse of its heart, every little twitch and contraction of its battered body.

And there. Just like that, she felt something deeper inside herself. It was like becoming aware of her own tongue: never quite in focus, but always there, and once her attention got ahold of it, it was the only thing she could think about.

"Lee?" Xiulan said. "What's happening? Are you—?"

"I . . . I think I'm doing it," Lee said. Chasing that feeling felt like diving into a dark pool. She didn't know how deep it went, but it felt like she could follow it down forever. As she dove deeper, she became vaguely aware of something diving next to her. Even with her eyes closed, she could sense feelings radiating from it: Fear. That was the main one, by far. But there was also confusion there, and sadness. The dog didn't know what was happening to her, didn't know why she'd just been attacked, just wanted the pain to stop.

It's okay, little friend, Lee told her. *I'm scared, too.*

She felt the dog's spirit waiting for something. And then Lee remembered what she was supposed to do next.

What do you want me to be? she asked.

Rather than answer, Lee felt a dull throb from within the dog: a sensation as real as the waning heartbeat Lee felt in the palm she'd pressed to the dog's furry chest. And when Lee focused on it, she was surprised to find that it resonated with a similar throbbing inside herself, like two notes joining in harmony.

When she turned her focus to that part of herself, that throbbing turned into an ache. Once again, she saw her dying mother. Her siblings leaving her on a darkened doorstep. The partners she'd had over the years, when things were good.

You want me to help you find that? Lee asked. This dog wasn't nearly as articulate as the rooster had been, but Lee understood her so much better. *You're looking for . . . love?*

Another feeling, and Lee knew the dog's answer to her question was *Yes.*

Lee gripped her tight. *Then I'll help you find it.*

She felt something give way beneath her palm, and then she was grasping only at open air.

Lee's eyes opened. Her lap was empty. In place of the dog, Lee felt a tingling . . . there, hovering somewhere around her midsection. She tugged at her neckline and peered down her dress. To her surprise, she saw something that hadn't been there this morning: a bright-white chevron mark, splashed across her stomach. "Is . . . is that . . . ?"

"Your pactmark," Xiulan said. Her voice was quiet, but in the rearview mirror her eye danced with excitement. "She'll have one to match it . . . once you seal the pact."

Right. Lee needed a name and now she was back to freezing up. Naming something was more responsibility than she liked to shoulder. She flipped through the mental record of every name she'd ever heard, from every person she could remember meeting. Not a one that came to mind felt as if it'd be enough to encompass what this new companion was supposed to be to her.

She didn't know if it would work, but she thought to herself, *I don't know. What do you think?*

The response she got back wasn't words so much as feelings and ideas. There was still confusion there, but all the sadness and fear were gone. In their place: a rush of gratitude, and happiness, and excitement. It was every good feeling Lee had ever come to associate with a dog, and now a bundle of them just sat there inside her, bubbling just below the surface. She imagined the dog now, as it used to be: the way it would probably run through these fields, getting mud on its already-dark . . .

. . . *Ah*, Lee thought. *That'll do.* "Pull over," she said.

"Strange name for a shade," said Xiulan. "But I suppose she's your shade, and—"

"No, you. Pull over."

The car glided to a stop next to some tall grass by the side of the highway. Lee vaulted out the gaping hole where the door had been, feeling like she was fit to burst. She pointed her finger at the ground and shouted, *"Bootstrap!"*

A jagged white bolt of energy shot from her, slicing through the night like a gleaming silver knife. It solidified into a creature at least three times larger than it had been in its previous life as a mere dog. Her distinctive coloring remained: gold-brown fur and bootlike dark legs. But her fangs now jutted out from the bottom of her jaw, curving up like shark's fins. Her pointed ears now had tufts of fur adorning their tips like little baubles. Before she'd had one tail; now she had three, all curled up tightly against her back. She was no dog anymore, but a dog-shade, and she looked every bit the fearsome spirit that Lee had always fantasized about.

Then her mouth opened, and a long pink tongue flopped out. She sat, giving Lee a glimpse of the white chevron mark adorning the fur of her belly. Her eyes met Lee's, and all three of her tails thumped the ground excitedly.

Lee smiled—not a calculated gesture meant to unsettle or posture, but a genuine expression that welled up irresistibly from inside her. Gently, she placed a hand between Bootstrap's eyes. Sensing what Lee wanted to do, Bootstrap dipped her head and panted happily. As Lee ran her fingers through Bootstrap's fur, she was struck by how soft it was. Had Bootstrap always been this way? Had that piece of Lee's soul done that to her? She brimmed with so many questions about this new part of herself.

"She's beautiful," Xiulan said. When Lee turned, the princess wasn't looking at Bootstrap, but at her.

Lee let her hand fall away from Bootstrap's head. "I . . . I can't believe it."

Xiulan's eye glinted with moonlight. "What you have now is far more than a mere pet, or servant," she said. "Bootstrap is a fundamental part of you now. The bond between you is soul-deep. You won't just carry her; you'll have her feelings, her memories . . . everything that made her, her."

Lee nodded. Her eyes flickered between the shade before her—*her* shade—and the hands that had wrought her.

Xiulan pulled her pipe out of her coat. "Inspector Lee, that was superlative work," she said. "Not only are you the first of your people known to be granted the honor of a shade, but you rose to the challenge so ably. So naturally." She produced a matchbook. "You'll be a living testament to the worth of the Jeongsonese people, which even the most strident critic—"

"Princess," Lee said, "don't you dare light that pipe."

Xiulan, who had the flame halfway tipped to her tobacco, shot her a questioning look.

Lee slipped a practiced hand around Xiulan's waist.

Xiulan's flame went out. "Ah."

This kiss wasn't a surprise like the last one, and it didn't have that same urgency. But there was hunger there, and that did surprise Lee. She closed her eyes and let herself wander through it as her fingers slipped inside Xiulan's coat and began to toy with her suspenders.

Xiulan's whole body stiffened, but with surprise, not reluctance. The moment passed, and she melted back into Lee's arms, her hands tugging at the bottom hem of Lee's skirt.

Lee herself didn't really know what they were about to do. They were two fugitives on the side of the road, driving just about the most recognizable car in Tomoda. Lee didn't know how much of this was feeling, or the sheer thrill of the night they'd had, or just something about the smell of Xiulan's hair. All she knew was the script she always followed when she was with a woman, and her hands, her lips, her tongue were already playing their parts.

A flood of images spiked in her mind, so suddenly that she tore herself away from Xiulan and staggered back.

"Lee?" Xiulan said, reaching for her. "What's wrong? Is there a problem with my technique? If you just show me how—"

Lee squeezed her eyes shut and held up one hand while she cradled her head with the other. "Stop talking," she said. She wasn't in pain, but her whole head suddenly felt heavy.

"Of course!" Xiulan said. "Bootstrap is responding to your heightened feelings. She'll be trying to connect with you. What you're seeing and feeling now are her thoughts and emotions and memories. What do you see?"

Lee gritted her teeth rather than reply, but the answer was *a lot*. Images flitted by her, almost too fast to grasp. She was running in the garden again as that same young boy, now in a different yukata, threw a stick to her. She was doing her little shuffling dance as the boy, now older, bent over his desk and sketched intently. She was curled up on top of his bed, perking up her ears when his bedroom door slid open and his mother stood silhouetted in the doorway. She was—

"The dogs take me," Lee said, and pulled herself out of Bootstrap's stream of consciousness. She looked at the shade, who sat patiently waiting for pets with her tongue flapping out of her mouth. She thought back to the sketchbook she'd seen. To the painting in Kohoyama. There was no mistaking it.

"Are you going to tell me what's going on?" Xiulan said irritably, but Lee held up another finger.

And then she dove back into Bootstrap's mind.

Again, she was buried under a deluge of images. But the next time she saw one of the boy, she seized on it and presented it back to Bootstrap, with as vague a question as she could manage: *Where?*

She had no idea what she'd get in response. But to her surprise, a scent filled her nostrils. It smelled like man—not the scuzzy sort of musk she got from the types she met in the gutter, but something refined, like a twisted, distorted version of the scent that wafted off Xiulan when they were close enough. And there were other scents: Gunpowder. Tire rubber. Money.

And it was all almost exactly due east.

Lee dipped back out of Bootstrap's consciousness again. *"The dogs take me!"* she shouted at the night sky.

"The dogs take you indeed, Inspector Lee," Xiulan said, now with naked impatience. "I entreat you to enlighten me: *Where are they taking you?*"

Lee chuckled in disbelief. "Princess," she said, "wait till you hear whose dog she used to be."

CHAPTER TWELVE

JIMURO

Jimuro had heard of the Steel Cicadas. Since Erega made a point of visiting him in his cells to discuss world affairs, he'd made a point of having the newspaper delivered, so he would actually have something to discuss. He had to adjust for the level of jingoism and libel endemic in the Sanbuna press, but it had nonetheless been a relatively reliable conduit of information.

Every so often in the pages of the *Lisan City Star,* he would come across a reference to or a brief news story about the Steel Cicadas. They were patriots (his translation for the Sanbuna term *terrorist*) fighting small battles all over the island of Tomoda to strike back against the occupying foreign powers. The *Star* dismissed them as neo-monarchists and thugs.

But witnessing them in action now, Jimuro saw only heroes.

Sergeant Tala yanked him so hard, he lost his footing. "We're *going,* Your Brilliance," she snapped. Clearly, she'd read the news stories about the Steel Cicadas, too.

Jimuro yanked back, slipping his hand free of her grasp. "They're helping my people," he said. "I have to help them."

"*Help them from the throne,*" Tala said.

That was perhaps the only thing she could have said to give Jimuro pause. After the fight they'd had, he was beginning to truly understand what the sergeant had given up to restore him to a throne she didn't even want him to claim. And there was something to be said about the good he could do once he ascended to the Mountain Throne.

But the Mountain Throne was leagues away, and the people who needed him most were here right now.

"I have to help them!" Jimuro said, then tore away from Tala and charged for the nearest Shang soldier.

Growing up in the Court of Steel meant Prince Jimuro had had the benefit of the finest martial arts tutors in Tomoda. His basic training as an officer had further sharpened his theoretical combat skills into something street-practical. While Fumiko had excelled at the showy disciplines centered on striking, he had developed a much stronger affinity for throws, joint locks, and turning an opponent's own weight and momentum against them.

He'd felt self-conscious at first, that he wasn't as skilled at laying people out in a single punch the way Fumiko could on a good day. But his mother had confided in him once that a Steel Lord had little use for their fists.

"Challenges faced by the Mountain Throne seldom go away after merely being struck once," Steel Lord Yoshiko had told him as the two of them watched Fumiko flatten their sparring instructor. "But they can be redirected. Repurposed. And more often than not, two of your problems may solve each other while you do nothing . . . or appear to."

The young Iron Prince had taken this in, and mostly understood it. "But what about the times when you do need to punch somebody?" he'd asked eventually.

"Hn." It had been his mother's favorite all-purpose noise. "Those are the times you light incense at my shrine and thank me for giving you a sister."

He fell upon the Shang soldier before the woman even realized what was happening. He grabbed her gun arm and twisted it behind her back, then slipped his finger over hers and pulled the trigger. She collapsed to the ground with a shout, but by then Jimuro already had her pistol in hand, its steel singing to him as he poured his spirit into it. In his hands, every metal felt different: iron stubborn, gold relaxed, copper bright and friendly, but all yielded to his spirit's will eventually. And true to his birthright, none did so more readily than steel.

He fired off two more shots in short order, each one finding a mark in another Shang soldier. He felt the gun's mechanics beginning to jam as he readied his third shot—typical cheap Shang manufacture—but he channeled more of his spirit and coaxed the gun into firing smoothly a fourth time.

In mere seconds, he'd cleared away an entire carful of Shang soldiers. They lay bleeding at his feet, either dead or dying. It was justice for the innocent people they had brutalized.

But, he realized all too late, he'd also thrown himself into an exposed position right in the middle of the road.

Tala tackled him to the ground just before the air above him was rent with return fire. "*Beaky!*" she shouted, and a gust of wind whooshed past Jimuro's face as the crow-shade took shape, and then flight. All at once the air came alive with more noise: Gunshots. Battle cries. The crackle of magic. Pinging metal, shattering glass.

And then, just like that, it all stopped.

"Don't shoot!" Tala shouted, putting her hands up. She was getting to her feet, and tugged on his collar to indicate he should do the same.

"Yes, listen to her!" Jimuro said. The scene before him looked like something straight out of the war: Shang troops dead, Cicadas dead, and cars riddled with bullet holes. Tala stood back-to-back with him, while Beaky flew a tight circle around them both, cawing at the top of its little bird lungs. Three of the Cicadas had broken open the armored car and were busily relieving it of its contents. The rest ringed them, guns and swords leveled. Their steel masks glinted under the streetlights overhead. Prince Jimuro caught snatches of what they were shouting:

"*She's got a slave! She's one of them!*"

"*She's not Shang, look at her!*"

"*Take her down, save her hostage—*"

And then a new voice cut through the din: "*Spirits take me, put your weapons down, you idiots!*" Their leader appeared through the crowd a second later, megaphone dangling by his side. It was hard to gauge his expression beneath his cicada mask, but his mouth hung open in disbelief.

"If any of you shoot," Jimuro said carefully, "you'll regret it deeply."

"*Your Brilliance, wait—*" Tala hissed.

"My name is Jimuro, son of Yoshiko, Iron Prince and heir to the Mountain Throne of Tomoda," he plowed on, his voice ringing like steel on steel.

He expected awe, or perhaps an outbreak of bowing. What he didn't expect was for the leader of the Steel Cicadas to say, "I'd never forget your face, Your Brilliance. Why do you think I just ordered everybody to put down their weapons?" He glanced back over his shoulder at the armored car. "Harada! How're we doing?"

"You want it to go faster, you can come and help!" said Harada, the bony woman with the sword who'd beheaded the rider at the start of the battle.

The leader gritted his teeth, then nodded to his two nearest comrades. They bowed (from the waist, Jimuro noted, which meant they were of lower birth), then slung up their guns and ran to help empty the truck.

"We have to go now, Your Brilliance," said the man. "It's not safe here." The more Jimuro observed him, the more he saw the man sketched in familiar lines. He squinted carefully. Where had he seen this man before? Where had he observed those movements, that posture? Where had he heard that voice . . . ?

"We just want to be on our way," Tala said carefully. "We have—"

"I don't negotiate with slavers," the man spat. "My offer for salvation doesn't extend to you, barbarian."

Jimuro drew himself up as regally as he could. "I go nowhere without Sergeant Tala."

That took the Cicada leader aback. "But, Your Brilliance—"

"Am I your Iron Prince, or am I not?" Jimuro said, in what he hoped was a passable impression of his mother.

The man hesitated only a little before bowing gently. "Of course. Your will is unquestionable, my liege." He raised the megaphone to his mouth again. *"Move out!"* Then he dropped the megaphone again and pointed to his waiting vehicle at the intersection. "With me!"

As they broke into a run, Tala returned Beaky to its place within her body. Jimuro could feel her reluctance to let it go, but he respected her for doing it anyway. He knew the creature well enough by now, and he still had misgivings about it. He could only imagine how its presence would've colored the conversation that was to follow.

The car's interior was black, velvety, and lush: Not the kind of strictly utilitarian, disposable vehicle he would've expected a resistance effort to use. The addition of himself and Tala made the backseat cramped, but he appreciated the comfort of the familiar.

Tala seemed far less impressed. "These aren't soldiers," she muttered in Sanbuna.

The Cicada shrugged and looked vaguely amused. "No, we're not," he said mildly. He jerked his head out the window, at the red-coated corpses lying in the street. "They were." He switched back to Tomodanese to address his driver. "Go."

Tires screeched as the car peeled away. Other cars fell in behind it, and traffic swerved to avoid them as Cicadas leaned out from the car windows, firing wild rounds of bullets into the air.

Jimuro had to wonder about where those bullets might land, but the Cicada leader seemed unbothered. He leaned back in his seat, then removed his steel mask at last to reveal a handsome and surprisingly youthful face. But his thick, slanted eyebrows made Jimuro's own knit with thought. Those were Kurihara eyebrows, through and through.

The young man appeared to be studying Jimuro with equal curiosity. "I'm sorry for staring, Your Brilliance," he said. "It's just . . . I wasn't certain I'd see you again." He smiled a bit coyly before adding, "And besides, you're a bit more handsome than I remember."

Tala scowled, but that was nothing new. Tala scowled at everything.

Still, the man's comments did nothing to clear matters up for

Jimuro. "Forgive me, sir," he said carefully, "but do we know each other?"

A light flickered behind his eyes. "Of course," the man said. "I'm Kurihara Kosuke, son of Lord Daisuke."

Recognition flitted across Tala's face. Not the pleasant kind. "The Red Tide."

Kosuke's mouth took a satisfied slant. "The only person to ever defeat General Erega in open battle."

"The general won a war," Tala said. "What's your father won lately?"

Kosuke's amusement instantly snuffed.

"Both of you, stop it," Jimuro said. He was thinking. The name Kurihara was of course familiar, but the name Kosuke was new. "I see your resemblance to Lord Daisuke, but he only ever had a daughter, Keiko. Are you . . . forgive me, but are you some bastard son of his?" Bastards weren't unheard of in Tomoda, and the stigma was highly regionalized. In some prefectures, a competent or charismatic bastard could rise quite high in society. But as it happened, the Kurihara clan did not govern such a place.

Kosuke ran his fingers through his short-cropped hair. "Lord Kurihara has only ever had a son," he said simply. "He just needed some time to understand that." His expression lightened. "Though in fairness to him, I needed some time, too."

Jimuro's eyes widened. *"Kei—"*

"Kosuke, if you please, Your Brilliance," he said. "Keiko is a beautiful name, and my mother honored me by choosing it, but it's not mine anymore."

Jimuro nodded. His mind spun wildly with questions, but he wouldn't give voice to them. "Kosuke," he agreed.

Kosuke beamed, before his attention slid past Jimuro to his glowering bodyguard. "I disgust you, do I, savage?"

Tala grunted. "All terrorists do."

"'Terrorist,'" Kosuke repeated. "The Steel Cicadas are the children and retainers of the great houses of Tomoda. Our parents rot in prison while they await farce trials. The Copper Sages have bent their necks to foreign occupiers, the better for those outsiders to lop off their heads. Our great military has been forcibly disbanded by those who rightfully fear its might. Only we remain to keep the out-landers' boot off Tomoda's neck. We fight for our country and its people, and we'll continue to fight for them until Tomoda is reborn, like a glistening cicada crawling up from the soil to cry its song to the heavens." His momentum had picked up the more he'd talked, and now intensity radiated off him like heat from a car hood.

Jimuro couldn't help but grin. "Am I supposed to believe you came up with that off the cuff?"

Kosuke matched the grin with one of his own. "Of course not. With a speech that good, why leave anything to chance?"

Tala remained unmoved by his charm. "All your speechifying doesn't change what you are," she said. "How many Tomodanese have you killed in your little raids?"

"Sergeant—" Jimuro began, but Kosuke rose to the bait.

"As if Erega's jungle-runners never sent a Sanbuna citizen to an early grave." Haughtily, he folded his arms over his chest and tossed his head. The gesture looked odd now, but with a head of long hair it would've made perfect sense. Jimuro could recognize that easily enough, given his own long hair. "The Shang we killed today robbed the Tomodanese people. We merely took back our riches, and will redistribute them to those who need and deserve them . . ."

Tala's eyes flashed, steely. "After a cut off the top?"

The accusation didn't appear to wound Kosuke at all. "Wars are expensive, Your Brilliance," he said, ignoring Tala now. "You know that even better than I. The Steel Cicadas take only what we need, and use the rest to buy up food for the hungry, clothing for the cold, or else we just give it back directly. You'll see soon enough: The Ci-cadas are fighting your good fight, Your Brilliance.

"In the meantime, though, I have to ask how you came to be re-turned to us here in Tajiri, and what you intend to do now that you're home. Whatever your goals, the Steel Cicadas are behind you."

Tala caught Jimuro's eye and gave him a tiny shake of her head. And most of the time, Jimuro would've agreed with her. But they were fighting at a fraction of a fraction of the strength Erega had as-signed to ensure the completion of Operation: Grand Tour. And here was a group of trained fighters with resources, offering themselves up to aid him. He would've been a fool to say no to that.

And besides, Kosuke was an old friend, and Jimuro was tired of being surrounded by enemies.

When Jimuro had finished with his tale, Kosuke sat heavily back in his seat. Jimuro expected him to sag under the weight of what he'd just heard, but when his eyes met Jimuro's, they brimmed with earnestness and urgency. "Prince Jimuro," he said, "this is a burden the Steel Cicadas were born to shoulder for you." He reached into his kimono and pulled out a shiny black gun. Tala stirred, but Jimuro waved her off as Kosuke laid it flat across both his palms before bowing gently and offering it up to Jimuro. It was a formal offer of his service, and that of his allies: as solemn a promise as he could make. The implication of offering up his weapon was that if his service ever displeased his liege in any way, this was the tool that would be used to punish him for it.

Jimuro glanced over at the sergeant one last time, and once again she shook her head. He could understand why. Politics had conspired to make her grow up hating the Tomodanese, and being surrounded by them couldn't possibly be comfortable for her. And he was sure in her heart of hearts, she would take Jimuro's acceptance of Kosuke's service as a tacit admission that she had failed in her duties.

But he was a prince in his own country again. He was destined to live a life serving his people. What kind of Steel Lord would he be if he turned his back on them now, when they wanted nothing more than to help him?

He took the pistol in hand, closed his eyes, and touched its cool surface to his face, so its length ran along the ridge of his nose. It was a ritual meant to symbolize him accepting the metal as a vessel in his service, and its master by proxy. After a long second, he opened his eyes again and handed it back. Kosuke accepted it gratefully with another bow.

"Our headquarters isn't far from here," he said. "I'll have the Cicadas spread the word that tonight, we welcome our Iron Prince back where he belongs." Once again, his coy smile emerged. "Tell me, Your Brilliance: Have your years away robbed you of your taste for sake?"

Tala turned away in disgust, glaring out the window as if willing the passing cityscape to light itself on fire.

Jimuro ignored her. He was too taken now with memories of the sips of sake that he, Kosuke, and Fumiko would sneak as children when they thought their parents weren't paying attention.

"I still have a taste for a lot of things," he said.

"To the memories of Steel Lord Yoshiko and Steel Consort Soujiro!" Kosuke cried, raising his steel sake cup aloft.

Up and down the long, low table, two dozen more raised in response. *"May they live ten thousand years!"* the Steel Cicadas chorused.

They had gathered in the Steel Cicadas' headquarters: a temple built atop a low mountain some thirty kilometers outside Tajiri. The Sages of the past had dotted the countryside with temples just like it, each built over a major nexus of the spirits. Jimuro knelt at the head of a long, low table of copper and wood, a full Tomodanese feast laid out before him. Normally, such tables would be used for solemn gatherings of meditation, but there was nothing solemn about the raucous gathering of Cicadas over which he presided.

At his right stood Kosuke, who like his cohorts had changed from his black kimono to a sapphire one for the occasion. Its cotton folds draped appealingly over his slight figure, making him look every bit the image of dashing Tomodanese gentry.

And to Jimuro's left seethed Tala. It was customary in Tomoda to receive meals by kneeling on the floor, but the stubborn sergeant was used to chairs. She sat defiantly cross-legged, and hadn't even bothered to remove her hat. Instead, she just glowered down at the collection of plates in front of her.

Kosuke, to Jimuro's relief, ignored the slight. "To the memory of Iron Princess Fumiko!"

Once again, the response arose: *"May she live ten thousand years!"*

Kosuke let his hand fall onto Jimuro's shoulder. Jimuro felt some color rise to his face.

Next to him, Tala glared into the depths of her metal cup, as if willing her sake to boil.

"And to the greatest blessing," Kosuke said, as a low rumble of cheers spread through those assembled. "Returned to our sacred soil at last, the divine vessel of the spirits, beating heart of our people . . ."

The cheers crescendoed.

". . . our great Steel-Lord-to-be and the instrument of Tomoda's rebirth, *Iron Prince Jimuro!*"

And the Cicadas all cried out: *"May he live ten thousand years!"*

With a *clink* that echoed around the dining room, the Steel Cicadas tapped their sake cups to the table, drained them, then slammed them back down in front of them. A throaty cheer went up, and Jimuro joined in as he savored the familiar crisp burning in his throat and on his tongue.

Tala sat still, her sake untouched.

He shot her a beseeching look: *Please don't make this weird for me.*

But she just sat there, arms folded. The brim of her hat shaded her eyes, but he could see them reflected in the surface of her soup.

He opened his mouth to say something to her, then realized he didn't hear the scrape of chopsticks in bowls. When he looked up, he saw everyone staring at him expectantly.

Of course, he realized. He was so used to eating with his family, where he was the lowest, or among his own troops, where he insisted on eating when they ate. But now he wasn't a captain anymore; he was a prince, and his subjects wouldn't eat before he did.

With dignified delicacy, he picked up his chopsticks, then scooped a glob of rice into his mouth.

Once he did that, the Steel Cicadas dug in with gusto. There was rice with sweet pickled plum paste, seared tofu, tempura-fried peapods, seaweed salad, and—spirits bless Kosuke and the House of Kurihara—big, steaming bowls of his favorite, mushroom udon.

He fed himself some of the noodles, and luxuriated in the familiar earthy flavors washing over his palate. During his long captivity, he'd grown used to the bold, punchy tastes favored by the Sanbuna tongue. But there was something so refreshing and refined about the clean, light flavors and dining presentation of his own people. Sanbuna food may have fed his body, but the elegant fare of Tomoda nourished his soul.

"I hope the spread's to your liking, Your Brilliance," Kosuke said. He beckoned a servant over, and the young man hurried to refill their sake cups.

"It's wonderful," Jimuro said. "And all this in a temporary base, no less?"

Kosuke raised his cup in offer. "Like my father always said: Wars aren't won by the hungry."

Jimuro grinned, thinking of his own father's paunch. "What your father said, mine lived." He clinked his cup against Kosuke's.

The two drank, and once again Jimuro savored the burn of good sake.

"And it's not just food," Kosuke went on. "We've stockpiled a good amount of munitions and vehicles. We have agents and bases across the country. We continue to provide for the people, so they know who their true friends are. With a word from you, Your Brilliance, we could rise up and take our country back."

"Tch."

Jimuro's whole body went hot as he heard Tala make the noise. With painstaking slowness, he turned back to her. She'd lifted up her rice bowl with her right hand, then dug directly into the rice with her left. Her chopsticks lay forgotten on the table as the Cicadas stared on in disgust.

A chill settled over Kosuke, and he sat up a little straighter. "You may have gotten used to treating our prince so poorly, slaver, but I'm the son of one of Tomoda's great clans, and you're in my house. You will not scoff at me."

Tala looked unconcerned, which Jimuro saw only deepened Kosuke's antipathy. "Well, it's not your house," she said, gesturing to their surroundings. "You said it was a temple, didn't you?" She put the rice down, only to pick up the bowl of udon and slurp some broth from it as if it were a cup. Jimuro winced.

"And what's more," Tala said, "you're barking if you think that's what Jimuro's going to do when he's got the Mountain Throne."

Jimuro opened his mouth to speak, but Kosuke spoke first.

"It's not up to you, telling the Steel Lord what he does with his divinely ordained birthright," said Kosuke. "You're not in your own country anymore, you savage, and the steel of the Tomodanese people won't bend to you." Cheers greeted his words.

Tala rolled her eyes. "Tell them, Your Brilliance," she said. "Tell them this uprising's a quick way to get people killed, nothing more. Tell them about the world Steel Lord Jimuro wants to build."

Jimuro shifted in his seat and said nothing. In the corner of his eye, Kosuke's face lit up.

Tala stared at him in disbelief. "Iron Prince Jimuro," she said. "You can't be serious."

Jimuro's eyes flickered between Tala and Kosuke, both of whom looked up at him with expectation: Tala's irate, Kosuke's smug.

At long last, he said, "I have several matters to consider before the Sages crown me, and even more for afterward. After the day I've had, for now I'd rather just consider the food."

An approving cheer rose up again from the Cicadas. Kosuke smiled, though there was a new tightness in his expression that hadn't been there before. Tala's expression, on the other hand, was an unchanging portrait of disapproval.

She plucked a fistful of tempura radishes from her bowl, and popped one into her mouth. She rose. "I need air."

"How dare you rise before the Iron Prince," Kosuke said, but he fell silent when Jimuro rose, too.

"I'll walk with you a moment," he said, before telling the rest of the Cicadas, "Please continue without me. I'll return shortly."

Kosuke still had his misgivings drawn on his face when Jimuro slid the door shut behind him, leaving him and Tala alone in the long, narrow hallway. "Sergeant, do you care to explain what it is you're playing at?" he said, switching to Sanbuna. The last thing he needed was her starting trouble, and it seemed like an easy enough measure to placate her.

Its effectiveness was limited, though, because she snapped back in

Tomodanese: "You can't seriously expect to just throw the world back into war."

"What? Of course not," Jimuro said. He was so confused. What in the spirits' name had set her off like this?

"Then why aren't you telling them that?" Tala said, jabbing a finger at the closed door. "Why aren't you telling them to lay down their weapons and help this peace happen?"

Jimuro bristled and folded his arms over his chest. "Don't tell me how to govern my people," he said.

"You serve them," Tala said. "Don't you? Isn't that what you were going on about earlier? How is going along with *that* plan serving them?"

"Why do you even care?" said Jimuro. "From what I've seen so far, another war with Tomoda would be your fondest wish."

He'd expected a snarling rejoinder, but to his surprise some of the light dimmed behind her fierce, hawklike eyes. "Is that really what you think of me?" she said. "That I'm just hanging on until my next fight?"

Jimuro's laugh was mirthless and heavy with disbelief. "Sergeant," he said, "when have you ever tried to convince me you were any other sort of person?"

He trusted Tala enough to believe that no matter how enraged the sergeant became, his life was never endangered in her company. But as he asked the question, he felt the thrill of fear anyway, as he firmly set foot across some invisible line between them.

Yet again, she didn't rise to the provocation. The light in her gaze dulled further, as if his words had dealt her some hidden wound. "Fine," she said quietly. "But if you're giving the Steel Cicadas even some false hope about a new Tomodanese Empire . . . what about General Erega?"

For only a moment, he felt a stab of guilt as he considered Erega's craggy face, stony in its disappointment.

"The general committed to building a peace with Tomoda," Tala went on. "That's the whole reason we brought you here instead of leaving you in a ditch somewhere. And I don't care if they're your old friends. Those guys are terrorists, Your Brilliance."

"'Those guys' are doing the job I should be doing, as Iron Prince and Steel Lord," Jimuro said. "Protecting my people. Standing up for my country."

"Protecting your people?" the sergeant sneered. "The only reason we have clothes and a car is because you took them from your people at gunpoint."

That took him by genuine surprise. "What?"

"Don't waste time treating me like an idiot," Tala said. "How else could you have gotten all those plus antivenin with empty pockets?"

A dry cackle of disbelief escaped his throat. "It's not often you maneuver yourself into defeat, Sergeant."

She narrowed her eyes. "What the fuck do you—?"

"My mother, the late Steel Lord, kept a box of her jewelry hidden beneath the floorboards at Kinzokita," he said, with a mirthless laugh that just edged on taunting her. "I peddled away my children's birthright to save your life. And I didn't tell you," he added to head off her question, "because I didn't want you to feel beholden to me."

The stunned sergeant's mouth opened and closed and opened again, as if she couldn't quite form whatever words she wanted to say next. He knew it was inelegant of him to say anything else, but he found himself too incensed by how easily she'd believed the worst of him.

So he leaned forward and offered quietly: "I believe the phrase you're seeking is *Thank you, Your Brilliance.*"

Chill settled between himself and Tala: first a frost, then rapidly solidifying into a wall of ice. "Of course," she said eventually. He had to stop himself from flinching; there was something of his mother lurking in her cold, controlled tone. "Thank you for saving my tiny, worthless life . . . *Your Brilliance.*" Somehow, she'd found a way to make his honorific sound like an epithet. With that, she bowed stiffly, then turned on her heel and left.

For a long time, Jimuro stood in that dark hallway, watching her go.

And then he slid the door open and let the warmth of Kosuke and the other Cicadas wash over him as they welcomed him back.

"What did the savage have to say for herself?" Kosuke said as Jimuro reclaimed his spot at the head of the table.

"Please don't call her that," Jimuro said. For some reason, he didn't feel so much like a returning hero anymore. He felt small.

"As Your Brilliance commands," Kosuke said with a shrug. The light caught his face like it would the edge of a blade, and the look he gave Jimuro cut just as deep.

The prince dropped his voice. "Don't do that, either," he said. "Don't talk to me like you're other people. I'm not 'His Brilliance' to you. I'm Jimuro. I've always been Jimuro."

Kosuke favored him with a sake-slanted smile. "I've never thought of you as anything else."

Nonchalantly, his friend reached for a bottle of sake and poured out two fresh cups. He placed his fingers on the metal cups and concentrated a moment. Faint tendrils of steam wafted up from the sake. Satisfied, he handed one to Jimuro, who took it gratefully.

Jimuro glanced around the room again. The air was thick with excited Tomodanese chatter, and the smells of well-cooked Tomodanese food. The sight of so many happy Tomodanese faces, the warm weight of the sake in his hand, even the distinct way the electric lights shone off the high, pointed ceiling . . . they all made his heart swell.

"Now, my liege," Kosuke said, catching the prince's eye. "Clearly, you've missed the taste of sake. Is there anything else you've missed?" Hope glinted in his gaze: a hope Jimuro recognized.

He studied Kosuke for a moment. The young noble put up a confident, easy air, but Jimuro saw stiffness in how he sat as he waited for his prince to respond. He was struck by the genuine admiration that shone in the other man's eyes. After the flat-eyed disdain he'd weathered from Tala, it felt more nourishing than udon broth.

He clinked his cup against Kosuke's. "I could do with a bath," he said simply. Kosuke's entire face lit up, and by the spirits was it a good feeling. "Why don't you join me?"

CHAPTER THIRTEEN

XIULAN

She drove the car until its meager supply of gasoline gave out. There was supposed to be a spare canister of the stuff in the trunk, but a few too many hexbolts had fused it shut. So when the car finally sputtered to a stop by the side of the road, they simply abandoned it and started walking in silence. Xiulan didn't have a paucity of things to say; when did she ever? But at this hour apparently Lee did, and a lifetime in the cutthroat court of Shang meant the princess knew how to read a room. So instead they walked side by side behind the huge dog-shade that lumbered through the trees ahead of them.

But after another hour or so, exhaustion finally took its toll on both of them. When they were far enough away from the roadside, Xiulan suggested at last that they stop for the night.

"Thank the dogs," Lee said, immediately plopping down where she stood. "Thought you'd never quit." Her new shade, Bootstrap, had wandered ahead, but now she ambled back over and nudged Lee with her huge wet nose. "That's enough out of you," the thief said sleepily. "C'mon, lie down." Obediently, the dog-shade folded her legs beneath her body. Lee leaned up next to her, stretching, before casting a look Xiulan's way. "What?"

Xiulan had been caught breathless by the sight of Lee. When she stretched, the moonlight bathed her every angle and contour in a soft silver sheen. Xiulan found her eye tracing the shadows cast by Lee's wristbones, the way her hair fell back from her face with every tilt of her head, the inviting curve of the spot where her neck and shoulder met . . .

Xiulan coughed and shrugged out of her overcoat. "One of us should take watch."

"You," Lee said, lying down against Bootstrap's huge furry flank and closing her eyes.

Xiulan snorted. "What ever happened to gallantry, Inspector Lee?"

"Right, Princess," Lee yawned. "That's why I've got a price on my head in ten cities: gallantry." She stretched out again, apparently not even slightly concerned with getting dirt on her dress. "Wake me up if there's danger or breakfast. Preferably the second thing." And then her entire body relaxed.

Xiulan blinked. They'd slept in separate cabins aboard the *Wave Falcon*, so this was her first time seeing Lee Yeon-Ji at rest. It was like she'd just seen her become a completely different person. Without the veneer of cunning she wore on her face like a second layer of makeup, the thief looked so much younger. How much did she carry on her shoulders when she was awake? Xiulan wondered. What invisible weight did she drag behind her each day, that made her seem so old?

It was incredible how easily Lee could shrug it all off. Xiulan would've thought a thief like her would need to be on edge at all times, sleeping with one eye open and the like. Even the refined gentleman thief of *White Diamond in a Black Glove* had always kept his wits about him, and he slept in a gilded penthouse.

So did you, once upon a time, she reminded herself. *How're you sleeping now, White Rat?*

"*Kou,*" she whispered, and her own white rat appeared. A warm wave of happiness rolled through her; Kou was always happy to see her. She patted the spot behind his ears that he liked. "Thank you for earlier."

He made a low chittering noise.

"My associate here and I will be quite hungry come the morning," she said. "Would you be so kind as to forage for some provisions?"

Kou's nose twitched, and then he turned and surged into the trees. In moments he was out of sight completely. She hoped he would bring back something other than mushrooms. He was quite fond of them, even though he was bonded to the soul of a woman who despised little more.

Growing up, she'd kept her distaste for mushrooms secret. She ate around them when she could, or else smothered them in so much sauce that she'd be able to swallow them whole without getting any of the actual mushroom experience. She wasn't certain how Ruomei had found out, though she'd developed a few theories over the years. All she knew was that one day, the amount of mushrooms the kitchen was putting out fairly well doubled. Dishes that once had small pieces of mushroom now had caps the size of the plates they were served on. Sauces became sparser. And soon enough, Xiulan found herself going to bed hungrier and hungrier.

Her stomach twisted at the memory. It wasn't so hard to believe that the girl who did that would grow up to be the woman who put a bounty on her own sister.

She glanced back up at the moon and closed her eyes. She felt the cool light on her face as she dreamed of the day she would drag the Iron Prince into her father's throne room, right past Ruomei's stunned face, before she dropped him at the Crane Emperor's royal feet. She wondered if there was some way she could arrange to have Ruomei be the one to crown her. It wasn't really protocol, and she was just as likely to slip a garrote around Xiulan's throat as she was a crown on her head. But after everything she'd endured at her sister's hands, Xiulan felt she was due a bit of payback.

She opened her eye. Her gaze fell back to the sleeping form of Lee. That was one of the reasons she enjoyed the thief's company, come to think of it. Protocol dictated that she couldn't speak ill of any of her siblings, let alone Ruomei. In that respect, Lee's lack of regard for protocol was refreshing. For the first time in her life, she had someone in her life besides an easily bullied sibling, or a court-appointed playmate, or a loose-lipped servant. She had a friend. A partner. Someone she could trust.

She heard the woman's own voice in her head: *Trusting a thief. That'll get you far in life, Princess.*

She smiled at the memory.

A medley of birds and bugs called in the darkness, including the famous singing beetles of Tomoda's trees. But as time went on their voices became less and less distinct. After a few minutes, they had all coalesced into a single noise, and one she found oddly soothing. The only other sound was Lee's soft, sleepy breathing, and the princess let the sound gently lap at her ears like a warm tide at her toes.

In a gentle flash of white light, Bootstrap disappeared out from beneath Lee as she finally slipped into full unconsciousness. Proudly, Xiulan surveyed the matted ground where the shade had just been. Truly, she thought, today had been remarkable.

She balled her coat up, then knelt next to her partner. Carefully, she slid her coat toward Lee, unsure of how best to wedge it beneath her head without waking her.

Lee grunted. "Get on with it, then," she muttered, lifting her head up.

Xiulan smiled and slid her coat into place. Lee's head dropped back down onto its folds, and her body relaxed once more.

Xiulan busied herself with her pipe. Tomorrow, she promised herself, they would finally catch up to Prince Jimuro. They would sneak past his legion of Sanbuna escorts and steal him away right under their noses. There were Shang garrisons stationed nearby, and any one of them would be more than grateful to receive the Twenty-Eighth Princess, let alone one who was an agent of the Li-Quan. The bounty was troublesome, but nothing she couldn't fix by showing up handcuffed to the most wanted man in the world.

It would be her greatest victory, one that Ruomei could never take from her. And once their father made her his new heir, she'd merely need to survive a few years of assassination attempts before she could take her rightful place.

She checked her tobacco case. She was starting to run low on the leaf. She thought she'd packed enough to last the whole trip, but she saw she'd been smoking it like it was going out of style. *I should cut back,* she thought as she lit up anyway.

. . .

Kou didn't bring back mushrooms, thankfully. He did find some clumps of berries that, according to her research on the native flora of Tomoda, were edible enough. She wished they could have had some fish or game to start the day off, but she was reluctant to make a fire. So when Lee shook her awake the next morning, they ate a hasty breakfast of bright-blue berries, then summoned up Bootstrap and got on their way.

"Far as I can tell, she's still got his scent," Lee said as they trailed behind the lumbering dog-shade. "How's that even work, then? She probably hasn't sniffed the guy for years, and he's got to be miles away."

Xiulan chewed thoughtfully on the button of her pipe. It wasn't lit; she'd resolved to save the last of her leaf as a personal reward for finally apprehending the Iron Prince, when the time came. "The phenomenon isn't unheard of," she said. "Animals who form close bonds with a person before pacting with a soul may carry a special attunement with them into their next life."

"Suppose that tracks," Lee allowed, with a shrug. "Because I'll tell you what, Princess: Royal pain in the ass that he is, the princeling loved the shit out of this dog."

Xiulan's eye sparked with curiosity. "What do you see?" she said eagerly. They couldn't have lucked into a better pipeline for insight into their quarry's thoughts. Bai Junjie could step into the criminal mind to make his brilliant deductions, but strictly on a metaphorical basis. When it came to detection and intuition, she and Lee Yeon-Ji stood alone.

Well, as alone as two people could be.

"Mostly, a whole lot of this and that," Lee said. "It's not like they sat this dog down and went over bank statements with her. It's mostly just her and Jimuro playing, her and Jimuro having a nap . . . Not sure how having a pet squares with this whole thing the Tomodanese are on with animals, though."

This, Xiulan's extensive readings on Tomodanese culture had prepared her for. "You're examining the matter from the wrong angle.

The Tomodanese believe in the primacy of the spirit, regardless of its vessel. In their eyes, the souls of man and dog command equal weight."

"Tch," Lee said. "Haven't met me a man yet who'd be worth half a dog."

"I hold men in similar esteem," Xiulan said with an appreciative smile. "But I'm hardly Tomodanese. I don't imagine the prince saw Bootstrap as his pet, during their companionship. It would be more in line with his beliefs to simply say she was his friend."

Lee patted Bootstrap's massive flank. "Reckon I can't fault him for that."

Xiulan eyed her partner thoughtfully. She almost didn't say anything, but then decided she was feeling bold at the moment. "Why did you save her?"

Lee didn't quite look at her. "Like I told you: I like dogs."

Xiulan shook her head and chewed on her pipe. "I thought we'd agreed to proceed with honesty, Inspector Lee."

Lee shrugged again. "I was honest."

"Ah, but not completely so," said Xiulan, wagging her slender finger. "You like money, too. But were it a sack of jian and not a dog lying there, you never would've coerced me into expediting its retrieval."

"I'm too hungry for this shit," Lee muttered with a pat of her stomach.

Feelings immediately arose and clashed within Xiulan. She worried she'd prodded her partner too far, while berating herself for being a princess of Shang who took no for an answer. Rather than act on either, she opted for diplomatic distance. "Very well."

It worked. Lee frowned and said, "You ordering me, as a princess?"

"I'm asking you, as . . ." *Your friend*, Xiulan thought. *Your comrade. Your companion. Your . . .* ". . . your partner."

Lee sighed. "All right, all right. You really want to know?"

Xiulan hoped her nod wasn't too eager.

"To the Jeongsonese," Lee said, "there're a finite number of souls in the world. Idea is, your soul cycles through each of the millions of roles it's got to play, across all the life spans it needs to do it. Once your soul's done everything it needs to do, though, you get a final reward: You get to come back as a dog."

Xiulan nodded. Her voracious reading had given her a keen feel for story structure, so she suspected she knew where this anecdote was going. But she didn't interrupt; she liked the way Lee sounded when she was telling a story.

"Now, my mom got herself the wasting cough when I was nine," Lee went on. "Wasn't a doctor in all of Shang who'd treat her, and it wasn't like the Tomodanese were treating us any better. So all we could do was make the wait comfortable. You want to know when I picked up thieving and swindling? That's when."

An uneasy chord of guilt rang through Xiulan. In the courts of her childhood, Jeongsonese affairs were either politely ignored or else blithely discussed with little respect or weight. The nonchalant way Lee cited Shang's abuses made Xiulan's whole being twist and squirm. She wanted to object, to assert that surely not all Shang were so callous to her, but she tamped that instinct down and listened.

"One day toward the end, mom calls me and my siblings in and says, 'I think I'm about done playing this part.' So we all have a cry about it. Does fuck-all for the blood pooling in her lungs, but at least it feels nice, you know? No one ever talks about that," she added suddenly. "How nice a good cry feels. Like ten stiff drinks, without the hangover."

Xiulan's smile was small and encouraging. "I'll have to do it more often. Please continue."

"Oh. Right," said Lee. "Point is, when we're all done crying, she pulls us close. She's got a mask on, so she won't cough blood on us, but she pulls it down off her mouth and says to us, 'Next time around, I'm gonna be a dog. I know it.'"

Xiulan blinked, and was surprised to feel tears against her lashes.

"She didn't die then. Held on for a good week longer. And when we went up on the roof to scatter her ashes, I'd swear up and down I heard a dog howling as the last of her faded into the air."

Xiulan's fingers twitched. She wanted to reach out and comfort Lee, but that was stupid. Childish. Lee had been carrying this around every day for more than half her life. It was arrogance, Xiulan berated herself, to think her touch could magically fix everything.

"Look, Princess," Lee said. "I know all that stuff about spirits and roles is a big, steaming load. For one thing, how's that idea track with exponential population growth?"

Xiulan kept her tone mild. "I suspect such matters were not on the minds of the ancient Jeongsonese."

"Right. Like I said: a big, steaming load." Lee's voice softened slightly. "But just in case, you know?"

Xiulan smiled to herself. She tried not to let herself get too excited, but she'd just learned something about Lee. More than just a clinical statistic she could've read in the woman's criminal record, Xiulan had managed to glean something *real*.

Feeling bold, she pressed ever so gently: "Where are your sisters and brothers now?"

Lee's expression dimmed slightly. "Not sure. I took off a few years later. They weren't keen on a thief in the family, you see."

Her tone made it perfectly clear she didn't want to delve into the matter any further. Panic shot through Xiulan once more.

But then Lee said, "Since we're playing 'asked and answered,' then, tell me: that kiss. The first one, back in the cell. Why'd you do it, Princess?"

Xiulan's face flushed so suddenly and forcefully, she felt like her entire head was glowing. It'd been foolish to hope she could elide the subject entirely, but she had, just the same.

"I've been thinking about that, Inspector Lee." And she had: often, and with detailed extrapolation of what might've followed. But she pushed that speculation to the back of her mind and continued: "And I've come to the conclusion that I owe you an apology."

Lee favored her with an amused slant of her eyebrow. "Do you now?"

Don't get flustered, Xiulan told herself as she descended into the deepest bowels of being flustered. Bai Junjie would've handled this with a cool head, like he had in his sixth case, *The Color of Drying Blood.* So she told herself: *Be cool. Be Junjie.*

"I've employed you as an inspector of the Li-Quan, and as my partner in this personal enterprise," Xiulan said, painfully aware of how fast she was talking. "Those are both professional entangle-ments, which I regard with the utmost respect. Furthermore—"

"Oh, good," Lee said with a smirk, "there's a 'furthermore.'"

"—I'm a member of the House of Shang, and bear the blood of a queen in my veins," Xiulan plowed on. "That status creates an un-fair imbalance in the power dynamic when I fraternize with one of my own subjects."

"Like me."

"Like you," Xiulan agreed. The end of her well-rehearsed speech lay in sight now. "So I wish to apologize for muddying those waters with my, ah, inappropriate advances. They were an aberrant behav-ior, and one that I promise will not happen again."

Lee nodded, absorbing this. Then she said with a smile, "Nice try, Princess."

Xiulan frowned. "'Nice try'?"

Lee smiled wider. "You didn't answer my fucking question."

The fading flush in Xiulan's cheeks came roaring back with full force. Her head felt like a paper lantern attached to a body. "Inspec-tor Lee—!"

"The question wasn't 'should,'" Lee said. "It was 'why.' And until you answer it head-on, I'm going to be a complete pill to you about it. You can't use your fancy courtly doublespeak on me. I'm too much of a rube to fool."

"You most certainly are not," Xiulan said, suddenly fierce. "Your wisdom and boldness are the only reasons we've made it as far as we have. And I envy your social acumen so much. I always calculate my every word with great care, in service to being the best version of myself for every given moment. But despite your skill in deception, I've never seen you be anything but yourself, and that person has fascinated me from minute one of our partnership."

Her eye went wide as she realized how much she'd just said. Her mouth hung open stupidly.

Lee slipped her hands out of her pockets. "Anything else?"

Xiulan resisted the urge to hang her head. She would meet her embarrassment like a princess. "Yes," she said. "You're also . . . really, really funny."

Bootstrap abruptly stopped and sat down. Xiulan opened her

mouth to ask what was the matter, but suddenly Lee Yeon-Ji filled her vision, their faces inches apart.

"Now, that was a proper answer," the thief said. "But I've still got a problem with your apology: Second time around, which of us did the kissing?"

Xiulan shifted her weight from foot to foot. "You did." She made to raise her pipe back to her mouth, but a hand on her wrist stopped it from rising above hip level.

"Who was it who put her arm on your waist?" Lee said, toying with the lapel of Xiulan's coat. "Was it you, prowling predator that you are?"

The challenge in her voice put fire in Xiulan's fingers. They dropped her pipe then slid around Lee's slender waist. She only trembled slightly as she felt the soft folds of Lee's dress, and the warmth of the skin lying in wait just beneath it. "I suppose this time, it is."

"*Finally,*" Lee said, leaning in until their lips met.

Xiulan had kissed her first girl at the age of ten: Song Lihua, daughter of one of her mother's many retainers. To Xiulan, it had been a magical, transportive experience, everything books had told her it would be, and also so much more than the page could ever encompass.

Afterward, Lihua had said to her, "You're not very good at that, are you?"

Since then, opportunities for practice had been fleeting at best. Shang didn't mind Xiulan's preferences, exactly. But with the Crane Emperor's official heir yet undesignated, there was still more prestige in offering up one's daughter to a royal son in the hope of getting a royal grandchild. As long as that hope was on the table for the various noble families of Shang, it left no prospective women of appropriate status for Xiulan. Consequently, like all other exciting prospects in life, kissing had become more of a theoretical pursuit for Xiulan than a practical one.

But with Lee, her lack of practice didn't matter.

The woman tasted like the world: the grit of its streets, the depth of its oceans, the weight of its history. Her fingers skillfully roamed Xiulan's body, dancing while Xiulan's own barely had the confidence to crawl. Her eyes closed as she let go of all the artifice she'd constructed around herself. Lee had no idea, but the woman she held in her arms was the real Xiulan—not the princess, not the detective, not even the sister or daughter. She was holding a woman who belonged to no one else.

Lee's fingers brushed through her hair and gently peeled her long bangs away from Xiulan's left eye. Slowly, Lee pulled away from their kiss. "Look at me."

Xiulan's pulse doubled. Her eyelids fluttered uncertainly as they opened, revealing a brown eye on her right, and a pure white one on her left. In place of an iris and pupil, it instead bore a black square divided into quarters, like a windowpane. It was the most visible part of her soul, and she'd grown out her hair specifically so no one could ever see it.

And now Lee Yeon-Ji was staring right into its depths.

Instinctively, Xiulan moved to brush her bangs back down, but once again Lee clamped down on her wrists. "I'm not done with those eyes yet."

Xiulan had read in books that to truly enjoy an intimate encounter, it was best to let go of one's thoughts and relax. And indeed, she'd felt herself begin to do just that a moment ago. It was a simple thing, she told herself as they slipped back into their kiss, to remove any barriers between oneself and the purity of an experience.

Naturally, she told herself this because her mind was racing.

This is hardly the time or place, said one voice.

This is the greatest feeling in the world, another chimed in.

Am I doing this right?

We have important work to do.

How hard would it be to undo that dress?

Why is she doing this?

Why am I doing this?

No, seriously, am I doing this right?

She broke contact and stared up into Lee's face again. The thief's canine charm was still there, but she looked off-balance in a way Xiulan hadn't seen before, as if Lee were as surprised by all of this as she was.

As one, they both turned to look at Bootstrap. The dog-shade sat patiently but expectantly with her gaze on them. Her tongue flapped from her open mouth like a pink banner, while her three tails thumped the trail excitedly.

They both burst out laughing. And as they laughed and laughed and laughed, they didn't let go.

But eventually, Xiulan sighed and said, "We should resume our pursuit."

"Reckon so."

They walked on in giddy, comfortable silence. At least, it was giddy to Xiulan, who felt as if her whole body were vibrating. Lee would flash her the occasional wolfish grin, though, and it would give her footsteps that much more spring as Xiulan took them.

Abruptly, Bootstrap stopped again. Her hackles rose, and she let out a thunderous bark into the distance.

A chill ran through Xiulan's body. She hadn't realized it until Bootstrap had barked, but the air around them had grown quiet. No birds sang. No squirrels scrabbled in the undergrowth. The world was too still.

The tight, searching look in Lee's face told Xiulan her partner was thinking along similar lines. "Best get your rat out," she said tightly. "Girl's smelling blood."

Xiulan's lips thinned as she whispered Kou's name and he appeared at her side. "We should find another way around."

"You'll get no disagreement here."

Despite their efforts, though, they soon came upon the source of the quiet just the same. When they saw the car through the trees, Xiulan's whole body tensed up, but then she saw the familiar white crane on its door. This was a Shang car. She felt a momentary trickle of relief. Much as she would've wanted to avoid all detection, at least Shang troops would be easier to deal with than Dahali or Sanbuna ones. They, at least, could be relied upon to respect her badge.

But as they drew closer, she saw the car's open door. Its shattered windshield. The long gouges and deep dents in its metal chassis. And of course, the mangled bodies of its occupants, who littered the ground around it like spent shells. Their limbs were snapped, their joints twisted, their faces carved by tooth and claw.

Her relief froze back into dread. She thought frantically of the many passages she'd read in her books, where Bai Junjie came upon a grisly crime scene and converted all his sorrow and disgust into some poetic insight that would inevitably end up helping him catch the killer. But here, Xiulan's prodigious wit and outsized vocabulary failed her.

"Lee," she said softly. "In your myriad criminal dealings, have you ever encountered anything like this?"

"You rescued me from an organ seller," she said. She kept her tone nonchalant as usual, but her ashen face betrayed her. "No two ways about it though, Princess: This is all kinds of fucked up."

Xiulan swallowed a long breath to calm her roiling stomach. She wanted her brain to start analyzing the scene before her, to construct the narrative that would explain this crime, but her eyes couldn't see any deeper than its viscera-slick surface.

"What does Bootstrap smell?" she said quietly.

"She's not getting a clear picture," Lee said, clearly disturbed. "Neither am I. She's smelling a lot of shades, though."

Kou's sense of smell wasn't nearly so strong as Bootstrap's, but what it could pick up fit with what Lee just told her. Xiulan could feel it beneath her own sense of smell, a steady bass line beneath her nose's treble. She smelled a suffusion of magic, possibly even an oversaturation. A truly remarkable amount of arcane energy had been unleashed in this area, in the form of a small horde of shades. It was the kind of thing Xiulan would have expected to find at the site of a pitched battle, not an ambush.

But as she switched her focus back to her own senses, she noticed something odd: only a single set of footprints in the dirt. A quick study of the corpses' boots told her they weren't a match.

"The footprint thing?" Lee said. There was a crispness to her demeanor that Xiulan hadn't seen before. She realized: This was Lee the professional. Xiulan had never seen her before. Not really.

She nodded. "One man—based on the size of the boot—walks in, offering himself up as bait. While he distracts the troops, his cohorts launch their attack from the safety of the trees." But even as she narrated it, the story didn't quite add up. The soldiers' weapons were intact, as were their pockets. They even still had their boots on their feet. There was no plundering here. These attackers had just wanted to kill.

"Think it's those masked fellas from the news?" Lee said. "The Steel Beetles?"

"Cicadas," Xiulan said. They would've been her first thought, too, but even with Tomoda laid low like this, she'd yet to hear any report of the Tomodanese capitulating on their beliefs and resorting to shadepacting. And she was going to trust that this hadn't been an act of treason, where Shang turned against Shang.

No, there was only one group of shadepacters in Tomoda that could have done this.

"I do believe, Inspector Lee," Xiulan said, "that we've stumbled upon the handiwork of the Iron Prince's honor guard." Her gut squeezed unpleasantly as she cast a fresh eye on the bloodshed. It took on a whole new sinister light when she considered that it could have been at General Erega's behest. Even though Xiulan sought to undercut their esteemed ally, she'd always held the general in high regard. To order such base slaughter . . . this was an act worthy of Ruomei, not the fabled Typhoon General.

"Bootstrap doesn't smell him here," Lee said uncertainly.

But the sight of her own dead countrymen had stirred something in Xiulan. While Ruomei was off playing pirate on the Sea of To-moda, Xiulan was the only one with boots on the ground. The only one who could put an end to this madness and secure the future Shang and its people deserved. And it started with putting an end to Erega's scheme before it claimed any more Shang lives: whether here on the road . . . or once that despot had been restored to his throne.

"Point me in the direction she does smell him," Xiulan said. "We haven't another minute to waste."

CHAPTER FOURTEEN

TALA

At dawn, Tala's eyes opened, to her great surprise. And when she'd determined that her throat hadn't been slit in the night, she sat up and set about getting dressed.

Sanbuna clothes were looser, made to be shed and donned quickly to accommodate the island weather's wild mood swings. But Tomoda was a different sort of island, with a climate and a people that were both temperate. So its clothes were complex things: elaborate kimonos donned in a process that had calcified over centuries of history, multilayered suits with endless buttons, clasps, and zippers. In Sanbu, clothing was a matter of practicality. But in Tomoda it was, like seemingly everything else, a ritual.

And more than that: It was a great way to piss Sergeant Tala off.

She swore fluently as she finished fumbling with her tie, only to see that it fell unevenly across her chest again. She kept cursing as she undid it for the third time, all while ignoring the growing throb of discontentment in the back of her head. If Mang wanted to weigh in on her vocabulary, he could go fuck himself.

She directed some of that ire to the prince down the hall. At first, as she lay on her lumpy, misshapen pallet—a gift from Kurihara himself, she was sure—she'd thought her anger stemmed from her proximity to the Steel Cicadas, and to Kurihara in particular. But the more she examined those feelings, the more she'd realized that it all came back to Jimuro.

Her feelings regarding the Iron Prince were always going to be complicated. But even though he was a smug, puckered asshole of a man, and even though he'd lived his life in a comfort bought with Sanbuna lives and suffering, he'd also proven his mettle in a fight. He'd saved her life several times over, once at the cost of his own heirlooms. He'd demonstrated a surprisingly big heart, at least when it came to his own people. He'd been brave enough to reveal to her the pain he carried with him, and either sly or persuasive enough to get her to do the same.

And to top it all off, he'd made adobo.

Mushroom adobo.

But adobo nevertheless.

She would've hesitated to call the man a friend, but she'd just started to come around to the idea that he might be a comrade. Sure, he hadn't stormed the shores of Katagawa at her side, running full-tilt across mortar-glassed sands. But the two of them had survived a hell of their own, and there was a special kind of bond that came along with that. Her comradeship with the 13-52-2 had been fire-forged; her bond with Jimuro, just an ember. Small, yes, but even the smallest ember could start a wildfire.

Unless, she thought sourly, some idiot pissed on it.

She wished she was more surprised by how easily he'd thrown in with the Steel Cicadas. He'd tricked her into siding with him, against her own brother. And the fucking thing of it was, she'd wanted so badly to be right about him. But while Iron Prince Jimuro might have been relatively decent as far as the Tomodanese went, he was still Tomodanese.

That's not why you're angry at him, she told herself. *You hate him for seeing through you.*

She hurled down her tie in frustration, took a deep breath, then stooped to collect it. She coiled it into a tight roll, then slipped it into her coat's breast pocket. It occurred to her the Tomodanese would say she was probably offending some ancient spirit by leaving the tie off and her top shirt button open.

Good, she thought.

But her mood tempered slightly as she stumped down the dark hallway to Prince Jimuro's quarters. She found herself still hoping he would end up surprising her. She'd seen the hurt in his face when she'd made her case to him last night. That wasn't the kind of hurt a person could feel if they didn't care. She needed to believe Prince Jimuro wouldn't, despite Kurihara's enthralling presence, fall prey to his rhetoric. She needed to believe that he would truly break from his ancestors and embrace peace.

You just like fighting. Mang's words echoed in her head. *You're terrified there won't be anything left over once you let it go.*

She growled to herself and shrugged off the memory. What did he know?

But another voice chimed in: *When have you ever tried to convince me you were any other sort of person?*

She squeezed her eyes shut to quiet both of them. "Shut up," she muttered as she reached Prince Jimuro's chambers at last. She composed herself, then slid his room door open. "Your Brilliance, I—"

She froze at the sight of the Iron Prince: snoring, naked, his long hair a mess and his tight, sinewy body twisted up in his sheets like a freshly caught barracuda. But her eye didn't have time to linger on the smooth, scarred ridges of his chest or the serene expression on his handsome face, because the prince was not alone in his chambers.

Kurihara Kosuke knelt before a mirror, binding his chest with a long, narrow strip of white cotton. Tala eyed his torso and noted his lack of battle scars with disapproval.

But Kurihara misread the expression on her face, because he stopped wrapping himself and mockingly threw his arms wide as if to say, *Behold.* "Does my form offend you, barbarian?"

Tala rolled her eyes. "For someone who says he fights for his country, you don't look like you've done much fighting."

"Maybe I just haven't lost any fights I've had," Kurihara said, flashing a bladed smile. But there was something defensive buried in his tone, and Tala smelled it as easily as a shark could blood.

"I've got a whole collection of scars," Tala said.

"I can't imagine you're much of a fighter, then," he sniffed, taking the bait.

"I'm here," Tala said, "and hundreds of you steelhounds aren't. So I guess I'm good enough."

And then she smiled, for that crucial extra layer of *fuck you*.

There was a deep, sick satisfaction in watching all the smugness drain from Kurihara's handsome face. His hand twitched at his side, ready to strike her.

"Try it," Tala said calmly. She pulled aside her open shirt placket to reveal the topmost rim of Beaky's pactmark. "My shade needs breakfast."

Kurihara turned as pale as his binder. His eyes narrowed. "Don't let yourself be found alone, slaver." He shrugged on his kimono and swept out of the room, slamming the door shut behind him.

Tala's rage subsided, and she felt fatigued again, as if she'd just taken another dose of spider venom. Her temples throbbed. How had that escalated so quickly? Was Kurihara just that adept at piercing her calm? Or had Mang been right?

"Kosuke . . . ?" Prince Jimuro said, voice still misty with sleep. When he saw who was standing over his bed, though, he let out a squawk of surprise. He sat up, then squawked again as his blankets slipped from his body. He moved hastily to re-cover himself.

Tala pointedly looked away. Life in the barracks had made her no stranger to the naked male form, but she wasn't dealing with a fellow soldier here. And after last night, she was feeling some desire to make nice. "Calm down." Inspiration encouraged her to add: "I didn't see anything."

"Ah," said Jimuro. He cleared his throat. "Of course. My apologies." When he spoke again, his tone was clipped and formal. "Would you mind giving me a moment, Sergeant?"

"Not yet, Your Brilliance," Tala said. "We have to talk about how today's going to go down."

"That's surprising," Prince Jimuro said mildly. "Considering the way you were acting last night, I didn't think you were in the mood to talk about much of anything."

Tala ground her molars. "That's why I want to talk to you," she said. "I don't care what kind of history you've got with this Kurihara guy. You can't trust him, or the Steel Cicadas. How's that going to play with the allies you sit down with at peace talks, when you look them in the eye and tell them you partnered with violent criminals? They're gangsters, Your Brilliance."

"Well, I suppose that's an upgrade from 'terrorists.' "

"Jimuro—"

"Tala, I can't have this discussion before tea." Prince Jimuro
sighed. "But I'd add that you're talking about the heir to the most
powerful and important clan in Tomoda after my own. If Lord
Daisuke is incarcerated or executed, Kosuke becomes the head of the
household. I need lords like Kosuke on my side if I'm to be an effective Steel Lord."

Tala's mouth hung open a little. What he said made perfect sense;
the notorious Red Tide was awaiting trial, and imprisonment for life
was the kindest possible future he could hope for. "That's what you
want to tell me all this was about?" she said, gesturing to his tangled
sheets. "Politics?"

The prince flushed and looked away. "I'm the Iron Prince of Tomoda," he said, a little too quickly. "In a position like mine, sex is
the most political act there is." He nudged his glasses up his nose, his
patience at an end. "Now, as I said, we will have this discussion. But
we will not have it before I've had tea. If you please, Sergeant."

Tala noted the change in his demeanor. He'd always been haughty,
but after two days in Tomoda he was already starting to sound like
an actual prince again. Certainly, she suddenly felt like some sort of
valet that had just talked out of turn.

Tala was no valet. She was a warrior. A survivor. A soldier.

But her mouth clamped into a tight frown as she bowed and left
the room.

Breakfast was another opulent affair that delayed them getting on
the road for a full hour. When Tala irritably pointed this out to the
prince, Kurihara waved off her concerns. "Forget the road, Your
Brilliance." A map of Tomoda was spread on the table before them,
and he traced a line down it with a slender finger. "We'll take the
southbound train out of Gorudo. You'll be in Hagane before daybreak, and waving the sword of Steel Lord Setsuko before your next
breakfast."

"Absolutely not," Tala said, slamming a palm flat on the map. "The prince has a thousand enemies—"

"The prince is right here, thanks," said Prince Jimuro.

"—and as his protector, I won't put him in a position where a potential enemy can know exactly where he is at all times."

"What is the Palace of Steel, if not that exact thing?" Kurihara said with an amused little smile. "Your plan's already beyond repair. Adhering to it because you're too slow to think of a better one is far more dangerous, if you ask me."

Tala's eyes narrowed. "I didn't."

Impatiently, the prince set his teacup down like a tiny gavel. "Sergeant. You're not helping."

Tala clamped her mouth shut. There was no point in showing her anger. Every time she did, Kurihara would just use it to build the case that she was the dangerous and unstable one, not him. But even with her composure and discipline, she found it trying. While Prince Jimuro had surprised her by occasionally subverting her worst expectations of what the Tomodanese were like, Kurihara seemed all too eager to confirm them.

"That said, Kosuke, I don't think the sergeant's wrong," Prince Jimuro continued. "General Erega and I considered using the rail system when we first hatched this plan, and rejected it as an option for similar reasons to the sergeant's."

Tala did an admirable job of hiding her satisfaction. Kurihara did a significantly poorer job of masking his displeasure.

The prince tapped a dot not too far from Gorudo, labeled NA-MARI. "There's our next safe house," he said. "And that will be our destination."

"Ah, but Your Brilliance . . ." Kurihara began, but Prince Jimuro cut him off with a small shake of his head. It was a nice change of pace for Tala to see him turning his princely act on someone else.

"We should be on the road soon," Jimuro said. He rose, and Kurihara pressed his forehead to the floor. Tala only gave the prince the shallow bow that one officer might another in passing, then rose with him and followed him out.

Though she felt as though she'd come out of the post-breakfast conversation with the upper hand, she was reminded shortly after that even if Jimuro could be made to see reason, they were still among enemies. As he and Kurihara ducked into the car at the front of the motorcade, Tala's attempt to follow was stymied by two Cicadas: Harada, the bony swordswoman from the day before, and Iwanbo, her pudgy comrade with a shotgun laid flat across his shoulders.

Tala rolled her eyes. "Out of my way."

"No slavers will sully His Brilliance's presence," said Harada.

Once again, Tala fought the temptation to summon Mang, or at least Beaky. But instead, she said, "I don't leave his side."

"We're all the protection our liege needs," said Iwanbo. He patted his shotgun with clumsy menace. "You can ride behind. Rearguard, *Sergeant.*"

Tala flexed her right hand and considered her options. Even though it was two-on-one, they were spoiled children playing soldier. She was the real thing. Any fight among the three of them would be brief and unpleasant for everyone involved . . . except for her.

Iwanbo giggled, but Harada at least seemed to be measuring Tala up like a serious opponent. Tala saw her thumb twitch, and with a soft *click* her hilt slid free of the mouth of its sheath, revealing an inch of bare steel.

Tala clenched her hand into a fist. She couldn't get to her gun in time, but she wouldn't need it.

But then from inside the car Kurihara called, "Oh, we can let her in. She's tame, after all."

The Cicadas exchanged a sneer, and Tala realized she'd been played. She narrowed her eyes. She knew little of courtly graces, but this game she recognized. Kurihara was going to take every opportunity to jab at her and undermine her credibility with the prince, brick by brick.

Let him, Tala thought as she settled into her window seat in the back. *You don't have any reason to care.*

An hour later, she was still telling herself that much more insistently as Kurihara laughed too loudly at another of the prince's stories.

"Lord Miyamoto would kill me if he ever found out what really happened to his wig." Prince Jimuro cackled.

"His nephew, Tsukasa, is one of our hands in the east," said Kurihara. "Maybe I should tell him this story sometime."

"Do it," said the prince. "I've always wanted a reason to order an execution."

The two men burst again into raucous laughter, while Tala simmered.

She remained silent, fedora angled down to discourage engagement. She hated everything about this blighted nation, she told herself as its countryside zoomed past. She hated the way its guttural language scratched at her eardrums. The hollowness its meatless food left in her stomach. The constricted feeling she got from knowing she couldn't summon her shades, let alone walk down the street with her face visible.

And most of all, she thought with a sidelong glance at Kurihara's laughing face, she hated the people: smug, scheming, and vile, down to the last steelhound.

Around midday, they stopped by the side of the road, and Tala finally broke her long silence. "Why're we stopping?" she said. "We're still miles from Namari."

She was relieved to see the prince looking as confused as she. "Yes, what's the meaning of this, Kosuke?"

"Apologies, Your Brilliance," said Kurihara, raking his fingers through his short-cropped hair. "I didn't want to mention operations in the presence of unreliable ears."

"Easy now," Prince Jimuro said. "Sergeant Tala's saved my life several times over by now. I trust her, and so should you."

"Of course, my liege," said Kurihara, though he looked hardly convinced, or contrite. "Our spies in the prefecture have received word of a Sanbuna garrison that's been menacing the locals. The Steel Cicadas intend to send them a message . . . one that requires no translation."

"Impossible," Tala said. "General Erega would never allow—"

"Your general 'doesn't allow' plenty of things," Kurihara sniped. "Still, they happen, and at our people's expense." He gave the prince an exasperated look. "You see why I didn't want to mention anything?"

Tala scowled. "We'll file a report with the general when we rendezvous with her in Hagane. We have to move on."

"I'd expect such callousness from you," Kurihara said. "The Steel Cicadas won't leave our people defenseless. Unless you expressly order us to abandon them, Your Brilliance, we're fighting."

Tala's heart sank. Framed that way, there was no question what Jimuro would do.

"He stays in the car," she said. "And none of the soldiers die. I'll make sure they face the republic's justice."

"I'll do no such thing," Prince Jimuro said. "The people need their prince to defend them."

Kurihara grinned.

"But heed the sergeant, Kosuke. No Sanbunas dead. They're our allies now."

That grin faded. He bowed. "I live to serve Your Brilliance," he said before hefting his gun and getting out of the car.

The town they'd stopped in was one Tala recognized from her old deployment maps: Shinku, named for the groves of sumac trees that grew nearby. It sat on the banks of the Hareyaka, where they'd erected an array of gleaming metal turbines to feed Tomoda's bottomless hunger for electricity. Sanbu's capture of it had been a major turning point in the homeland campaign, as it'd downed every phone, telegraph, and radio in the quadrant. Now, in the distance, the jade flag of the republic fluttered over Shinku. Tala's heart swelled just at the sight of it. She'd been surrounded by the Tomodanese for the past day and a half, and ill at ease the whole time.

"Keep your voice down," Kurihara interjected with theatrical cool. "The garrison is just around the corner."

There was indeed a Sanbuna motorcade stopped along the main street. Unlike the Shang, who had designed their own cars as a knockoff of the Dahali models, Sanbu had opted for a more direct revenge against Tomoda. They'd taken the Tomodanese vehicles captured during the war, then had them retrofitted for engines. Upon his capture by Sanbuna forces, the daito of Lisan had remarked that this was an uncivilized use of metal.

And if rumors were to be believed, General Erega had casually replied, "If you don't like Sanbuna iron, you should have left it in the ground."

Tala's eyes traced the familiar shapes of the vehicles: the way the peaked roofs had been beaten round, or the graffiti on the side of the largest truck, which screamed DEATH TO STEELHOUNDS. She hadn't realized how much she'd missed the familiar, rounded outlines of Sanbuna script.

Her thoughts leapt from there straight to Jimuro. Was that how he'd felt when he'd seen the Cicadas take the field last night? When he and Mang had waded into the shallows at Kinzokita? Was this why Kurihara had such a hold on him?

She shook her head to refocus herself on what was before her eyes. *Keep your head on straight, soldier.*

The day's commerce had ground to a dead halt, and every shop-keeper and customer had been herded out into the middle of the road. Sanbuna soldiers and their shades idled in a loose ring to keep everyone penned in. A hot snake of anger slithered through Tala's gut as she noticed how bored these soldiers seemed about taking in-nocent civilians prisoner.

Their commanding officer, a sergeant wearing an all-too-familiar uniform, strolled up and down the line, roaring at everyone in To-modanese, while his audience looked on in either fear or defiance. Tala couldn't hear what he was saying, but when a well-dressed woman spoke up to answer him, he smacked her across the face with his sidearm.

Tala's stomach clenched into a knot as the businesswoman buck-led and staggered back into the arms of her neighbors. If General Erega knew about this, she would have had that sergeant hanged for insubordination.

"Barbarians," Kurihara whispered next to her. Murmurs of agree-ment rippled in the word's wake.

Tala gritted her teeth, unable to deny the charge.

Kurihara turned to regard his fellow Cicadas. "Masks on."

As one, they donned their steel masks, and Tala found herself and Jimuro surrounded by the faceless . . . and the heavily armed.

"His Brilliance has ordered no Sanbunas dead," Kosuke said, to mutters from the Cicadas. "However, that gives us plenty of latitude in which to operate. Defend our people by any means necessary, sisters and brothers. Your Brilliance, the blessing?"

Jimuro stepped forward. "Children of Tomoda," he said as the Cicadas all bowed reverentially, "we are vessels of the spirits, and conduits of their will. Bright as copper."

"*Hard as iron*," they choroused back.

"Humble as lead."

"*Brilliant as steel.*"

Prince Jimuro's whole face came alive at the sound of their voices. "The battle is joined, children of Tomoda. Onward."

But as the Cicadas took the safeties off their guns and unsheathed their blades, all Tala could see was the bloodbath about to happen. Even with perfect Tomodanese sharpshooting, there was no guarantee against a stray bullet or rogue shade, and this was as target-rich an environment as she'd ever seen.

And then she glanced over at the richest target there was, in his blue jacket and glasses.

"Wait here," she said to him, then ducked around the corner before he could say anything else. She muttered a name, and Beaky popped into being next to her. He started to caw, but she sent a pulse of will, asking him to be silent. They had parts to play now. With sullen understanding, he acquiesced.

Satisfied, Tala called out in loud, clear Sanbuna: "*Hoy! What's the meaning of this?*"

Sanbuna soldiers hemming in all the civilians jumped in surprise. She smirked before she could stop herself, then after a moment of hesitation decided to lean into it. That was the persona she needed here: Haughty. Detached. Utterly assured in her superiority.

She grinned wider. She had just the model to follow.

When the soldiers nearest to her looked at her dumbfounded, she snapped: "What's wrong, soldier? Forgotten how to bow?"

They were either obedient or surprised. Whatever the reason, they both immediately sank into bows. Next to them, their shades— a buffalo and a flamingo—bent the knee as well. Tala strode past them like she'd already forgotten about them.

The Tomodanese eyed the newcomer warily. She felt their collective gaze prickle all over her body, even as she felt the Cicadas staring at the back of her neck. She imagined Jimuro was probably furious, and that Kurihara definitely was. But she knew how to talk her way through this. No one had to die. She could do this without a fight. She had to.

The sergeant with the gun in his hand whirled around to face her. "Who're you supposed to be?" he bellowed.

"Lieutenant Riza, Special Division," she said, borrowing the name from her hawk-eyed firing instructor. "Who's in charge here? Don't be so quick to volunteer yourself, Sergeant. You probably won't like what I have to say."

"These are my troops." The sergeant reminded Tala of the small, snub-nosed white dogs they bred in Shang, complete with bugging eyes and a nasal, breathy voice. "And they listen to me, not you. Where's your rank ID?"

"Get a line open to General Erega. She's all the rank ID I need. Tell her it's for Operation: Grand Tour. I can wait all day, though if you make me do it, she won't be happy."

The sergeant hesitated, then showed her a mouthful of crooked teeth. "You expect me to just call up the mother of the republic because you say to? Like I'm supposed to believe you're not some kind of spy?"

"Yes," Tala said with a showy roll of her eyes. "A Sanbuna woman, speaking fluent Sanbuna, with a shade in tow, who marches right up to a stranger in the middle of a foreign country and clearly identifies herself. That's who I'd choose as a spy. Have you ever considered moving over to the Special Division, Sergeant? We could use your keen intellect."

The sergeant snarled. "What do you want, anyway? I don't have time for you."

"But clearly you have time for this charade," Tala said, waving to the civilians huddled together. "What are you doing to these people? They're not enemy combatants." She found herself actively working to believe the words she was saying, and was surprised at how easy it was. "If they've committed no crime, then we can't detain them."

"They're all under suspicion," the sergeant growled.

" 'Sir,' " Tala said carefully. " 'They're all under suspicion, sir.' "

The sergeant looked as if he'd just swallowed a pint of medicine.

"What crime are they under suspicion for?"

"What do you think?" the sergeant said. "The Steel Cicadas are all over this area, and we got a tip that they—"

A gunshot rang out, and he spun to the ground with blood spurting from his shoulder. Before anyone could react, more shots followed from every which direction, and the entire scene devolved into chaos as more Sanbuna soldiers dropped. Their shades rippled with impact after impact as the Steel Cicadas poured fire into them. The civilians screamed, some trying to run and some throwing themselves flat to the ground. The Sanbuna troops returned fire blindly, chipping walls and shattering windows, while their shades charged headlong into the teeth of the incoming fire.

"Beaky, up!" Tala shouted, then ducked low and threw herself behind a parked car as Beaky took to the sky. She made herself as small as possible, while around her the air grew thick with flying bullets. Every so often she glimpsed a steel mask or the flash of a blade as the Cicadas closed in from all sides. She felt like a coward, crouching here, but her hands were tied.

A fresh wave of battle cries arose, and Tala's focus snapped left just in time to see a contingent of Steel Cicadas in close combat with the remaining Sanbuna troops and shades. She scanned the crowd for Prince Jimuro. Surely Kurihara had the wisdom to keep him back and safe, at least. Surely he—

The shriek of steel on steel filled her ears, and she rolled aside just in time to see a sword blade slice neatly through the car she was leaning against. The blade left a smoking, glowing trail of metal where it parted the car, and the machine split to reveal Harada. She wore her cicada mask, but there was no mistaking the weapon in her hands or the practiced way she held it.

"You're alone, slaver," she spat, then swung it straight for Tala's neck.

Tala threw herself straight at Harada's ankles, the blade passing inches over her back. Harada shuffled back to avoid getting taken down, then slashed down at Tala. Once again the sergeant just barely rolled aside in time, her fedora falling off her head. The sword sliced through it, neat as scissors through paper, and the hat hit the ground in two smoldering halves.

Tala leapt to her feet more clumsily than she would've liked. This was hardly her first time facing a metalpacted blade in combat. As with all metal objects, the Tomodanese could channel themselves into their swords: to make the blade diamond-hard, to heat it hot as dragon's breath, to sharpen its edge well past the point of absurdity.

Or, as Harada seemed to be doing right now, all three.

"Prince Jimuro!" Tala shouted. She made to draw her gun from her coat, but already Harada renewed her attack. Tala just managed to get her gun clear of her coat, but before she could pull the trigger, Harada brought down her blade, cleanly severing the barrel in two and just barely missing Tala's finger. Tala cursed and sidestepped the follow-up slash, but only just. She had to admit: She'd underestimated Harada, and it took all her skill to keep ahead of the other woman's blade. "Stop!" she cried. "Your Iron Prince would want you to stop!"

Harada shook her head. "My Iron Prince isn't here right now."

She caught Tala with her third strike, slicing a long gash down the sergeant's left arm. Her ruined coat and shirtsleeves flapped like flags, while a fresh burn carved itself across what had been a bleeding slash wound a moment ago. Tala was grateful she wasn't bleeding out, but blinding pain along an entire side of her body was hardly better.

Harada pressed the attack with a shout, her sword bright as a flame. She brought it down, ready to cleave Tala in two. A wave of desperation hit Tala, and with it her combat instinct. Almost as if it belonged to someone else, she watched her hand shoot out and wrap itself around the blade.

Instead of slicing through her hand, the sword blade caught the skin of her palm bloodlessly and with a soft *clang*.

Both Harada and Tala stared in disbelief.

And then Harada yanked her blade free of Tala's grip and leapt back, pointing the katana straight out at Tala.

As Harada tried to circle her, Tala circled to match. She risked a glance at her own palm. She wanted to tell herself the blade had somehow rebounded off the bones in her hand, but katana had famously keen edges and her skin wasn't even pierced. Was it some strange metalpacting malfunction by Harada, who looked just as rattled as Tala? Or . . .

She pushed the question away. She couldn't focus on it now. She was down her good gun arm, and a hat besides. Her stamina was still a wreck from the spider venom. All around her, the battle raged, but the Sanbuna resistance had dwindled to almost nothing. Most lay wounded on the ground, but a few were already dead. Those left standing were fighting alongside their shades for their lives, their odds steepening with each passing second. They couldn't help her. Prince Jimuro hadn't come running, either. And if she did take down Harada, she would still be surrounded by plenty of other hostiles.

The thought should have filled her with dread, not relief. But the moment she embraced the idea that the Steel Cicadas were her enemy, her world became so much more clear. Prince Jimuro confused her. The new approaching world confused her.

But enemies, she understood.

She pushed those vague, shapeless future enemies from her mind, and with them her pain. She could worry about winning those battles once she'd won the one in front of her.

"His Brilliance said no Sanbunas dead," Tala said.

"Tragic, unavoidable accident," Harada said, with a showy twirl of her sword.

Tala shook her head. "He didn't say anything about Tomodanese." And she glanced just over Harada's shoulder.

Beaky descended behind her with a loud *caw,* and with a shout Harada whirled around, bringing up her sword to block his outstretched talons.

That was what doomed her.

As Beaky wrapped his talons around the blade, pinning it in place, Tala pulled from her coat the only weapon she had left: a black silk tie.

She stretched it taut, then expertly looped it tight around Harada's throat and pulled.

Harada's hands fell away from her sword hilt and flew to her throat, but the tie was narrow and its silk tightly woven. Already, Harada's face had begun to redden. Soon enough, it would be blue.

Her sword clattered to the ground as Beaky let go of it, his feet crackling with healing wounds.

Though Tala was expertly choking the air from her, Harada was just able to rasp out a word. It took Tala a moment to realize she was speaking in Sanbuna. And the word she said was "Mercy." She said it again, and then a third time. The fourth, she had no more breath, but her lips formed the word anyway.

And then her hands dropped to her sides, limp and lifeless.

Tala let go of the tie, and Harada fell heavily to the asphalt. She wasn't dead, but even a few seconds completely cut off from air didn't do wonders for one's health. In that moment, Tala saw the woman for who she was: a noble's daughter, trying to be someone. An untested girl, who'd never undergone the trials that had turned Tala into a woman. A girl who had used Tala's own native tongue to beg for mercy.

A girl who would try to kill her again if she ever got the chance.

By the time her fingers wrapped themselves around the hilt of Harada's sword, it had cooled. Given how delicate the weapon looked, Tala was surprised at how heavy it felt in her grip. But the world had made her strong enough to wield it.

The girl lay unconscious, but the word *mercy* hung on the air. Its phantom echo was enough to still Tala for a moment. By now, though, she knew all too well that she could never give a steelhound another chance.

The blade was sharp enough to bite into the pavement when Tala brought it down.

And then it was as if she'd cut all sound from the air itself, because she realized that the battle was over. The Cicadas had triumphed.

She stabbed the bloody sword straight into the asphalt. It stood upright like a stick of funerary incense.

Beaky landed in front of her, turning his head sideways to give her a concerned look. Gently, she patted his beak. She willed him to return, but he resisted. The concern she saw in his eye shone even brighter.

She patted his beak again in gratitude, then straightened up to face whatever came next.

Before she knew it, she was staring down gun barrels in every direction. They were shouting in fury: at Tala, still standing, or at the thing lying in her shadow that had only just been a girl.

"*All of you, lower your weapons in the name of your prince!*" Prince Jimuro roared as he shoved his way to the forefront. Every gun lowered itself: either with immediate obedience or with reluctant slowness. "Sergeant Tala, what happened here?"

"I had the situation under control," Tala said. "Before the Cicadas opened fire, that sergeant there was telling me they'd been lured here by a report that the Steel Cicadas were active here. That was what they were up to in this town, Your Brilliance. They were provoked here."

"*Provoked?*" Kurihara shouted, stepping to the front and pulling up his cicada mask. "Yes, that sergeant was *provoked* into pistol-whipping that woman! Into corralling those innocent people! And just as you were *provoked* into murdering Harada!"

"Not murder," Tala said, careful to address only Prince Jimuro. "She attacked me. On *his* orders," she added with a jab of her finger at Kurihara. Her whole arm screamed in protest, and she dropped it back to her side. "She challenged a soldier. I finish my fights."

"Let me be the one to finish it, Prince Jimuro," Kurihara said, hefting his pistol. "If she wants to accuse me, then let me try her."

Beaky hopped in front of Tala, his feathers ruffled and an angry squawk in his throat. Mutters rippled through the remaining Cicadas, and some of them started to raise their guns again. Only Tala remained absolutely still, her expression steely.

"Enough, both of you!" Prince Jimuro called again. "Kosuke, look at the car around her. Something sliced it clean in half. No Sanbuna could've done that."

"Because Harada was defending herself from this barbarian and her slave!" Kurihara said.

"Your Brilliance," Tala said. "You know me. Would I attack first? You've seen me in battle. Fought alongside me, even. *Would I attack first?*" But even as she asked that question, she heard another in her head:

When have you ever tried to convince me you were any other sort of person?

And from the look in his eyes, she knew Prince Jimuro could hear it, too.

But eventually, he said, "It's true. Sergeant Tala is a woman of honor. She wouldn't have initiated the attack here. And surely if Harada had asked to be spared, Sergeant Tala would have let her live."

Something hitched in the back of Tala's throat.

"Prince Jimuro," she said carefully. "We need to get out of here. We have a plan, and we're so close to the end of it. We need to stick with it. Come on."

Prince Jimuro hesitated.

"She's wanted to separate you from your people from the moment we could embrace you again," Kurihara spat.

Tala ignored him. "What if that man attacks again? The splinter-soul?" she said, which put a spark of fear behind Jimuro's glasses. "I know he's dead. I saw it. But what if he's not? Do you think these toy soldiers can protect you from him?" Memories flashed across her mind like lightning, as she saw him tear apart her squad again, and again, and again.

Kurihara drew himself up proudly. "We're the only ones fighting for the people. What better champions could you need against this man, or any other?"

Tala looked past the prince's glasses, straight into the amber eyes that shone behind them. "I get why you'd want to take his word over mine. But think, Jimuro: When have I ever done anything without a reason?"

But at those words, the prince's gaze didn't clear up. In fact, it got even cloudier.

"Sergeant," he said, nodding to her hand. "Why is your tie wrapped around your fingers?"

Tala stared back, defiant. "I was using it to choke her."

"You had her helpless," Prince Jimuro said, voice beginning to rise, "and then you beheaded her?"

"She would've just tried again," said Tala. "Did you hear what I just said, Your Brilliance? *I finish my fights.*"

The cloudy expression on the prince's face had begun to darken into a storm. "Do you have so little faith in my sense of justice that you don't believe I'd have had her punished fairly once you came to me with her betrayal?" His voice shook. "Do you really believe I'd be so poor a Steel Lord?"

Tala couldn't believe what she was hearing. "She tried to *kill me*," Tala said, while Harada's last word echoed in her ear: *mercy,* in the tongue of her enemy. "Forgive me if I didn't have your feelings on my mind, but this wasn't about you." She expected Kurihara to chime in, but he'd visibly stepped back. He was getting out of her way.

That was how Tala knew that no matter what she said to the prince next, she'd already lost him.

"You had one of my subjects at your mercy." Jimuro's tone was so cold, his breath was practically visible. "She was helpless . . . and then you murdered her. You," he added quietly, "who never does anything without a reason."

"You idiot," Tala snarled at him. "There's no murder in a war."

"But we're not at war, Sergeant Tala," the prince said tightly. "Or had you forgotten again already?"

That brought Tala up short. Her mind throbbed from the sheer tonnage of fury it shouldered, and she wanted to direct it at every Tomodanese person she saw. "I know we're not at war," she said eventually, keenly aware of all the eyes on her.

"Then you just confessed to murdering a citizen of Tomoda in peacetime," Prince Jimuro said. "Under the Code of Steel, that crime carries a death sentence."

Behind him, Kurihara took a step forward, gun at the ready.

"But," the prince continued, "you've also been my diligent protector. That's earned you my clemency. Lord Kurihara."

Kurihara took another step forward, his disappointment plain. "My liege."

"See to it that the Steel Cicadas allow the sergeant to depart safely with a functional weapon," he said. "I'll personally look into her safe arrival back to Sanbu, and if I hear any harm has befallen her, I'll hold all of you responsible. Is that understood?"

Kurihara looked as if he'd swallowed blood. "Your Brilliance," he said, bowing.

Every part of Tala stung. "Prince Jimuro," she said. "Are you really putting your trust in them over me?"

"In my own people," Prince Jimuro said, "over a foreign soldier who until two days ago . . . had never even talked to me?"

For a long moment, they held each other's gaze. The other Cicadas seemed to fade from the corners of Tala's vision, as did the Sanbuna casualties at her feet. For that moment, Shinku—and with it, the world—was empty, but for Jimuro and her.

Everything she wanted to tell him hung in her throat.

She limped away from him without saying any of it.

PART FOUR

• • •

THE CROW'S FLIGHT

CHAPTER FIFTEEN

JIMURO

It had been Jimuro's grandfather, Steel Lord Kenjiro, who had introduced railroads to the people of Tomoda. Building railroads had always been theoretically possible, but the scarcity of metal on the home island had rendered it impractical. The conquest of the Sanbu Islands had changed that. The rich ore mined there had been used to mass-produce automobiles, to improve the weapons in Tomoda's national armory . . . and to finally realize the dream of a Tomoda tattooed with latticeworks of steel.

Though Kenjiro was lionized as the father of the Tomodanese railroad, the work had largely been completed after his death, by his daughter. So it shouldn't have been surprising for Jimuro to find massive portraits of his grandfather and mother hanging in the main atrium of Yatsura Memorial Station in Gorudo.

And yet, there they were.

Kenjiro was plump and jovial, more like the country's indulgent uncle than its leader. Next to him, Yoshiko more looked the part of Steel Lord: regal and . . . well, steely. Something caught in Jimuro's heart, to recognize his own narrow face in the brushstrokes of her portrait. He thought of her ashes, resting in state at the Palace of

Steel. Before he took the throne, he would have to visit her first. And his father.

And Fumiko.

He had to say goodbye.

Kosuke clapped a hand bracingly on Jimuro's shoulder, shaking him from his reverie. He pointed to a spot on the wall next to Steel Lord Yoshiko's. "That's where they'll hang yours." Jimuro could hear the *Your Brilliance* on the back of Kosuke's voice, but he'd caught himself just in time. He grew somber. "Do you miss them?"

"Him, I never knew," Jimuro said, nodding deferentially to his grandfather before regarding his mother's likeness. "Her . . . every day."

His stomach clenched into a knot as he recalled the reports of how his mother had died: in their garden, a place of quiet contemplation, as she was attempting to usher the household staff through one of the many secret passages that would get them safely out of the palace. Reports were inconsistent as to how many Shang she'd taken with her when they fell upon her, but Jimuro knew in his bones that no matter the number, his mother had died well.

Of course, not dying at all would have been preferable.

He let his gaze fall from the portraits. They were the only thing worth looking at inside the cramped train station, but he didn't want to look at them anymore. "Let's wait on the platform."

The air outside hung heavy with humidity, the sky above thick with bulbous gray clouds. The passengers already waiting by the side of the tracks exchanged idle chatter as they stared up at the sky and clutched at their umbrellas. Not a one of them noticed as he and Kosuke casually took places in their midst.

Jimuro felt a thrill of excitement as he listened to the distant rumble of thunder. The rains in Sanbu were frequent, but rarely refreshing. No matter how long they lasted, they only served to make the world heavier and stickier when they finally subsided. The Tomodanese rains—the rains he'd grown up listening to, feeling on his skin, tasting on his tongue—were crisp and clean. Before each came anticipation, and after each came renewal.

The land wasn't all that had been renewed. The station now had an outdoor platform with a handsome wooden awning stretched over a poured concrete floor. Old photographs showed the station had barely been a lean-to in his grandfather's day. In his mother's, it had been rebuilt into the small yet impressive structure it was today. Jimuro could only wonder: What sort of station would it grow into under his rule? Would it even grow? Or would his mismanagement reduce it to rubble and splinters?

Good, he heard Tala say in the back of his head. *Everything here was stolen, anyway.*

He squeezed his eyes shut and shook his head to clear away her voice. What was he doing listening to her? These rails were a symbol of Tomodanese ingenuity. If Sanbu wanted to hang on to its metal, he thought savagely, they should've fought harder to defend it.

You just called it our *metal,* her voice chimed in again. *Doesn't that say everything?*

"Shut up," Jimuro growled to himself.

Kosuke opened his mouth, then shut it again and flashed him a brief look of concern. Jimuro realized, sheepishly, that he'd just said that aloud. He shook his head to signal to his friend that everything was fine. And everything was, he knew. He was about to speed things up by abandoning Erega's glacially paced plan and traveling by train instead. He had a small but fierce squad of loyal subjects at his back, though they'd broken into duos and trios to avoid attracting suspicion. He was in as strong a position as he'd been since the day Sanbu had captured him. He just had some lingering anger toward Tala, and he would let that go soon enough. What did he care what she thought of him? He was a prince, soon to be a king, with his own subjects to mind. From now on, his people would always come first.

A gentle patter overhead heralded the arrival of the rain at last. Umbrellas mushroomed above the waiting travelers all around Jimuro, while other passengers simply muttered and migrated to the awning. They were all waiting so . . . normally. They had no idea their prince walked among them. They didn't even act like they were living in a country under occupation. The sight gave him hope. Truly, his people were as resilient as the steel they revered.

He smiled wanly at Kosuke, who grinned right back. Finding him had been a gift from the spirits themselves. When formulating the plan, General Erega had insisted that Jimuro put no trust in the loyal noble houses of Tomoda, but he saw now that Erega had just been trying to control him. He'd been a fool to put his trust in anyone but his own fellow children of Tomoda.

A rumble in the distance drowned out the cicadas' song. At first Jimuro thought it was more thunder, but then he felt the ground tremble beneath his feet. Just over the horizon, a solitary white light appeared in the gloom: the southbound train that would take them from the midlands straight down to Hagane. His heart swelled at the sight. At long last, he'd laid eyes on his final deliverance, and what more fitting shape for it to take than a piece of Tomodanese engineering excellence?

The train hissed to a gentle stop in front of him. The machine was like a steel serpent, its hide shiny and black. Its fine copper detailing gleamed beneath the dull gray sky. And the frontmost car, which housed the crew whose metalpacting moved the train, had dazzling veins of gold on its side that spelled out the train's name. Jimuro took a few steps over to read it.

In glittering characters, it declared itself to be the *Crow's Flight*.

He frowned.

Raindrops streamed down the train windows as Gorudo slowly receded into the darkness and fog. The lights had just begun to come on for the night when the town disappeared from sight completely.

The train was six cars long: the lead, a diner car sandwiched between two passenger cars, a sleeper car, and a freight car at the very rear. Jimuro would've been fine with a more utilitarian option, but Kosuke had insisted that they travel in comfort. "You're about to come into your birthright," he'd said. "Why not ride into your city like the hero you are?"

So he and the Cicadas settled in the frontmost passenger car. They broke apart into separate compartments, leaving him and Kosuke to share one together: cozy, with long, soft cushions like benches, and a table between them. When a woman appeared in the doorway to take a seat with them, Jimuro scooted aside to make room, but Kosuke frowned ever so slightly and gave a tiny shake of his head. The woman reddened, then bowed in apology and excused herself without a word.

"You didn't have to do that," Jimuro said. "She just wanted a place to sit. She was probably going to get off soon, anyway."

"You'll have the rest of your life to glad-hand the people, Your Brilliance," he said. He seemed relieved to be able to address Jimuro formally once more. "After the ordeal you've been through in the clutches of those savages, you deserve a bit of time to just be yourself again."

Jimuro noticed Kosuke's hand hovering tentatively near his knee. He gave Kosuke a nod, and with visible relief Kosuke laid his hand on Jimuro's thigh. The rest of Kosuke's body relaxed, and he slumped gently into Jimuro, resting his head on the prince's shoulder. "I can't believe the spirits gave you back to me, my liege."

"I told you, enough of that," Jimuro said, sighing. "You've known me since we were children. We've shared a bed. You can at least call me by the name my mother gave me." Something about his own words felt like an icicle to his heart.

"May she—" Kosuke caught himself. "That reminds me, we need some sake." He slid the compartment door open and hailed a crew member. "A bottle of sake and two cups," he told her. "Warm."

Jimuro didn't mean to say it. He had no intention of saying it. But when Kosuke shut the door and turned back to him, the words tumbled out of his mouth just the same: "My coronation's tomorrow." Saying the words aloud let him feel their weight for the first time. He tried to think of them as a cloak draped across his shoulders, and not a boot hovering over his throat.

"Spirits willing, yes," Kosuke said. "All the more reason to drink."

"No, you don't understand," Jimuro said. "I was never supposed to be the Steel Lord so young. My mother—"

He tamped down his words as the door slid open again. The uniformed attendant had returned bearing a metal tray, upon which rested a small sake bottle and a pair of cups. She placed them on the table, bowed, and departed once more.

"My mother was supposed to teach me so many things before I assumed her throne," Jimuro went on as Kosuke filled their cups. "*I* was supposed to do more before I assumed her throne. I was supposed to have a *life*, Kosuke."

Kosuke stopped mid-pour and looked at Jimuro with concern. "Are you saying you don't want to be our Steel Lord?"

"*No,*" Jimuro said. It sounded more heated than he'd meant it to. He softened his tone. "I do want to be the Steel Lord. I want to serve. I just . . . I never really gave it that much thought until now. Even after I heard that she was dead, I didn't let myself think about it. Now I have no room to think about anything else. Tomoda needs a great Steel Lord more than ever, and tomorrow all it's going to get is me."

"Jimuro." Kosuke patted Jimuro's leg affectionately. "I'm no monarch, but I have experience with floating in the gulf between who I am and who people think I am. Would you concede that much, at least?"

Jimuro grunted, staring into the shallow cup Kosuke had placed in his hands. "Fair."

"I know it is," Kosuke said, tempering his bluntness with a perfectly shaped grin. "But you need to set those fears aside. When you lead us into the bright future of our reborn empire, we'll need you at your bravest and boldest. If you show the world any less, they'll take it as a license to tear you apart."

Jimuro's voice caught in his throat. Despite his best efforts, Tala's words from the night before snaked through his head again. "We should talk about that," he said quietly.

Kosuke's face darkened. "The barbarian again," he sighed. "Is she whispering in your ear?"

"I don't see her here," Jimuro said, trying his best not to consider the part he'd played on that count.

Kosuke was uncowed. "Why else would you doubt our ability to come back from this? You're the divine vessel of the spirits, and the beating heart of our people. If anyone's supposed to believe in our future, it's you."

"I do believe in our future," Jimuro said. "But another war won't get us there."

Kosuke stiffened and sat upright. His hand withdrew, taking its warmth with it. "I see."

"Think, Kosuke. We're surrounded by our former enemies, our vaults are empty, and the people are exhausted." Jimuro ticked each item off on his fingers. "I may have spent more time in a cell than on the battlefield, but even I know those aren't the conditions for winning a war. Our best hopes for any future rest on the mercy of Shang, Sanbu, and Dahal."

Kosuke looked as if he were seeing Jimuro for the first time. He smiled unsteadily, then bowed. "Well. You have a lot on your mind. I'm sure we can talk it all out." He raised his cup. "May you live ten thousand years."

"Ten thousand years," Jimuro said automatically. They clinked their cups, thumped them against the wooden table, then drained them. Saying the number almost made him shudder. At that point, he would've been tired of the very act of being alive.

Kosuke sighed. "You're my friend, and you know I'll follow you no matter where you lead," he said. "I want you to remember that when I tell you: You aren't trusting in us the way you need to, and it's disrespectful to every child of Tomoda who's ever made sacrifices in your name." He coughed. "Don't forget that first bit I said, now."

Jimuro made to pour himself another drink, only for Kosuke to snatch the bottle away and fill his cup for him. He slid his fingers beneath his glasses and massaged the bridge of his nose. This place wasn't doing anything to help his nerves at all, but the train was up to full speed. He could hardly leave now. "Please don't lecture me on how I see my people."

"You *don't* trust us," Kosuke said. "Just today, you put more faith in that barbarian soldier to solve problems than you did in the Steel Cicadas."

"Back in Shinku?" said Jimuro. "Of course I did. She was Sanbuna. They were Sanbuna. And do you know something? Tala had the situation under control. I couldn't hear what they were saying, but I saw what I saw, Kosuke. She was handling things, until you opened fire."

"She's a mad dog," Kosuke said. "One who murdered Harada, in case you'd forgotten."

"Don't talk about dogs that way. One of my best friends was a dog." Ignoring the sting brought about by the invocation of another one of his dead subjects, he went on: "Before I dismissed her, Sergeant Tala claimed you'd ordered her death. Why would she think that?"

He watched Kosuke carefully, and sure enough, Kosuke gave up the biggest tell of all: a complete, studious absence of tells. Jimuro recognized the posture well; it was a common one in courtly intrigue, when one wished to carefully cultivate information and its flow.

"Like I told you," said Kosuke with practiced inscrutability, "she's a—*do you mind?*"

The compartment door had slid open yet again. A tall young woman with a black dress and black boots abruptly sank into a bow of apology and then excused herself, leaving the door slightly open.

Irritably, Kosuke rose and slid it all the way shut. He didn't speak again until he'd resumed kneeling next to Jimuro. "The slaver was a mad dog, Your Brilliance," he said. "Who's to say what went through that mind of hers when she was full of bloodlust?"

Jimuro knew Tala to be a fierce fighter—in fact, he'd experienced it firsthand. But there was a gulf between "fierce" and "vicious," and in his mind Tala never crossed it, even at her ugliest. Still, he kept that to himself. The more he prodded at the subject, the deeper Kosuke would entrench himself, and any further conversation would be pointless.

Kosuke sensed his disquiet. "Some food, perhaps," he said bracingly. He slid the door open and poked a head out. When he couldn't find an attendant, he said, "I'll look for someone in the dining car." His expression gentled. "Whatever you're going through, I want to help you. Just tell me what I need to do."

Jimuro nodded, smiling tightly as he tapped his cup to the table and took a sip of sake. Kosuke gave him a lingering glance of concern, then slid the door shut yet again.

The prince slumped back against the compartment wall with a sigh. He was so rarely alone these days. Kosuke would only be gone for a minute, but he was grateful for even that amount of respite.

So. His friend had tried to have his bodyguard killed. The only thing about it that surprised him was how unsurprised he was. It didn't absolve Tala of Harada's murder, but it did make the waters even murkier than they already were. Tala was right: Kosuke had been far too willing to casually resort to murder himself.

And now you've made him the only one you can rely on, his mother's voice snapped.

He's no threat to me, Jimuro reminded himself.

The world is more than you, came back her stern reply. *What of them?*

Out the window, night fell, and the rain fell with it. It streaked on the train's windows, blurring the distant lights of the towns they passed. He wondered who was currently in those homes and buildings, living by those lights. Did they know their prince walked among them again at last? Would they be heartened to learn that he had returned to serve and protect them? Or would they just see him for the incompetent boy-king he knew he was? Would he be yet another problem heaped onto their shoulders, when they already had enough to be getting on with?

And just like that, the town was gone again, the lights of its train station already a memory. Once again, the outside was nothing but darkness and falling rain.

He closed his eyes, looking to conjure up his mother again so he could draw from what strength and wisdom she'd been able to pass on to him.

But the only face that swam before him was Tala's, eyes glinting with stern disappointment.

His eyes flew open.

The compartment door slid open. "That was fast," Jimuro said, turning around. "I suppose you—"

But instead of Kosuke, a short young woman stood there, wearing a long white overcoat, a white hat, and a shiny cicada mask. She bowed, though not even half as low as she should have to greet a man of his station. She straightened back up, and from her coat produced a large pipe that she lit with a match.

"Iron Prince Jimuro," she said. "It is a genuine honor to make your acquaintance at last."

CHAPTER SIXTEEN

LEE

When Lee had left Danggae for good, shown the door by siblings who didn't like the heat she brought home with her, she'd hopped a train that same night. Since then, life had been one boxcar after another for her. That was how things always went for her: Find a new place, find a new partner. Fall into bed, fall out of love, then follow her one rule right to the nearest train yard. So Lee Yeon-Ji was no stranger to riding the rails.

She'd just never ridden them quite like this.

This was no cramped, smelly freight car. She stood in the dining car, smack in the middle of the train. A phonograph piped moody jazz into the room, and the lights had been dimmed and small candles laid out to cultivate a sense of atmosphere. Fashionable riders knelt on cushions behind low, polished tables, chatting away over smoldering cigarettes and plates of steaming food. Still more well-heeled patrons crowded the bar, where a woman in a bow tie doled out cocktails in every color and shape of glass. Impeccably uniformed waiters hurried in and out of the galley, deftly navigating the narrow space while balancing entire courses on a single tray. Through the galley door, Lee could even glimpse a small walk-in fridge, the kind of thing she'd never seen on a Shang train. Even while traveling, it seemed, the Tomodanese ate in style.

Lee was unable to keep a grin off her face as she sauntered into the thick of it. The aromas of Tomodanese food twisted her hungry stomach into knots, even though none of them contained a scrap of meat. But the real feast was for her eyes: Pretty men in suits. Handsome women in smart gowns.

And most important, all the shiny things they had.

Her fingers twitched with the longing to stick themselves into pockets and take whatever they could. She knew it would be so easy. Every mark in here had their guard down. By the time the first of them realized they didn't have their wallet or watch, Lee would be the smallest shadow in their memory.

But she stilled her fingers. Now that she'd ID'd the Iron Prince, she and Xiulan had reached a delicate part of their operation. And unfortunately, Lee's part in what came next didn't involve paying herself an early bonus for her good work.

She felt an unfamiliar pressure on the skin of her stomach, just as she felt a matching flutter of excitement from someplace that was both inside her head and not. That was Bootstrap, and Lee could feel her excitedly pawing at the door that separated Lee's mind from hers. Without Bootstrap summoned, her desires were more abstract, but Lee knew what she wanted: for Lee to turn right back around and bring her to her old friend, the Iron Prince. She was a good dog (though what dog wasn't?), but this close to their target she was getting excitable. When Lee had actually laid eyes on the guy, it'd taken all her willpower not to just say her name.

Easy, girl, Lee thought. *This goes off right, and we'll have plenty of time with your pal ahead of us.* She didn't know if Bootstrap could actually hear her words, but the sensation subsided enough for Lee to get her head back in the game.

At the bar, she spotted her target. He was a big guy with wispy hair, whose name she'd picked up at the train station earlier: Iwanbo. The man was already in his cups, hunched over the counter and beckoning the bartender for another round with a snap of his fingers.

Lee indulged in a small scowl. While she was working her first hustles, her brother Yeon-Ha had waited tables to keep the family fed. It wasn't the kind of job they normally gave to Jeongsonese people, but he was quite handsome, and his features had been Shang enough so that, with a fake Shang name, he passed as long as no one paid too close attention to him. But even when they thought he was one of them, Shang customers would treat him no better than these sake-guzzling steelhounds treated their own servants. It squared pretty neatly with Lee's understanding of how the world worked: Folks were always on the lookout for any reason to treat someone else like shit.

Her scowl reversed itself as she imagined exacting some indirect payback all these years later.

Unlike Yeon-Ha, Lee had never been prized for her looks. That, she'd decided at an early age, was to her great benefit. One bad day was all it took to rob someone of a pretty face. But twenty years of bad days hadn't robbed Lee of her own brand of charm.

As she approached him, she adjusted her posture, her gait, even the swing of her hips. She grinned at the familiar sight of heads turning in her peripheral vision. If she could grab that kind of attention without saying a word, this Iwanbo guy stood no chance.

She didn't walk to the bar so much as saunter, but she was careful not to be too showy about it. It took a light touch to avoid the act coming off like a put-on—or even worse, as desperate. But fortunately, a light touch was Lee's whole thing.

She held up a bill to the bartender. "Whiskey and a smoke," she said. "But skip the light."

The whiskey was brown as a cigar and tasted like smoke. Before she set about her con, Lee treated herself to a quiet moment so she could savor that experience: a mouthful of whiskey that cost more than her childhood apartment. She slipped the cigarette between her lips at an enticing angle, then turned to Iwanbo next to her. "Trouble you for a light, soldier?"

With a casual motion, he produced a metal lighter from his pocket. It sparked on its own, and Lee guided the cigarette's tip to the flame. She was careful to keep the smoke in her mouth, rather than inhaling it. Smoking wasn't her thing. But twenty years of movies had cemented the allure of smoking forever, so it never hurt to lean into it when she wanted something.

"Thanks," she said. "You headed down Hagane way, too?"

That drew his attention for the first time. "How did you know I was going to Hagane?"

"You look like an interesting guy, and it's an interesting town. Not the hardest math I've ever done." It was a well-practiced line, though of course she changed the place depending on who she was talking to. "Now, as it happens, I like interesting guys." She cast a meaningful glance down at his empty cup. "And especially interesting guys who know how to drink. So I guess—"

"I'm sorry," Iwanbo said. "I understand what you're doing."

A jolt of anxiety shot through Lee. She never got nervous when she was on the clock, but this had caught her by genuine surprise.

"I genuinely appreciate your interest, but I love my wife far too much to even think about other women. It's not a reflection on you, and I'm sure there are other men on this train your charm wouldn't be wasted on."

Lee blinked. This, she could genuinely say had never happened to her before. "I, uh . . . thanks?" she said.

Iwanbo nodded somberly and turned his attention back to his drink.

Lee wasn't about to give up just yet. She'd broken up marriages before. And besides, she didn't even need to break up this one. She just needed to lure him into the baggage car so she could knock him out. He was Kurihara's right hand, and with Kurihara himself nowhere to be seen, she'd switched to her secondary target.

"You miss her, huh?" Lee said.

"Every day." Iwanbo sighed. "I never wanted to leave her side, but she insisted I had important work to do. I lost a good friend today, though, and I've found myself taking stock of what really matters. We all have such finite time, even when the spirits are kind. If I'm only given this one chance to walk the paths of the world, I won't ever do it again without her at my side, and she at mine." He slurped his sake. "Forgive me; my wife says I would talk to an empty chair if it looked friendly enough. I'm sorry to unburden myself on your shoulders."

"Don't worry about it," Lee said, still trying to feel out what her angle was here. "I've been told I've got one of those faces."

"In this low light, I can hardly see yours," Iwanbo chuckled.

Lee grinned and sipped her whiskey. "You're missing out."

"So long as I have Nagisa, I'll disagree. Have you ever been in love, Ms. . . . ?"

"Rai," Lee said. A Tomodanese surname for her was a tricky thing, since the Tomodanese language didn't have an *L* sound. *Rai,* she'd come to understand, was the closest translation she could get.

"Rai what?"

"Just Rai's good."

In the dim light, she saw Iwanbo's brow wrinkle, not unpleasantly. "My friend that I lost today . . . she also went by her family name, rather than the one her parents gave her."

"If you think about it, they gave her the other name, too."

Iwanbo chuckled again, but it was a melancholy sound. "I guess they did. Why do you go by your surname, Ms. Rai?"

A pack of colorful lies leapt to Lee's mouth, but she held off. She could sell a lie to Iwanbo as easily as she could a few acres of farmland to a dentist with some disposable income. But when you were reeling someone in, the trick was to be strategic about where you let in the truth.

"I miss my family," she said. "We don't talk much. They weren't sad to see the back of me, but I still think about them. I guess it's my way of keeping that torch burning." She felt like she'd just taken off an article of clothing.

Iwanbo considered this for a moment, then nodded. "That seems a fair answer," he said. "And as for my other question?"

"Which one?"

"Have you ever been in love?"

Lee swayed on the spot as she considered the question, and it wasn't from the whiskey.

"Tough question?" Iwanbo said mildly.

"No," Lee said. "Leastwise, I don't think so." But she considered all the partners she'd had first. Here before her was a guy so devoted to his wife, he'd only left her side because she'd told him to. She'd enjoyed her time with, say, Lefty, and his smile had always had a way of making her heart beat faster. But if he hadn't screwed her over and fled to Jungshao; if the idiot hadn't run his mouth and lost his guts; would they still be together now? And it wasn't just Lefty. He'd had a healthy number of predecessors.

Which meant Xiulan had a healthy number of predecessors, plus one.

Iwanbo checked his watch, then drained the last of his sake and placed the cup facedown on the countertop. "Maybe you should go consider your answer to my question back in the quiet of your compartment."

Lee plastered on a grin and gestured out to the dining car. "And miss all the wining and dining? Not on your life."

Iwanbo frowned. "You seem like a nice woman," he said. "Please consider taking my advice."

Lee balked. Who was in charge of this conversation, anyway? "Let me get the next round."

"I'm sorry," Iwanbo said. He pulled something shiny from his coat and pressed it to his face: a metal mask in the shape of a spread-winged cicada. "Perhaps another time." And then he produced a sawed-off shotgun from the folds of his coat, held it aloft, and cocked it loudly. *Nobody move.*

CHAPTER SEVENTEEN

XIULAN

Despite Xiulan's long years of practice at maintaining a royal composure, she couldn't keep her mouth from bending into her most savage, triumphant smile as she knelt opposite the Iron Prince. It was an indulgence she felt was well earned. Because after all, there he was: the most wanted man in the world, the scion of her country's greatest scourge, and the ticket to her ascendancy and Ruomei's downfall.

"Whose acquaintance am I making?" Prince Jimuro said with a shrewd narrowing of his eyes. "I don't recognize you from earlier."

Xiulan supposed there was no point in holding out the secret of her identity any longer. Not everyone could be Bai Junjie, whose showmanship let him go entire chapters incognito without anyone noticing a thing.

Well, she was young yet. She would get there someday.

She swept the mask off. "Your Brilliance, you are in the presence of Her Majesty Twenty-Eighth Princess Shang Xiulan, agent of the Li-Quan and Lady of Moonlight. And considering that I'm the one person in the world who wants you alive rather than dead, I think it would be prudent if you were to come with me."

She expected him to posture. After all, she'd just revealed herself as one of his enemies, come for him at last. But after only a moment, he slumped back against his compartment wall and rubbed the bridge of his nose with two fingers. "I can't deal with this right now."

Xiulan stared. "What part of my introduction suggested to you that you had a choice in the matter?"

"I'm the Iron Prince of Tomoda," he said. "I always have a choice." He waved a hand at her. "Go away. I have enough going on."

Xiulan felt like her teeth were about to snap her pipe in two. She knew not everything could be like it was for Bai Junjie, but in the myriad novels, short stories, radio plays, and movies that made up his canon, this conversation was something she'd never seen. She hoped fleetingly that Lee was having better luck neutralizing the other Cicadas.

"What you have, ah, 'going on' is of as little concern to me as the well-being of the Shang people was to your ancestors," Xiulan said coldly. "I was hoping that, monarch-to-monarch, we could comport ourselves with civility. But in lieu of your cooperation, I'm willing to use force to expedite proceedings."

"And I thought I talked a lot."

"I'm sure we can compare our relative levels of loquaciousness at whatever depth you like . . . once we exit the vehicle at the next stop," Xiulan said tersely. She kept an eye on the door, but so far it hadn't opened. Good. Lee was holding up her end of the plan. That thought was enough on its own to spur Xiulan to try harder to meet her halfway.

"How do you imagine this power play of yours will bear out for Shang at the negotiating table?" Prince Jimuro said, not moving an inch.

She caught herself before she could say anything too specific. "I have my own reasons for doing this," she said. "And someday, Shang and the rest of the world will be grateful I did. Now, I believe that's all the explanation you require to proceed with this endeavor, so if you would be so kind . . ."

Prince Jimuro tapped his cup to the table, then knocked back its remaining sake and folded his arms over his chest. "You've already told me you need me alive," he said. "That doesn't leave you with much bargaining power, Your Majesty."

At last, they were on territory she was more prepared to face. Each time she'd fantasized about finally apprehending Iron Prince Jimuro, Xiulan had imagined some version of this conversation. So she leaned forward and said, "Your safety *is* guaranteed, Your Brilliance." She glanced meaningfully over her shoulder. "But such a bargain includes no provisions for the safety of your subjects . . ."

In truth, she had no idea if the gambit would work, because she had no idea what sort of man the Iron Prince was. If she'd issued that threat to Ruomei, her dear sister would have gladly let a hundred Shang citizens die if the net balance still tipped in her favor. If Prince Jimuro ended up being cut from the same cloth, it diminished her power in this moment, but surely she was doing the world a service by removing him from his seat of power anyway.

That said, Xiulan had done her detective work. She was not without a good guess.

Prince Jimuro glared at her. "My subjects are—"

"Are you on the verge of saying *innocent,* Your Brilliance?" said Xiulan. "Because if that's indeed your assertion, I could gladly produce half a billion children of Shang who would dispute that . . ." Her mind flashed to that clearing in the woods, and the small massacre that had greeted her sight. ". . . to say nothing of the ones who specifically owe grievance to the Steel Cicadas. Tell me, where *is* the rest of your guard? I've seen the murderers and cutthroats whose company you crave, but I've yet to see a single Sanbuna on this train."

The prince's expression darkened. "No plan survives contact with reality."

"Spare me," Xiulan said. "I know you were in the company of General Erega's troops as recently as this afternoon. I've observed the evidence personally."

For the first time, the prince looked more than vaguely antagonistic. His entire body stiffened. "If you've done anything to hurt her—"

"Don't insult my formidable intelligence, Your Brilliance," Xiulan said. "I know you departed from Lisan City in the company of an entire squad of Erega's finest marines. And I saw the massacre they wrought in the woods north by northeast of here."

The Iron Prince's expression clouded. "What are you talking about?"

"A whole contingent of Shang soldiers, slaughtered where they sat," Xiulan said, "their deaths clearly the work of shades charged with murderous intent. And when one knows the Republic of Sanbu doesn't have any outposts stationed so far inland, the culprit becomes all too easy to deduce."

Prince Jimuro paled. "Wait a moment," he said. "Did you see who did it?"

"Deduction is its own manner of seeing," Xiulan recited. One of Bai Junjie's catchphrases, but she doubted the Iron Prince would recognize it.

"No, you don't understand," Prince Jimuro said. Xiulan was taken aback by how urgent he'd become, and how suddenly he'd become it. "On the voyage here, we were attacked by a man who broke the laws of magic. A man who chewed through my entire complement of Sanbuna protectors, save for one. A man whom I'd hoped with all my heart was dead. If he's nearby, we're all in danger."

Xiulan cocked her head. Everything he said sounded too outlandish to believe. And yet . . . the manner in which he said it. The ease with which he called up details, rather than taking the time to concoct them. Those lent credence to the idea that he just might be telling the truth.

But then her heart hardened. What was she doing? He was the Iron Prince of Tomoda. There was nothing he wouldn't say to get himself out of this situation. "If what you say is true," she said, "then you really should come with me at the next—"

The door slid open, and she jammed her mask back onto her face just as Kurihara Kosuke swept into the room. Xiulan suppressed a squawk of surprise. It had been Lee's job to waylay him and the other Cicadas in the back of the train. Why hadn't she succeeded? Had the worst happened to her partner?

No, she thought, with a quick glance at Kurihara. His clothes were in good order and he wasn't out of breath, so he hadn't been in a fight. There had been no noises from the adjoining train car, either. Suffice it to say, she told herself with some relief, she could assume Lee was still safe and actively in operation. This was a minor setback, but one they could work around.

"Food is on its way," Kurihara said, bowing from his waist, then straightening up once he noticed Xiulan. "Who the hell are you?"

Xiulan leveled a meaningful stare at Prince Jimuro.

For a long moment, the Iron Prince said nothing.

Xiulan tensed. If he didn't play along, she would have to act quickly. Kou's name hung heavy on her tongue, a drop of dew waiting to fall.

"She can stay, Kosuke," said the prince eventually. "I was . . . rather enjoying her company."

Kurihara blinked. "Your Brilliance . . . ?"

"If you *insist,* my liege," Xiulan said brightly, though inside her mind spun like a machine. She was trying her best not to get swallowed by her prodigious imagination as it considered every worst-case scenario she could be stuck in. But then, she considered what Lee would do in her shoes. She thought of her partner's easy smile. Her loose, confident stride. Her unshakable confidence that no matter how high the world stacked things against her, she would always be good enough to jump higher.

She sucked in a breath.

She exhaled blue smoke.

She could do this.

She had no other choice.

She reached for the bottle of sake on the table. It wasn't much of a plan, but it would do for now. "May I humbly request the honor of filling your cups, my lords?"

CHAPTER EIGHTEEN

JIMURO

Outside, the Iron Prince was calm and collected.

Inside, he screamed.

He slipped his hands below the table before clenching them as hard as he could. He felt his own fingernails dig into the sweaty palms of his hands, but he squeezed anyway. There were too many variables at play. He was certain this princess had a shade, but he had no idea what shape it would take, or if she would even need to summon it. For all he knew, it was already prowling the train, menacing his subjects and waiting for the order to make good on her threats. And even if it was yet to be summoned, he didn't like his and Kosuke's odds against a bloodthirsty, semi-immortal beast when they had a single gun between them.

He glanced out the window of the compartment, though he wasn't sure why. Maybe he'd hoped to see some kind of inspiration lurking there in the rainy dark. Maybe he'd feared he would see the man in the purple coat, who was closer at hand than anyone else realized.

All that stared back at him was the dark.

"Your Brilliance." Kosuke cut into his thoughts by offering a cup of warm sake. Jimuro considered taking it and hurling that sake in the Shang woman's eye, but that wouldn't freeze her tongue. No, as tempting as it was to seize an opportunity, he had to accept that he had no opportunity to seize. He had to be as the mountain, and sit with patience.

Kosuke tapped his own cup to the table, then drained it and slammed it back down. He ran his fingers through his hair and gave Xiulan a distracted, thoughtful look. "I must confess, I'm not familiar with you."

Jimuro's heart leapt into his throat. He resisted the urge to pump his fist. Of course Kosuke would notice something was off right away. All Jimuro needed to do was wait for him to work it out for himself.

"I'm afraid you wouldn't be, my lord," said Princess Xiulan with a modest bow. "I was a household servant for Lord Iida. After his children both fell in the defense of our homeland, I wished nothing more than to avenge them. That was why I joined the Cicadas' cause."

Jimuro had to admit: For a non-Tomodanese, her performance was impeccable. She spoke with perfect grammar and adjusted her tenses with native fluency. She'd localized her accent, but with the kind of stiffness that could be explained away as servant-class awkwardness. She bowed when she was supposed to, and to the exact degree that custom called. Whatever else she was, she was at the very least a good student.

"I see," Kosuke said. He scratched his head again. "So that means you've had the privilege of fighting alongside my old friend Komachi Tsubame?"

Jimuro studied his old friend, looking for any kind of tell. Was he just making small talk? Was he suspicious, and probing their new companion?

Princess Xiulan let out a sigh. "Not since she died last year."

"I'm sorry to hear that," Jimuro said. "How did she die?" No reason not to speed things up, he figured.

Princess Xiulan turned to look at him full-on. Her one eye not obscured by her hair glinted with a sinister intelligence. "Childbirth."

From Kosuke's reaction, that was apparently the correct response. Jimuro barely resisted the urge to curse aloud. How could she have possibly known that?

"Apologies for the dressing-down," Kosuke said, accepting another pour of sake from Xiulan. "Nothing matters more than His Brilliance's safety."

"Oh, I quite agree," said Princess Xiulan.

Jimuro bit down to stop his teeth from gnashing into stumps. Beneath the table, his fists trembled against his thighs.

Kosuke tapped his cup against the table, then drank again. He squinted at Princess Xiulan's face. "What are you doing, still wearing your mask? We're all patriots here. Take it off, take it off."

Within the depths of that mask, Jimuro saw that one eye glint again. The princess's entire posture stiffened ever so slightly within her coat, so acutely that Jimuro never would've noticed if he weren't looking for it.

"She can keep it on," Jimuro said, gamely attempting a genial tone. "Clearly, she's more comfortable with it on." *Coward,* he told himself.

"Thank you, Your Brilliance," Princess Xiulan said, topped off with another immaculately performed bow. "I'm self-conscious of my face, especially in the presence of our Iron Prince. I know, it's awfully silly of me . . ."

Kosuke shrugged. "What'd you say your name was?"

"Oh, I didn't," Xiulan said. She'd pitched her voice up, the way one was supposed to when conversing with one's elders. Of course she'd think to do that, Jimuro thought; Shang was a tonal language. If anyone was going to have an ear for intonation, he supposed it would be a woman whose language was named for her own family. "My name is Hayama Izumi, though the name's not much worth knowing." She poured another round of sake: one for Kosuke, and one for Jimuro himself. "Though I suppose for now, I can at least be known as the one with the sake . . ."

This was absurd, Jimuro thought. Tomodanese culture was a collection of customs, each embedded with micro-customs. There were a dozen points in even the most mundane conversation where a masquerading foreigner should have tripped up. How could this princess possibly be so good at it?

He caught Kosuke's eye and, in his desperation, willed Kosuke to see what he saw. He strained his mind, trying to broadcast thoughts that would shout to his friend the true nature of what was happening. Surprise was the only way they would get the upper hand on her.

Kosuke frowned at him: *What?*

Jimuro tried to indicate Xiulan with a flicker of his eyes, and hoped Kosuke would understand him as he thought, *She's an enemy foreign agent holding me hostage.*

Kosuke squinted: *You're not making any sense.*

"May you reign ten thousand years," Princess Xiulan cut in, bowing to him.

"Ten thousand years," Kosuke echoed. Jimuro had no choice but to clink cups with him, then rap his cup against the table before downing it. The smooth burn of sake, normally such a comfort to him, now just made him aware of how the stuff curdled and roiled in the pit of his nervous stomach.

It's a shame we're not having tea, Jimuro thought. The Tomodanese tea ceremony was as tedious and complicated as anything in their entire culture. If ever there were a way to expose an outlander, watching them attempt teatime would be second only to watching them attempt to navigate Hagane's subway system.

You're an idiot, he thought. *Tala would've found a way out by now.* Of course, there was a good chance Tala's way would be reaching across the table and throttling Xiulan.

That's the difference between you and the savage sergeant, his mother's voice hissed to him. *Whatever you threaten, my sweet son, she has the spine to see through.*

"Your Brilliance?" said Kosuke. "Your Brilliance, what's the matter?"

With a start, Jimuro became aware of his own face. His eyes were wide, his mouth drooped open. Even his glasses had slid down his slight nose, and they were what he adjusted first.

"Nothing," he said gruffly, with a passing glance at Xiulan to warn her not to act up just yet. "Just . . . Steel Lord things." His gaze drifted away from the masked interloper in front of him, away from his friend to his right, to the lacquered bottle of sake in the center of the table.

He blinked, as a thought occurred to him.

"Friends," he said, "I'd like to propose a toast."

CHAPTER NINETEEN

XIULAN

Xiulan smiled when the prince raised the bottle. She'd made it plain that she was not a foe who could be outwitted, so she'd left him with only a single option: help her get Kurihara so stinking drunk he could barely stand, let alone stop them from leaving.

"We'll need another cup," Kurihara said, frowning. Xiulan studied him a moment. It was surprising to be in such casual company with so vicious a criminal, and in another time and place she would've been all too glad to exercise her powers as an agent of the law. Even adjusting for the exuberance of the Shang propaganda machine, Kurihara still had a lot of dead Shang to answer for.

The prince laid a hand on his shoulder. "No," he said. He picked up the bottle. "When I was a young boy, my mother, Steel Lord Yoshiko, told me that rather than rule her people, it was the Steel Lord's job to serve them." He flashed his teeth. "Let . . . Izumi, was it?"

Xiulan gave him a tight nod to encourage him to move it along already.

"The lady can drink from my cup," Prince Jimuro said, filling it and sliding it toward her. "I will drink from the bottle. Hardly polite, but I suppose royalty has its privileges, doesn't it?"

Kurihara grunted in assent. "I'm sure this is just a game you're running so you can get more sake," he said with a grin. "But I'll always turn a blind eye for you, my liege."

Xiulan saw the creases on the shoulder of Kurihara's kimono deepen as Prince Jimuro gave him an affectionate squeeze. In her brain, the puzzle pieces slotted neatly together. So it was romantic, then, this bond between prince and terrorist. It explained perfectly why he would abandon his Sanbuna guards, if he knew this option was waiting for him once he reached home.

Already, the story in her head was revising itself. He'd tricked Erega into this plan, knowing full well he would have the Cicadas to find him when he returned home. She wasn't sure when the prince would have had time to arrange things with Kurihara, but Erega's regime no doubt had its share of leaks and spies. After all, hadn't that been what had driven Erega into this mad plan in the first place?

Her mind whirred as she twisted every disparate thread into a thick cord of narrative worthy of Bai Junjie. Perhaps someday, she thought, she'd even write a book and tell this story herself.

"What would you like us to toast to, Your Brilliance?" she said, careful to hold her cup the formal way: right hand grasping, left hand supporting from beneath. Kurihara held his similarly, both vessels prodded toward Prince Jimuro like offerings.

Prince Jimuro studied the bottle of sake in his hand pensively for a moment. "We're a culture of small things," he said eventually. "We are a people who always seek the good in the granular. That is the Tomodanese way.

"Everything has a spirit," he continued, gesturing to the room around them. "Every floorboard that was a tree, every mushroom that once grew wild, every grain of dirt lying beneath the rails. With everything we do, we seek to pay tribute to them. It's in the precision of our rituals, and in the eloquence of our language, and in . . ." Inspiration seemed to strike him. ". . . in the very food we eat."

Xiulan glanced at Kurihara. He seemed to be hanging on to every word, albeit with some small measure of confusion. Likely, he was wondering why the prince was lecturing on the basics of Tomodanese philosophy and values. And to be fair to him, Xiulan was starting to wonder that herself.

She leveled her eye at him and jerked her head softly, but with a clear meaning: *Wrap this up*.

"When Sanbu first took me, I refused to eat their food," he said. "They're a loud people who have no patience for the delicate umami of a perfectly fried tempura, or the depths that can be found in even a shallow bowl of udon. They just drown everything in vinegar, and salt, and pepper sauce . . . most of the time, all at once. I even know one dish they have where they stew the flesh of a pig in its own blood."

Kurihara pulled a face, and Xiulan made sure to copy him. In truth, she was actually rather fond of the taste of blood.

"So I insisted that I would only eat food prepared in the Tomodanese style. For three days, I starved myself, until General Erega relented and instructed her cooks to serve me civilized meals. And when she wasn't fighting on the front, Erega would make a point of joining me at mealtimes: me with my food, and she with hers."

Xiulan tapped her finger against the table three times to indicate urgency. She hadn't signed on for a whole speech. She studied Kurihara again, watching for signs that there was some sort of code embedded in this diatribe. But Kurihara continued to listen with polite confusion, so Xiulan saw no need to speak up just yet.

"Most times, we merely discussed matters of state. I asked her for news from the front, and she obliged me. She would gripe to me about the headaches of establishing a new republic, and I obliged her. But no matter the topic of our conversation, it would always play against the backdrop of whatever pungent thing she'd deigned to eat that day. She never said anything about it. I . . . may have been less than gracious once or twice, but for the most part I comported myself like a prince. One day, though, my curiosity got the better of me, and I asked her what she was eating."

A faraway smile dawned on the prince's face. The genuineness of it made Xiulan tense up just a hair. If he was this comfortable in a standoff, then she had to be that much more vigilant.

"I wish either of you could have seen the way her eye lit up," he said. "She told me it was called bistek, and that it was made by stewing cow flesh in calamansi juice and soy sauce. She asked me if I wished to taste it. When I told her I couldn't, she told me she would instruct her cooks to create a batch made with mushrooms instead of cow, and that we would share it at dinner. And come dinnertime, she arrived with two bowls of bistek. Then she set mine in front of me, and waited for me to take my first bite."

The sake was beginning to cool in Xiulan's grip. She kept up her polite, attentive smile, but inside she roiled. She'd never encountered anything about this in her readings. Was this how long all Tomodanese toasts went on? Was he baiting her, hoping she would panic and make a mistake in her impatience?

"The bistek was . . ." Prince Jimuro closed his eyes, remembering. "Earthy. But it was salty, and sweet, and sour, all at once. I'd thought it would just taste like a bowlful of noise, but the flavors . . . they were bigger. Certainly, they were noisier. And yet, somehow, they were balanced. The elements were, against all odds, a harmonious whole."

"So the barbarians are wasteful and loud where we're understated and elegant?" Kurihara chuckled. "Illuminating, but hardly news."

Prince Jimuro shook his head. "Not quite, I'm afraid. I confess, the flavors were rather strong for my refined palate. I couldn't finish the bowl in front of me."

Xiulan suppressed a smug smile. She'd heard similar things about the Tomodanese and their inability to handle the powerful flavors of Shang cooking.

"But General Erega laughed and told me she was grateful I tried it at all. And when I asked why, she told me something I haven't forgotten: that to share a table with someone is to share everything." He hefted his bottle higher, inviting them to clink against it at last. "To sharing a table."

"*To sharing a table,*" she and Kurihara both echoed, touching their cups to the bottle. She brought her cup to her lips and tipped it back, trying not to grimace against the burning it left on her tongue and throat. She plastered a smile on as she set her cup down . . .

. . . and noticed that both Prince Jimuro and Kurihara were staring at her: Prince Jimuro with grim satisfaction, Kurihara with dawning fury.

"K—" Xiulan tried to shout, but Prince Jimuro hurled the bottle of sake straight at her face. She only barely ducked it in time, and the bottle swept the trilby right off the top of her head. It shattered against the compartment wall, showering the floor with porcelain and sake. She threw her metal cup back at him, but despite their closeness it went three full feet wide of his head.

With a roar, Kurihara plunged his hand into his kimono. Xiulan threw a long punch at the point of his elbow, which jammed his hand deeper into its folds. By the time she turned her attention back to the Iron Prince, he'd vaulted over the table, cutting off her access to the door. He braced himself against the wall and threw a punch. She snatched her sake-soaked hat off the table where it'd landed, and shoved its open mouth straight into the path of his fist. The hat swallowed the prince's fist just long enough for her to finally shout, "*Kou!*"

The small compartment was showered in black light. And then the light was gone, replaced with a whippy tail and gnashing teeth.

At her direction, Kou flung himself at Kurihara, who screamed as the rat-shade pinned him to the floor. Jimuro made to do the same to Xiulan, but she held up a finger. "Not so fast, Your Brilliance," she said.

When Prince Jimuro's eyes flickered to the other side of the table, they would see that his lover's throat was nestled just beneath Kou's sharp teeth. The terrorist had frozen where he lay. His hand was clear of his kimono, but his gun only half raised. He gritted his teeth and held his breath.

A near-identical expression looked out at Xiulan from behind the prince's glasses. But thankfully, he was staying put. She exhaled a sigh of relief, and retrieved her pipe from where it had fallen to the floor. She slipped it back into her coat and rose. Now that the immediate danger was over, they could find Lee and get off this abominable train at last.

"A wise choice, Prince Jimuro," she said. Already, she felt her confidence returning to her. "Now, as I was saying before, we really must—"

From the adjoining car, she heard glass shattering and a high scream. For just a moment, her attention strayed. Had that been Lee's voice? What was going on? Was there—?

There was the roar of a gunshot. The flash of a muzzle.

Then, nothing.

CHAPTER TWENTY

LEE

Steel Cicadas materialized in every corner of the dining car, donning masks as they rose. Some appeared from the adjacent passenger cars. Some even stood up from the tables at which they'd been kneeling and eating. Screams erupted, then died just as quickly once people saw the glint of gun barrels and the shimmer of sword blades.

At the bar, Lee had already altered her posture. Gone was the woman whose charm could open any door or any dress. She was back to her natural state: a shadow, seldom considered but always there.

She snatched up a small paring knife from the bar, which the bartender had been using to slice fruit. Its blade was short, barely the size of a shiv, but it would do. She palmed it and hugged the wall.

"We don't wish to harm anyone," said a woman with sharp, beautiful features that were apparent even beneath her cicada mask. She held a pistol in each hand, thumbs on hammers. "We, the Steel Cicadas, are fighting for your freedom!"

"But freedom requires sacrifice from everyone," Iwanbo chimed in. "With apologies to everyone looking to get off before, this train will now be going express to Hagane. We apologize for the inconvenience, but this is the only way."

Worried murmurs kicked up around the room. Iwanbo only let them continue for a few moments before he held up his gun again. Silence fell like a curtain.

"As long as you cooperate," the first Cicada said, "you have nothing to fear from us. What we're doing is for the good of the future of Tomoda. The Steel Cicadas thank you."

Iwanbo grunted. "Return to your meals," he said, as if their interruption had been no more than a random burst of dinner theater.

Passengers exchanged uneasy glances. Some continued to murmur. One child had started to cry into the folds of his father's coat. Nonetheless, they stayed put. No one looked like they were ready to try their luck at being a hero.

Lee cursed her luck. A would-be hero would've been the perfect distraction. Now she was just going to have to make one of her own.

She eyed the cigarette in her one hand, and the whiskey in the other.

Quietly, she tipped the rest of the whiskey onto the floor, the sound of its splash swallowed by the grinding of train wheels. She flicked off all the excess ash from her cigarette into the nearest ashtray, leaving behind a glowing orange tip. And then she let it fall from her fingers. It tumbled end over end as it fell to the floor, seemingly in slow motion—

—and immediately fizzled on contact with the liquid before going out with a tiny stream of smoke.

Lee sighed. "Just my fucking luck," she muttered, before seizing a glass candle off the countertop and hurling it to the floor. The glass shattered hard enough to make every head turn her way, and the fire bloomed fast enough to keep every head turned her way.

But by the time they were all looking at her, she wasn't there anymore.

As screams and shouts erupted in her wake, she slid past the metal galley door, toward the narrow walkway that would connect her with the rear passenger and baggage cars. But as she reached for the door that would take her to the back of the train, it slammed open.

A broad-shouldered woman in a soaked gray suit and a cicada mask bulled right past her, not even bothering to close the door behind her as she ran.

Lee didn't stop to consider her good luck. She just ran for it.

Her short hair was caught between the wind whipping through it and the rain that plastered it to her face. She pushed heavy strands out of her eyes and tottered on, her normally sure feet unsteady on the slick iron walkway.

The door was heavy and meant to be metalpacted, so she struggled to slide it open by hand. She had to put her whole body into it. When it finally shuddered open wide enough for her to slip through, she threw herself in, didn't bother to shut it behind her, and shouted: "*Bootst—*"

She caught herself just in time. She'd been expecting a fight, having given up the element of surprise. But instead of Cicada hijackers, she saw the bodies of three well-dressed women and men strewn across the floor. Two were still breathing, but one lay in a pool of her own blood, a fresh gunshot in her chest.

Lee's breath caught. She was getting flashbacks to the slaughterhouse again. The smell of blood was as sharp in her nostrils as chopsticks scraping on a plate. It wasn't like she couldn't handle blood, but somehow all she could think of was Lefty, and what had remained of him when she'd finally found him.

As she stumbled through the car, one of the seating compartments slid open. A scared-looking man with a thick mustache raised an umbrella with a shout, and then brought it down on her head. But even in her rattled state, she batted him aside with ease, and he spilled right to the floor. "Please don't hurt me!" he cried.

Lee bit back the rejoinder on her tongue. Far as she was concerned, the wallet she'd lifted from him was enough of a comeback. She slammed the door shut in his face and continued on.

The rearmost car was for baggage. In the dim, flickering light, she saw stacks on stacks of bags and trunks. A thin stream of water traced its way down the center of the floor, leading straight back to the wide-open door at the very back of the train. Already her mind was at work: Someone had forced their way onto the *Crow's Flight,* taken out the three guards in the adjoining car, and was probably fighting their way to the front of the train right now, where lay the ultimate prize: the princeling.

And, Lee thought with a sudden chill, Xiulan.

For the first time, she realized that when she'd seen trouble just now, she'd run straight for the exit. It was the smart thing to do. It was the kind of thing that let her walk away from bad times, while others didn't.

But that left Xiulan in the lurch.

Heh, she thought. *Looks like you haven't forgotten the rule after all.*

No, this was different, Lee tried to assure herself. The princess was a capable young woman. Didn't have the street smarts to know a shadow from a shade, but she'd read enough books to get by. She'd proven herself a capable fighter, a better linguist than Lee ever could've been, and on top of all that she had Kou watching her back. So Lee wasn't running out on Xiulan; she was just respecting the princess's skills by trusting her to get the job done. It was what she would've done with Lefty, or any of her partners that had come before. What was any different about this time?

She felt another twinge along her pactmark. Bootstrap was pawing at her again, barking to be let out. With growing unease, Lee pushed her aside again so she could think.

Her mind flitted to the forest last night. To a small body, slipping into her arms as easily as a blade between her ribs. To soft fingers in her hair. To lips, parted with inviting shyness. To—

She shook herself out of the memory's grasp. She'd kissed plenty of her partners. More of them than not, and she'd done plenty more besides. But a kiss wasn't a contract. It didn't compel her to walk herself right back into a death trap, especially after she'd just gotten away clean.

Carefully, she stepped across the baggage car to the open doorway. She squinted against the steady spray of rain and wind in her face, and felt her dress sag as it took on more and more water. The clouds above had blotted out the stars and the moon, but one glance at the wooden railroad ties below was all she needed to tell her how fast the train was going. They looked as if they were being thrown out behind the *Crow's Flight* one by one, like scraps of meat tossed into the snapping jaws of the dark.

Her first thought was that she could never make the jump. Even if she tucked and rolled, like she'd done so often back when she was riding the rails, at this speed she'd break half her bones. In the old days, that had meant she would just stick it out and hope the train would wind up somewhere with good weather.

But while she could never make that jump . . . Bootstrap could.

At least, she was pretty sure. Having a shade was new for her, so she wasn't completely clear on the limits of her partner's body just yet. Shades were physical, but they were also magical, and that meant things got kind of fuzzy when you wanted to talk limits. Riding Bootstrap didn't feel right; Lee knew in her gut that the two of them just didn't have that kind of bond. But if she did saddle up, at least for a minute, she knew Bootstrap could get her a safe landing.

An ache grew inside her as she felt Bootstrap barking again. Even without her summoned, Lee could understand her. *This isn't the pact.* Not an accusation. Just a fact.

Anger and annoyance surged through her—not Bootstrap's, but her own. There was a time when she wouldn't have even hesitated to take this way out. Only royals did stupid things like risking their necks, since they always knew deep down that, in the end, things would fall in their favor. Women like Lee didn't have that luxury. So just because Heaven hadn't blessed Xiulan with the wits to keep her head down, now that was Lee's problem?

She looked to her right: to the closed door, beyond which lay her partner, her pact . . . and certain danger.

She looked to her left: out the open door, to the rainy night and the freedom that awaited her past its threshold.

And she tasted vomit in her throat as she remembered her only rule.

CHAPTER TWENTY-ONE

JIMURO

The gunshot rang out.

The rat-shade disappeared in a flash of inky black light.

The Shang princess crumpled to the floor.

"*Kosuke!*" Jimuro screamed. "*What did you do?*"

Spirits take him. The Shang princess lay dead, and with her died any hopes Tomoda had of leniency from their former enemies. If it had been Erega's daughter at his feet, he could have expected terrifying wrath from the general, and she was a reasonable woman. The Crane Emperor of Shang, by all reports, was anything but. It didn't matter how much both of their nations had been bled dry by the war. It didn't matter how much Sanbu and Dahal might object. It didn't even matter if this princess, twenty-eighth as she was, was one of his lesser children. The Crane Emperor didn't tolerate weakness, and he would go to any lengths to avenge a slight.

With a twitch of his finger, Kurihara Kosuke had just doomed Tomoda.

"Jimuro," Kosuke said. "Are you all right? Did she—?"

"*You idiot!*" Jimuro roared. "*You just murdered the Crane Emperor's daughter! Do you have any idea what you've just done?*"

"Saved your life, for one thing," Kosuke said, his demeanor chilling. "And for another, I didn't kill her."

With a mad surge of hope, Jimuro swung his head back toward the princess. Sure enough, beneath the voluminous folds of her coat, he could see her chest rising and falling.

"I shot her mask," Kosuke said quietly. "They're not just for show, you know. We knew going into this that we'd be going to war. So we dressed for the occasion."

Gingerly, Jimuro approached the princess. He peeled back her long bang to reveal that her mask was dented but not broken. Carefully, he removed it from her face, where a palm-sized bruise the color of a plum had begun to form. She looked as if someone had spilled wine on her face, but otherwise she was intact.

He breathed deep and nearly collapsed to the floor with relief. The room started to come back into focus. His country wasn't doomed. He wouldn't go down in history as the last Steel Lord. He spared a pittance of concern for the Shang princess, but that only went so far. After all, she had just been trying to arrest him.

"If you're done having your panic attack, Jimuro . . ." Kosuke said, "I can handle things from here." He stepped forward, holding a hand out for the mask.

Jimuro frowned but handed over the mask anyway. "What's going on out there?" he said. "I heard a woman screaming."

A fleeting look of . . . something . . . crossed Kosuke's face. It was gone before Jimuro could identify it, but he didn't have to identify it to raise his suspicions.

Slowly, Jimuro rose back to his feet. He swayed gently to keep his footing on the moving train. "Kosuke," he said carefully. "This train has now passed four stations it was supposed to stop at. Would you know anything about that?"

"You've just been through an attack," Kosuke said. "You shouldn't worry yourself with—"

"I need you to look me in the eye right now," Jimuro said, summoning up his mother's mettle. "And I need you to tell your Iron Prince that you didn't hijack this train."

Kosuke swallowed, annoyed. He bowed his head. "I can't lie to my prince."

"Spirits take us both, Kosuke!" Jimuro said, blood rising in his ears. He wanted to kick the table, even though he knew it would only lead to a set of broken toes. "There are innocent people on this train who were just trying to go home to their families. We're supposed to be protecting and serving these people, not holding them hostage."

"The Steel Cicadas are protecting them," Kosuke said. "We're asking a small sacrifice from relatively few citizens, in order to ensure your safe and speedy return to Hagane. It's no different than levying a new tax."

"This isn't a *tax*," Jimuro growled. He could hear his mother's voice in the back of his head warning him to keep his temper in check, but he was far past that now. "It's a crime."

Kosuke laughed. "They're the same thing, to hear Lord Sugayama talk about it."

"I don't care what Lord Sugayama thinks, and I don't care what you have to say about this, either," Jimuro said. "I'm your prince, soon to be your Steel Lord, and I order you to stop this train at once."

"I'm afraid not, Your Brilliance," Kosuke said, bowing again. "Apologies. We captured the engine room as soon as we boarded. The crew are unharmed," he added hastily, "but we'd rather they suffer in the name of a greater cause, instead of for nothing at all."

Jimuro gritted his teeth. He didn't want to believe what he was hearing, but there was absolutely no way around it. Tala had been right. Spirits take him, Tala had been right about everything. "I could order you to take your own life, and you'd be honor-bound to obey."

Kosuke paled for just a moment, but he held strong. "That's true," he allowed. "But you won't do that. We're fighting for the same side, and we share far more than just a cause. Even when we were kids, I always knew I'd be your right hand someday." He reached for Jimuro's hand. "You wouldn't cut off your right hand, would you?"

Jimuro snarled with disgust and yanked his hand out of Kosuke's reach. He was so frustrated, so furious, so consumed by rage that he just wanted to scream and cry. He had faced his first challenge as a ruler: knowing who to trust. And right out the gate, he'd failed. This was all his people had to look forward to: failure after failure. The cumulative weight of his failures would press Tomoda deeper into the sea, and at their center, collapsing beneath their bulk, would be Jimuro, the last Steel Lord.

His shoulders slumped. If he was going to be pathetic, at least he could also be useful. "That doesn't change the fact that a woman screamed just now," Jimuro said. "I'm going to go check on her."

Kosuke sidled between the door and Jimuro. He tapped it, and the metal lock clicked shut. "We don't know if there are other hostiles on this train, Your Brilliance," he said. "Until my Cicadas have come to let me know the train is secure, I can't let you out of my sight."

"You don't think I could force my way out?" said Jimuro.

"I think you don't want to leave me alone with an enemy of the state."

Jimuro's eyes narrowed. "You wouldn't."

"You're on this train because you've shown, time and time again, that you don't understand what I would or wouldn't do for my country. And maybe you'll get even with me once you sit the throne I'm helping you take back. But when you leave a room, people will always whisper to each other: *There's the Steel Lord who was afraid to rule.*" And then he knelt next to the Shang princess and rapped the bruised half of her face with his knuckles. "Wake up, Princess."

Princess Xiulan groaned to life, her body twitching and folding in on itself as if she were a swatted fly. Prince Jimuro watched, rooted to the spot.

"You speak good Tomodanese, but you don't know how to drink like one," Kosuke crooned. "You didn't realize we tap our cups to the table before we sip, as a sign of respect for its spirit. So perhaps your understanding of our culture isn't as complete as you thought. That's why I'm going to teach you about it." And he held up the steel cicada mask.

"Kosuke . . ." Jimuro said.

Kosuke ignored him. "The Tomodanese people can bond with the bones of the world," he said with deadly softness. "We can command their shape, their hardness . . . or even their temperature."

The princess surged up, trying to escape, but Kosuke slammed the steel mask hard onto her face and shoved her back down to the floor, pinning her there with one arm.

"I'm going to ask you some questions now," said Kosuke. "For every one you answer falsely, I'll raise the temperature of your mask twenty degrees. Did you know that skin starts to burn just after forty? It takes nearly four times that much to burn hair. I could leave your little bang here completely intact, if I wanted to. And that'd be just as well for you; you'd have to grow out a whole lot more hair to hide the boiling ruin that would be your face."

"Wait a moment," said Jimuro. His stomach had turned from Kosuke's little speech, but he forced gruff, regal strength into his voice as he continued: "She's a princess, clearly operating outside her father's permission. I have to treat with her father tomorrow. Our negotiations won't go well if I begin them by returning his daughter to him well done."

"You don't need to know anything about it, Jimuro," Kosuke said, not breaking his stare into the helpless princess's mask. In its smooth, shiny surface, Jimuro could just make out his friend's twisted reflection. "Officially, you were never here. You've never met Princess Xiulan in your life. Your hands will be clean, and Tomoda's future will be secure." His grip tightened on the mask. "Now, Princess: Tell us how you found His Brilliance."

"No," Jimuro said sharply, and this time he meant it. He'd already caved to Kosuke once. He wasn't about to let himself do it again. "This country will be mine to govern tomorrow, and I will not allow my subjects to torture in my name."

"These outlanders deserve worse than torture," Kosuke spat. "The Shang, the Sanbunas, the spirits-forsaken Dahali . . . we showed them a better way to live, and they butchered us in gratitude. They don't deserve our decency or our mercy, and they should live in eternal fear of the day we have the strength to strike back again."

"If you do this," Jimuro whispered, "they'll do everything they can to make sure we never do."

"Tomoda is the steel of the world," Kosuke said. "And steel does not break."

The door tore itself off its own frame, revealing a stooped, monstrous figure of muscle and bare bone that had to duck under the train's ceiling. Before Kosuke could even react, Dimangan batted him aside with a swat of his huge hand. Kosuke was lifted off his feet, slamming so hard into the window that it cracked where he hit it. He slid to the floor with a groan, unconscious.

Another hand wrapped itself around Jimuro's forearm. One with strong, callused fingers.

One he'd recognize anywhere.

"We have to go, Your Brilliance," said Sergeant Tala, yanking off the cicada mask she'd been wearing. A thrill ran through Jimuro at the sight of her. Until he felt her hawklike stare pierce him, he didn't realize how much he'd missed it.

He wanted to ask how she'd found him. How she'd caught up to him.

Why she'd come back for him again.

Instead, they ran.

CHAPTER TWENTY-TWO

TALA

HOURS AGO

She was an hour off the main road when she finally gave in.

There were no convenient woods to use for cover, so she had to content herself with the miles of gently swaying grass that rippled in every direction. The only breaks in the scenery were the distant road to her left, and the even more distant mountains to her right, whose faces the summertime had turned green.

It was here that she finally pointed to the ground, braced herself for the pain, and muttered, "Dimangan."

Mang came out ready for a fight: fists clenched, muscles bunched, head on a swivel. "Report," he rumbled in his low, deep voice. "Where is he?"

"You know what he did?" Tala said. "How?"

"I don't know what the bastard did," Mang said, "but I know how he made you feel." He trailed off, finally noticing the empty field they stood in. "Wait. Where is he, actually?"

"Among the Cicadas," Tala said bitterly. She was already in rough shape, but now with Mang out she could barely see straight for the pain.

"Yeah, I don't know what that means," Mang said. Then he finally caught sight of her tattered sleeve and the long, cauterized cut beneath it. *"Your arm!"* He looked around wildly again. "If that steelhound scum was the one who cut you, I—"

"She's not a problem anymore," Tala said quietly. A vision of Harada flashed in front of her, face blueing as the noose around her neck tightened. Though Tala's hands were empty, she could almost feel the tightness of the garrote on her fingers, the heaviness of her blade—

"Stop it," she growled at herself.

"Stop what?" Mang said, still looking around. "What happened to the prince? Where did he go? *What did he do?*"

Rather than at Mang, Tala looked at the ground. The ground wouldn't judge her. "He made a choice."

She waited for him to say something, but when she finally looked up, she saw that he was just standing there, staring at her. He frowned tightly, but his huge brown eyes glinted with something else: pity.

An irritated urge arose in her to fill the silence. " 'You'll fight alongside them, as long as it means you get to fight,' " she quoted.

"Lala—" Mang began, but Tala held up a hand, and he gave her a respectful nod before falling silent again.

"It got under my skin, Mang. Worse than any steelhound's bullet or blade. But I couldn't just drag you back out to prove you wrong, so . . ." She waded through the sharp pounding in her head. Having Mang out was never easy on her thoughts, but this was too important for her to get lost in the weeds. "I thought I could prove it to him. And for a second there, I really thought I was gonna. I thought he was more than just some steelhound, and he was seeing I wasn't just a savage."

She detected the scent of rain on the air, but when she breathed in, she could have sworn she smelled the tangy, salty aroma of adobo. When she blinked, for that brief moment she wasn't in the field anymore, but back in the cabin up north. The mist was clearing from her eyes as the venom left her system at last, and Jimuro was standing at the stove, humming to himself in the early-morning sun.

Her eyes opened. The grass around her bowed low as the wind picked up. Overhead, the clouds thickened like a broth on the boil. In the distance, thunder rumbled like a distant train.

"I can't believe I thought . . ." She trailed off. She wanted to be angry. Anger was a comfortable feeling that put warmth in her belly and strength in her limbs. But now she felt neither warmth nor strength.

"Disappointment," Mang rumbled at last. "That's the word you're looking for."

Tala frowned at him.

He shrugged and tapped the pactmark on the back of his head. "It's not like I can help it, Lala."

Her fingers raked through her hair, resting on the back of her scalp, where her own matching mark lay hidden. Pain radiated out from it as if it were an exit wound. He was right, of course. Disappointment hung on her like a stench, and she knew in her heart that its source was not Jimuro.

When have you ever tried to—

She swallowed. "You're right." At those words, something cracked inside her. "I've been a shit sister, Mang."

"I once read a play where a sister killed her brother, then slept with his son," he said. "By that metric, you're doing just fine."

She could sense his own feelings: that familiar concern that reared its head when anyone in his sight was displeased. That was her brother, all right. If anyone was unhappy, he had to do something about it. "Stop it," she said. "I'm serious. You were right the other day. I've been living like my soul's my own, and it hasn't been for ten years, not after what I did to you. That thing you said yesterday, about being afraid to stop fighting? That was true. I proved it."

It was her brother's turn to frown. "I said that because I was angry. I wanted to hurt you."

"The way I hear it, the truth hurts," said Tala. She sat down heavily in the grass, then lowered herself onto her back. Her arm throbbed from the cut Harada had scored on her, but the soft grass beneath it helped. Though the grass was tall enough to swallow her whole, it barely came up to Mang's chest when he sat down next to her.

For a long while they sat, brother and sister. The clouds darkened, the air grew heavier, and the cicadas sang on. She scowled at the noise. They were rotten bugs, inescapable on this shades-forsaken island. But she and Mang had grown used to the pain that bound them to each other, and in time she grew used to the cicadas' song as well.

"I did a terrible thing to you," she said at last.

Mang shifted. "I asked a terrible thing *of* you."

"And I said yes," Tala insisted.

"I wasn't your slave then, and I'm not now."

"I gave myself the power to make you one, if I wanted."

"And you've never used it."

She shook her head. "It doesn't matter. I should've known better. I was stupid."

"You were *ten*."

She lifted a hand and stared up at it. When she twitched her fingers, fresh shoots of pain accompanied each motion. "Do you remember the first time I summoned you back?"

"I thought I was going to pass out from the pain," Mang said. "I was certain you would. But you didn't. Not even then. You were a little girl covered in Ina and Ama's blood, and you carried my weight anyway."

She leaned against his shoulder, ignoring the way his spines dug into her sides. "You've been carrying mine." She stared at the swaying grass another long moment before asking, "If we could undo it . . ."

He shook his huge head. "We're not going down that road, Lala."

Her muscles protested, but she sat up just the same. Panic seized her. "Wait," she said. "Please, I—"

Dimangan shook his head. "You summoned me here because you needed me," he said. "And I came because I knew it was bad. This is a time when you need me to build you back up, Lala. That's what I'm going to do, and nothing else."

Fear bubbled to the surface of her mind. With it, she felt a spike of anxiety: Beaky, eager to get out. Him, she ignored. This moment didn't belong to him. "So if you answer my question, it'll tear me down, then?"

"I didn't say that," said Mang. "But I know no matter what I say, you'll find a way to take responsibility and beat yourself up over it. I swear to the shades, you were born scowling." He smiled, in a distant kind of way. "So, spill it: Why do you care what the prince of the world's worst kingdom thinks about you? Why do you care if he just sent away his best chance at seeing tomorrow? He doesn't even eat meat."

"I noticed," Tala said, thinking once more of the mushroom adobo, its bowl warm in her fingers. "It's just—no. It's stupid."

"Lala."

"I thought he was changing, too, okay?" The words burst from her like blood from a wound. "It was just small things, but I was starting to see why Erega trusted him. I was starting to have second thoughts. And do you know the one thing that's worse than being wrong?"

"Being right when you don't want to be?"

She shot him a look. "You reading my mind again?"

He shook his head again. "You're just predictable."

She chuckled mirthlessly, then lowered herself back into the grass. She wanted to lie here, letting the soil and grass creep up her body until the ground swallowed her whole. She wanted to just fucking disappear.

But even as she thought it, she knew she couldn't. She'd let herself forget before, but she never could forget again: Her soul was not her own to waste.

"Where do you want to go?" she said.

Mang's head turned. "What?"

"We're partners, but I've never let you drive," she said. "The way the prince chose Kurihara over me . . . it's not that different from me choosing him over you. In fact, it's pretty much fucked."

"Language, Lala."

"You didn't ding me when I said 'shit' earlier."

"I was going to bring it up later."

"Point is." She tensed, suddenly full of energy. This was something she could do. If she couldn't be a soldier anymore, then she could be a sister. It was the job she should've been doing all along. "It's your turn to choose, Mang. We're free. Dandelions in the wind. Where do you want to drift?"

Mang was thoughtful. And then he stood and said, "We're going to find Iron Prince Jimuro."

Tala would've fallen over with surprise, if she hadn't already been lying down. She sat right up again, certain the thrashing pool of pain in her head had addled her hearing. "What?"

"You heard me." Through their emotional connection, she felt resolve ripple off him. "We're going to find him. We're going to pull his head out of his . . . *ass*. And then we're going to drag him to Hagane by his ear if we have to."

Tala stared. "But . . . you hate the Tomodanese. And swearing."

"Of course I do," he said. "But I love you more, Lala. It matters to you to see this through, and that means it matters to me." He stretched. "Which way is Gorudo?"

She sat there, overwhelmed by the love she felt for her brother. She couldn't fathom what it must have taken for him to make this choice. What—

"Lala," Mang said gently. "Time's of the essence. Which way is Gorudo?"

He must have pulled the name from her thoughts, she decided. Still numb with affection and disbelief, she pointed.

In the direction she'd been walking.

His gaze followed her finger. "You were heading there anyway."

She hung her head as a bitter laugh escaped her. "I was really hoping you'd talk me out of it." She blinked, her lashes suddenly heavy with tears. She had a lot of feelings happening at once, and she was no great multitasker. She didn't know which of those feelings had triggered her tears, but she was grateful for the release.

She needed to be clear-eyed and sharp when she saw the prince again.

She started to stand, but suddenly Mang reached down and scooped her right off the ground and placed her on his shoulders. She sat uneasily on the slabs of muscle there. *"Mang!"*

"Only way we'll get there in time," her brother said. "You point, I'll run."

She pointed.

He ran.

With no cash, she'd resorted to sneaking onto the train platform at Kuronaga. It wasn't difficult; the rain had scared all the other passengers indoors, leaving her to lurk in the shadows just at the platform's edge.

She shivered against the cold and pulled her tattered suit jacket tighter to her body. It was beyond waterlogged by now, but it was the only protection she had. She hoped the train would come soon. The last thing she needed was to fight her way back from the brink of despair, only to die of a fucking cold.

In the dark, she acutely felt Mang's absence. But once they'd reached civilization, she'd reluctantly put him back. The absence of pain would have been a relief, but now more than ever she felt like it was something she deserved to live with all the time. After all, Mang had to.

But any kind of shade would have drawn unwanted attention. Mang would have drawn that, plus blazing guns. So, away he went.

A separate pulse in her chest told her Beaky was in a fine mood. She sent back some annoyance of her own, along with an image of the rain falling all around her. What bird in his right mind would even want to be out in this?

Resigned grumbling from Beaky was her reply. She did feel bad for not letting him out, but now wasn't the right time. She relented, and sent him a feeling of reassurance: If things went bad on this train, he'd be stretching his wings sooner rather than later.

This was madness, she told herself. She was going to sneak right onto a train full of dangerous terrorists who specifically hated her. She was going to march right up to their leader, who hated her most of all, and demand he release the world's most valuable hostage. And if he wasn't charmed by her good looks and pleasant tone, she was going to have to fight her way back off the train with one hand, while using the other to drag the Iron Prince of Tomoda behind her.

And somehow, she was going to do it all after two days without coffee.

Fuck. Coffee, she thought. That was what she could go for now. Warm, with some of the sweetened canned milk they'd started getting in their rations at the end of the war. The boost to her brain would've been nice, but at this point she just missed the taste of it. It was how she'd started almost every day of her life since she'd begun this fight. Its absence, more than almost anything else, had underlined for her just how far into the weeds she'd gone.

A distant rumble shook the ground beneath her feet. A blade of light slashed at her eyes. Her stomach tightened as she turned to face the source. There was no mistaking it: That was the southbound train, all right. She wasn't completely certain it was the right train. But based on the train schedule she'd consulted at the station, this was the only one that could have been coming from Gorudo. It was a good ten minutes early, but if that meant ten fewer minutes shivering in the rain, she wasn't about to complain.

A few passengers began to stream out of the station and onto the platform, though they still huddled beneath its bowed awnings. She caught snatches of them muttering to one another, mostly wondering why the train had come so early. But Tala was clued in when she didn't hear the telltale screech of the brakes on the rails: The train was early because it hadn't made any stops before, and it wasn't about to stop here, either.

Despite the rain, her mouth instantly went dry. The train's haste erased all doubt in her mind that this was the right one, but that presented a new challenge: How was she supposed to get on?

The train's wake hit her like a wall of wind, nearly blowing her off her feet. She staggered to keep her footing, then gritted her teeth. She was in no kind of shape to do this, but she couldn't see any other choice.

As the train sped past, she glanced warily at the bystanders on the platform. They were about to see a hell of a show.

She broke into a run, then threw out a hand behind her. *"Dimangan!"* she yelled, and resisted crying out as her brother erupted out from behind her. He stumbled on his first step, but picked up speed until he was easily keeping up with her.

"The train?" he shouted.

She gritted her teeth, unable to trust her voice, and nodded.

He shot her one look of warning, then nodded, picked her up, and hurled her at the train's receding rear car.

She threw her arm out behind her and willed for Mang to withdraw. He disappeared in a flash of light, and she felt his spirit rejoin hers. It was reassuring, but only as long as she didn't consider how fast she was hurtling toward the back of the train.

For a long moment, she hung in the air, legs and arms pumping desperately to give her as much lift as she could get. She kept her eyes riveted on the metal ladder rungs above the train's back landing, praying as she sank to the ground that she would be close enough to—

Her right hand managed to close itself around a rung, but her left arm was still weak from her duel with Harada. The metal ladder was slick with rain, and her fingers slipped right off it. She tried to swing her feet onto one of the lower rungs, but her boots' old soles were too smooth to get purchase. She was holding on to the train by a single arm, and already she felt its strength failing as she dangled mere feet from the speeding ground.

She screwed up her face with concentration. *"Beaky!"* she shouted, then sent him as strong a pulse of will as she could manage.

For a long moment, she felt nothing except the gradual slip of her fingers as her fist unraveled.

And then a beak closed around her ankle. Fighting the momentum the train had given Tala, Beaky flapped his wings as hard as he could. And with each passing second, he shoved her boot closer and closer to the ladder. Tala pulled with all her strength, as every muscle in her core lit up with soreness and pain.

Then relief flooded her as she felt her boot sole get a grip on the ladder at last.

Beaky released her, and she braced herself against the ladder to swing the rest of herself aboard the train. As her heart pounded against her ribs, Beaky settled on the back railing of the train and clacked his beak with disapproval.

Tala swung herself onto the landing, bending her knees to absorb the impact. "I," she panted, "probably deserved that."

Beaky's head whipped around, slapping her palm with the flat of his beak.

"Ow!" Tala said, yanking her stinging hand away from him. She glared at him for a moment, then sighed. "Yeah, that too." She reached into her coat and pulled out the heavy Tomodanese pistol she'd been given as a parting present. She was all too eager to return it to sender.

She and Beaky exchanged a nod. She threw open the door and rushed in.

Dimangan gave her a fleeting look of understanding as she recalled him again, leaving her alone with the prince.

Well, Kurihara was on the floor, as was some other Cicada in white she hadn't seen before. But Tala didn't give a shit about them.

She ran, Jimuro at her side. Summoning and dismissing her shades so many times in a row was taking a toll on her spirit, but she forced herself to run just the same. She was so far down the path now, she was officially out of other choices.

"Your timing's impeccable," Jimuro said. "I've had quite a day."

"Yeah?" Tala said, grabbing the handle of the door that would lead them back to the dining car. "And whose fault is that, then?" She immediately regretted it. Crazy as it was, she was actually happy to see him, and even happier that he was as keen to escape as she was. Why did she always fall back on snapping at him like this?

Jimuro tapped the door, and it sprang open at his touch. "I'm too glad to see you to have a good comeback."

Tala grinned. "Your comebacks are shit, anyway."

It wasn't until they'd burst into the dining car that she realized she'd just smiled at him.

The first time she'd come through here, she'd dashed through with her head down and her borrowed mask on. She would've demolished anyone who got in her way, but no one in the whole dining car had even tried. Now, though, she burst back into the worst kind of target-rich environment: a relatively small number of hostiles, scattered among a few dozen innocents. One of them was beating out the dying remains of a fire, but the rest immediately turned their eyes right to herself and the prince.

Fortunately, she figured, Jimuro had juice. The Cicadas were fanatics, but they were fanatics loyal to him. If he ordered them to let him pass, they would.

Iwanbo reacted with a start when he saw Jimuro. "Your Bril—sir!" he said. "What's going on? Where is Lord Kurihara?"

To his credit, Tala didn't have to prompt the prince. Jimuro stepped forward and said, "There's been a change of plans. Let these people go and let me pass."

But Iwanbo's gaze had strayed from him, landing squarely on Tala. "The slaver," he spat.

"There's no time for that," Jimuro said as the word *slaver* sent ripples of whispers across the hostages. And more than a few, Tala saw, were beginning to eye the prince with more than a passing curiosity.

"Move it along," she muttered to him in Sanbuna.

He nodded, then addressed Iwanbo again. "You heard my orders, Iwanbo. Do it."

Iwanbo frowned. "I'm sorry, Your—sir. I can't let you leave in the company of that barbarian. You have to—"

Tala moved like chain lightning. Iwanbo tried to snap his shotgun up and fire at her, but Tala brought her leg down on its barrel just as he pulled the trigger. The gun roared and spat flame at the floor, and with a scream Iwanbo collapsed, clutching at the bloody ruins of his foot.

The air filled with more shouts and screams. Some passengers hit the deck, while others fled to one end of the car or another. Tala cursed. The prince was her first priority, but she didn't want anyone getting hurt if she could help it.

Even if they're Tomodanese, she added sourly.

Another Cicada whipped up a pair of revolvers. But before she could pull their triggers, Prince Jimuro was there. With expert finesse, he grabbed one gun and twisted it hard. The woman's finger caught on the trigger guard and broke with a *snap* even Tala could hear. The gun fell off her broken finger, and Jimuro nimbly caught it by the barrel. The Cicada only had a moment to gawk at her own prince before he caught her under the chin with a fierce uppercut. She fell to the floor, her metal mask clanging against a table as she hit her head on the way down.

Tala gaped. He'd just attacked one of his own subjects.

To save *her*.

Prince Jimuro flipped the gun, caught it, and fired a round straight into the ceiling. "Get to the front of the train!" he shouted to the civilians, though they were already fleeing in both directions. But as Tala eyed the crowd heading for the front of the train, she saw something: a small woman in a white coat and fedora, pushing back against the crowd and heading for them.

Tala whipped up her gun, ready to fire on her, but the woman had already raised a hand and shouted, *"Kou!"*

Tala did a double take as a white rat-shade materialized in front of her. "Jimuro!" she shouted, moving to put herself in the rat-shade's path. *"Beaky!"*

Black feathers collided with white fur as the two shades fell to the floor in a tangle of wing and fang. She felt Beaky's ferocity in her own heart, but she had to leave him to his own fight. She hefted her gun—

"Don't shoot!" Jimuro shouted. "She's a princess!"

"And I thought one of you was bad enough!" Tala snapped, but she lowered her gun anyway. Jimuro was right. She couldn't risk a diplomatic emergency right now. Her top priority was getting Jimuro off this train.

The princess—Shang, now that Tala had a good look at her—stepped farther into the light. "You are interfering in official Li-Quan business, brave soldier," she said in slurred Tomodanese. She staggered back a step, then caught herself. "I must insist the Iron Prince come with us."

"'Us'?" Tala glanced around for signs of any other Shang. "I don't see an 'us.'"

The Shang princess's expression turned ugly and dark. "I need the Iron Prince alive, soldier. I saw your handiwork in the woods. I have no qualms about avenging it on you, especially if you visited similar atrocities on my partner."

Tala couldn't make heads or tails of what that all was supposed to mean. "This one talks even more than you," Tala said to Jimuro.

"That's what I said."

"Soldier," the princess cut in, and now her voice took on an uncertain edge. She swayed where she stood, like a dry reed in the wind. "I will allow you to leave this train alive if you can give me your assurances that you've left my partner Lee Yeon-Ji unharmed. Is that clear?"

"I don't know shit about your partner!" Tala snapped. "And I don't have time for you." She aimed high and fired off two rapid shots. The lights above the princess's head exploded in sparks, and she recoiled. Tala yanked at Jimuro's arm. *"Go!"*

But then she felt the familiar tingle of spirit energy rejoining with her body, and the pactmark on her chest pulsed. She glanced over her shoulder. Her heart sank. Beaky had discorporated. In the corner of her vision, she saw a white blur as the rat-shade scrabbled over dining tabletops and came to a skidding stop on the hard wooden floor. Its tail lashed and its fangs flashed as it stood its ground, barring their way out.

Tala glanced this way and that. She didn't want to summon Mang, not for this. She was already on her last legs. But that left her with a human opponent she couldn't shoot, and a shade she couldn't beat one-on-one. Tough as she was, you needed to be someone like Kapona to take on a shade by yourself.

The memory of that last night aboard the *Marlin* hung in her head. And just like that, Tala knew what she had to do.

She swiveled herself so that she was facing the princess, leaving Jimuro squared off against the rat-shade. "Jimuro," she muttered. "I've got this."

Jimuro peeked over his shoulder. "What are you—?" he began.

But Tala, the memory of Private Kapona fresh on her mind, charged straight for the Shang princess with a shout.

The princess started, but she was too unsteady on her feet. In a second Tala was on her, a hand on each of the princess's shoulders, lining her up for the perfect headbutt.

Tala saw stars and spots with the impact, but the princess collapsed like a pyramid of mah-jongg tiles. In an eruption of black light, her rat-shade disintegrated. Just as Tala had suspected, she'd taken some kind of head injury, probably a concussion. She wouldn't be out for long, Tala was sure, but it'd be enough for she and Jimuro to make good their escape. Yet somehow, despite the secrecy of their mission, this woman had found them. That meant Tala couldn't just leave her lying there.

She hefted the Shang princess and nodded to the walk-in fridge. "Get the door."

Jimuro looked as if he wanted to object, but clearly he wasn't feeling up to second-guessing Tala at the moment. He tapped it, and it slid open. Unceremoniously, Tala tossed the princess inside, then nodded to Jimuro. The prince looked reluctant for a moment, but nonetheless he tapped the door again, then held his hand on the lock for a moment once it had sealed shut. "I fused the lock, but broke the air lock. She won't escape, but she won't suffocate, either."

This Shang princess's well-being was about as low on Tala's list of priorities as anything, but she needed to be helpful now. "Good enough," she said. "Let's move."

When they charged into the rear passenger car, Tala raised her gun skyward and fired off another shot, which was enough to scatter the frightened passengers in their way. She heard Jimuro calling out apologies as they passed, and suppressed the urge to grin again. Once was quite enough for today.

Then at last, they reached the baggage car. All she had to do was summon Mang one more time, and they'd be home free. In fact, they'd even gained some time thanks to the train's swiftness. She had to give Kurihara credit for that, at least.

But then Jimuro whispered, "No."

Silhouetted in the far doorway—the door she'd ripped open on her way in—was a tall, gaunt man in a sodden coat the color of the night sky. His long black hair hung lank from grease and rain. The stolen pactmarks studding his torso pulsed in a hundred different colors. His lips peeled back, and his guttural voice formed words that fell from his mouth like rotten teeth.

"Give him to me."

CHAPTER TWENTY-THREE

JIMURO

Before Jimuro could do anything, Tala grabbed him by the front of his shirt and shoved him back. She pointed at the man in the purple coat and called, *"Dimangan!"*

As the shade's massive shape solidified, their attacker's eyes narrowed. "The abomination," he growled in Sanbuna. Glowing shapes erupted from his fingertips, solidifying into three shades clustered around him: the snapping turtle, a tiger, and a bear—the black-and-white kind from Shang.

But by then, Dimangan had already re-formed and dropped into the crouch of an angry hound. "You again, huh?" he said to the man in the purple coat. "Guess I didn't hit you hard enough—!"

The tiger-shade pounced, wrapping its huge jaws around the arm Dimangan used to block it. Its teeth sank straight into his flesh, and the wounds began to spark bright magical energy as they closed up. Dimangan roared with pain and thundered forward, grabbing the tiger-shade's body and slamming it down on the spider-shade that had tried to creep past him.

Jimuro couldn't stop staring at the chaos unfolding. The tight quarters gave Dimangan a slight advantage, since only one or two shades could come at him at a time. But tough as he was, he wouldn't be able to keep this up forever. Eventually, the magic keeping him corporeal would exhaust itself, and Jimuro didn't know how long it would be before Tala could summon him again. They had to get out, now.

"Back this way!" he said, pointing to the doors through which they'd just come. Beyond lay the dining and passenger cars, with Kosuke and the others. He didn't know where he stood with them at the moment, but he surely knew where he stood with this man, and it made his choices rather clear.

He expected the sergeant to resist, but she didn't hesitate. "Hold the line!" she shouted to Dimangan as she and Jimuro broke for the door.

Her brother bellowed in reply, but his words turned to a shout as the bear-shade reared up and clawed four wide slashes across his chest.

Tala didn't look back. She gritted her teeth, and a faraway look settled in her eyes, but her strides were steady.

Jimuro cast one last fleeting glance at Dimangan's wide, muscled back as he disappeared through the train doors again. The sight of him fighting so fiercely against overwhelming odds, just to protect Tala . . . even now, as they fled for their lives, all he could think of was his sister Fumiko, and the doomed rescue mission she'd led for him.

He lengthened his own strides. He wouldn't let another sibling's sacrifice be in vain because of him.

He whirled around just as they reached the doors. "What are you doing?" Tala shouted.

"Buying us more time!" Jimuro said, kneeling. He placed his hand on the metal join that tied the baggage car to the rest of the train, and poured his spirit into it. It groaned and creaked as he bonded with it, its iron stubborn in its desire to keep its shape.

But Jimuro was more than iron, he reminded it. He was steel.

The join broke with a loud *clang*, and suddenly the baggage car receded into the dark.

"Come on!" Tala said, grabbing him by the shoulder. "That won't stop him for long!"

His glasses fogged over as he thundered into the passenger car, but even through the haze he could see the naked fear on the passengers' faces. It turned his stomach to look upon them all. They were his people, and they were all in this position because of him. He had to do something.

"Children of Tomoda!" he cried out. Passengers looked up at him, though their panic didn't subside. He exhaled. "My name is Iron Prince Jimuro, son of Steel Lord Yoshiko and rightful heir to the Mountain Throne!"

Now he had their attention. A few compartment doors had opened, their passengers trying to hear better. But Jimuro was most conscious of Tala, who was pointing to the front door imploringly.

"I will offer up full explanations later," Jimuro said, "but right now you are all in the gravest danger you've ever known. I need everyone to get to the front of the train as quickly as you can."

"I'm not going there!" cried one woman. Jimuro recognized her as the one who'd tried to sit with himself and Kosuke. "Those masked people are at the front!"

Jimuro turned to face her, hoping his glasses had unfogged enough for her to see the earnestness in his eyes. "I won't let them hurt you, madam," he said. "You have that promise, on my honor as your prince and Steel Lord . . ." His gaze slid past her to Tala, who stood ready. "I will give you all the best protection that I can."

The woman stared at him for a moment, dumbfounded.

And then she sank into a waist-deep bow. "Your Brilliance," she said, then straightened and ran for the door.

There was a fresh chorus of shouts and screams as people surged after her. Tala tried to yank Jimuro along with them, but he shook his head. "Not until they're clear!"

"Jimuro, this isn't the time!"

"The best time to put your people first is when they're in danger, Tala! There's no time better!"

Tala scowled, then leveled her gun at the back door of the cabin. "What's your plan?"

"We get everyone to the front of the train."

"I was clear on that part."

"And then we detach every car but the first two. If we get everyone aboard to pact with the train's metal and we reduce the weight to just two cars—"

"—we could go fast enough to outrun him," Tala finished. Her scowl lessened, if only a degree. "Smart."

"I have my moments." He fixed his eyes on the door. "Can you feel how he's doing?"

Her annoyance evaporated, replaced by worry. "He's fighting hard," she said. "But he's not invincible. He—"

A bolt of blue energy shot straight through the sealed door, hitting Tala. She staggered back a step, as if the aura had actually had an impact on her. Jimuro knew what that meant: It was what happened when a shade discorporated and rejoined its human partner.

"Sergeant!" Jimuro said. "Are you all right?"

"That was Mang." She glared at the door and steadied herself. "He's coming."

Jimuro knew that when Tala said *he*, she wasn't talking about her brother.

His stomach knotted itself. He looked down at his hands and saw that they were dewy and shaking, like a pair of pale spiders.

"Then we should be going." He nodded to the open door. The passenger car was empty of civilians now. It was just them.

As they stepped out into the rain once more, he saw that the door to the dining car was wide open. The low, warm light within beckoned them forward.

He swallowed. "I'm sorry for everything, Tala," he said. "I mean it: everything."

"There's no time for that now!" said Tala. "We need—"

Jimuro swallowed again, then planted both of his hands on the sergeant's back and shoved her forward as hard as he could.

She stumbled forward onto the landing of the dining car, already pivoting back toward him with a stricken look on her face.

But he'd knelt, laid his hand on the join between cars, and flooded it with his will.

With a *clang,* the join sundered.

Tala was two feet from him. In a heartbeat, twenty feet. In another, a hundred. She was screaming at him, but soon enough her voice was swallowed by the thunder of the rails and its echo in the clouds above.

This man, this *splintersoul,* had defied death to find him. It was clear to Jimuro now that this man would go to any lengths to avenge whatever crimes he considered Jimuro guilty of. And that meant that no matter where Jimuro went, even in the safety of the Palace of Steel, he would always be endangering the people he was sworn to protect and serve.

So here he would wait for the end. Either he would kill the man in the purple coat, ending his threat forever . . . or he would die, and hopefully his death would slake the man's bloodthirst. This was, as far as Jimuro could see, the only winning play.

As the world slowed around him, he closed his eyes and bowed his head. He offered up a prayer to the spirits of his ancestors, that they'd guide his hand. He offered up another to the spirits of the Copper Sages, that if his line ended tonight, they would be able to guide Tomoda toward a brighter future. And he offered up a final one to the spirit of Tala, that she'd forgive him for leaving her again.

From the darkness at the end of the train car, a shadow unfolded with a rustle of wings. The man in the purple coat landed on the deck outside, carried by his massive owl-shade. It disappeared behind him as he strode into the car. He glared at Jimuro with furious, bloodshot eyes, as Jimuro scanned the pactmarks on his skin. He understood now what he was looking at: a graveyard of Sanbunas and Shang, wrought in brown flesh.

With this, Jimuro prayed to each departed soul, *I will either avenge you . . . or join you.*

"Whatever you want with me," he called to the man, "whatever crime I or my family may have committed to incense you so . . ." He spread his arms wide. "I'm here to answer for it."

The man stopped and looked at Jimuro as if he weren't quite sure what to make of him.

Jimuro walked toward him with big, confident strides. "You've stalked me all across the world, sir," he continued. "You've slaughtered my guards, and the spirits only know how many of my subjects. But your hunt is over. You stand in the presence of Iron Prince Jimuro, son of Steel Lord Yoshiko, divine vessel of the spirits, beating heart of the Tomodanese people, and heir to the Mountain Throne." He came to a stop a scant meter from the man, then straightened his glasses and drew himself up as regally as he could muster. "So let us end this."

The man stared down at Jimuro for a long moment, his expression inscrutable.

Then he lunged. His hand wrapped itself around Jimuro's throat. He yanked Jimuro close. And radiating low-simmering contempt from every line of his weathered face, he rasped, "I don't give a fuck who you are."

Jimuro's eyes widened as the man lifted him off his feet and tossed him aside like garbage. He skidded across the wet wooden floor, throat burning as he scrambled to regain his breath. When he blinked back tears of pain, he saw a long vertical crack down the center of his left glasses lens.

He staggered back up just in time to see the man in the purple coat stalk right over to the open door at the front of the passenger car. He turned to face Jimuro once more, his coat billowing in the wind despite the fact that the train car had slid to a stop.

And then there was a flash of light behind the man. A pair of talons wrapped themselves around his shoulders and pulled him back into the darkness.

"*No!*" Jimuro shouted to the empty train car. This couldn't be happening. He'd meant to sacrifice himself in service to his people. All he'd done was doom them, and now he couldn't even catch up to try to make things right.

But it didn't make any sense. The man in the purple coat had chased him across an ocean. He'd carved his way through an entire shipful of Erega's finest. And all of it had been because he wanted to get his hands on Jimuro. So why now, when he'd had his quarry dead to rights, had the man in the purple coat passed him by?

Behind him, he heard the click of a compartment door.

He whirled around to see one of the passengers who'd interrupted him and Kosuke earlier: the tall woman in the fitted black dress, with a sharp haircut framing a sharper face. He was about to shout at her for disobeying his orders to evacuate, but he stopped himself when he saw she was no daughter of Tomoda.

"I hear that right?" she said in accented Tomodanese. "You're really the princeling?"

On the best day, he would've rankled at how casually this outlander addressed him. Today, in this very moment, he couldn't bring himself to care. Not when so much else was at stake.

"I don't know who you are," he said, "and I don't know how long you've been there. But if you've been here the entire time, then you saw how dangerous that man can be. And if you saw how dangerous that man can be, then you understand why I have to find a way to catch up to that train and stop him, right now."

But the woman rolled her shoulders and sauntered toward him. Jimuro at last noticed something dangling from her hands: a thick strip of cloth, the same color and pattern as the train's seating upholstery.

And then, just a moment too late, he remembered what Princess Xiulan had said about her missing partner.

"Well," said the woman who could only be Lee Yeon-Ji. "That's a long walk to 'yes.'"

CHAPTER TWENTY-FOUR

TALA

"*Jimuro!*" she shouted into the dark, though of course it was already too late. That idiot. Shades take him, what had he been thinking? But even as she asked the question, she knew the answer: He was trying to do something noble and selfless, like a fucking idiot.

She howled her rage as the rain fell around her. She'd explained this so many times: With him dead, this whole mission was for nothing. Did he know something she didn't? Did he have some kind of cunning plan to get the better of the splintersoul? Or was he really as dense as the steel his crazy family loved to worship?

Frantically, she ran her mind through the options. Mang had just discorporated, so she couldn't summon him back until he'd recovered. Beaky was out of commission, too, and wouldn't have been able to help her anyway. She could rush to the front car and try to get the Cicadas to stop the train. There was a chance they might, if she told Kurihara what kind of danger Jimuro was in. But to do that, she would have to get more than three words out before one of them just beheaded her on principle.

She shook her head, splashing rainwater everywhere. Every second she hesitated took her miles farther from Jimuro.

She ran into the dining car, grateful to see the place empty of civilians.

Unfortunately, it wasn't empty.

"*You!*" bellowed Kurihara, limping toward her with a gun in hand. He had a few Cicadas at his back, while others were busy helping the maimed Iwanbo off the floor. "What did you do to His Brilliance?"

"Listen to me," Tala said, putting her hands up. At least he'd saved her the trouble of finding him. "You need to stop this train right now, or else Prince Jimuro is going to die."

"I won't allow you to make idle threats on his life, slaver," Kurihara snarled, hefting his pistol and cocking back the hammer.

"I'm not," Tala said, fighting to keep her voice even. "I'm just telling you what's going to happen if you don't stop the train right now. He's in danger."

"I don't know what you barbarians did to him," Kurihara said, "but you broke something in him. I know Iron Prince Jimuro, and the man you brought back here isn't him."

Color rose in Tala's face. Her head spun just from thinking about how much farther they'd gotten from Jimuro. "Will you listen to me for a *second*, you—"

"I'm going to bring him back," Kurihara raved, eyes wide and unfocused with rage. "I'm going to make him remember who he is. So you have one chance, Sergeant Tala. I demand that you—"

"*Give him to me!*" bellowed a voice on the wind.

Tala's heart tripped over its own beat. *No.*

She dove away from the door, and Kurihara opened fire. She tried to yell a warning as bullets slammed into the wall, but then it was too late. A green flash of light heralded the arrival of a snapping-turtle-shade; yellow, a giant wasp. A fox-shade with a teeming mass of tails stepped out of a cloud of red light.

And striding behind them through the doorway was the other splintersoul.

"*Give him to me,*" he said again, searching the train car with frantic eyes.

The bottom of Tala's stomach dropped out. For him to be here . . . was Jimuro dead? Had her mission been for nothing?

A cry of fury escaped her throat as she whipped up her pistol and opened fire. But the wasp-shade flitted right into her line of fire, its body crackling with yellow energy as it absorbed bullet after bullet.

"Who is that?" said one Cicada.

"Another barbarian!" said Kurihara. "Light him up!"

But the man moved like violet flame. The walls splintered in a trail of bullet holes behind him as his shades moved to engage the Cicadas. He muttered another name, and a hog-shade with four tusks appeared, charging at a full gallop toward the embattled Steel Cicadas.

Tala tossed her gun aside and darted for the serving counter of the dining car. She made to vault over it and get herself into cover, but a hand wrapped itself around her ankle like a manacle, stopping her mid-dive. Her gut slammed into the bar's corner, driving all the wind from her lungs.

She rolled hard, yanking herself free of the man's grip and kicking up at him. Her boot caught him in the jaw, and he staggered back with a groan. But before she could capitalize on the opportunity she'd just created, he came right back at her, that greedy glint in his eye. *Shades take me,* she thought. *Is he made of iron?*

"Give him back to—"

Tala swung herself off the counter, fist cocked for a punch right to his gut. He reeled back from the impact, and she swung at him again. "You should've thought about what you wanted from me before you took my squad," she spat.

Their faces flashed before her: Kapona. Minip. Ompaco. Maki, even though he and his crew hadn't been 13-52-2.

But neither had Jimuro, and she saw his face, too.

She lunged, and even though she was at the end of her rope, she still had those hard reserves of rage to fuel her. They burned bright, hot, and brief, but this didn't need to be a long fight. Not as long as she won it.

He blocked her first punch, but she just used her momentum to pull herself in closer, aiming her knee for his solar plexus. If she could disrupt his breathing, she could stop him from summoning any more shades. Either she took him out, or she stalled long enough for the Cicadas to dispatch the other shades in the car and help her out.

He turned his body aside and leaned, so that she caught his ribs instead of his gut. But already she was throwing another punch, and another, and another. The more punches she threw, the harder her blood pounded in her ears. This man had killed her squad, then rendered their deaths pointless. The only thing she cared about now was making him bleed.

But while she landed her first three punches, on her fourth the man seemed to come awake. With the speed of a striking viper, he leaned away from her blow, then darted right inside her guard and slammed a palm hard into her chest. For such a weedy frame, the man had surprising strength, and it broke Tala's footing. *"Give him to me!"* the man shouted again. *"Give him back!"*

As he showered her with punches, she was barely able to stay ahead of him. She felt herself backing up into the counter again. "He's not here!" she screamed. "You're fighting for nothing!"

"I can feel him!" the man in the purple coat roared. *"Give me back my bird!"*

Tala's entire body froze, and she felt like the floor of the train had dropped out from under her. But the man didn't wait for her to process his words; his hand wrapped around her throat and shoved her backward onto the counter.

Spots burst before her eyes as her brain, heart, and lungs abruptly lost their air. She fought against the urge to panic, but it grew stronger and steadier with each second. She thought fleetingly of Harada, only for a moment. It felt like it stretched on longer, though, because moments were now all she had left.

Harada receded, swallowed by questions. *His bird?* But she hadn't . . . she'd made sure that . . . it couldn't be . . .

She brought her failing eyes up to meet those of the man, and instantly she realized she'd seen him before. Not three nights ago, aboard the *Marlin*; years ago. In Lisan City. Before she was a soldier, but after she'd become a fighter.

She expected revulsion on his face. Perhaps hatred. Maybe even just blind rage.

But instead, even as chaos swirled all around them both, she saw tears of joy roll down his cheeks.

"I've found you," he whispered, not at her or to her so much as through her. "I can be whole again . . ."

And then her entire body was immersed in a deep, dark pool of agony.

In her tours of duty, Tala had been shot, stabbed, sliced up, and scorched. She'd had bombs dropped on her, shrapnel dug out of her, and even once survived getting hit head-on by a car. Some of her scars ran so deep, even her bones bore them. Those scars were formidable, but she'd thought none could eclipse the pain she felt when she invoked Mang.

This hurt more than all of those wounds put together.

Every inch of her body felt as if it were being clawed and burned at the same time. It was as if something horrible had been lurking inside her that at the man's touch finally came alive, eager to rip its way into the world. She screamed, and she could hardly hear herself over the noise of her mind tearing itself apart.

Her vision slipped. When she blinked, it was the man in the purple coat choking her. She blinked again, and it was Maki. She blinked, and it was Mang, with his arms like oaks. She blinked, and it was her mother. The man again. Her father. Kurihara Kosuke. The man again.

And then she blinked, and saw Prince Jimuro pinning her, rapturous and ecstatic pleasure etched onto his face.

Whatever he was doing, it would be over soon, she knew. The pain hadn't tapered, but she felt her ability to perceive it dimming. Perhaps this wasn't something that would have killed her normally. But after everything else she'd been dragged through, she knew she wouldn't have the strength to continue.

Was this what I did to you? she thought. *Was this how it felt when I last touched you?* Surely, it couldn't have hurt so much. And yet here she was, her every nerve aflame.

She stared up into the prince's face. She tried to will herself to see her killer for who he really was. But her mind was gone, and it'd taken her eyes with it. So she was doomed to die, staring into the face of Prince Jimuro, while the stranger who wore it twisted it into something unrecognizably cruel.

But something stirred in her as that thought skittered across her dying mind like a roach. She'd seen Iron Prince Jimuro be arrogant, nationalistic, proud, and flinty to the point of stupidity. But she'd never known him to be cruel.

She felt as if she'd had a bag over her head, and someone had just yanked it off. She was splayed out on the train's kitchen counter, staring up into the eyes of the man in the purple coat, as his tears leaked down onto her. His teeth were gritted, the lines in his face drawing deeper by the second.

She turned her head to the left, and saw abandoned cooking tools. To the right, she saw the same. Frantically, she searched: for pans, for pots, for particularly pointy chopsticks, for—

There. Not perfect, but it would have to do.

She thrust out her right hand, and her fingers wrapped uneasily around the metal-and-wood hilt of a square-bladed vegetable knife. She only had enough strength in her left for one swing, and she squeezed her eyes shut with effort as she spent it at last.

Tomodanese steel was sharp, but brittle. She expected its blade to bite into his flesh and stop at the bone. But then her nose filled with the familiar unpleasant odor of burning flesh, and she felt the vegetable knife pass effortlessly through sinew and bone alike.

The man in the purple coat staggered back with a scream, and Tala felt the hand drop off her neck like tags with a broken chain. As it fell to the floor, Tala saw one of the shades in the dining car abruptly disappear.

Coughing and sputtering, she forced herself upright. Every part of her still burned, but she felt that fire inside cooling to embers.

The man in the purple coat stood mere feet from her, staring in disbelief: at his stump of a wrist, and at her.

No, Tala realized. At the knife in her hand.

Whose blade was still red with heat.

The Steel Cicadas were still fighting the remaining shades, but she saw Kurihara looking on, similarly stricken.

"What are you?" said the man in the purple coat.

Staring down at the knife in her hand, Tala had the same question.

But just as the steel in her grip cooled, so too did her curiosity. It could wait.

She raised the knife and leveled a glare at him that was just as steely and sharp. She snarled. "The last thing you'll ever see."

The blade flashed as she clutched it tight and charged. The man in the purple coat growled, then turned and fled for the door.

"Kurihara!" Tala shouted. "He's getting away! Shoot him!"

"I will not take orders from—!"

"Just shoot him, you upper-class twit!"

Kurihara opened fire, as did the other Cicadas. But the man was zigzagging, the way Tala had learned to as a jungle-runner. Without even breaking stride, he threw himself out the door in a dive, his coat fluttering behind him like wings. In a flash of light, his owl-shade appeared again, yanking him away from the rails and up into the night sky.

Tala charged to the door. She glared out at his retreating form. And in that moment, she decided that she had no intention of fighting another day.

"Beaky!" she shouted, only to feel a tiny pulse on the pactmark on her chest. It was an indicator that her crow-shade still hadn't recovered enough of his magical energy to sustain a physical form. But that was fine. Now that she remembered, he wouldn't have been any help against the man in the purple coat anyway. No, there was only one shade for this job.

She gripped the cleaver in her hand tightly and shouted: *"Dimangan!"*

She waited for the burst of light, or else the pulse of pressure on the back of her head that would tell her he was still in recovery, like Beaky.

But when she invoked her brother's name, she felt nothing at all.

A tiny flame of panic sparked to life inside Tala. *"Dimangan!"* she tried again.

Again, she felt nothing.

Her panic roared into a full inferno. She remembered aboard the *Marlin*, seeing shades like Sunny and Tivron stolen from their rightful partners. Hell, she had more than just witnessed shades being stolen; she'd done it herself.

"Dimangan!" she shouted into the night sky, at the receding figure of the man in the purple coat. *"Mang! Di—"*

At last, she felt something on the back of her head. But it wasn't something magical; it was the familiar weight of a pistol butt, rammed right into the base of her skull.

The cleaver clattered to the iron landing, and Tala's limp body followed.

PART FIVE

· · ·

Ashes and Embers

CHAPTER TWENTY-FIVE

DIMANGAN

Dimangan heard his name and came when he was called.

He careened into the world with a scream. Something about this journey had been different. Suddenly existing after long periods of not existing was rarely a smooth experience, but this one was rougher than most. It was the difference between a car stopping because someone had slammed on the brakes, and one stopping because it had run headlong into a wall.

The first thing he noticed was the pain: his constant companion since that fateful day. He'd fled his body, desperate to escape the agony visited upon him by that Tomodanese bomb, only to wake to something far, far worse. He'd never said anything about it, to spare Lala, but he knew she felt it, too. It was the weight they carried between them, and now it settled on him once more.

The second thing he noticed was that he was nowhere near the train car he last remembered standing in, before he'd been overwhelmed by the splintersoul's personal army. He stood in what appeared to be a run-down Tomodanese house, its contents in disarray. The sun was just beginning to rise out the window, and the rain appeared to have finally stopped.

As a magical being, he no longer had a stomach. Nonetheless, he felt it twist as he considered how long he'd been out. Lala had been fighting for hours without his help, and he'd promised to protect her.

Easy, he reminded himself. He was still standing here. That meant she'd gotten out all right. And of course she had. His sister was the most stubborn survivor he'd ever known. At the end of the world, there would be the cockroaches, and there would be Tala, their fearsome warrior-queen.

But when he turned around with a relieved grin and said, "Report," it wasn't the sight of his sister that greeted him.

It was the other splintersoul.

Without hesitation, Dimangan launched himself at the man with a roar, eager to get his huge hands around the man's head so he could pop it like a melon.

But then something shuddered in his veins, cold like poison. He still wanted to kill this man, but suddenly he . . . also didn't. He came to a hard stop, and his arms fell placidly to his sides. He hunched forward onto his forearms in a restful, bestial crouch.

He tried to move his legs. Nothing. His head: nothing. Not even his eyes could twitch. They had to remain fixed on the man in the purple coat, and on the house around him. A house that Dimangan now saw was not run-down after all; its furniture was too freshly smashed, its walls too recently gouged by claw and fang. In the center of the floor, amid their broken things, an old man and woman lay together in a bloody heap.

The breath left Dimangan's throat. He felt a sharper, renewed horror as his attention slid back to the man in the purple coat.

He tried to contort his face with fury, but found he couldn't even do that. "What did you just do to me?" he thundered. "Where's Tala?"

"Tala." The man repeated the name, as if tasting it. The flavor wasn't to his liking, because he grimaced. When he did, hatred sliced through Dimangan's mind like a red-hot Tomodanese blade. The pain of it was so intense, even against the backdrop that was his existence, it forced him to his knees.

"Get up," the man growled, and though Dimangan wanted to defy him, he also wanted to obey. Shaking, he stood. Panic bubbled up in Dimangan's mind like water in a hot pot.

The man began to pace, cradling his right hand close to his body. Except no, there wasn't even a right hand to be found; just a messy, burnt stump. "My sister did that to you?"

The man didn't answer, but more seething hatred spilled over into Dimangan's mind. He felt as if his brain were being struck by lightning, over and over. But the man had bade him to stand, and so this time he did not fall.

He couldn't.

"Where's my sister?" he said. He forced his voice into a tightly controlled register, the sort of deadly calm meant to communicate that he meant business.

Once again, the man did not answer. But eventually, he did speak: "I took you from her."

Dimangan's whole body seized up as he fought to break free of the man's thrall and throttle the life out of him. He was desperate for even one of his fingers to move, to so much as twitch.

He remained crouched.

The man narrowed his eyes at Dimangan, unimpressed. "You'd end my life, even knowing our souls are now tethered?"

Dimangan hadn't even considered that aspect of things, but it didn't give him any pause. He fought all the fiercer, certain that if he just tried hard enough, he could overwhelm the geas on him . . .

"Your resolve's admirable," said the man, eyeing him carefully. "It's the hardness in both of our bones that's allowed us to endure a world that would pulverize us if we were even slightly weaker. That's why you and I were able to pact."

Dimangan's eyes widened. "I never pacted with you."

"Your soul cried out for revenge, and I promised it," said the man, flexing the fingers of his remaining hand. A rainbow of magical energy arced between his fingertips. "You found resonance within me. Otherwise, our union would be impossible. I've bonded with dozens of souls. Do you have any idea how many hundreds I've left behind?"

Horror spread through Dimangan's mind like blood through water.

"I was asleep when she took him from me," the man said. He tapped his temple, which bore a small blotch of scar tissue that stood naked in his hair, like an island in black water. "Shrapnel to the skull. Not enough to kill me, but enough to hollow me out. They put me in a hospital bed in Lisan City with other soldiers who would never wake up, and they left me there to sleep."

As he spoke, fleeting images coursed through Dimangan's head, each one bitter and wholly without warmth. He saw burned-out cityscapes, the buildings riddled with bullet holes and blood spatters. He smelled burning hair and flash-boiled blood. His mouth filled with the taste of soot and steel. And at the center of it, he saw the man: not in his purple coat, but in the ratty, soiled fatigues and drab green bandanna that marked him as a jungle-runner. He fought against a tide of Tomodanese like a demon: first with his gun, then with his machete, and eventually with his bare hands.

And ever at his side was a familiar black bird: a crested crow-shade with a trio of interlocking purple rings splashed across his breast feathers.

"Every day I slept, I dreamed of that," said the man. "Every day, I fought that battle. And no matter how I fought it, no matter how many enemies lay dead at my feet, I could never win it. But one day, my fighting stopped. One day, a Tomodanese officer got past my guard, put her gun to my head, and pulled the trigger. But instead of dying again . . . I woke up."

The memories were less distinct now: the hospital bed. The orderly who came in at the wrong moment. The clatter of his falling tray as his patient lunged forward, hunger in his heart and hate in his veins . . .

"I've lived two years with a starving soul," the man said, glaring balefully up into Dimangan's eyes. "I've followed the thin thread that ties my soul to hers, the cord she couldn't sever. And when someone stood in my way . . ."

More images flitted through Dimangan's head. Ones he wished he could shut out.

"I dreamed of finding her and making her suffer exactly as much as she had made me." He stopped pacing to look Dimangan over again. "But I never dreamed I'd find someone like you waiting for me at the end of my trail."

Dimangan found himself free to move his head at last, and he shook his head in disgust. "Why are you telling me this?"

"Because you're the first person who can feel that hunger as closely as I do," the man said with sudden intensity. He surged toward Dimangan, grabbing his paralyzed forearm with his one remaining hand. "You're the first person I can be honest with. The first person who has no choice but to understand me, because now you and I are one."

Dimangan couldn't move his arm, but he did turn his head away. "You don't know what you're talking about."

"*Don't I?*" shouted the man. "When I called you, *you came.* When I bid you stay, *you stayed.* And when I reached into your sister's soul to find what was mine, *I found your hatred and pulled it out of her like a beating heart.*"

Dimangan squeezed his eyes shut, as if that would stop things somehow. For so long, his problems and Tala's had been one and the same, and he'd only needed his two fists to solve most of them. But with that taken from him, he had no idea what to do now.

"Look at me," the man said in a low, deadly voice.

Dimangan squeezed his eyes tighter. He felt the desire to obey on the fringes of his mind, like a wolf pawing at his door. He had to have this. He had to have some shred of resistance, because if there was so much as a seed of it within him, one day it could flower into something breathing and alive. And when it bloomed, he could find Tala again at last.

"Dimangan." His name sounded like a curse on the man's chapped, bloody lips. "Look. At. Me."

The desire to obey was overwhelming now, a smell that choked away all the air in the small room. It was the only thing he could breathe, and after several long moments, his eyelids slowly fluttered open. His huge head turned, until the man in the purple coat was the only thing he saw.

The man's nod was long, slow, and satisfied.

Dimangan nodded to the scorched stump of his right wrist. "If you don't get that treated," he said, "infection may set in. You'd die."

"So would you," said the man.

"Infection would be too gentle a death," Dimangan spat.

The man in the purple coat smirked. "Nothing will kill me until I'm whole again," he said with an unshakable confidence that Dimangan could feel in his own gigantic bones. "I could follow the thread your sister trails everywhere, but I'd rather you just tell me where she's going. So tell me: Where in Tomoda is Sergeant Tala headed?"

I'm sorry, Lala, Dimangan thought, while his traitor tongue immediately answered: "Hagane. The Palace of Steel in Hagane."

"Why?"

"She's escorting Iron Prince Jimuro of Tomoda. He's set to take the throne tomorrow. My sister was charged with making sure he gets there in one piece."

The man considered this, then at last examined his stump more closely. Dimangan could feel the wheels turning in his head. "Dahali magic can treat this," he said at last.

"And if we found a Dahali hexcrafter," Dimangan sneered, "how exactly do you expect to get her to cooperate with you . . . Mayon?"

The man raised a thick eyebrow. "What did you . . . ?"

"I saw your memories," Dimangan said. "Including the name on your dog tags. Mayon."

Mayon took no apparent pleasure in hearing the name. "That was a name given to a boy and inherited by a man," he said. "I've become much more than either."

"Whatever," Dimangan said. "That still doesn't answer my question."

Mayon sneered. "You enjoy getting in my head, boy? How do you like it . . . now?"

And just like that, the pain that engulfed Dimangan's body reached torturous new heights.

Though he no longer had true lungs, he found his breath completely taken from him as the room spun. The curse of his monstrous form had come with the gift of incredible strength, but now he felt like thin, flimsy paper being undone fiber by fiber.

He gasped. "You feel it," he said with what was left of his voice. "Not just for me. For . . ."

"Every single one." Mayon slowly crossed to him. The light shifted with each step, so that he looked like an ever-changing monster.

Through the miasma of hurt, that stray line from Dimangan's reading floated to the top of his mind.

Sanbuna lore had countless monsters, but the worst of them wore a human face.

"This is my everyday, Dimangan," said Mayon. "This is the life I have left. It tests me every day, and every day I prove I'm stronger: stronger than my fractured soul. Stronger than the remnants that rattle inside me like shrapnel. Stronger than you."

The shreds of humanity Dimangan held on to fled him. He tilted his head back and screamed until he felt the floorboards shake beneath him.

And then, just like that, the man in the purple coat gestured, and Dimangan stopped. The pain was still there, but now his voice was caged inside his throat, rattling ineffectually at the bars.

Mayon turned his back on him, looking out the window at the dawning new day. "I'm not going to get a Dahali hexcrafter to cooperate with me," he said simply. "You are."

And the moment he heard the words, Dimangan knew he would obey.

CHAPTER TWENTY-SIX

XIULAN

Her entire head felt as if it were aflame.

Which was quite the achievement, considering her frigid locale.

Memories swirled inside her skull like leaves on the wind, and she frantically snatched at them as she oriented herself. The Sanbuna skull bash. The Iron Prince, key to Ruomei's downfall, mere inches from her grasp at last. Lee, disappearing into the dining car to distract the other—

Lee.

Desperately, she surged to her feet, but fell flat onto her stomach before she got halfway up. She exhaled a long, shuddering sigh, punctuated by a small puff of steam. Her eye had adjusted to the dark, so she could see the metal shelves lining the walls, and the carefully secured crates of foodstuffs on them. She was in the galley. Specifically, in its fridge. In the cold dark, she felt as if she'd been swallowed by some great and chilly beast.

Stupid White Rat, she cursed herself. *Stuck in a trap, the stupid rat who was born doomed to die.* She heaped curses onto her own slim shoulders, even as she clawed her way toward the nearest crate on the floor. She grabbed at it and levered herself up onto her knees, her stomach resting atop it. She was breathing hard and her head was pounding and all she could think about was that she had to get out, had to capture the prince, had to find Lee, had to find a new way for this story to end.

Her gaze fell to the friendly yellow Tomodanese script on the box. In her addled state, it took her a moment to translate it:

MUSHROOMS

A groan gained power in her throat, rising until it was a pure, primal growl of frustration. She unleashed it, leaving her formidable vocabulary by the wayside. Everything she had was in that growl. It reached from so deep inside her that it brought tears to her eyes just to let it out. But even as she vented all her fury and frustration, she felt the refrigerator walls stifling her voice, like a glass placed over a candle flame.

She glared tearfully at the crate's label. "I was . . . so close," she whispered to it with a shaking voice.

Cheerfully, the crate replied:

MUSHROOMS

Her skin was cold, but her tears were colder still. She wiped them away with her sleeve, then drew her coat's folds tighter around herself. And with the dented, sputtering machine that her mind had become, she tried to think of any moments in the formidable canon of Bai Junjie where the great detective had been in similarly dire straits. To be sure, he always found himself in peril in the course of his investigations. But what she needed now was to remember a moment when he had been at his very lowest, without recourse or resource. And she needed to remember how he'd gotten out, because if Bai Junjie could do it, then surely she, Twenty-Eighth Princess Shang Xiulan, could as well.

But every time she found an example, she found one common thread between them all: the timely intervention of his trusty partner, Kou.

She eyed the heavy metal door. *Her* Kou could do nothing about that. The only hope she had left was her other partner.

Worry blossomed anew in her chest. Surely, the Steel Cicadas had discovered Lee. That was the only thing that could have kept her from Xiulan's side. No, it was a question now of whether or not they had allowed Lee to live.

She dared not allow herself to feel despair. The only thing she had room for right now was hope.

Her gaze slid over to the crate on which she lay, which chimed in once again with:

MUSHROOMS

She slid off the crate and back onto the floor. Her head was starting to clear, if only a little, but the headache had not subsided in the least, and it sapped the rest of her body of its strength. She tried to lay her cheek on the floor, only for that whole side of her face to suddenly blaze with pain. She whipped her head away from the floor, certain it had been heated or something as a way to torture her.

Then it swam back to her: a foggy, distorted vision of Kurihara Kosuke, gun raised, pulling the trigger, muzzle flashing—

Her cheek throbbed all over again, as if she'd just been shot a second time. She tried to grasp at the memory, but it danced away from her. She had to focus. If she didn't focus, she wouldn't be able to help Lee when her partner arrived to retrieve her. Why was it so hard to—

The lock on the fridge opened, and hope bloomed in her chest, bright and fresh as spring flowers. *"Lee!"* she said from the floor. "I'm in here, I'm—"

But the woman who entered was not her exquisite partner, but the Sanbuna brute that had locked her in here in the first place. And she didn't walk into the fridge, despite the appliance's rather descriptive name. Instead, she was hurled in by a pair of Steel Cicadas, one of whom spat on her back before sliding the door shut again. A loud click told Xiulan that it had been metalpacted shut.

The Sanbuna woman groaned, the same noise over and over again. It took Xiulan a moment to realize it was no mere grunt, but rather a word in its own right.

"Mang . . ." the woman said. "Mang . . . Mang . . ."

Even with all her mental faculties intact, Xiulan still wouldn't have understood what the woman was saying. And since she felt as though her brains had been pulverized into congee, she said in To-modanese: "Do you mind?"

She'd tried to keep her tone polite, but the woman's eyes snapped open. She scrambled to her feet and shouted: *"Mang! Dimangan! Mang!"*

Xiulan didn't know Sanbuna, but she was aware of their wide-spread practice of nicknaming. So *Mang* was a name, then, diminutive of *Dimangan*. And using that key piece of information, she could use her formidable detective acumen to deduce . . .

. . . not a blasted thing.

"He's not here," she said, taking a stab in the dark on the gender. "I fear the only companionship Heaven has seen fit to provide you is my own." She was frustrated by her own tongue. She'd put a great deal of practice into her elocution, but suddenly her mouth felt like too clumsy and blunt an instrument to express her words.

When the door didn't budge, the Sanbuna slumped down it until she was sitting on the floor, mere feet from Xiulan. Her broad shoulders heaved with effort, and beneath her hair Xiulan spied a thin trickle of blood. She was about to point it out. Then another memory formed: the soldier, seizing her by the shoulders and ramming her skull into Xiulan's hard enough to turn the world dark.

But Xiulan was a woman above spite. So she said, "You're bleeding."

The soldier dabbed at the back of her head with her fingers, inspected the blood on them, then smeared it irritably on the door. "I've had worse."

Xiulan nodded—a difficult thing to do, lying down as she was. "I know I have little in the way of credit with you," she said, "but may I ask you to do me the favor of sitting me up?"

The soldier scowled and said nothing. Xiulan was about to resign herself to a facedown view of the refrigerator and a sullen companion with which to share it. But then one hand wedged itself beneath her like a spatula, the other carefully supporting her head as the Sanbuna forced her upright and leaned her against a nearby shelf.

"I don't believe we were formally introduced," Xiulan said. She'd been in such a haze when she made her last-ditch effort to capture the Iron Prince, she had no clue what she'd said and what she hadn't.

The woman grunted.

"I'll assume that to be a Sanbuna colloquialism in the negative," Xiulan said. Her mouth continued to form the words clumsily, slurring one into the other, but she refused to truncate her vocabulary. This was merely something else to be overcome, just as she'd clawed through everything else in her way. "In which case, I believe it would behoove me to introduce myself as Twenty-Eighth Princess Shang Xiulan, Lady of Moonlight, and an agent of the Li-Quan in . . . well, not the best of standing."

The woman scowled, then muttered: "Sergeant Tala. Thirteenth Regiment, Fifty-Second Company, Second Platoon."

"Tala what?"

"Just Tala."

Xiulan nodded, then decided to prod. "And who is Mang?"

Tala grew even colder than their surroundings. "Get fucked, Your Majesty."

The brusqueness cut through her mental fog the way pepper oil cut through a stuffy nose. "Lee," she said, with sudden urgency. "Sergeant, I know we engaged each other in an adversarial capacity, but in our current predicament, I hope we can speak with candor. On your way to the scene of battle, did you by any chance encounter a tall, striking woman of Jeongsonese descent?"

Tala shrugged.

Xiulan cursed under her breath in Shang. "You're certain?" she said. "Not among the hostages? Not in the clutches of Kurihara and his comrades?"

Tala shook her head. But then Xiulan saw something change about the way the light hit her eyes. Her expression softened a degree. "I was distracted when I made my way through. I could've missed her."

Xiulan's mind worked furiously, though forming thoughts was like trying to ride a bicycle through a muddy field. If Tala hadn't seen Lee, then there was hope yet. But perhaps she'd gotten waylaid in some other manner.

Or perhaps she's just a criminal who remembered who she really was.

Xiulan dismissed the thought immediately. She'd never felt for anyone what she felt for Lee Yeon-Ji. If she seriously considered that line of thinking, she would poison all of those deep, genuine feelings. Xiulan had already worked so hard to undo her prejudices just by taking the woman on as her partner, and this choice had rewarded her in all the best ways. She refused to regress now.

But none of that changed the fact that Lee wasn't here, and she was trapped in a refrigerator.

"What happened to the Iron Prince?" she said.

Tala glared at her. "I know we're stuck in the same tight spot, but that doesn't mean I've forgotten you were here to kill him."

"Quite the contrary," Xiulan said. "My father's preferred heir wishes to kill him. I merely wished to present him as a gift to my father."

"Who would kill him."

Xiulan shrugged. "Perhaps. I'll confess, the Iron Prince's well-being was a secondary concern here."

Tala narrowed her eyes. "What was the main one?"

"Saving my country from misrule that would take a generation to undo," Xiulan said. "I don't expect a soldier such as yourself to be concerned with the larger diplomatic field, but you should take it to heart when I say that you'll thank me someday."

"And what about the Tomodanese?" Tala said.

"What about them?" Xiulan said. "We Shang have a rather old and famous saying about victors and spoils."

" 'To the victor goes the spoils'?"

"Yes, that's the one." She reached into her coat and found her pipe still there, mercifully intact. The leaf was all spent now, but even the weight of it on her teeth was a comfort when precious little else was. "Tomoda inflicted all manner of horrors upon Shang and its people. I don't feel particularly beholden to their well-being in turn. In truth, I'm surprised that you appear to. The atrocities the Mountain Throne visited upon the Sanbu Islands are not unknown to me, Sergeant."

Tala's mouth tightened. She stared down at her hands and said nothing.

Xiulan rolled her eye, but was rewarded with a headache that immediately made her regret the gesture. "We can negotiate a truce of sorts," Xiulan said. "But that can't happen without key information. So again I ask: What happened to the Iron Prince?"

Tala didn't meet her eye. "I don't know," she said. "He shoved me onto this car, then cut the joins so he could sacrifice himself. The idiot. It didn't even work."

Xiulan fiddled with her pipe, agitated. "Sacrifice himself?" she said. "To what?"

At last, Tala looked at her. "You wouldn't believe me if I told you."

Despite everything, Xiulan found it in herself to muster up a very Lee-like smirk. "Try me."

So Tala told her.

"I don't believe you," said Xiulan.

"I don't care," Tala said.

"Surely you must appreciate how preposterous that sounds," Xiulan said. "The soul can't fracture more than once. And it certainly can't steal shades from another one." But even as she said it, more hazy memories floated to the surface of her mind . . . a wholesale slaughter in the woods, a mass shade attack whose forensic evidence didn't add up to any logical conclusions . . .

"It can," Tala said quietly.

"I'm not unfamiliar with the Sanbuna folklore on the subject. What is the term you use? *Splintered soul?*"

Tala grimaced. "Your accent sucks." She began unbuttoning her shirt.

Xiulan made to avert her eyes. "I fear you've misread the situation, Sergeant."

"No, you idiot," Tala said, pointing to her chest. When Xiulan looked, she saw a trio of interlocked purple rings across her upper sternum. A pactmark.

"Yes," Xiulan said irritably as Tala turned around. "I have one of my own."

"That's the thing," Tala said, pulling up her hair. "I don't have just *one*."

Xiulan squinted her eye to see better in the dark fridge. But when she caught sight of it, she gasped. It was mostly hidden by the sergeant's hair, but just beneath, barely visible, she could just make out the lines of . . .

"A second pactmark?" Xiulan gasped. "How?" In all her reading, she'd never encountered any reports of people whose soul bore more than a single pact.

Tala scowled.

Xiulan decided not to press that, but her curiosity was too powerful to be tamped down on entirely. "Can either of them get us out?"

Tala scowled further.

The pieces all felt as if they were hovering just out of Xiulan's mental reach. A man who could steal shades. A soldier with two pactmarks.

And the name *Dimangan*.

A vision slammed into her skull like a bullet. She was on the floor of the compartment where she'd had the Iron Prince and Kurihara cornered. Though she'd been incapacitated, she hadn't been knocked unconscious. So she'd seen it: the wall being torn apart by huge hands. And the monster on the other side . . . human-shaped, but inhumanly huge, his skin pocked with bony plates and wounds fizzing with purple sparks.

And at his side, a Sanbuna woman in a sodden gray suit.

Just like that, the pieces fell into place. Xiulan's horror deepened. A person with more than one shade was impossible.

But a person with a human shade was unthinkable.

"Sergeant Tala," she said slowly. "Did the man in the purple coat . . . is Mang with him?"

The sergeant was a gray blur, and then Xiulan's entire body jerked up by her coat lapels. Tala was in her face, hatred and hunger mingling in her eyes. Danger wafted off her like a bad smell. *"You don't get to talk about him,"* she rasped.

Xiulan's eye widened with fear. She tried to wriggle free, but the soldier was far stronger than she. Her pipe clattered from her teeth to the ground.

The noise seemed to bring Tala back to her senses. She looked at Xiulan as if she were only seeing her for the first time. Carefully, she lowered Xiulan back to the floor, then staggered back in a daze. "I'm sorry," she muttered. Then again, slightly louder: "Sorry." She fell back against the shelf opposite Xiulan, suddenly out of breath. Frantically, she tugged at the collar of her shirt again, and Xiulan could see that despite the chill in the fridge, her whole body was covered in sweat.

Xiulan's misgivings had only magnified in the last ten seconds, but once again she forced herself to set them aside. Heaven had seen fit to drop her into this situation and provide her with only the sergeant as a potential ally. She knew she was in no shape to escape on her own. And she needed to escape. She needed to re-secure the Iron Prince and dethrone Ruomei once and for all.

But more important, she needed to feel the delicate touch of a thief's hands across the small of her back once more.

Her eyelid felt heavy, and she indulged by letting it fall closed. Even shutting out the dim light of the fridge's inside eased her headache, if only an iota.

Snap.

She started back to wakefulness, to see Sergeant Tala's hand hovering an inch from her face, fingers primed to snap again. "You can't fall asleep," she said. She tapped her temple. "You're concussed. I've seen it before."

Xiulan wanted to snipe that what Tala had just said was a common misconception about the proper treatment of concussions, and that she'd read many books by credible experts that would testify as such. But the truth was, she hadn't wanted to fall asleep anyway. Not when there was work to be done. And step one was getting the sergeant on her side.

So instead, Xiulan settled back and kept her eye visibly wide open. "Thank you," she said carefully.

The sergeant gave her a slow, careful nod and sat back.

For a long while, the air held only the hum of the refrigerator's motor and the rumble of the rails.

Then Xiulan carefully picked up her pipe and slotted it back between her teeth. "What's happening to you?" she said.

At last, Tala seemed to notice that she was sweating. She wiped her brow with the sleeve of her coat, but already Xiulan could see new beads forming. "I don't know," she said, and Xiulan heard the tiny chord of fear in the back of her voice. "This is new. I've seen all kinds of shit, Princess, and I've never seen this."

Xiulan nodded. "I understand." She inhaled from her pipe, savoring the stale echoes of flavor trapped inside it. "Perhaps you should tell me just the same."

Tala rubbed her eyes with the heels of her palms. When she looked back up, her gaze was clear and collected.

And when she spoke, it was to answer Xiulan's question.

CHAPTER TWENTY-SEVEN

LEE

The sun was up and the clouds were gone, but the air was still heavy the way it always got after a good, hard rain. The bugs in the trees had just begun to sing for the day, a grating counterpoint to the trills of the morning birds. The countryside had been verdant enough yesterday, but last night's rain had made the grass and the leaves much more vibrant. If Lee were the kind of woman who enjoyed nature, she might have found it peaceful.

But even if she were that kind of woman, it still wouldn't have been truly peaceful, because she wasn't alone. She had Bootstrap barking away inside her, begging to be let out. And Lee wanted to. Really, she did. She was feeling bad enough about what kind of partner she was, and she didn't want to let a second one down. But she knew if she did that, it'd grind their whole morning to a halt. And for whatever reason, Lee was feeling a powerful urge to make good time.

Not that her other companion was being much help on that front.

"Where are you even taking me?" Prince Jimuro said. He marched in front of her, his hands bound behind his back by a scrap of upholstery from the train. His blue suit was rumpled, his glasses scratched and cracked. His topknot was sloppy and dissolved more with each passing minute, while a thin dusting of stubble had appeared on his chin and upper lip. And yet despite looking like shit, he still talked like he was better than her.

"You're the most valuable beating heart on this shitheap of an island," Lee said. "I could take you to any street corner in the country, start the bidding at ten thousand masu, and someone would offer me twenty."

"Is every agent of the Li-Quan so noble?" Prince Jimuro sniffed.

"No," Lee said. "But they're not the ones who've got you, are they?"

That shut him up for a moment, so Lee could think a bit, hard as it was with Bootstrap intruding into her every stray thought. After her rough night, Lee figured she'd earned the fun she was having, playing the rogue. But that didn't change the fact that she'd been pondering the same question since they'd hopped off the abandoned train car: What *was* she going to do here?

Xiulan would know, her traitor mind hissed, but she tamped those thoughts down. Xiulan was fine. She was capable of looking after herself, and she would find Lee soon enough. After all, she'd found Lee the once, hadn't she?

"You're not Shang, are you?" the princeling said eventually.

"Took you that long to figure it out?" said Lee. "What, do we all look the same to you?"

An uncomfortable silence followed.

"You're not serious," Lee said. "We all look the same to you?"

"I've learned much in the past three years," the princeling said, a little defensively. "Even more so in the past three days. So you're what? Yu-Kung?"

Lee rolled her eyes at his back. "Yu-Kung? You see me stopping to pray at the sun?" They were another set of folks that Shang didn't like to talk about, a people in the kingdom's far west who rejected Heaven's primacy in favor of the sun's warmth.

"Fine. Jeongsonese, then."

Lee couldn't help but be a little bit impressed. Normally, it took people twice as long when they got it in their heads to play this guessing game. "So I might have roots in Danggae. What's it to you?"

"I've heard of your people. The Shang have mistreated you for centuries. You don't have to listen to that princess anymore."

Frost spread all across the inside of Lee's chest at the mention of her.

But then she hardened her heart against that cold. "You think I'm doing this for her?"

"She identified herself as your partner and seemed quite concerned with your well-being, so yes, I thought that was a reasonable assumption to make."

His description of Xiulan sent blades of guilt carving through Lee. "The dogs take me, you talk as much as she does," she snapped. "Were you both born that way, or does that just happen when you grow up around people who aren't allowed to tell you to shut it?"

"You seem to have no shortage of things to say," the princeling said tightly.

"I didn't pass up the last chance I got to tell a royal what I thought of them. What makes you think I'd pass up this one?" said Lee. "You don't get to call up the ghosts of my people when you couldn't even see me for who I was. And you don't get to tell me about how the Shang are when the Tomodanese were just as bad."

"We weren't—" The princeling hung his head. "Never mind. I suspect you're right. So I suppose there's no point in appealing to you on my honor as a son of Tomoda?"

Lee snorted.

"Fair enough." He resumed walking. "Then allow me to make an appeal to you on logical grounds. Did you see the man who attacked the train?"

An involuntary shudder passed through Lee's body. She'd seen him, all right. But while fleeing such a man who defied all the known laws of magic squared neatly with her rogue persona, being afraid of him didn't. So she affected an easygoing tone as she said, "Nice coat, bad hair, lots of tattoos, scary beyond all reason? I might've caught me a glimpse."

"Then you know what danger your partner is in," said Prince Jimuro. "If you let me loose, I can get us a car, and we can race ahead. They were following a train track, after all. It wouldn't be hard to find them, even after all this time."

For a moment, she was tempted. Obviously, she wanted to know that Xiulan was alive and okay. Lee would even be able to spin it perfectly: that she hadn't fled in fear, but rather had seized an opportunity and merely gotten separated. She and Xiulan could reunite, their prize finally in tow, and then present him to the Crane Emperor together. Xiulan would become First Princess and someday Crane Empress, and Lee would get her promised kickbacks. Everything would come together, neat as the folds of a paper crane.

If she's alive, that voice in her head hissed again.

She shut it out. Of course Xiulan was alive. She had to be. She was the cleverest woman Lee had ever known. If Lee had to stack her up against whatever Sanbuna meathead or Cicada fanatics were still on that train, her money was on Xiulan.

And the purple guy?

She refocused. The purple guy wasn't a problem. Xiulan was smart enough to know he wasn't worth fighting. She would've gotten herself clear.

Somehow.

"Keep walking," Lee muttered. Her stomach growled softly, but she ignored it. She'd eaten relatively well since joining Xiulan's company, but before all that had been a lifetime full of missed meals. Hunger was an old friend, and like Lee's other old friends, it was an opportunistic shit who'd tried to sell her out at one point or another.

"Do you even know where the nearest Shang military base is?" the princeling said. "And when you show up on their doorstep, how do you suppose they'll greet you, a daughter of Jeongson with neither a badge to flash nor a princess in your pocket?"

The thought had crossed Lee's mind, but she was annoyed that it had crossed his, too. She was winging it here, and the last thing she needed was the princeling picking at her while she was trying to think. "That's not your problem."

The prince sighed. "Given that you're trying to off-load me, I'd disagree. But fair enough. Allow me to offer one further perspective."

And then the bastard just turned and ran.

"Hey!" Lee shouted. "Get back here, you royal idiot!"

She rushed to follow, but her boots were meant more for sneaking than running, and only on good ground, at that. The waterlogged dirt tugged greedily at her feet every time she picked them up.

She'd thought that three years in a Sanbuna prison would take the edge off Prince Jimuro, but he moved faster than she ever would have thought possible. She was out of her element in nature. There was no way she'd catch him.

She stopped and rolled her eyes. She'd officially run out of time for this. *You wanted to come out and play, girl?* she thought. *Well, here you go. "Bootstrap!"*

A flare of white light appeared, followed by a big, galumphing dog-shade. "Get him, girl," Lee said.

Bootstrap barked, then hared off after the princeling. He only had a moment to look over his shoulder, eyes widening in surprise as he was engulfed by the shadow of the leaping dog . . .

. . . who pinned him right to the ground and began showering his face with licks. As she did, images flitted through Lee's head. She saw Bootstrap the way she used to be: a small dog, thigh-high to the boy she lived with, tackling him to the grass of their palace and sitting on his chest to pin him in place. As the boy laughed, she frantically licked every inch of his face clean, eager to show him how much she loved him . . .

Something caught in Lee's breath, and it dropped her hard back into the moment unfolding in front of her. The Iron Prince was squirming and sputtering as a tongue larger than his own head matted down his hair and sent his glasses flying into the grass. *"Ah!"* he cried out between licks. *"Down! Kohaku, down!"*

Lee felt a little pulse from her dog-shade. Before she could unpack what it meant, though, she watched in surprise as Bootstrap immediately stopped licking the Iron Prince and sat down on top of him. She waited there expectantly, as her three tails pounded the grass flat with their wagging.

Jimuro sat up, breathing hard. "My glasses," he said. "Please, my—"

Lee had already picked them up. "Hold still," she said, then jammed them awkwardly onto his face.

He blinked owlishly, trying to see through cracked lenses that were smeared with drool. But apparently he could see well enough, because he squinted up at the shade pinning him in place, a spark of recognition dawning in his eyes. "What . . . ?" He squirmed to get out from under her, but Bootstrap sat obediently, tongue lolling and tails wagging excitedly. Lee was about to will Bootstrap to let him up, but then the princeling said, "Kohaku?"

Bootstrap whined. Her huge paws shuffled on either side of the prince's prone form in an excited little dance . . . or at least, what had been a little dance in her previous life. Now she ran the very real risk of popping Prince Jimuro's head like a grape.

"Bootstrap," Lee said in Jeongsonese. "Back it off."

Bootstrap shot an imploring look at Lee. Couldn't she see, her friend was *right there*! He was *right there,* and what in the world could possibly be more exciting? The dog-shade's heart was swollen to bursting with how much she cherished the princeling's sight and scent, and even the faint echoes of her joy that Lee felt hit her somewhere deep.

Jimuro rolled over, offering up his bonds. "Would you mind?" he said in a quiet, choked voice. "I promise, I'm not going to run." He coughed. "Again."

Lee's mouth twisted. This went against all of her instincts. But either she was in a soft mood, or Bootstrap's joy had put her in one. So she knelt and undid the knot, and then the Iron Prince's hands were free. She backed away before he could attack her, but he didn't even try. Instead, he picked himself up off the ground, wiping off his glasses with the tattered remains of his tie. She figured it would only take a few moments for his surprise and joy to turn into outrage. That, she was ready for.

What she wasn't ready for were the tears.

Rather than recoil, he wandered forward two steps, an arm outstretched. And with ginger gentleness, he laid a hand on Bootstrap's snout, just past her huge, wet nose. "Kohaku," he whispered.

Her eyes stared back at his, bright and brown like amber in sunlight.

He threw his arms around her thick neck in a tight hug, burying his face in her fur. Lee kept watching for the telltale signs of Tomodanese disgust or disdain; after all, this wasn't just any animal she'd pacted with.

But all she saw was a boy and a dog who loved each other very much.

Eventually, Prince Jimuro pulled himself away. He stared at Bootstrap, drinking in the dog-shade's face greedily, as if he still couldn't quite believe he was seeing her. "Where did you find her?" he said.

"Kohoyama," Lee said carefully. A bubble of discomfort hovered somewhere around her gut, and it grew larger with each passing second. "The Dahali there were taking care of her."

Jimuro nodded, accepting this. "And your . . . pact?"

Lee hesitated. "She got caught in some crossfire. I couldn't leave her behind, and I couldn't let her die. She made me promise to help her find you. That was our pact."

She expected the princeling to be moved by this, but the asshole looked away, chuckling.

Heat rose in her ears. "What?" she said. "There something funny about that to you?"

He waved her off and shook his head no. "You're not dissimilar to someone very important to me, that's all."

"The hell's that supposed to mean?"

"That it's difficult to compliment someone who could find an insult in a bouquet of peonies."

It wasn't lost on her, how he'd chosen to use the Shang national flower for his example. Mentally, she took a step back. There she was, getting defensive again. It wasn't like her to get hot under the collar. The dogs take her, why did she feel so off-balance?

"I'm not a flowers kind of girl," Lee said, hoping her tone would convey enough of an apology that she wouldn't need to offer up a verbal one. "And I'm not too wild about peonies in particular, if you get my drift."

Prince Jimuro inclined his head, as if to say *Fair enough*. "My whole family's dead," he said simply, running his fingers through Bootstrap's thick golden fur.

"I know," Lee said. "Local kids got the day off from school after the news broke about your old man."

Jimuro shot her a narrow-eyed look, and the bubble of discomfort inside her inflated a little more.

"When we held court, I always had people around me: servants, friends, playmates. There were hundreds of them at all times, and they always wanted something from me. Captain Sakura wanted to protect me, Lord Kurihara wanted me to fall in love with his son so he could marry into the family, and my mother wanted me to pay attention so someday I could be the greatest Steel Lord in history. There were only two people who never wanted anything from me except my companionship. One died on a mission to rescue me from Sanbu. The other, I thought would be dead for sure. I would've given anything to see her again. I can't believe I'm saying this, Inspector, but . . . thank you."

Lee shifted her weight uncomfortably. "Lee," she said. "It's 'Lee,' not 'Inspector.'"

"Lee? Just Lee?"

She tried to smile. "Lee's all you need to know." Normally, her roguish grin would've come so easily to her right about now. But her smile faltered as she found herself staring at this man and her dog.

Images flashed through her head: her mother, spending her dying breaths on children who wouldn't even be talking to one another two years later. Petting every dog she passed on the street, just in case. Half throwing herself out of a speeding car to scoop up Bootstrap's magic-addled body, feeling the flutter of her failing heart just beneath her chest . . .

. . . and of course, the woman in the driver's seat.

At the thought of Xiulan's one-eyed smile, Bootstrap's ears pricked up. Her tails grew still. And her head cocked hard to the south. She barked once, just once.

"What is it?" Prince Jimuro said. "What's gotten into Kohaku?"

Lee ignored him. She had eyes only for the southbound road. Was it possible? Bootstrap's impeccable nose had managed to pick up Prince Jimuro's scent from half a country away, just because of the connection between the two of them. Was her nose even better than Lee had thought? Had it managed to dig up yet another connection that was stronger than the miles that separated one end of it from the other?

And yet, despite her doubts, she could feel it . . . the stink of axle grease, the vaguely fiery smell of metal on metal, the earthiness of . . . mushrooms?

Still, there was no mistaking it: It was her. Relief flooded Lee's body as she noted the absence of the telltale stench of death. Shang Xiulan was alive, and she was headed south.

But the longer Lee stared southward, the larger that bubble of discomfort inside her grew. She felt as if something inside her needed to be washed and scrubbed away, with the roughest steel wool she could find in Tomoda.

That bubble didn't pop when she said to the princeling, "Come on, then."

It didn't pop when she nodded to Bootstrap and said, "Lead the way."

It didn't pop when she took her first step on the road to Hagane, or her second, or her fifth, or her tenth. In fact, the more she considered having to look Xiulan in the face again at the end of this journey, the bigger still the bubble became.

Lee Yeon-Ji walked on just the same.

CHAPTER TWENTY-EIGHT

TALA

*T*he hospital stank of blood, and shit, and scorched flesh, and always death.

The last one, Tala never could've described precisely. But she always knew it when she smelled it, and never was it stronger than in places like this. The staff had gamely attempted to cover it with flowers, and then with industrial bleaches and chemicals, but those scents had merely draped over the hospital's true stench like an ill-fitting dress.

It didn't help that it was a typically sweltering day in Lisan City. The heat seemed to agitate all the bad smells, and the humidity ensured that they hung in the air, heavy as a body in a noose. She wiped sweat from her forehead with a small hand and felt a fresh layer replace it almost instantly. She wiped her hand on her dress, then shook its top hem a few times to give the rest of her body a momentary respite from the roasting heat.

When her hands came away, they were still covered in sweat.

Tala gulped. That wasn't from the heat, and she knew it.

All around her, she saw bloody, burnt, and bandaged people. Most, she knew, were civilians. But among them were members of the resistance: the bravest of Sanbu's children, who had grown increasingly bold in their efforts to pry open Tomoda's steel grip. Just *two weeks ago, reports had emerged that Erega had personally led a raid on a Tomodanese supply depot, making off with a huge stockpile of weapons. Now, in an irony that appealed deeply to twelve-year-old Tala's sense of justice, they were being turned on the hands that had forged them.*

Reading that report had been what had finally decided things for Tala. She'd kept her head down for a few years, but now she was certain: She wanted to join the jungle-runners of the resistance. She would live to see the day Tomoda was cast out of the Sanbu Islands forever, and she wanted to be part of the reason why.

But if she was going to fight, she needed a shade.

She already had a shade, of course. Not two years ago, she'd done something desperate. Something so unheard-of and taboo, even at age ten she'd known not to tell a single soul about it. Mang would've been a force to reckon with on the battlefield. For the outgunned and outmanned jungle-runners, he might have even become indispensable, if they were willing to use him. But Tala knew that one glimpse of him was all it would take to guarantee her a swift death warrant, even from Erega. A splintersoul—a real, living one—was an enemy to all nations.

So, no. If she was going to join the fight and avenge her family, Mang included, then she had no choice but to find another. To her, it seemed so obvious. She couldn't retreat from being a splintersoul. Since shades were the thing Tomoda reviled most of all, Tala could think of no better monster to become.

"You don't need to become a monster," Mang had told her one night as she puzzled over how to make this happen. "There's plenty of other good you can do."

Through their connection, she'd felt a low-bubbling current of guilt. What he'd meant to say was, You don't need to become a monster because of me.

She pushed past that. "Our parents were doing good," she'd said savagely, ignoring the way her legs shook with the effort it took just to stay standing. She'd gotten better at bearing the pain that came with summoning him, but it was still overpowering. "Look where it got them."

He leveled a huge frown at her. "What happened to them wasn't their fault."

Tala clenched her fists and glanced down at her bare, dirty feet. "I know," she said. "Why do you think I want to be a monster?"

But despite her conviction, the path to it eluded her. She couldn't go to a library to learn about it; the Tomodanese had removed as much information about shadepacting as they could from the public's reach. And while there were a few adults in her life, mostly shopkeepers who were friendly when she needed food, this was hardly the sort of thing she could talk to any of them about. She'd even tried capturing rats and pigeons and even stray cats, hoping she could find one to pact with. But without her dying brother to steady her focus, she couldn't reconnect with her own soul.

But then she'd remembered what Mang had explained to her about pacting. It wasn't as simple as finding an animal you liked and petting it. There had to be resonance between one soul and another. Right now, her soul was consumed with the fires of rage, and the only thing that could feed it was war. What she needed was the soul of a warrior.

No. Of a soldier.

She was proud of the plan she'd landed on. She was going to be smart about this. If her suspicions were true, she would be reinstating a shade to service, to continue the fight that its partner no longer could. And if they weren't true, then all she'd cost herself was an unpleasant visit to the hospital.

"It won't work," Mang had told her the night before, when she'd been going over the plan with him.

"It might not work," Tala said. "I won't know until I've tried."

"But pacting directly with a shade?" he said. "A shade already bonded to someone else's soul?"

"You've heard we can only pact with animals," Tala said to him. "Did you also hear that we can't pact with people?"

Mang had fallen silent. She'd been stung by the sadness in his eyes, but not enough to be dissuaded. More than anything, what she wanted now was to finish what Tomoda had started.

So in the light of day, she crept past the nurses and orderlies, down the stairs to the wing for "honored citizens." Or at least, that was what the official signs declared it to be, so as not to arouse Tomodanese suspicion. But everyone on the street knew what the wing really housed: resistance fighters who'd almost died in the line of duty, but *not quite made it all the way there. Rumor had it that Erega was using her own personal wealth to fund the wing and see that these fighters were cared for. Whether it was true or not, it inflated the woman to even greater stature in Tala's mind. How incredibly noble was she, to be so dedicated to her troops even after their fight was over?*

The floors down here were wooden, slick with varnish so they could be easily cleaned. The walls were white, and absent dust or errant droplets of blood. Even the bare lightbulbs seemed . . . not gentler, but at least less harsh. And yet these did nothing to still her heart, which only beat faster with each step she took.

She stopped in the middle of the corridor and sniffed deeply. Though its denizens were closer to death than any upstairs, the telltale scent was nowhere to be found.

There were no private rooms here, just a line of beds along either wall, with simple white curtains to separate them. In each bed was a woman or man wrapped in a clean white linen gown. Their sheets had been stripped away to protect them from the heat. Some had their eyes closed. Some stared with wide-open, bloodshot eyes at the ceiling above. But none of them moved.

Nurses bustled about from bed to bed, adjusting machinery and fluffing pillows. They chattered away to one another in medical jargon that went over Tala's head. She stood there watching them for almost a full minute before one of them noticed she was there.

"Hello there!" he said pleasantly. It rankled Tala to hear him pitching his voice up at her like she was a child, even though she was a child. "Are you lost, little girl?"

Tala forced herself to undo her default scowl. Smiles never sat comfortably on her lips, so she had to rely on her youthful charms to make up the difference. "I'm here to see my . . . brother," she said, then cursed. Why did she have to say "brother"? That already cut down half her choices in this ward. She would've kept her options open if she'd just said something like cousin *or* friend.

"Oh, of course," said the nurse, widening his eyes and mouth into what he probably thought was a reassuring display. Tala appreciated that he meant well, but already her patience had worn thin.

She glanced at the nearest bed, where an older man lay at peace. The side of his face was a scabbed-over ruin. Her stomach turned at the sight of him. She glanced quickly at the chart hanging from the foot of his bed. It listed his cause of injury as "industrial accident," but there was no mistaking a wound like that.

The nurse frowned for the first time. "He's your brother?"

Immediately she reached for his limp hand, tamping down on how much the touch made her skin crawl. She squeezed it gently. "No one saw me coming. Not even our parents."

The nurse studied her a long moment, then nodded. "Your parents haven't been by."

Tala didn't have to fake the distant look in her eyes when she said, "They won't be."

The nurse blinked, tears forming in the corners of his eyes. Inwardly, Tala groaned. That was the last thing she needed right now.

"You poor thing," he whispered to himself, clutching his heart. He looked down at the bed's occupant, her "brother." "All those bad things happening out there? They'll be over soon, I promise."

Tala squeezed the sleeping man's hand tighter, began to search for that warm place inside herself, and hoped he was wrong.

Xiulan had listened politely while Tala relayed all this to her. It had felt strange, voicing all of it aloud, like she had a splinter in her foot and she had felt it with every step she'd taken for the past ten years. Telling Xiulan hadn't been like removing the splinter so much as finally taking medicine to dull the pain.

"It sounds as if you already have a steady grounding in the facts of the matter," Xiulan said when Tala was done. Tala appreciated how attentive she'd been, but she was rapidly tiring of the princess's ability to turn a three-word thought into a thirty-word sentence. "What benefit do you foresee from consulting with me?"

"I learned that day I could take someone's shade if I wanted," Tala said. "Making Dimangan into one changed something about me. But I never wanted to do it again, after the first time."

"And now?"

Tala stared at her with haunted eyes. "It's taking everything I have not to reach over and rip that rat out of you."

Xiulan shrank back.

Tala held up a hand in apology. "I'm a soldier, Princess. I'm not going to touch you."

"Anymore," Xiulan grumbled, rubbing her forehead.

"I'm not going to apologize for that," Tala said simply. "So, do you have an idea of what's going on with me, or not?"

Xiulan sucked thoughtfully on her empty pipe. "This shade of yours . . . Beaky . . . he doesn't originate from your own soul, correct? His origins lie with the man in the purple coat?"

Tala nodded.

"Then perhaps, ah, Beaky's removal had an adverse effect on his own soul," Xiulan said. "An adverse effect that's been the proverbial engine under his equally proverbial hood, all these years."

Tala narrowed her eyes. "Then you mean . . . ?"

"I suppose what I'm saying," Xiulan said carefully, "is that by removing Dimangan from you, he tore your own soul asunder . . . and that until you've been made whole once more, no other cure will suffice."

Slow as a sinking balloon, Tala's gaze drifted down to her hands.

Xiulan frowned. "I understand much of what I've said may be disturbing to you," she said, ever sharp on the uptake. "I would remind you that the information I've given you here, despite my diversity of sources, is still at best a mix of reasonable guesswork, analogies based in folktales, and the occasional barely corroborated historical record. Which is to say, Sergeant Tala, that I can always be wrong."

Tala glanced up at Xiulan, who fiddled with the pipe she clung to like a child with their favorite blanket. "That a habit of yours? Being wrong?"

"Not as such, no," Xiulan said. "My educated guesses tend to be so well educated that the designation of 'guess' is more a matter of etiquette. But I remind you that the possibility—however slim—does exist. I would hope that a woman as resilient as you wouldn't lose heart."

Tala cocked an eyebrow. "So you care about the state of my heart now?"

"Of course I do," the princess said. "If you didn't notice, Sergeant, we're in a fridge together."

Tala snorted. Compared with all the other shit she'd been through in the past week, being trapped in a fridge seemed downright ordinary.

But the amusement lasted only a moment before it was drowned out again by the howling hunger inside her head. She tried not to think about it, but trying just made her think about it more. Warily, she eyed her twitching fingers. She needed to keep them under control, not consider how easily they would slip around Princess Xiulan's throat and—

No, she said forcefully, bringing her mind to heel. She couldn't let herself fall into this. She was too disciplined to become a mad dog like the splintersoul. She was a soldier.

But a voice in the back of her head whispered: *So was he.*

Tala wasn't sure how much time passed before the door opened again, revealing Kurihara Kosuke. He glanced over her and the Shang princess a moment before gesturing to someone out of Tala's line of sight. "Get them out here and bind them," he said. "Use wood cuffs for the Sanbuna."

Xiulan shot her a questioning look, but Tala avoided making eye contact. She'd neglected to fill Xiulan in on that detail, because the truth was that she hadn't quite wrapped her mind around it, herself. She'd had long years to make peace with the reality of splintersouls, and that had been easy enough. Xiulan's guesswork about her current condition even lined up pretty well with all that. But shadepacting and metalpacting? There was no precedent for that at all. Not in myth, not in movies, not in yesterday's paper. Hell, Tala wouldn't have been convinced of it herself, if she hadn't seen the knife with her own eyes, and the cauterized stump it had left behind.

And not just that, a nagging voice in her head said as she remembered her fingers bloodlessly closing around Harada's blade.

They were cuffed and hauled out of the fridge, then shoved to their knees in the middle of the dining car. The place was still in disarray from last night, the floors and walls covered in bloodstains and battle damage. But mercifully, it was at least empty of civilians.

"Lord Kurihara," Xiulan said without preamble. "I know we've only recently made each other's acquaintance, but I think it fair to remind you here of the stature I occupy in my native land of Shang."

But Kurihara didn't even bother to look at her. He was staring hard at Tala, his hands folded into the flowing sleeves of his kimono.

"However you may feel about Shang or its ruler—and rest assured, on the subject of my father you would likely find me a kindred spirit—you can't deny the delicate diplomatic position in which Tomoda finds itself. Any harm that befalls me would doubtless be reflected in the tenor of the ensuing peace talks, which will surely determine—"

Kurihara's hands withdrew from his sleeves. Tala steeled herself for the glint of his gun, ready to make a desperate bid for freedom before she got a bullet between the eyes. But rather than a heavy Tomodanese pistol, his hand held . . .

. . . another hand, covered in pactmarks.

The hand fell heavily to the floor in front of her. Tala stopped herself from reacting to the sight of it, but Xiulan didn't have her discipline. She let out a curse in Shang and recoiled from it, as if she expected it to start crawling across the floor like a crab.

The Cicadas exchanged sneers, but Kurihara alone was unamused. He had eyes only for Tala. "Explain this," he said. "All of it. You lie, I take a finger. You insult me, I take a finger. You call your slave, I take an eye."

"Lord Kurihara," Xiulan said insistently, "you should know that this woman has been taken on as a member of my personal retinue, and as such is subject to the same protections—"

With casual contempt, Kurihara backhanded her. From where Tala knelt, it didn't look like much more than a light cuff, but it was enough to get Xiulan sputtering with outrage.

"Your father's name is the only reason you're still alive," Kurihara said, still not deigning even to look at her. "Show your gratitude by not interrupting the adults while they're talking." He nodded to Tala. "Speaking of which: Start talking."

Beaky's name was half formed on Tala's tongue before she caught herself. Her head had been consumed with vivid fantasies of setting him on the nearest Cicadas while she lunged straight for Kurihara, ready to wrap both hands around his throat—

And then what had seemed so appealing a second ago made her

stomach turn. *For shades' sake, Tala,* she told herself as she fought back the throbbing in her head, *keep it the fuck together.*

So instead of Beaky's name, she said, "I don't know his name. All I know is that he steals shades from others with a touch." She nodded to the disembodied hand, which itself bore three pactmarks that she could see. "From what I've seen, he's got a big collection."

Kurihara eyed her, as if tasting her words for the telltale flavor of falsehood. "Hn," he said eventually. "Fine. What does he want with the Iron Prince?"

Tala hesitated. The last bits of information had been easy enough to give up. But the truth here would complicate things.

She swallowed. "Nothing," she said. "He's been after me."

Kurihara adopted a very ugly look. "Your so-called protection was endangering His Brilliance the entire time, then?"

"We didn't know," Tala said. "We both thought he was after Jimu—"

The backhand that came for her was much harder than the one Kurihara used on Xiulan. It nearly sent Tala to the floor, and made her vision pop with stars. When she blinked to steady her sight, she saw Kurihara had leaned down next to her, so their faces were mere inches apart.

"You don't get to speak his name," he hissed to her. "You think you know him? You know less than nothing, slaver. *You don't get to speak his name.*"

He leaned back, and his composure seemed to return more and more with each inch he put between them.

"Now," he said. "How did you come to learn our sacred and noble art of metalpacting?"

Once again, Xiulan stared at Tala, now in disbelief.

Once again, Tala refused to meet her eye. One problem at a time, and right now Kurihara was her biggest one.

She chose her words carefully. She'd been truthful so far, and Kurihara had believed her. So it didn't immediately lose her a finger when she said, "He taught me."

Xiulan's eye widened.

So did both of Kurihara's, before falling back into a suspicious squint. "Who's 'he'?"

Tala grinned. "Who do you think?"

Kurihara gaped.

"Think about it," she said to him. "How many other Tomodanese could I possibly know? How many would I have time to take lessons from? How many," she added, "would I be comfortable calling by their name?"

Kurihara looked as if he'd just swallowed soap.

"If I might intrude now," Xiulan said.

With labored slowness, Kurihara at last turned to face her.

"May I inquire as to where you intend to take us?"

Kurihara scowled, but at last he answered. "You, we intend to sell you back to your family in Hagane, at a premium. And you," he said, turning his attention back to Tala. "You . . . you . . . *abomination.*"

The translation wasn't perfect between Tomodanese and San-buna, but the word was similar enough to what the man in the pur-ple coat had called Mang. Once again, Tala felt the throbbing in the back of her head, and with it the rising urge to rip her cuffs to splin-ters, tackle Kurihara to the ground, and slip her thumbs into his stupid eyes and just . . . *push* . . .

"The only reason you're still alive," Kurihara said, "the *only* rea-son, is because His Brilliance specifically tasked me with your well-being. If any harm befalls you, he said he would hold me personally responsible. So you live until I can present you to him myself and prove to His Brilliance that I've kept my word."

Tala's bloodlust receded slightly. But it didn't stray far, as if it weren't yet convinced it wouldn't be needed.

"Why?" Kurihara said eventually. "Why would he teach you metalpacting? What could you possibly have done to convince him that . . ." He trailed off, as if the question were too painful for him to finish.

Tala got it. But her inability to care about Kurihara's feelings had reached spectacular new heights in the past minute or so.

"That's between us," she said. "But you're close to him. I'm sure he'll tell you the story himself someday."

Kurihara gnashed his teeth, then gestured at the open refrigerator door. "Throw them back in," he said.

"Lord Kurihara," Xiulan said. "I hardly think that necessary, given that you've already secured our cooperation."

"You, perhaps," Kurihara said. "But this one would eat my heart if she could. Probably stewed in my own blood, if the rumors I hear about Sanbuna cooking are true."

What he said about neither her nor Sanbuna cooking was untrue, but Tala's nostrils flared in rage anyway.

"Wait!" Xiulan said, now urgent. "Among your prisoners, is there a tall, striking woman of Jeongsonese descent? I beg you, I must know."

Kurihara squinted at her. "Jeongsonese? I thought you people killed all those dogfuckers."

As he chuckled, Xiulan deflated. Tala felt an annoying spike of sympathy for the verbose Shang princess.

"So. As I said: the fridge." At that, the Cicadas grabbed Tala's hands and hauled her back up to her feet. "But think of it this way," he added with a smile as they were led back to their chilly prison. "At least when you reach Hagane, you'll be nice and fresh."

And so she and the princess landed right back where they'd started, in the dark confines of a walk-in refrigerator on a battered train as it sped south to Hagane.

"It is a truly breathtaking thing, the number of times I've found myself in one manner of cell or another over the course of this journey," Xiulan said. She toyed with the long bang that obscured her left eye. "I'd never expected to do so much of my traveling in them."

Tala laid back and closed her eyes. She was so tired, and the throbbing hole in her soul where Dimangan belonged meant that even if she managed to get some sleep now, there was no way it would be restful. She'd never experienced anything like this, but she could see a few moves ahead. Until she was whole again, this was going to eat at her from the inside out.

"So," the Shang princess said. "Metalpacting. Perhaps you might expound on how you came by such a rare skill for a Sanbuna?"

Slowly, Tala's eyes opened. "There's such a thing as being too curious, Your Majesty."

"Nonetheless, my curiosity persists."

Tala scowled. She didn't owe this Shang her honesty, but if it would shut her up . . .

"Fine," she said. "You want to know?"

"I believe I've adequately communicated that."

Tala shrugged. "Beats the hell out of me. One second, I couldn't do it; the next, he didn't have a hand."

"I see, I see," said Princess Xiulan, before dissolving into a thoughtful silence.

After a few moments, Tala said, "If you've got a theory, share it before I come over there and beat it out of you."

"There's no need for that, Sergeant," she said. "I was merely reluctant to postulate with so little data from which to extrapolate."

"Then give me your best hunch," Tala said, struggling to hear her own thoughts over the snarling rage in the back of her throbbing head.

Princess Xiulan's mouth twisted. "I once read that all the world's known disciplines of magic were fruits hanging from different branches of the human soul. It posited that when one climbed far enough out onto the branch to, ah, pick the fruit, so to speak, one made it impossible to climb back to the tree. Does that make sense?"

"Only kind of."

"That will suffice. The author went on to suppose that while going back the way one came on an individual branch was impossible, there were extraordinary life-or-death situations in which a person might, ah, jump."

Tala raised an eyebrow. "Did he give any examples?"

"They," Xiulan corrected. "And I'm afraid not. When it comes to the interdisciplinary approach to magic, you're quite unique. It takes a particular rigidity to pact with metal."

Unsatisfied, Tala muttered her thanks and closed her eyes again. As the pain returned, she kept it at bay by letting her thoughts wander to the other royal she'd spent time with: His eyes, their intelligence sharpened by the glasses that framed them. His voice, and the surprisingly skilled way it spoke Sanbuna. His body, tangled in his sheets—

Her eyes opened again. That wasn't helping, either.

She sighed, settling back against a shelf of food (with no meat or coffee, she noted sourly). Wherever Jimuro was, she hoped he was better off than she was.

CHAPTER TWENTY-NINE

JIMURO

Jimuro liked the *idea* of walking.

He was entranced by the fantasy of having his home soil underfoot and his native sky overhead. He liked the stories he'd read of heroes striding on the road toward their destinies, and the romantic visions of soldiers marching in lockstep, singing songs of bravery and valor. And when he'd crashed his and Tala's car into those Shang, he'd told himself that now would be the time for him to finally experience the magic of a long journey on foot for himself. But after two (non-consecutive) days on foot, Jimuro could admit: Walking sucked.

His feet had been sore enough the night they'd met up with Kosuke. A day spent riding around in his motorcade and aboard the *Crow's Flight* had allowed his body to recover some, but by midday of his southward trek with Lee, he felt like he'd already burned through every reserve of energy he had.

"There's one," Lee said, pointing down the road. Jimuro squinted through his cracked lenses, and sure enough the high-noon sun glinted off a distant windshield.

"No," Jimuro said flatly, while his feet throbbed in outrage.

"You're *limping*," Lee said.

"Your sudden concern for my gait is touching."

"Yeah, that's me," Lee said, frowning at the car as it zipped right by them. "A big, bleeding heart."

Jimuro measured his new companion with a look. She certainly wasn't what he expected from an agent of the Li-Quan, though he did admire her ability to keep an air of dignity about herself, even as they trudged through muck and mire. In the hours since they'd gotten to know each other, she'd been sharp-tongued, sullen, impatient, and he was pretty certain he would've been relieved of his wallet by now if he were still carrying one. Her Jeongsonese heritage notwithstanding, he suspected she might have actually done well in the Court of Steel, in another lifetime. He wasn't totally sure what had made her decide to take him to Hagane, and not knowing where she stood meant he had no reason to really trust her.

But then she'd introduced him to the third member of their party.

Jimuro didn't understand Jeongsonese, so he couldn't quite make out the name that Lee had given his old friend. But he'd known the dog in her previous life as Kohaku, and the amber color of her fur meant that the name still applied. Besides, while Kohaku had more than tripled in size as a shade, it took only one look at her face for Jimuro to see that she was still the same friend she'd always been.

Apparently, Kohaku felt the same way. The way Lee described it, she and Xiulan had been able to find him because Kohaku had scented him out all the way from Kohoyama.

"But that's hundreds of kilometers," Jimuro had said when Lee had dropped that particular grenade.

"I know," she'd said. "Not like I traveled them all, or anything."

"I just . . . I didn't realize that shades could do that."

Lee had smirked at him. "For the prince of a country whose whole thing is how much you hate shades," she'd said, "you're sure interested in them."

Jimuro had caught himself. "Hating shades is not our 'whole thing,'" he'd bristled. "And Kohaku isn't just any shade."

Lee had crooked an eyebrow at that, but she let it lie.

That conversation had happened hours ago, when the sun was still low in the sky. Now it beat down from its highest perch, but Jimuro's mind was still on the matter of Kohaku. If someone trust-

worthy had told him ahead of time that when he next saw his beloved friend she would be a thrall to an outlander thief, he would've
been hard-pressed to pick out which part of that prophecy disgusted
him the most. Enslaving any creature's spirit was an affront to nature, but enslaving one of his friends was an affront to him.

And yet when the moment had come, there had been no disgust
anywhere in his body. He'd just been so happy to see a familiar face.
To see someone who was just happy to see *him*.

And now, her nose was leading them to Hagane.

To his crown and throne.

To the rest of his life.

His breath turned sour in the back of his throat.

To the rest of his life.

The ground was rushing to meet him.

To the rest of his life.

And the midday sun was turning dark . . .

*His cell in Lisan City hadn't really been much of a cell. He'd had
three rooms to himself on the Erega estate. Every way in and out
had been under heavy guard, but even a man as privileged as Jimuro
was aware that his own troops were being kept by Sanbu in much
worse conditions. He'd tried to escape twice, and been easily foiled
both times. After the second failure, he'd settled in for the long haul.
He quietly hoped his mother might open the floor for a hostage exchange of some kind, but he knew her unyielding nature too well to
seriously put stock in the idea.*

*And besides, what combination of prisoners in Tomoda's dun-
geons could have possibly measured equal to him?*

*When Erega came to visit him, which was often enough, it was
usually in the sitting room, where he spent his time drawing, filling
up sketchbook after sketchbook all day long. The staff would bring
him meals there twice a day, and fresh paper or brushes when he
requested them. At first, it had started as a ploy to get his hands on
lead-based paint, in the hope of eventually accruing enough metal to
effect an escape. But Erega was too wily for that, and neither his
paints nor brushes contained so much as a molecule of metal. So as*

the months of his imprisonment wore on and turned into years, he was no closer to finding a way home, but he'd gotten reasonably good at capturing the essence on paper of each guard assigned to his detail. When Erega came in to visit him that day, however, he was in the middle of painting his new favorite subject: himself.

Despite his promises that he couldn't manipulate the metal in a mirrored surface, the Sanbuna military had allowed him no mirrors. So as a challenge to himself, he'd begun to paint his own face from memory, guessing at the ways in which captivity might have aged him. He tried watercolors, pencils, even charcoal. But that day, his challenge had just been plain black ink on plain white paper, with only one wrinkle: He had to draw the portrait in a single, unbroken line.

"General," he said, not looking up from his paper. "I'm glad you chose now to come in, and not when I was working my way around the glasses. If I'd known I would be drawing these someday, I would've chosen round frames . . ."

"Your Brilliance." Though Jimuro had seen the woman face-to-face hundreds of times, for some reason he couldn't conjure her visage inside this dream.

Dream? *he thought.* Am I dreaming?

"But we're out of the woods," he said to the general, "and I think this might be one of my better renderings." He frowned thoughtfully as his brush slid across the page, laying down another contour of his pointed chin. "Actually, perhaps not. But when they write the history of my artistic progression, they'll call this an important stepping-stone."

"Your Brilliance, there's no easy way to say this, especially if you won't listen to me," said Erega. "The Palace of Steel has fallen, Tomoda has surrendered, and your mother is dead."

Jimuro froze. At last he looked up from the paper spread out before him, though somehow the sight of Erega's face slid off his mind like a slick of spilled oil. "What?"

The general's grip tightened on her cane. She bowed—not in the collegial way that two equals might, but deeply from the waist. Though it was an appropriately respectful gesture, it wasn't one typical of the general, who'd begun to develop a bad back.

And it was how Jimuro knew that she was telling the truth, that it wasn't some sort of mistake. His mother, the great Steel Lord Yo-shiko, was dead. He was vaguely aware of Erega's voice as it sketched in further details: that it had happened in the palace's beautiful royal garden, that she'd been caught by Shang forces while trying to help the household staff evacuate, that she'd earned herself a good death. But while he heard those words, he'd stopped listening after "Your mother is dead." It had been Fumiko, and then his father, and now the indomitable Steel Lord herself.

Now there was only him.

"Your Brilliance," said General Erega. "Your brush."

Jimuro glanced down. His brush tip had frozen at the precise spot where it had been when he'd heard the news. The fibers of the paper had wicked black ink farther and farther away from that spot, so that half his face was now covered in a cancerous blotch.

"Your Brilliance," said General Erega again, except her voice sounded different. When Jimuro blinked, her face at last came into focus. Except he didn't see the craggy, tired eye of Tomoda's most notorious and legendary foe, but the eyes of a young woman, whose hawklike focus had always been able to pierce right through him.

His pulse quickened at the sight of her. "Tala," he whispered.

And then the sergeant gave a very un-Tala-like roll of her eyes. "Oh, fuck this."

A sharp pain shot up and down his ribs, and he sat right up with a loud *"Ow!"* A few decimeters away, Kohaku barked loud enough to ripple Jimuro's hair.

Lee, who was poised to kick him again, put her foot down. "Easy, girl," she said. "Just needed to get him awake. We're good here."

"What happened?" Jimuro said, climbing to his feet. His forehead throbbed. "Did we come under attack?"

"Yeah," said Lee. "You fell right into your enemies' trap of being a stubborn dumbass."

"Your sarcasm is neither helpful nor appreciated."

"Nothing I do is ever helpful or appreciated."

Jimuro rolled his eyes. The woman had an answer to everything, it seemed. "Very well. We can continue now."

Lee snorted. "You're in no kind of shape."

"I'll be the judge of that. I'm stronger than you think."

She shook her head. "Wasn't your strength that failed you, just now."

Jimuro felt stricken. "What would you know about it?" he said, too quickly.

"I've seen it before," Lee said. "Had a friend who was always a bit twitchy, but fun when you wanted a drink or a turn in bed. Saw her try to lift a wallet once—"

"You associated with criminals?"

"I wasn't always a cop, Princeling."

"How long have you been one?"

"Two weeks and change," she breezed. "Point is, she froze up with her hand halfway out the man's pocket. I'll never forget it. She had this look in her eyes, like the ground had just dropped out from under her feet and the air had sucked itself back out her lungs."

The familiarity of her words chilled him.

"So you're found seized up, your hand on a wallet halfway out its owner's pocket, and you're Jeongsonese in a country that doesn't give a shit about you, occupied by another country that doesn't give a shit about you," Lee said. "What d'you think happened to her?"

Jimuro's stomach turned again.

"If I'm gonna throw myself into the teeth of mortal peril, I don't want to do it when the only person I've got to rely on is twitchy," Lee said. "So what gives? Last night, knowing that come tomorrow you get to sit in a big chair and wear a shiny hat—"

"—the Steel Lord doesn't do either of those things—" Jimuro tried to interject.

"—you instead decide to turn around and walk right into the jaws of a homicidal maniac?" Lee cut across him.

Jimuro froze. "I was doing the right thing."

Lee waved his words off like they were gnats. "Right thing would've been to get your sorry ass out of there, Princeling . . . and it ended up working out that way," she added with a wolfish grin. "But that man was a factory-grade sausage grinder, and you were going to feed yourself to him anyway. And you did it without even thinking, too."

Jimuro exhaled. "I was doing what I thought was best for my people. I was serving them."

"Can't serve them when you're dead, idiot."

"You will not address me as—"

"I'm taking you south to get kinged up, so I'll address you however the fuck I want," Lee said.

"No, you're going south to find your partner. You just don't care enough about my own mission to stop it."

"The dogs take me, I haven't even known you a whole day and I'm already tired of you. Out with it: You don't want to be Steel Lord, do you?"

"Of course I do!" Jimuro snapped, color flooding to his ears and cheeks.

Lee glanced at Kohaku, then said, "Not according to her, you don't. She can smell it on you, Princeling. The way she tells it, the throne scares you shitless."

Scared? Impossible. The throne was his birthright. As far back as he could remember, he'd always known that his mother's throne would one day be his own.

But not so soon, whispered his mother's flinty voice. *Not before you were ready.*

He gritted his teeth and tried to shut her out.

"Be straight with me, Princeling," said Lee. "How many other times on this trip have you tried to off yourself?"

"I would never be so irresponsible with my life when it's not my own to spend," Jimuro bristled. "And even if I'd wanted to, Tala never would have let me come even close."

But suddenly he was thinking of that moment in the hold of the *Marlin* when he felt the breeze of Tala's bullet zipping past his temple. He remembered, with chilling clarity, how readily she'd pulled that trigger at his goading. He considered, with solidifying certainty, how easily she could have ended him. Of the favor she'd almost done his country.

The moment the thought crossed his mind, he felt flat-footed. Where had that come from?

His mother's voice chimed in again, distant and cold: *Where do you think?*

Memories of the last few days flashed through his head. Driving a car headlong into a Shang barricade. Giving himself up to the man in the purple coat. Taunting Tala in that hold, to the point that she'd been willing to throw away her duty.

Pushing her again in Shinku until she, his staunchest guard, finally left him in a pit of vipers.

". . . Spirits take me," he muttered.

"Yeah, that's what I thought," Lee said. "Look, I'm not saying I blame you. Your family's dead. The world hates your guts. And once you take that throne of yours, if you don't watch your step, that blows back on your people. Shit, if I was in your fancy boots, I'd think really hard about eating my gun, too."

Jimuro's jaw dropped. "How can you say such things?" he said. "How callous a woman are you?"

Lee shrugged. "I'm not saying you should. In fact, I'd rather you didn't, because I'd be pissed if I went through all this trouble for nothing. But I get it. And sticking around's gotta be your decision. If I try to take it out of your hands, you'll just get it in your head to find some way to try again." She narrowed her eyes at him appraisingly. "Probably doing something you'd tell yourself was a noble sacrifice, but really was just fucking stupid. So what's it going to be? You actually want to do this, or not?"

And just like that, his vision swam again, his breaths shortening by the moment. He'd only just understood this about himself. How was he supposed to have a cohesive answer already?

A vision of his mother's throne room floated before him. *Because, Your Brilliance,* said a strong voice that was neither his mother's nor his own, *you have to.*

"I'm not ready for this, Lee," he said eventually. "I never even got to say goodbye to my family, and now I have to carry on their legacy all by myself. And if I fail, my whole country pays the price for it. What if I can't be the Steel Lord they need? What if everyone at these peace talks is just setting me up to fail?"

"Getting boxed in by powerful people who don't give a shit about you?" said Lee. "Sounds *awful*. What d'you think that's like?"

"I just thought . . ." He hesitated, then forced himself to say the words. "I thought a dead hero would be worth more to the people of Tomoda than a living fool. I thought the world would be better off without me."

"Well, to be fair," Lee said, "you're not wrong."

Jimuro recoiled as if he'd been slapped. "By the spirits, what's wrong with you?"

"What?" Lee said. "It's not your fault. Well, you're prince of the worst empire in the history of the world, so I guess it kind of is. But what I meant was, you're a king, or you're about to be. Not a country in the world that wouldn't be better off without one, if you ask me. Whole point of this, though, isn't to get my input." She placed a hand on Kohaku's flank, and the dog-shade disappeared in a flash of white light. Jimuro wanted to say something in protest, but no words came. "Do it or don't. But whatever it is, choose it now."

Jimuro stared at the empty space on the gravel where Kohaku—or whatever her name was now—had just sat. There were still indentations in the pebbles from where her tails had rested. Carefully, he knelt down to feel the stones, and found that they were still warm to his touch.

He wished Kohaku were here still. He wished his father were, to tell one of his long, meandering stories that inevitably ended with the phrase, . . . *and then I found five masu.*

He wished Fumiko were, to smack him upside the head and tell him to get ahold of himself before their mother saw him like this.

He wished the Steel Lord were here herself, to tell him that there'd been some huge misunderstanding, and that he had time yet to learn how to be a good king.

He wished Tala were here. For several reasons.

He sucked in a breath to steady himself, then walked to the side of the road. Already, another car approached. When he saw it, he smiled wanly to himself, and calmly stepped out into the middle of the road.

Lee's eyes went wide, and she muttered some kind of curse in her native tongue and darted out into the road. "*Hey!*" she roared, switching to Tomodanese.

Jimuro only smiled wider as the car approached. He'd already done this before, hadn't he? Last night on the train, he'd done what needed to be done, because circumstance hadn't allowed him the chance to second-guess himself. In the moment, he'd just acted, with full conviction, to do the right thing.

"*You idiot, you weren't supposed to take any of that shit seriously—!*"

The car came to an abrupt stop, its tires screeching on the asphalt. The driver leaned her head out her window and shouted, "*What's wrong with you? What if I hadn't stopped? Do you have some kind of death—*"

Jimuro held up two hands, and both the driver and Lee fell silent. Both women looked at him as if he were crazy, but the truth was that he was calmer than he'd been in days. He'd realized it once before, when he'd thrown his lot in with Kosuke, but now he meant it for real: It was time to stop relying on his own strength, and look to his people for power. "My name is Iron Prince Jimuro, son of Steel Lord Yoshiko and rightful heir to the Mountain Throne."

The driver squinted skeptically, then drew back in surprise as recognition dawned. She paled and gasped.

Jimuro fought the urge to be alarmed. "I'll offer up full explanations later," he said in his most calming voice. "But in the meantime, my friend and I could use a ride."

CHAPTER THIRTY

XIULAN

The floor of the fridge lurched beneath them as the *Crow's Flight* finally came to a stop. Tala perked up. "We're here."

Xiulan's imagination burst to life. Even with full knowledge of where she'd been headed these past few hours or so, she could hardly believe she was actually in the cradle of the demon Tomodanese. The legendary Shining City of Steel.

Hagane.

Xiulan had only read about the place, or seen intricate models in films, made to look large through the magic of forced perspective. It was said to be a world-class megalopolis, and that even before Tomoda's imperial era it had glimmered with all the metal the island had to offer from its meager veins. With decades' worth of ore mined from Shang and Sanbu, not to mention whatever they'd plundered from intercepted Dahali shipments, she could only imagine what the grand capital looked like today.

"Sergeant," she said. "You fought in Hagane before, did you not?"

Sergeant Tala grunted. "Sure enough."

"What was it like, when you first saw it?"

The sergeant got a faraway look in her eyes as she lost herself in memories for a moment. "The first time I laid eyes on the place, it was Operation: Anvil. Do you know about Operation: Anvil?"

Xiulan did. Following a full retreat of the beleaguered Tomodanese forces to Hagane, General Erega had concocted a pair of complementary operations that were meant to at last bring the impregnable Hagane to its knees: Operation: Hammer, conducted on land, and Operation: Anvil, conducted by sea.

"The Thirteenth Regiment, Fifty-Second Company, Second Platoon was sailing with Captain Maki. He was the bravest sailor General Erega ever had. Give it ten years, and someone will make a movie about him. I'm sure of it."

Xiulan caught the sudden fondness in her tone, as well as the use of past tense following this captain's name.

"The point is," Tala said, "there we are, sailing in, flags flying high. I'm standing on Maki's deck, and before me I see . . . you know, Lisan City's pretty big. Millions of Sanbunas live there."

"I'm not unaware," Xiulan said.

"I'm telling you that so you get my meaning when I say Hagane made Lisan City look like a sand castle," Tala said flatly. "It was a big, glittery sprawl everywhere I could see, spread over the land like oil spilled on water. There were a load of tall, shiny buildings right in the middle, where the palace was. And straight ahead, stretching across Hagane Bay, there was the Bridge of Brass."

Understanding dawned. The Bridge of Brass had been a massive suspension bridge, remarkable in both its scope and its beauty. It had once been a marvel of engineering so unparalleled that even Shang's engineers had to concede its superiority.

And as with Tala's captain, Maki, the key to understanding the bridge came in referring to it in the past tense.

"Right when the first wave of ships passed under, I saw them: explosions. Big ones, like . . . I don't know. Angry orange flowers, blooming just like *that,*" she said with a snap of her fingers. "A whole row of them went off, all up and down the bridge. So I had front-row seats when all that fire and twisted metal rained down on our fleet, and sent our ships to the bottom of the bay by the dozen."

Xiulan smiled mirthlessly. "The moment Steel Lord Yoshiko cut off her country's nose to spite its face."

"If that's how you want to see it, knock yourself out," Tala said, shrugging. "It was just a good place to fight and a bad place to die."

The fridge door opened, and the Cicadas once again yanked them to their feet and marched them out. This time, though, she and Sergeant Tala were led to an open door that led to a train platform of poured concrete, with brightly painted signs everywhere for out-of-towners and tourists. Along the far wall, she saw propaganda posters behind glass: images of brave Tomodanese soldiers, terrifying metal war machines, and noble portraits of an angular woman with a topknot and a pointed face: Steel Lord Yoshiko. There were other portraits, too: Yoshiko's father, Steel Lord something-ro, as well as the local lord of the prefecture. But none commanded Xiulan's attention so strongly as Yoshiko.

Xiulan had hoped fervently that it would be the Dahali to greet them at the platform, or even, against all odds, the Sanbunas. But already present on the platform were crisply assembled ranks of red-uniformed Shang soldiers, their shades at their sides and standing at attention. In contrast with most of the platoons she had seen in Tomoda, these soldiers had shades that were all as uniform as their partners: Each one was a tiger. The pacting process had changed them in different ways, but each was a tiger nonetheless. Their presence didn't bode well for her and Tala. The tiger was the divine protector of Heaven's Menagerie, and there was one sort of person in Shang who warranted divine protection . . .

Next to Xiulan, Tala uttered a Sanbuna curse under her breath.

"What's the matter, Sergeant?" whispered Xiulan.

"I was hoping it'd be my guys," she said.

Xiulan sighed. "So was I."

The sergeant nodded appreciatively, and her frown deepened.

Kurihara Kosuke waited on the platform, as well. He wore his steel battle-mask, as did the two Cicadas flanking him as an honor guard of sorts. Xiulan could see the lordling was attempting to look impressive, but it was difficult with his crew so beaten up. "As you can see," he said theatrically, "I present to you the Twenty-Eighth Princess, whole and unharmed."

Xiulan's throbbing, bruised forehead begged to differ. She opened her mouth to relate as much, but an elbow to her side directed her attention to Tala, who shook her head. Xiulan frowned, and wished her hands were free to smoke her pipe.

"The agreed-upon price for her capture was a hundred thousand jian," Kurihara continued. He'd narrowed his tone to address a single woman in a captain's uniform at the head of the formation. "Normally, I would demand to be paid in masu. But given the shambles you barbarians have made of our once-robust economy, the jian will be acceptable. I'll have to see it before we continue."

The captain he was addressing didn't answer him, instead studying Xiulan closely.

Kurihara noticed. "Ah, the bruise. An unavoidable consequence of the suddenness with which she ambushed us. She's been dealt no lasting harm," said the man who, just last night, had shot her in the face and then tried to burn it off.

Once again, the captain didn't answer him. She just squinted harder at Xiulan.

"Well?" Kurihara said. "Aren't you going to say something? I have your princess. I know you have thirty of them lying around, but the least you could do is pretend to be grateful."

The captain glared at him, then turned to the formation behind her and said in Shang: "It's her, Your Majesty."

Xiulan's whole body felt as if it had been dunked in ice water. There were thirty-three people in the vast nation of Shang who could rightfully be addressed with the style *Your Majesty,* but she knew in her bones exactly which one was making her way through the parting ranks of soldiers at this very moment.

When the House of Shang had taken the country over from the Serpent Emperor and the House of Zhou, they had done away with the model of the small royal family. The new Crane Emperor was expected to take several husbands or wives and to produce heirs from each, as a way of preventing the stagnant bloodlines that had doomed the dynasties that had come before.

But while that meant she and her sister bore half the same blood in their veins and chromosomes in their genes, Shang Xiulan and Shang Ruomei couldn't have possibly been more different. Where Xiulan was slender and slight, Ruomei was generously built, with a moonlike face and thick limbs that made her the envy of the Crane

Emperor's other daughters. And while Xiulan bobbed and bounced like the lid on a boiling pot of rice, Ruomei moved through the world with the calculated grace of a surgeon's knife parting flesh.

She wore a streamlined dress of pink-and-white silk, and her tightly wound black hair only barely peeped out from beneath an ostentatiously wide-brimmed hat. She tilted her dark round glasses down her delicate nose so she could look upon her sister with the appropriate amount of disapproval.

"You stand," the captain said in Tomodanese, "in the presence of Her Majesty Second Princess Shang Ruomei, the Flowering Flame."

Customarily, this would have been the place for subjects to bow, if not kneel. But while the soldiers all followed the protocol, Kurihara and his cohorts remained defiantly straight-backed.

Like her captain, Ruomei ignored Kurihara in favor of Xiulan. "Well, meimei, you've certainly outdone yourself," she said in Shang. "Given the magnitude of the mess you've made, I don't know if I've been over- or underestimating you all these years."

Xiulan glared up at her. All the years of childhood cruelty came rushing back to her: The vandalized books.

The whispers at court.

The mushrooms.

"Sneer at me all you'd like, jiejie," she said. "I was several steps ahead of you throughout this whole endeavor. I came far closer to capturing the Iron Prince than you ever came to killing him."

Ruomei's eyebrows arched up a degree. To most, it would have been a mild reaction at best, but Xiulan knew her sister's stoic nature well enough to understand it as a look of abject shock and surprise. But then her face resettled, and Ruomei replied by glancing at Tala and saying, "If the woman with you is supposed to be Iron Prince Jimuro, then he's much more handsome than I've been led to believe."

"*Enough,*" Kurihara snapped in Tomodanese. "This is my parley, and the terms are mine to set here. And term number-fucking-one: *We all speak the same language.*"

Ruomei regarded Kurihara, her nose just barely wrinkled enough to make her disdain noticeable. "You harmed my sister. You're lucky you still have a tongue with which to speak any language."

Kurihara paled but held fast. "I won't apologize for how I fight for my country. Now, I've honored your terms. Do you intend to honor yours, or will this meeting take an unfortunate turn?"

"Kurihara—" Tala growled.

"You haven't been allowed to speak yet, Sanbuna," Ruomei said before returning her attention to Kurihara. "If my troops open fire, the misfortune would surely fall heaviest on the dozens of innocents crowded in that train behind you. And if I ordered my guards' shades to search the train thoroughly for other potential dissidents, I assure you: They would not do so gently."

The assembled Cicadas muttered in outrage. Kurihara, never one for muttering, growled: *"You wouldn't!"*

Xiulan, on the other hand, knew with grim certainty what Ruomei would and wouldn't do.

"As I understand it," Ruomei said, "you were the one who dragged these innocents by the dozen into a battle you were fighting. To act surprised that they might be in danger now . . . one would almost think that you and your little band of freedom fighters don't actually have the Tomodanese people's best interests at heart." She took a step forward, and her pleasantly polite tone took on an edge sharp enough to shave with. "Because I can assure you, Kurihara Kosuke, son of Kurihara Daisuke: I certainly don't."

"Lord Kurihara, if I may?" Xiulan piped up. "I would put stock in her sincerity, were I in your position."

Kurihara gritted his teeth. "The Steel Cicadas fight tirelessly for the future of Tomoda and its people," he said. "There's no need for bloodshed. Give us our reward money, and we'll be on our way."

"If we deduct that reward of jian from the sum total of bounties that have been placed for your own head," Ruomei said mildly, "you would see that you actually still owe the Snow-Feather Throne four thousand jian." She turned to her soldiers and didn't even bother to change languages as she continued: "Soldiers, collect it for me."

In perfect lockstep, her troops and their tiger-shades took one step forward, the collective footfall echoing through the empty train platform as a single noise.

Tala gritted her teeth. "Is she trying to get us killed?"

Xiulan shook her head. "What others try, Ruomei does."

Kurihara seemed to be running the odds himself. "You may have numbers," he said, "but we would make your cost of victory dear. We would die as heroes."

Xiulan's mouth was dry with fear. Even though she knew her life was valuable to the Shang troops assembled, all it would take was a single stray bullet to make an already-bad day a hall-of-fame worst.

She swallowed. Now wasn't the time to think like a person, she told herself. Now was the time to think like a rat. And if there was one thing rats always did, it was survive.

"But you have no wish to die a hero, do you not?" Xiulan said. "Or indeed, to die at all. Not when you're a young man in love."

Kurihara's spine stiffened.

"Do you really wish to go to your grave without seeing your beloved prince again?" Xiulan said. "To let these fine Shang soldiers—and they are fine Shang soldiers—fill your body with shard after shard of the metal you worship, when instead there lies the tantalizing possibility that one day, you might once again have the chance to run your fingers through Prince Jimuro's hair, or savor his touch on the small of your back, or enjoy the thrill that races through you when he laughs at something you've said?"

Tala stared. "How did you say that all in one breath?"

"How I feel about His Brilliance is hardly relevant!" Kurihara protested, glancing around uneasily. For her part, Ruomei said nothing, retreating behind her own dark glasses and an inscrutable smile.

Xiulan shrugged. "I merely wish to remind you that you have more at stake in this very moment than you might first assume."

"And besides," Tala added, "I saw what I saw. You're way past the 'feelings' stage, Kurihara."

Kurihara glanced around helplessly. Xiulan was struck by how young he looked, suddenly. He was a few years her senior, but in this moment he exuded the vague aura of a child, lost in the woods and trying his best not to fear the distant snapping of twigs.

"Release my sister and drop your weapons," Ruomei said simply. "I'll see you and your . . . comrades . . . returned to your individual families, where dealing with you can be their problem. Or I can make it my problem, and you can see a firsthand demonstration of my effective problem-solving skills."

Kurihara puffed up his chest like a proud rooster, and for a moment Xiulan was certain that even after all that, he would force the issue. But then he deflated, and the proud rooster became a lame duck. "Weapons down," he said quietly to his Cicadas. "Weapons down."

As Shang soldiers moved forward to take them into custody, Tala caught Xiulan's eye. "How'd you know that would work?"

Xiulan grinned. "We Shang have a rather old and famous saying about one's enemies, and the knowing thereof."

" 'Know thy enemy'?"

"Yes, that's the one. And speaking of . . ." She nodded to her approaching sister.

"Unbind them at once," Ruomei said to the nearest soldier, and moments later both Xiulan and Tala had free hands again. "Come along, meimei. You've caused the family enough problems and embarrassment for one lifetime." She regarded Tala. "And as for this one . . ."

"Ah, forgive me," Xiulan said, pointedly sticking to Tomodanese so Tala could understand. She and Tala had only recently met, but she trusted the sergeant to safeguard her well-being far more than she did her sister. "Allow me to introduce Sergeant Tala, daughter of . . ." She trailed off and cast a questioning glance Tala's way.

". . . two people," the sergeant finished. "And I'll be thrilled to report to General Erega that you were here to rescue me, and not waiting to assassinate the Iron Prince like our intelligence suggested."

"I don't know what you're talking about," Ruomei said, predictably. "But I'm glad to have been here to prove in person how incorrect those awful rumors were. Shang holds only the highest regard for its cherished ally, the Republic of Sanbu, and wishes for nothing more than productive and expedient peace talks."

As Ruomei was talking, a realization fell into Xiulan's mind, heavy and juicy as a ripe fruit. She couldn't believe it. Now was the perfect time.

"It's funny you should mention those," Xiulan said. "I take it that you mean to attend them yourself?"

"Of course," Ruomei said. "I'll be at Father's side the entire time."

"I find the prospect of that to be dubious at best," said Xiulan.

"I know you deliberately stopped speaking just then because you're hoping I'll ask you something like, *And why is that?*" said Ruomei.

"Because, Second Princess Shang Ruomei," Xiulan said, "I, Twenty-Eighth Princess Shang Xiulan, in my capacity as your sister and peer, challenge you to gui juedou."

The soldiers within earshot may not have necessarily understood Tomodanese, but they all knew the phrase *gui juedou*. They looked at one another uncertainly, a few muttering among themselves.

"What do you think you're doing, Princess?" Tala said, but Xiulan's focus was riveted on her older sister.

The Second Princess returned that attention in kind. And then she gently tilted her head back and began to laugh. It was a delicate sound, like a razor being scraped across skin, and it made Xiulan's blood boil. It was the exact same laugh she'd heard when Ruomei had bestowed upon her the soubriquet that had haunted her until she'd turned it into an armor unto itself.

"Meimei," Ruomei said, "I don't have time for your storybook nonsense. I have a consulate to run. A staff I should be getting back to. Piles of paperwork that require my personal attention."

"I'm an officer of the law," Xiulan said, "and no stranger to paperwork. I speak with authority when I tell you: It can wait."

Ruomei reached for Xiulan's long bang. "You've had an ordeal. Self-inflicted, but an ordeal nonetheless. Come home. Rest. We can discuss—"

A hand shot out, grabbing Ruomei's wrist before it could touch Xiulan. And there, slightly interposed between one sister and another, was Sergeant Tala. She wore a glare that looked downright murderous. For a moment Xiulan saw something deeper behind her eyes, too: a hunger, deep and primal.

She remembered what Tala had told her about her fantastical condition. Was this an expression of it? Was she about to rip Ruomei's soul in two?

At once shouts arose from her sister's guards. In a heartbeat Tala found herself surrounded by a trio of roaring tiger-shades. Ruomei's calm shattered completely, a stricken look of panic on her face. Xiulan couldn't see her own face, but she imagined her expression was much the same.

Sergeant Tala didn't so much as flinch.

"Sergeant," Xiulan said slowly. "Think very carefully about what you're doing . . ."

The film of rage that had settled on Tala's face disappeared. She let go of Ruomei's wrist, then took two steps back and sank into a Shang-style bow, with her hands clasped together and offered forward. "Uh, sorry, Your Majesty," she said. "No one touches Princess Xiulan."

She straightened and took her place slightly in front of Xiulan, whose mood was currently transitioning from shocked to downright gleeful. She could barely believe what she'd just seen. In Shang, Ruomei commanded the adoration of the people, the respect of their siblings, and the distant passive aggression from their father that was supposed to pass for approval. What with her heritage, the vast personal wealth she had begun to accrue with the reopening of Shang's national markets, and the network of political connections she commanded, the Second Princess was virtually untouchable.

Except the good sergeant had just disproven that in the most delightfully literal way possible.

Ruomei did an admirable job of regaining her composure, though Xiulan noted with satisfaction that the slight tremor in her hands betrayed her. "Why do you even *want* a gui juedou, meimei?"

"If I win," Xiulan said, "you will relinquish your post as diplomat in chief, citing . . . I suppose whichever cause you prefer. I won't be so cruel as to stipulate. But you will nominate me to serve in your stead."

Ruomei bristled. "This is absolutely ridiculous, mei—"

"You don't have permission to refer to me that way," Xiulan said coldly. "Not after everything."

Slowly, Ruomei reached up and pulled her glasses off her face. Her eyes regarded Xiulan with some kind of pity, and it stung like a slap in the face. "If you're sure you want to go down this path—"

"I am quite so," Xiulan said, more vehemently than she'd meant.

"—then for me to accept the challenge, you would have to offer up something of commensurate value as your stake. What do you have to offer, m—Xiulan?"

Xiulan was ready for this question. "I'll wager you my claim to the throne."

Next to her, Tala twitched in surprise. Xiulan felt fleeting appreciation for the soldier's discipline that stopped the sergeant from undermining her.

She expected Ruomei to jump at the chance, but to her surprise the Second Princess looked uncomfortable. "You have no claim to the throne. Not really."

"You've always been scared of the ways I am uniquely capable of disrupting your position," Xiulan said. "Wouldn't you like the permanent assurance of my neutrality?"

"Only if I believed for a moment that, should you lose, you would remain neutral," Ruomei said before softening her tone and switching back to Shang. "Xiulan, please consider what you're giving up."

"I have considered it," Xiulan said, stubbornly remaining in Tomodanese. "I've considered it every day of my life for nineteen years. Now, do you find the terms agreeable or not?"

Ruomei's mouth twisted. "I don't find them agreeable," she said. Then she sighed. "But I do agree." She gestured to the train platform. "Given your love of slumming, I imagine this will be a suitable venue for you."

Xiulan beamed. "You do care, after all."

Ruomei shook her head, then turned on her heel and began issuing orders in Shang. She didn't raise her voice, but she didn't have to. The soldiers all jumped to obey, practically falling over themselves as they fanned out to clear space on the platform.

"Okay," Tala said, "I'm going to need a quick explanation, right now, of what the fuck just happened here."

"Gui juedou," Xiulan said simply. "An honor duel between peers of privilege, to settle disputes. The practice has become archaic and fallen out of common usage. But," she added with a twinkle in her eye, "a careful reading of the Crane's Law would reveal that it was never formally superseded by our more traditional judiciary. Once she provides her assent, the duel and its results become legally binding."

Tala nodded, then frowned. "Hang on," she said. "Ruomei's been giving you trouble for years."

Xiulan's expression darkened. "Indeed."

"So if you're so sure you'll beat her now, and the law was always there," Tala said, "why didn't you challenge her before?"

"Because," Xiulan said, "I never had an adequate champion before."

"Champion . . . ?" Tala said. But Xiulan knew that in moments, she would notice that it was not Ruomei striding to the center of the ring created by the Shang soldiers, but rather the captain who had first treated with Kurihara. And for that matter, all the expectant eyes that had fallen on Sergeant Tala.

And just like that, Tala noticed.

By the time she leveled a glare at Xiulan, she had already retreated a good twenty feet from the sergeant. "All part of my grand plan, good Sergeant!" she called from a safe distance, though she got the distinct impression that Tala was trying to set her aflame with her mind.

Tala sighed and rolled her broad shoulders. "You're lucky I'm in a fighting mood, Princess." Then she called: *"Beaky!"*

Violet light heralded the arrival of a black bird. Next to the tiger-shade he was up against, Tala's own shade didn't look too impressive. Certainly, Ruomei didn't think so, from the lopsided smile she exchanged with a nearby aide.

Xiulan, on the other hand, calmly removed her pipe from her coat, then tipped her hat to her older sister.

As Ruomei's champion and Tala squared off, Xiulan felt a current of electricity running just beneath her skin. All over her body, her hair stood on end, and she felt her pactmark throb on the surface of her eye. Nestled in the depths of her soul, Kou seemed to feel the significance of what was about to happen here.

She glared across the ad hoc arena at Ruomei, who stood with her arms folded while a servant cooled her with a large peacock-feather fan. After a lifetime of being at each other's throats, this would be it: the long-awaited reckoning in this struggle of sisterhood. In her head, she already saw it playing out like Bai Junjie's final reckoning with Professor Sakini, the fiendish Tomodanese mastermind who had been his archenemy for most of the series. Theirs had been a dramatic showdown, a deadly game of wits inside an abandoned mansion that had ended, after great struggle, with the professor outwitted at last.

Going in, Xiulan knew it wouldn't be the same. For one thing, there was always a whiff of jingoism about Bai Junjie's stories that hardly applied here. But beyond that, this would be all the more satisfying. The great detective had had to fake his death for a year following his triumph. Xiulan would be able to revel in hers straightaway.

Got it figured out already, then? Lee snarked in her head. *Why not just save some time and skip the fight, then?*

She smiled at even the illusory sound of Lee's voice. Once all this business with Ruomei was settled, she would be able to find Lee at last . . . and if necessary, she thought as she glared at the retreating figure of Kurihara Kosuke, avenge her. But first, there was a long, hard battle to be fought and won.

The tiger-shade barely made it halfway across the platform when Beaky swooped down, just barely grazing the creature's back with his talons. The tiger-shade turned and snapped its jaws ineffectually at the crow-shade, but Beaky had already gained altitude again, and the tiger's teeth closed over only open air.

Ground attacks against a flying shade? Xiulan thought with a smirk. *It's not very effective . . .*

She had no idea how right she was.

Suddenly Beaky dropped from above, wings folded to his sides and beak forward like a rocket. The tiger-shade leapt up, ready to intercept the smaller shade in midair. But at the last moment, Beaky flared out his wings and whipped his talons forward, raking them across the tiger-shade's face before latching onto its upper brow. He gripped tightly, then bent forward and sent a savage peck right into the base of the other shade's neck. The shade cried out as its entire body stiffened and convulsed. Its legs collapsed out from under it.

Energy crackled over the wound as it began to heal, but by then Beaky had repositioned himself. He drove his beak right into the creature's skull again. And when that wound began to heal up, Beaky pecked it again.

Sergeant Tala had her back to Xiulan, but Xiulan didn't need to see her face. The tight fists clenched at her sides told her everything she needed to know about the sergeant's mental state.

"Yield!" Xiulan called across the platform.

Ruomei's champion stared at her shade with wide, horrified eyes, even as the tiger-shade suffered having one of its own pecked out. She glanced back over her shoulder at Ruomei.

Ruomei frowned. And then at long last, she gave a single curt nod.

The champion hung her head and reached out a hand. As quickly as the tiger-shade had appeared, it dissipated into a cloud of light.

A terrified, awful hush fell over the Shang troops, and Xiulan became keenly aware that all the eyes on the platform were squarely on her.

The sergeant was breathing hard, as if she'd been the one in the ring instead of Beaky. She'd broken out in sweats again, and when Xiulan approached her, she whirled entirely too fast to face her. Beaky hopped to her side, and though he couldn't emote in a way Xiulan understood, she got the message anyway.

"Sergeant," Xiulan said slowly. "Are you . . . calm?"

Tala nodded, shoulders heaving. "I am now." She looked around. "So what happens now?"

Xiulan blinked in disbelief. "I do think," she said, "that I've just won."

CHAPTER THIRTY-ONE

LEE

In contrast to the clouds and rain of the previous day, today the sky couldn't have possibly been any clearer. The roads had been relatively clear, too, but the closer Lee and Jimuro got to Hagane, the more congested they became. A sign by the side of the road declared them to be ten miles outside the city limits, and the traffic had cut their cruising speed in half.

Lee glanced out the window at the cars crawling past them. There were Tomodanese cars, of course, but also the beetle-like automobiles of Dahal, and the boxier models favored by Shang and, to a much lesser extent, Sanbu. The two nations had only developed the ability to mass-produce motorized cars toward the end of the war, with designs purchased from Dahal. It always made their vehicles look a bit primitive by comparison, though the way Lee saw it, at least they didn't require the presence of a Tomodanese person.

Still, she thought as she regarded her driver, as far as Tomodanese went, he was about as good as she could hope for.

"You ever think about how anyone could look out their window right now, see you, and call it in?" Lee said.

Prince Jimuro's mouth tightened as he shifted over a lane to the right. "My likeness has never been available for public consumption."

"That doesn't help you much. I've been with you a day, and I've already noticed that you look at the world like you expect it to be handed to you." Lee smirked. "Never had to keep your head down before, eh?"

"I'm beginning to think I'd be better off if I had some practice." The princeling checked his mirrors, then shifted over another lane. "I imagine you *are* well practiced in the art."

"Of not getting dead?" Lee said. "I know a thing or two."

Prince Jimuro frowned, then hesitated. "I have a question, but I don't know how to ask it without sounding rude."

"Oh no, not a rude question," Lee deadpanned.

The princeling sighed. "Fine. Why *do* the Shang hate you so much?"

Lee's grin was without satisfaction or mirth. It was the very question she'd been expecting. "You think we Jeongsonese haven't asked one another that?"

"I'm sorry," Prince Jimuro said, color rushing to his ears. "Forget I asked."

"Don't think I will," Lee said. "Far as I know, we were just living on land they wanted. Or maybe they thought our language was stupid. Or one of us tried to tell them our whole idea of what happens when you die, and they said, 'You're wrong, see for yourself.' " She chuckled ruefully. "Whichever one it actually was, it doesn't really matter. If it hadn't been that reason, they would've just picked one of the others. But it's not just Shang, you know."

Prince Jimuro nodded, eyes riveted on the road ahead. "I do."

"When Tomoda showed up and kicked Shang's teeth in, we even helped you people do it, a little. We figured anyone who wanted to beat up the guys who were beating us up couldn't be that bad, right? But once you got what you wanted from Shang, you turned around and started beating on us, too. Between the two of you, there's barely a Jeongson left. Hell, once we'd booted you people completely out, I wouldn't be surprised if General Erega swung by with her whole army, just to piss on our soil. It's probably her turn. Do you guys keep a chart or something?"

Jimuro swallowed, a lump visibly bouncing in his throat. "I wish

I could apologize enough," he said carefully. "I may not have personally had a hand in Jeongson's suffering, but as Steel Lord I'll bear responsibility for everything my people have done."

Lee studied his hands for so much as a tremor, and found none. Just a few hours ago, he'd admitted he didn't think he was up to ruling, or living. Now he was talking a big game about what he would and wouldn't do with his fancy new job. Unsure of how to respond to all that, she contented herself with a slow nod, and no words.

Prince Jimuro flicked a switch near the steering wheel, and the air filled with a soft clicking.

Lee snorted. "You actually use your turn signal?" On Shang's roads, the blinker lights ended up being more of a suggestion.

Prince Jimuro nodded. "My mother once told me that people who don't use their turn signals are people who spit on the spirits and deserve to be shunned by their ancestors after death." He nosed the car off the main road and onto a thin dirt path branching off away from Hagane.

Lee sat up a little straighter. "Not that I want to be the one telling you how to navigate your own backyard," she said, "but you do remember the city's *that* way, right?"

"There's more than one way to enter the great city of Hagane," Prince Jimuro said.

Before Lee could ask what he meant, the princeling jerked the steering wheel and sent the car straight off the road and careening for a nearby hill.

Lee jumped up. *"What're you doing?"* she shouted. "I thought we were past this!" She threw herself at the wheel, trying to wrestle it from his grip, but he fought her off.

"Stop that!" Prince Jimuro shouted. "I need you to trust me!"

Lee saw the wall of grass looming larger and larger in the windshield. What the hell was there to trust?

But then the hillside disappeared, sliding out of their way to reveal the mouth of a tunnel that had been dug directly into the hill.

Lee looked around wildly. "What the—?"

"I told you," Jimuro said. He twisted a knob on the dashboard, and the car's headlights came to life just as the door closed behind them, plunging them into darkness. "You needed to trust me."

"It's a lot easier to trust a guy if he tells you there's a fucking door in the hill!"

"I'll admit, I may have been having a bit of fun," Prince Jimuro said. "It's an ingenious design, don't you think? There's a pressure-sensitive plate buried beneath the grass outside. My mother had it and others like it installed around the city limits, to hasten evacuations. One of these routes should take us directly to the palace."

"And to your big chair and shiny hat?"

Jimuro grinned wanly. "Something like that."

The tunnel ended up being the smoothest part of their journey, by far. Lee hardly would've believed it at the outset. But then again, she hardly would've believed she'd be road-tripping with the Iron Prince of Tomoda.

Or that she would have a shade.

Who used to be the prince's dog.

She'd been having a weird week.

Imagine going back to Danggae now, she thought. *What would they think of you, Lee?*

That brought her up short. She hadn't really given it a lot of thought, but with the end of her journey looming, she had to wonder: What *would* she do now? She guessed she could squeeze some back pay out of the Li-Quan for her services here, but it wasn't like she had another gig lined up. And once the story of the past few days became known, she figured she'd be too recognizable to go back to petty thieving. That one hit her hard, once she thought of it. She hadn't even realized what she'd be giving up when she signed on with Xiulan.

As thoughts of the Twenty-Eighth Princess surfaced, that bubble in her chest appeared again. A quick roadside check-in with Bootstrap had confirmed that yes, her partner had made it into the city. But her relief was numbed by that damn bubble. It swelled and swelled, swallowing everything in its path until it was the only thing Lee had room for inside herself anymore. And at the center of it: an acutely imagined rendering of the hurt in Xiulan's eye when Lee looked into it again.

"You look pensive," Jimuro said.

Lee leveled a glare at him. "Eyes on the road, not my face."

They rode the rest of the way in silence.

. . .

The tunnel came to its end so abruptly, Lee didn't notice it until Jimuro slowed the car to a stop. "We're here," he said, letting his hands fall from the steering wheel. Lee could see the trails of sweat on it that he'd left behind, and how his fingers twitched nervously against his thighs as he wiped his palms dry.

Stepping out, Lee saw now that while the floor of the tunnel had been paved in concrete, the walls were merely packed earth, with rows of iron support beams stretching back into the distance like the ribs of a dragon. And hanging directly in front of the car was a simple steel ladder.

Lee stared up as high as she could, until the darkness swallowed the ladder's rungs. "That's it?"

"You were expecting a grand entrance hall, perhaps?" said Prince Jimuro.

"I'm just saying, if you're going to steal the rest of the world's metal, might as well be doing something interesting with it," she said, and then climbed.

At the top of the ladder was a heavy steel hatch with a release valve. "You need to metalpact this?" she called down to Prince Jimuro.

"No," he replied from a few rungs below. "My mother took great pains to ensure that as many facilities as possible were universally accessible."

"Nice of her," Lee muttered, reaching for the hatch.

But just then, it flipped itself open with a loud *clank*. Before Lee could react, a steel cable whipped down, wrapped itself around her outstretched wrist, and yanked her right through the open hatch and into the light.

The room looked small and out-of-the-way, but Lee didn't have much time to appreciate it, what with the flying through the air and all. She landed hard on the floor like a fresh-caught fish, and even as a guard in a blue kimono stepped forward to demand who she was, she managed to gasp out: *"Bootstrap!"*

The space was a little too small for the dog-shade, and Lee acutely felt Bootstrap's anger as she closed her jaws around the forearm of the nearest guard and slammed him into a wall with a toss of her head.

"*Wait!*" Prince Jimuro called from the ladder.

"*Slavers!*" cried a tall, older woman with a sharp gray undercut and a weather-beaten face. Lee saw now that the cable wound around her wrist was tied to an apparatus on the woman's wrist. When the woman clenched her fist, a spike of heat ran through the cable, and Lee's wrist burned with pain.

With a shout, Lee tried to rip her hand free, but the cable just wound itself tighter. Another one snaked through the air, wrapping itself around her other wrist, and the two yanked her feet off the ground. "Bootstrap, help!" she yelled, but her shade was surrounded by four more guards, all dressed in the same blue-and-white kimonos. In unison, they hurled out more cables, which wrapped themselves around Bootstrap's legs and flanks and pinned her in place.

And then Prince Jimuro popped out of the hatch like a mole and roared, "*Will everybody kindly stop trying to murder one another in my palace?*"

At the sight of him, the guards all chorused: "*Your Brilliance!*" At once, the cables retreated, depositing Lee roughly on the floor. Bootstrap stood and shook, a ripple running through her fur. And the guards who'd had her completely dead to rights had all sunk to their knees and abased themselves, their foreheads pressed to the floor.

Lee blinked. She'd spent the past week of her life hobnobbing with royalty, but this was the first time it had really sunk in for her how much power one of them could wield if they were allowed to.

Prince Jimuro had pulled himself entirely out of the hole and gotten to his feet. "Captain Sakura."

The tall woman rose to one knee, though her head remained bowed. "Your Brilliance. Words can't express how happy I am to see you here again."

"I've missed you, too," he said gently. "I'm glad the Kobaruto has stayed sharp in my absence."

"True steel never loses its edge," Captain Sakura said. She cast a wary glance Lee's way. "Your Brilliance, may I ask who . . . ?"

"Lee's fine," Lee said cheerfully. "That's what it says on all the wanted posters, anyway."

"Lee was one of my escorts," said Prince Jimuro. "You have her to thank for my safe delivery home."

If Captain Sakura had any more reservations, she didn't show them. "How may the Kobaruto serve you?"

"Send word to the Copper Sages. Tell them that General Erega has kept her word, and that they should make preparations for the coronation immediately. The rest of you, escort me to my chambers. We'll use the servants' corridors."

Captain Sakura pointed to one of her guards. "Tamaki."

"My captain," they replied, before bowing to Sakura and Jimuro in turn and hurrying out of sight.

The rest rose, though a few cast long, lingering looks of horror and recognition toward Bootstrap.

Despite herself, Lee rankled at such visible distaste. "Stare all you want, steelhounds," she snapped. "She stays with us."

In unison, every guard's head swiveled toward Prince Jimuro.

He nodded: just once, but with the kind of regality that meant he didn't need to do it again.

Lee had to give them credit. However they may have really felt about the situation, not a one of them betrayed it in expression or stance. She grinned in thanks to the prince as she scratched Bootstrap between her huge pointed ears.

"Who're these fanatics, anyway?" Lee whispered as they began their march through the bowels of the Palace of Steel. "And how can they all do such cool rope tricks?"

"These *fanatics* are the Kobaruto," Prince Jimuro said with bristle in his voice. "They're the honor guard of the royal family, who rank among its most dedicated servants. And with the forced demilitarization, they currently represent the only armed strength I have left to command. Is that correct, Captain?"

Captain Sakura nodded. "Yes, my liege. The provisional deal the Sages struck forbids us from carrying firearms anymore. But," she added, holding up a wrist to show the cable rigging there, "we are far from defenseless."

"So you get ropes while everyone else gets shades and guns?" Lee said. "Sounds fair."

The captain drew herself up proudly. "The Kobaruto would defend His Brilliance's life with sticks if that were all we were granted. We would defend it with our bare hands. And against any threat, we would prevail."

Lee smirked.

But as they walked along, she found herself glancing sidelong at the captain every now and then. Assuming everything worked out with her and Xiulan (*there was that damnable bubble again*), was that a potential future for her? An ever-present attack dog at Xiulan's side, to chill the princess's enemies by day and warm her bed by night? In her gut, Lee felt a sense of recoil. She only had so long before she shuffled along to play her next role. In that life, where would there be room to play this one?

They stopped outside a wooden sliding door, and Jimuro frowned. He looked as if he were trying to work something out. "These aren't my chambers," he said.

The captain bowed low and slid the door open. "Yes, Your Brilliance. They are."

The room she revealed made Lee's jaw drop, if only from the sheer size of it. Like the palace in Kohoyama, it was sparsely decorated, but that did nothing to diminish the sense of awe she felt. If anything, it only increased it. The lack of clutter made it clear that the power and weight she felt came not from furniture and knickknacks, but from the actual space itself.

A low bed floated like an island in the center of the bare wooden floor, its black polished surface inlaid with simple, stark streaks of silver. Rather than gaudy red silk, there were plain blue linen sheets neatly folded atop the mattress. The walls were decorated not with massive tapestries but simple, solid blue hangings. A long table along the far wall held a collection of small sculptures rendered in jade and obsidian, and directly above that hung a pair of crossed swords. Along the next wall over sat a simple wooden desk. A stack of paper lay atop it, pinned in place by the weight of a shiny steel pen.

But what really caught Lee's eye was the low table next to the side of the bed. It bore only a single thing on it: a small framed photograph of a short, round man with a beaming smile; a tall and severe woman whose face Lee had seen exaggerated and caricatured in years of propaganda newsreels; and two young children, a boy and a girl, kneeling in front of them in yukata. The boy, skinny and be-spectacled, frowned with a tight, closed mouth. But the girl beamed out at the world with a big, wide smile that proudly showed off her missing teeth.

Jimuro wandered into the room as if in a daze. Right at the door, he stopped to remove his shoes, then carefully, quietly made his way across the floor. The Kobaruto hung back at a respectful distance, and Lee did the same. She was someone who had made her living by taking from others. But for the first time maybe in her entire life, she felt as if she were intruding.

Next to her, Bootstrap stared longingly at Prince Jimuro's back. She let out a soft whine, and a little ripple of concern lapped at Lee's consciousness, followed by another of uncertainty.

Lee patted her flank and nodded.

As if Bootstrap understood the solemnity the occasion called for, she didn't bound for Prince Jimuro. She padded across the floor with the same deliberateness that he had. The Kobaruto watched her warily, but none of them moved to intercede as she came to rest be-side the prince. Wordlessly, he reached out and began to stroke the back of her neck, and the dog-shade sat at his touch and bowed her head.

Lee stooped to remove her own boots. But Jimuro turned around and held up a hand. "Not so fast," he said. She saw he wasn't crying just yet, but his eyes had already turned red and he was blinking very rapidly. "I have a job for you, Inspector Lee."

"Your Brilliance," said the Kobaruto captain, dropping to one knee and thumping her fist to her shoulder. "I beg you, allow the Kobaruto to serve you. Your will is the flame that drives us."

"Kiss-ass," Lee muttered in Jeongsonese. The glares she got from the Kobaruto told her that whether they spoke her language or not, they understood her just fine.

"Apologies, Captain, but this task is one that only Inspector Lee can fulfill for me." He crossed to the desk and knelt before it. He bowed, then began to write something on the top piece of paper. Satisfied, he slid open a compartment in the desk and withdrew a small silver box. Lee couldn't see what he was doing exactly, but when he rose and turned around, he held out a neatly folded letter bearing a fresh blue wax seal. He crossed the floor, Bootstrap at his side, and handed it to Lee. When she inspected the seal, she saw the image of a stark, simple mountain staring back at her.

"I need you to deliver that to the Shang delegation," he said. She made to take the letter, but Jimuro didn't give up his grip on it just yet. He caught her eye. *"Personally,"* he added carefully.

She grinned as she took his meaning: an uncalculated expression of happiness and gratitude. She tucked the letter into her dress, and then with only a tiny hesitation bowed to him. "Thanks . . . Your Brilliance." She straightened. "What do I tell them if they ask what all this is about?"

Gently, Jimuro picked up the photograph on the bedside table and stared intently into it. "I suppose by the time you deliver the message, it won't be a lie to say so," he mused. "So if they ask . . . tell them the Steel Lord wishes to talk."

PART SIX

. . .

THE BRILLIANT BLADE

CHAPTER THIRTY-TWO

TALA

The car glided to a stop at the curb. "We're here," the driver said. His Sanbuna wasn't great, but Tala appreciated the effort.

She nodded and summoned up the best Shang she could recall. "Thanks for the ride, soldier."

He flashed her a fleeting smile in his rearview mirror as she opened the door and ducked out.

The sounds and smells of downtown Hagane hit her like a punch in the brain. There was cigarette smoke, and car exhaust, and the faint but distinct scent of sewage and trash. Foreign cars rumbled down the road, a lumbering invasive species next to the sleek, quiet native ones, their metal chassis awash in neon lights. All around her, people chattered away: in Tomodanese, in Shang, and in, shades preserve her, her own mother tongue of Sanbuna.

It was a far cry from the last time she'd been in Hagane. Last time, the air had been thick with fire and smoke and flash-boiled blood. It had carried the roar of shades, and the screams of soldiers, and the steady patter of gunfire. That had been mere months ago, but now the street on which she stood looked as if it had never borne witness to anything more hostile than a bit of road rage. It was beyond her how the place could have already been scrubbed so clean, when all the dirt was still caked on and piled up in her head.

The Sanbuna consulate had been established in a steel-and-glass office building. Five tall flags had been planted on either side of the front entrance, each bearing the ten stars of the Republic. Tala's heart swelled at the sight of them flying overhead. It wasn't home, but it was as close as she'd get in this country. She remembered how hard they'd had to fight to raise even one of these flags in the heart of Hagane, how dear the cost had been. And now she stood in the fluttering shadows of ten.

Standing there, she offered up a quiet prayer to the memories of the 13-52-2, and the crew of the *Marlin*. This moment here had been everything they'd fought for. Everything they'd died for. She muttered their names, one by one: Kapona. Minip. Maki. And on and on she went, until eventually she ran out of names and just started offering up vague descriptors, like *the short one with the good cheek-bones*. And eventually, after she'd run out of other names to call, she whispered one last one:

"*Beaky.*"

The crow-shade appeared in a flash of violet and a flutter of wings, and the thrumming annoyance he always exuded. It clashed with the empty throbbing in the back of her head, like discordant notes slamming into one another.

"I know, I know," she said, putting a hand up. "We have a lot to talk about. Can you please . . . ?"

Beaky cocked his head to fix one eye on her, and the annoyance backed down to a low simmer.

"I never asked you about your life before . . . before me," Tala said. "Kept the door closed between us. I told myself it was because it wasn't my business, and it didn't matter as long as I was fighting like you asked. But I think I didn't want to know. I think there's a reason we call splintersouls monsters, and I didn't want to make it easier to believe I was one, too. I told Mang I hadn't been a good partner to him, but I've been even worse to you."

His feathers ruffled, and a low croak escaped his throat.

"I took you from him," Tala said. "Your soul was twined with his, and I ripped you in half."

He dipped his head once in an unmistakable nod.

"So before anything else happens, I needed to tell you that I'm sorry, Beaky. And whatever happens next, I'm going to make it up to you however I can."

He clacked his beak thoughtfully. Doubt filtered into her heart: his.

"I know I said that to Mang," she said. "I know. But I mean it. If you've got anything you want to say to me, I'm ready to listen."

At first, there was nothing.

Then she was plunged into an ice-cold pool of fear.

It caught her so off guard, her knees buckled. The memories surged through her head: of last night, with that hand around her throat and her vision fading to purple. Of her soul tearing roughly, fiber by fiber. Every single nuance of that pain came back to her, real as if it were happening again.

She was about to push it away and demand to know why Beaky was doing this to her. But then her memories shifted. She wasn't a soldier on a train; she was a girl in a hospital, clutching a hand twice as large as her own, and Beaky's soul felt as if it were aflame.

The girl who summoned him was unfamiliar, and panic fluttered in his chest like a smaller bird. Where was Mayon? Why did he feel this way? How had she known to call him?

And why could he feel something else inside her?

The girl spoke to him, and he felt the echoes of her feelings beneath his chest feathers. But it was impossible to understand any of it; his fear muddled everything, like he was looking through a greasy window.

When it got to be too much, he took to the air.

She screamed for him to wait, but already she was receding into the distance below him. He was back where he belonged: the city beneath his belly, the sun on his back, the wind ruffling his feathers like gentle fingers.

He wheeled around and quickly assessed his surroundings. Good. He was still in the same city, the one that Mayon had taken him to all that time ago. How long had it been? He didn't know. When he went away, he couldn't keep track of days and nights anymore. All he had was the vague sense that however long he'd been gone, it had been a while.

But just as he started to think ahead, something snagged him. In his old-old days, when he was small and wild, he wouldn't have known the word for it. But Mayon had taught it to him, like he'd taught so many other things. It was sad. He was feeling sad, and it was a sadness that wasn't his.

It wasn't a sadness directed at him, the kind that would plead for him to come back.

But after a moment, he banked left and turned around anyway.

As he flew back to her side, he understood that things had changed. There had been a rope tying him to Mayon, but he could only feel the faintest threads of it anymore. The thicker cord led directly to the little girl, and he was able to follow it right back to her.

Her eyes were dry by the time he returned, but there was no disguising their redness. "Thank you for coming back," she said, and for the first time Beaky really understood her words—if not the sounds, then at least the feelings beneath them. "We're going to have to do a lot of fighting. But I promise I'll be good to you. And when we're done fighting, you'll be able to fly all you want."

The familiarity caught him off guard. He had never seen this girl before in his life, but the things she said, and more important the things she felt . . . That certainty. That drive. That commitment to the fight. Beaky knew now: This girl was a branch who would not bend in a storm. It was what he had asked Mayon to be all those years ago, when they had first forged their pact.

And he understood now that when he had asked this girl to be the same thing, she had said yes.

Tala surfaced from the memory with a deep, sharp breath. Concern radiated off Beaky, but Tala waved him off. "I'm okay," she rasped, then gathered herself. In a more certain voice, she said again: "I'm okay."

Her head spun, her limbs were weak, and she felt more thin-worn than the soles of her own boots. When she blinked, tears appeared on her lashes. "I'm sorry," she whispered to him again. She felt like she would never be able to say it enough times for it to really matter. She knelt and tentatively reached a hand out to him. "I'm so, so sorry."

Beaky didn't exactly nuzzle her; even on their best days, he'd never been affectionate. But he gently laid his feathery cheek in her palm, just for a moment, and left it there. A quiet trickle of affirmation flowed from his heart to her own. It wasn't certain, but it was strong.

Tala could live with that. Strength had gotten her this far.

As she collected herself, she felt a growing resignation within Beaky. When she understood what it meant, she shook her head.

"No," she said.

A pulse of questioning.

Tala nodded once. "I mean it."

And so Sergeant Tala, formerly of the 13-52-2, staggered into the front lobby of the Sanbuna consulate in Hagane with a crested crow-shade at her side.

The man behind the front desk wasn't military, and so he didn't snap to a salute as he took in the sight of her. "May I . . . help you?"

She caught sight of herself in the metal doors of a nearby elevator and realized that she still looked pretty chewed-up from the past few days. The quicker she got out of these damnable Tomodanese clothes, the better. "My name's Sergeant Tala," she said. "This is my shade, Beaky. We're the sole survivors of Operation: Grand Tour, and we need to see General Erega right now."

The man eyed her skeptically. "The general is a very busy woman . . . Sergeant. You can have a seat over there—"

"Call up to her office right now and tell her Sergeant Tala is in the lobby, ready to file a report," Tala said. "See how busy the general is then."

The man frowned, but nonetheless picked up the phone at his desk and dialed. He began to relay Tala's story to the person on the other end with a patronizing smirk, but after a moment he fell silent. The longer the silence stretched, the more his smirk melted away, until it had disappeared entirely.

He hung up the phone and swallowed. "My apologies, Sergeant," he said sheepishly. "One can never be too careful . . ."

Tala merely waited.

"The general is in a meeting that cannot be interrupted, but her staff has told me once it ends you will be her highest priority. A soldier will be here momentarily to escort you to a private meeting room."

Tala nodded at last. "Thanks." She turned to head for the nearest bench.

"Wait," said the desk attendant. "I feel terrible about doubting you. While you wait, is there something I can get you?"

It had only been four days since she'd washed ashore on Tomoda, and during that time Tala had been torn up in just about every way possible. But every inch of hell she'd crawled through to get here was worth it now, because she was chewing on a steaming mouthful of garlic rice and some sweet, salty, honest-to-shades dead animal.

She'd been whisked to a private room that had been some mid-level executive's office during the war. She'd knelt behind the broad, fancy oak desk, and minutes later a steward had arrived bearing a tray of longganisa, rice, and fried eggs. The smell alone made her want to die of hunger, but the taste was strong enough to bring her back to life. And she was even eating it with her own fingers and hands, like a civilized human being. The steward had easily brought her enough food for two, but she was increasingly certain she was going to end up devouring it all.

Beaky perched on the desk, watching her with mounting disgust.

She eyed him back. "You can't judge me," she muttered through a full mouth.

In the corner of her vision, the door slid open. "Hoy," Tala said, swallowing. "How much do I have to bribe you to get some coffee in here?" Shades take her, the only thing sweeter to the tongue than longganisa was being able to speak Sanbuna again, and knowing she'd be understood.

The reply she got was a soft chuckle. "I'm sad to say, Sergeant, I won't come cheap."

Tala nearly choked on her half-swallowed food.

And then she rocketed to her feet, hands slapped to her sides, and pivoted to come face-to-face with General Erega herself.

The general was a surprisingly small woman, her stormcloud-colored hair in a tight bun. Her face was weathered and broad, its most distinguishing feature the brown leather patch she wore over where her right eye had once been. Despite her status as head of the Republic, the uniform she wore was barely more elaborate than a humble private's. Her only concessions to rank were the deep-green cape draped over one shoulder and the ten-star medal pinned to her chest.

"General Erega, sir!" Tala said with a hard swallow of rice. She bowed, aware of how little she looked the part of a good soldier. She still wore the tattered gray Tomodanese suit she'd acquired up north, for one thing, and she was sure she carried the kind of stench that would've fooled anyone into thinking she was still active on the front. "Apologies. No one told me you were on your way."

"Don't hold it against my staff," said General Erega. "They didn't know I'd be coming, either. At ease, Sergeant." When Tala relaxed her attention, the general shook her head. "I mean really at ease. Sit back down. Eat. And while you eat, give me your full report on Operation: Grand Tour. Even if you have to do it with your mouth full," she added, the gentlest sparkle in her eye.

Tala knelt. She bowed her head. "Sir, the operation . . . it was—"

"I know it was compromised early on," said the general. "But details beyond that are sparse. Which is why, among many other reasons, I'm glad to hear of your survival, Sergeant." She indicated the table again. "Tell me more, but please don't forget to eat."

But Tala could hardly consider eating now. "General," she said, hanging her head lower. "Operation: Grand Tour was a failure. We came under attack last night, and in the chaos I was separated from Iron Prince Jimuro. I rushed here in the hope of being able to meet him when he arrived, but the truth is . . ." Her head dipped even lower. ". . . I have no idea where he is, sir." She straightened, ready to receive whatever dressing-down she had in store.

And yet, General Erega smiled.

"I would've come to you sooner, Sergeant, but I was held up in my office just now. I received a very interesting phone call from the Palace of Steel."

Tala perked up. Was it possible?

General Erega seemed to be able to read her mind. "Congratulations, Lieutenant Tala. The Thirteen-Fifty-Two-Two succeeded in the safe return of Iron Prince Jimuro to Hagane."

"Then he's alive," Tala said, unable to keep the relief from her voice. "Jimuro—I mean, His Brilliance, has he been . . ."

"Soon, I think," said the general. "We were issued an official summons to the palace. I imagine by the time we arrive, we won't have a prince on our hands anymore. And speaking of 'on our hands' . . ." She stumped over to the table, then nonchalantly picked up a longganisa and popped it in her mouth. "Are you going to eat yet, or do I have to order you myself?"

Hastily, Tala crammed more rice in her mouth.

"Ordonia!" General Erega called.

A moment later a soldier appeared in the doorway and saluted. "General Erega, sir," she said.

"Bring us the hottest coffee this consulate has."

After Ordonia had gone, General Erega turned back to Tala. "Now then, Lieutenant Tala," she said, "I believe I requested a report . . . ?"

Tala told her almost everything, pausing only when Ordonia returned with the requested coffees. The only detail she left out was Dimangan, and by now she was well practiced in editing stories around him. By the time she was done, she'd downed the entire coffee, but her throat still felt parched.

General Erega drank the last of her own coffee, then frowned. "He's Sanbuna, this purple man?"

Tala nodded.

"And you're certain he survived his escape from the train?"

She felt the throbbing absence in the back of her head. "Absolutely, sir."

With a jolt, she realized that there was a better-than-even chance that the general probably even knew this man, if he was truly the resistance fighter from the hospital bed. But there was no way to ask that question without provoking all kinds of unwanted ones in return, so Tala remained silent.

"An actual splintersoul, then?" the general said. "Well. I guess that tracks."

Questions erupted in Tala's head. "Sir?"

"Yours isn't the first platoon this man's massacred, Lieutenant," said General Erega.

A chill ran through her. "You mean command knew about this man?"

The general shook her head. "We only guessed. They were all random massacres, mostly of Sanbuna or Shang troops caught unawares. Taken separately, they meant nothing. After all, it was a war. But eventually, we had a pattern that suggested we were dealing with something new . . . minus the proof, until now." She sighed, then rose. "I'll have security around the consulate doubled, then."

"Wait, sir," Tala said, getting to her feet. "Are you heading for the Palace of Steel right now?"

General Erega raised an amused eyebrow. "A rather direct question to pose your commanding officer and the head of your republic, don't you think?"

The rebuke was gentle, and not even unkindly meant. But still a thought snarled to life in Tala's mind: *I could rip your shade from your soul, you hag. How's that for direct?*

The general's expression frosted over. "Is something the matter, Lieutenant?"

The question spiked Tala back into the moment. Hastily, she composed herself as she stamped out those thoughts. "No, sir," she said, straightening up. "But respectfully, I'd like to attend as part of the delegation. The Thirteen-Fifty-Two-Two and the crew of the *Marlin* gave everything for this mission. Seeing it through to the end is the least I can do to honor their memories."

"You don't have to prove anything anymore, Tala," said General Erega. "You've been through enough. You should be resting. Eating me out of house and home. Switching to something harder than coffee," she added, nodding to the mugs on the table.

Let's see you try to stop me with your soul in tatters, Tala thought with sudden savagery, as her fingers flexed at her sides. But this time, she caught herself before the general noticed something was off about her. "The offer's appreciated, sir, but I have to do this. Sir."

General Erega sized her up a long moment. Then she said, "You're not going dressed like that, soldier. I'll have a uniform sent down. You and Lieutenant Barriga have about the same measurements. That'll do for tonight, I think."

The general was almost out the door when it finally sank in for Tala. "'Lieutenant,' sir?"

"I wondered how many more times I'd have to call you that before you noticed." The general chuckled. "After everything you've been through, you didn't really think I'd let you retire on an enlisted soldier's pension, did you? Finish your food. We hit the road in twenty minutes." The door shut behind her.

Tala only had three to herself before a woman, presumably Lieutenant Barriga, showed up carrying a neatly folded uniform. But she spent those three minutes staring at her hands and wondering what she'd almost done with them.

CHAPTER THIRTY-THREE

LEE

Her reception at the Shang consulate was chilly at best.
The hotel lobby was awash in pale-golden light, the kind
that was supposed to make plain stuff look sumptuous. Instead it
lent a strange hue to all the red rugs and wall hangings that had been
put in place, and it stained all the white crane insignias a dingy piss
yellow. In every direction, phones rang and consulate staffers rushed
back and forth with armfuls of papers and documents. But when Lee
strode in, they all turned to stare at her as if they were sharks who'd
just smelled her like a drop of blood in water.

Wonder who's less welcome here, she thought as she surveyed the
frowning people around her. *These two Kobaruto, or me?*

Then she heard someone nearby mutter the word "Dogfucker."

Definitely me.

"Who's in charge?" she said to the nearest office drone.

"Get out of this building before you stain the floor," the woman
spat in reply. She didn't even seem that curious about how a Jeongsonese person might have come to be all the way here in Hagane.

Her tone made Lee realize how much she'd been enjoying her little vacation from being surrounded by Shang. "Nothing I'd love
more," Lee said, then held up Prince Jimuro's letter. She flashed its

mountain seal. "But I'm not going anywhere until I deliver this, so if you're gonna make me wait, I hope you're all right never getting back your deposit on this place."

At the sight of the letter, the drone's eyebrows leapt straight up her forehead. "Give it here," she said, holding out a hand and snapping her fingers.

"Snap those again, and I'll bite one off," Lee said. "I'm supposed to deliver this personally to whoever's running things, and you look like you couldn't even run a ship into the ground. Now get me someone important, because I'm bored with you."

The woman sputtered in outrage, but abruptly turned on her heel and stormed off.

"That doesn't sound like it went well," one of the Kobaruto said mildly in Tomodanese.

"Oh, it went great," Lee replied, beaming. "You just missed all the cultural nuance."

When the drone returned, she had a pair of soldiers with her. "You come alone," she said.

Lee snorted. "Only if my other option is you." When the woman squinted at her, confused, Lee sighed. "Take my word for it: In Jeongsonese, that would've been hilarious." She nodded to the two Kobaruto. "Go on. Tell His Brilliance it's done."

The Kobaruto exchanged a look, shrugged, then left. The Shang gave them a wide berth as they swept out of the foyer.

Lee turned back to her new escorts. "Fair warning," she said. "If this is the part where you try to kill me, I won't go down easy, and someone pretty important will be pissed."

The dogs take me, Lee thought as the drone rolled her eyes and headed for the elevator. *Since when was I the one who never shut up?*

The elevator ride ended on the twelfth floor. The whole way up, Lee kept her eyes trained on the two soldiers with them. With luck, she'd be able to summon Bootstrap before either one could draw on her, and the shade's bulk would pin them to the wall long enough for Lee to make good her escape. Of course, that would present the thorny issue of actually making good her escape, but one thing at a time . . .

. . . except not even that, because the soldiers stayed right where they were. If anything, it seemed like they were the ones watching her.

She deflated a little inside. While she was relieved things weren't about to get messy, she was becoming reacquainted with the feeling of being watched everywhere she went. The Tomodanese hadn't cared, nor the crew of the *Wave Falcon* after a drink or two. But here, in the center of the Shang family's nonsense, she would have to reacclimate to the old way of doing things.

The elevator doors opened, and the four of them filed out. The drone turned to Lee once again and said with a long-suffering sigh: "This way."

The consulate, Lee knew, had been established in what had once been the finest hotel in Hagane. While General Erega and High Treasurer Bhavna Devarajah had each taken office facilities, the Crane Emperor had insisted on something more lavish for his headquarters. Lee smirked at the thought of the old bastard waddling into this place; after all, the Tomodanese idea of "lavish" was very different from the Shang's.

And sure enough, Lee saw a wide, sparse hallway, an inviting stretch of wood and metal that had been despoiled with red silks and gaudy, glittering furniture that stood too tall for the room around it. Not that she particularly cared about how the Crane Emperor came out of this, but she still felt vague embarrassment at the sight of it all. Lee knew she could be crass, but at least she wasn't inelegant.

She swallowed. She guessed that in a moment, she'd be able to complain about his taste in décor personally.

Two more guards were posted outside the room at the end of the hallway. "Just in here," the drone said. She looked deeply reluctant to humor this any further, but apparently she was even more reluctant to disobey orders. The guards, at least, showed more discipline: Their gaze barely flickered as she approached. Without breaking their forward stare, one of them reached out with their arm and effortlessly slid the door aside.

The drone put a firm hand on her shoulder, and it took all Lee's self-control not to break her fingers for it.

"Listen carefully," she said, as her glasses slid steadily down her nose. "You will announce yourself and your business, then bow from the waist. You will take two steps into the room, then bow from the waist again. You will take ten steps farther, with your head down to avoid direct eye contact. Upon taking the tenth step, you will slowly drop to your knees, press your forehead to the floor, and with both hands humbly offer up your message. *Do I make myself clear?*"

Every instinct in Lee whispered a different comeback in her ear. But it had occurred to her that while Xiulan's name would have kept her out of trouble with most people, the man who'd ranked her his twenty-eighth-favorite child probably wasn't one of them. So instead she just said, "I'll keep that in mind," and then brushed past her and into the doorway. But then, because she couldn't help herself, she added: "You're welcome."

The woman sputtered. "Don't you mean *thank you?*"

Lee glanced back over her shoulder at the woman's jacket pocket, which she had consciously decided not to relieve of its wallet. "No," she said, then stepped all the way past the threshold.

The door slid shut behind her.

She'd been let into what she imagined to be the penthouse suite. Lee was surprised to see that compared with the gaudy redecoration outside, the inside showed much more restraint. The tall Shang furniture still threw the room off-balance, but it was much less egregious to her eyes. Just beyond the narrow entryway (on which a narrower red silk carpet had been spread), she caught a glimpse of two chairs and the very corner of a desk. And though she couldn't quite see the Crane Emperor himself, she saw his shadow playing across the desk's wooden finish.

She felt a flutter in her stomach, just beneath her white pactmark. She did her best to ignore it, then sucked in a deep breath.

"Lee Yeon-Ji," she called into the room. "A deputized agent of the Li-Quan, bearing a personal message from the hand of the Steel Lord."

Within the room, he stilled. She had his attention.

Carefully, she took two steps forward, and got halfway to bowing before she stopped herself. Why bother with it when he couldn't even see her from here? So instead of bowing, she just walked the next few steps, keeping her head down. When she counted out to ten steps, she lowered herself to her knees and bent as low as she could go, offering up the letter with both hands. The dogs take her, they were shaking. What kind of thief was she, with fingers fluttering like a moth's wings?

Still, she supposed if there was any one person to bring it out in her, it would be the Crane fucking Emperor.

She heard the creak of his chair as the old man stood up. But when he came around the desk, she didn't hear any of the telltale signs of his approach. No rustle of dragging robes. No heavy, slow footsteps.

And then her nose filled with the scent of pipe smoke.

A small, familiar hand slipped beneath Lee's chin and gently pulled her head up to take in the full sight of Shang Xiulan, from her black boots to her brown eye. Her long coat hung on the wall, her suit jacket was draped over her chair, and her waistcoat hung open over her plain white shirt. Her sleeves were rolled up, and a lopsided smile peeked down at Lee from beneath the princess's long black half bang. Just beneath her hairline, Lee glimpsed the edge of a plum-colored bruise that she knew was far larger than it looked.

Her mouth went sandpaper-dry. "Xiu . . . Xiulan . . ."

Her partner smirked wider. "You neglected to perform the first bow."

And then she pulled Lee's mouth up to her own and kissed her.

At the first taste of tobacco, Lee melted. The letter fell from her fingertips as her hands wrapped themselves around Xiulan's waist. Gently, she guided the princess down to the floor with her. As Xiulan shrugged out of her waistcoat, the top two buttons of her shirt fell open with a bare touch from Lee's practiced fingers. Lee got an inviting glimpse of the way it draped over the princess's collarbone just before Xiulan buried her face in the base of Lee's neck.

"I thought I'd lost you," she sighed, gently kissing the skin between Lee's neck and shoulder.

Lee swallowed. She easily undid another shirt button, revealing the white bra beneath Xiulan's shirt, and the beautiful pale breasts just beneath it. *Lady of Moonlight*, she thought.

"White all the way down, eh?" she rasped. Her heart thundered, suddenly tight in her chest.

Xiulan kissed her again, slightly higher. "I thought I would never see you again."

Another button fell open. Tingles raced beneath Lee's skin as her fingers brushed against Xiulan's silk-soft midriff. She wanted to say something back, but her tongue felt paralyzed, which boded ill for the next few minutes if she didn't get her shit together.

The princess moaned in reply, and kissed Lee just below her ear, and pressed her body tight to Lee's. "I never want to lose you again."

Lee's fingers fell to the shirt's final button.

Xiulan leaned up and whispered right into her ear: "*I love you, Lee Yeon-Ji.*"

Lee's fingers slipped off the button, and it remained fastened where it was.

Her entire body screamed for her to keep going. She hadn't gotten laid since Lefty. But Shang Xiulan was so much more than a lay, and so much more than Lefty. And with her so close, Lee could practically smell Xiulan's desire in the air around her like it was a perfume she wore.

But when Lee opened her mouth to answer, she felt that bubble rise from her chest to her throat and choke away any words that might have been there.

Reluctantly, her fingers dropped away from Xiulan's shirt. She sighed, then placed a hand on each of Xiulan's shoulders and gently pushed the princess away.

Hurt stung in Xiulan's eye, small but deepening with each passing moment. "Lee . . . ?"

Lee swallowed, and a taste coated her tongue, bitter and filmy as motor oil. "Listen," she said. "This'll be a long walk to 'I'm sorry.' "

CHAPTER THIRTY-FOUR

XIULAN

As Lee's confession washed over Xiulan, a ringing rose in her ears. She heard what Lee was saying, understood what Lee was saying, but somehow it didn't quite land with full impact, each word only a gentle tap on the head with a mallet. Yet even with that light touch, every tap she endured drove her an inch deeper into the ground.

She'd only just begun to acclimate to her new office when the call had come through: a Jeongsonese woman was in the lobby, bearing a message from the Mountain Throne. Xiulan's heart had leapt out of her chest. On the whole island of Tomoda, there was only one person to whom that description could have applied.

Hurriedly, she'd set the scene appropriately: shedding her layers, but leaving a few because a gift was always more satisfying when it was presented with wrapping. She'd rolled up her sleeves, thrown on a bit of jazz, even lit her pipe again so the air would be filled with curls of smoke by the time Lee entered. So often, Lee was the cool one, the one in control. Just once, Xiulan wanted to feel like she'd impressed the thief. If her badge was a lie, she needed to feel like she'd earned *something*.

At first, it had gone so well. She'd been quietly proud of herself as she worked her way through her concussed state to play the picture of high-class nonchalance. When that character she'd been playing melted away, and Lee was left holding the truest, most distilled version of Shang Xiulan once more, she'd felt her entire body come alive at Lee's touch. With every button the thief had undone, her body had ached for another to follow it.

And then, she'd gambled on *I love you* . . . and lost.

She'd thought the worst of her concussion had passed, but now the pressure between her temples built. The ringing in her ears crescendoed. The hard lines that defined objects and spaces around her blurred and bled.

And Lee kept talking.

"I'm not trying to make excuses, you see?" she said. "I'm just trying to explain here. I've got this rule I keep to, the only code I follow: *Leave them before they leave me.* It's how I've kept myself alive. Back there on the train, I thought that was what I was doing. I saw you opening yourself to me, and I knew you were going to want me to do the same, and I knew I wanted to do that for you, and I thought I knew what you'd do once you saw what I'm really made of. So when shit went sideways, I went for the door."

She looked to Xiulan expectantly for a reaction, but Xiulan was too paralyzed by the sheer number she wanted to give that she was unable to yield even one. That was for the best; she could feel her face molding into the kind of removed, stoic mask that would have served her well in the royal court if she'd ever deigned to play its twisted games.

"But right away, I knew that was the wrong thing," the thief continued eventually. "Tried telling myself you would've taken off, too, but fuck, you're not me. You would've fought every Steel Cicada and that purple-coated psychopath to get to me. I had every chance to go back and save you like you would've for me, and I didn't, and I'm . . . sorry." The word sounded as if it had escaped her mouth only with great difficulty. "Not used to saying that, but I mean it here. I'm sorry for everything, Xiulan. And if you'll still take a thief's word, it won't ever happen again."

Xiulan fell back from her knees into a sitting position. Her skin had been tingling moments ago, but now it was all just numb. Every-thing was numb.

Stupid White Rat, she hissed to herself. *Thought she could have it all, but the sweet smell was only just bait for Heaven's trap. Stupid, stupid White Rat.*

"Xiulan?"

With painful slowness, she regarded Lee Yeon-Ji. *Heaven take me,* she thought. *Even when she's breaking my heart, she's breathtaking.*

But while her appealing angularity had not changed, her signature fierceness—the quality to which Xiulan was drawn like a proverbial moth to an equally proverbial flame—was dimmed. The woman be-fore her was a full head taller than she, but everything about her made her look so diminished: the limpness with which she held her-self. The dull sheen of her black hair. The fear that shone in her beau-tiful eyes.

An icy hand closed around Xiulan's heart. Lee was afraid of her.

Good, a voice snarled. *After you opened up to her the totality of your significant resources, this was how she repaid you. She should be terrified.*

That ice around her heart solidified and permeated deeper. She'd been a fool to open herself up so much. Of course Lee had run out on her. That was what people like Lee did. That was what everyone did.

A hundred fleeting fantasies raced through her, each of a different way she could exact vengeance. She could have Lee jailed again. She could have the pactmark carved out of the woman's skin, erasing Bootstrap from existence for good. She could use her formidable resources—the same ones she'd so generously offered Lee, stupid White Rat that she was—to track down the rest of Lee's family, and make their lives miserable, too. Her fury was a bottomless pit, and every fantasy was new fodder to feed it.

"What is it you were hoping to accomplish here?" she said at long last. "What is it you think you deserve for this little performance of yours?"

Lee met her gaze. Her eyes were dry, serious, haunted. "Nothing at all."

Xiulan didn't know what she'd expected Lee to say in that moment. But for some reason, she hadn't expected that.

Two Hours Ago

The prison wagon was made of heavy oak, drawn by an ox-shade the size of an elephant. Kurihara and the other Steel Cicadas were herded into its back door, encouraged to step lively by the snarling tiger-shades of their captors. Xiulan should have found the sight immensely satisfying: Was it not just like the climax of every Bai Junjie story, where the great detective successfully maneuvered his quarry into a cell?

But it was difficult for her to savor her victory when her sister refused to treat the afternoon's proceedings as a loss.

"I imagine your display of brinksmanship was meant to reprimand me for what I did to your friend in Jungshao," Xiulan tried as a guard locked the wagon doors tight.

"No reprimand necessary," said Ruomei. "Magistrate How was never nearly so important to my plans as he liked to imagine himself. Everything he could do for me, countless others could do as well."

Xiulan rolled her eyes. This went back to their childhood in the Palace of Glass. Anytime Ruomei had a setback, she would always claim it had been part of her grander plan to lose in the first place. It made her, among other things, the world's most frustrating person to play go against.

"So," Xiulan said, gesturing to the departing prisoners. "To which work camp do you intend to send our newly captured dissidents, once your new preferred magistrate finds them guilty?" Such duplicity was only to be expected of her dear older sister, but in this case she wasn't displeased to see Kurihara go. Instrumental as he'd been to getting them to Hagane so swiftly, that didn't change the fact that he was a criminal and a terrorist who had no place in the new order. And there was the small matter of threatening to melt her face off, which Xiulan wasn't likely to forget in a hurry, either.

Ruomei shook her head. "None of the above. I really am sending them back to their families."

"What families?" Xiulan spat. "Lord Daisuke of the Kurihara

clan festers in a cell like a cluster of mold, ready to hang for the thousands of war crimes on his shoulders."

"Your desire to be poetic's made you mix metaphors," Ruomei observed. "No mold I know has shoulders . . . or a neck."

"There's no family to give him back to, Ruomei," Xiulan said. "To say nothing of the other Steel Cicadas."

"Of course there is," her sister said with a shrug. "They *are* their families now."

Xiulan balked. "What?" she said. A blanket pardon? Unthinkable. "But the Shang they've killed—the damage they've done—the myriad ways in which they've jeopardized the peace!"

Ruomei shrugged. "All reprehensible. But the Steel Cicadas are from prominent, powerful families in the Tomodanese ruling class." She cocked her head Xiulan's way. Xiulan realized she was being challenged.

"So the ax of justice hangs over all," Xiulan said with a sneer, "but the rich are free to skirt its edge whenever they please?"

Whatever test Ruomei intended to set for her, Xiulan could tell she'd failed. Her sister rolled her eyes. "You let too many books do your thinking for you. Use your own brain for once, meimei. You got the best one out of all of us." The gentleness in her tone was gone, replaced with a hardness far more familiar to Xiulan's ears. "The Tomodanese have their own complex system of honor and face. The Steel Cicadas will face that judgment, and the consequences that come attached."

"So their parents will be mad at them on their way to the gallows," Xiulan scoffed, as the coachman shouted a command and his ox-shade pulled the wooden cart away from the train station. "How fearsome a fate. And I believe I made myself clear on the subject of the diminutive *meimei*," she added.

Ruomei let out an exasperated sigh. "Once again, you're not *thinking*. Say we do things your way and throw them down into the bottom of a zinc mine and have them work their fingers to the bone. We call the families of every soldier they hurt or killed, and tell them all about this mine we've put the Steel Cicadas into. What does that get us?"

"Justice," Xiulan said simply. "Albeit an ineffective one, considering we would be putting metalpacters in close contact with raw ore . . ."

"No," Ruomei said. "It empowers the remaining Tomodanese nobility, while giving them a convenient reason to be more anti-Shang than ever. They would be far more likely to back the plays of an anti-Shang Steel Lord, to say nothing of Sanbuna and Dahali interests they could advance at our expense. But by giving the new heads of houses back their lives when we had them dead to rights, we gain influence over them. And once we establish that credit with the Tomodanese and reinforce it with time . . . we have a lever to undermine the Steel Lord whenever we like."

Xiulan narrowed her eye. "And the dead soldiers these spoiled children have left in their wake? Are they merely acceptable sacrifices to offer up to the altar of your ambitions, then?"

"It's not *my* ambition." Ruomei sighed again. "It's *Shang's*. Our country's far larger than me, and it will outlast me. I only intend to be its steward for a time before I have to pass it on. And if ensuring its good condition means sacrificing a few hundred lives to avert a conflict that could one day take the lives of hundreds of thousands, I'll do that and consider it a bargain well struck."

Xiulan felt something harden in her gut at the sound of her sister's words. She felt a cold chain of logic running through them, and the moment she sensed herself understanding it, she recoiled. In her mind, it wasn't Ruomei's job to make sense, not even a little bit.

Ruomei produced a slim gold cigarette case and pulled two cigarettes from it. She offered one to Xiulan, who took it. She pulled out her pipe, clenched it in her teeth, and unrolled the cigarette, funneling the now-loose tobacco into the bowl. Ruomei wrinkled her nose. "I wish you wouldn't do that," she said. "It's disrespectful to the factory worker who rolled the cigarette, and it only makes the leaf taste worse."

Xiulan's defiant streak burned within her. She dropped the now-empty paper to the asphalt, then tipped a match into the bowl and took a puff. Sure enough, the leaf tasted foul, but at least she was smoking her pipe again, instead of just gnawing on its button.

Ruomei held out her cigarette for a light. Xiulan knew perfectly well she probably had a light of her own on her somewhere, or else that she could've ordered one from any of her retinue. But begrudgingly, she struck a second match and offered it up to her sister, and Ruomei cherried her cigarette on it. "Tell me," she said with her first sigh of smoke. "Why do you want to be Crane Empress?"

Tch, Xiulan thought. Such a typically small-minded view of her. Leave it to Ruomei to underestimate her. "Because I want what's best for the country, not just myself. While you were off playing games at court, I joined the Li-Quan to help reestablish law and order in our reborn country."

Ruomei chuckled. "My dear sister," she said with perfectly inflected condescension, "how do you think a princess got a job working in law enforcement?"

That brought Xiulan up short. "I . . ." She'd never even stopped to consider that it could have been anything other than her outstanding mental acumen. "What are you saying?"

"I'm saying," Ruomei said with a roll of her eyes, "that someone— even a princess—without any background in police work only gets recruited into an elite law enforcement agency if there's somebody behind the scenes. Somebody pulling strings. Valuable political connections," she added, "cultivated while playing games at court."

Xiulan reeled as if she'd been slapped. Her badge had always been a literal mark of pride for her. A bitter tide rose in her. She had to believe Ruomei was lying. She couldn't believe that the one thing that had been her very own had been given to her—and out of what? Pity? She felt ill in every cell of her battered body.

Next to her, Ruomei was oblivious to her inner turmoil. She sighed wistfully. "Why *have* we always been at each other's throats, Xiulan?"

Xiulan gaped in disbelief as Ruomei calmly took a drag.

"*Why?*" she said eventually.

"That was the question, yes," said Ruomei.

Xiulan chuckled in that way people only did when nothing was funny. "You want to know why the last person I wish to see sit the Snow-Feather Throne is the woman who spent my entire childhood terrorizing me? Who tried to quash any brightness I had within me, so she could shine above the others? Who arranged things so I couldn't even enjoy a meal in my own home?"

Ruomei only frowned at that last one. "I was young," she said. "Perhaps overzealous."

"Perhaps?"

"For Heaven's sake, they were *mushrooms.*"

"You starved your own sister! Just to maintain some semblance of dominance!" Xiulan couldn't believe she had to spell out something so patently obvious. "If you're willing to do that, what kind of a queen could you possibly be?"

"*The one Shang needs right now,*" Ruomei said, raising her voice for the first time. "Our father is a doddering old fool who finds more comfort in the stories grandmother told him of our past glory than he does in the potential of a bright new age. If he were a man with any vision or ambition left, we could have thrown off Tomodanese rule decades ago, and without Sanbu or Dahal to help us. *Decades.*"

Xiulan found herself without words for once. She wasn't certain she'd ever heard Ruomei speak so candidly in her entire life.

"Do you know why I'm designated Second Princess, and our oaf of an eldest brother is First Prince?" said Ruomei. "Because even though the old man knows I'm his best choice for successor, he still wants to make me fight for my position."

"Are you seriously trying to tell me you shouldn't have to?" Xiulan snorted with a healthy dose of contempt.

Ruomei was unfazed. "I'm saying I already won out long ago. I have thirty-two siblings, and the only one who's ever come close to being my equal is standing right here. And if that woman can't handle a few mushrooms in her soup," she added with sudden scorn, "then she's not really an equal candidate to begin with."

Xiulan almost looked around to see which of their siblings had joined them, before she realized how stupid that would make her look. She was so surprised by the compliment, backhanded as it was, that she couldn't even internalize it. "So," she said with a long pull from her pipe, "you worked to suppress me because you saw a threat in me?"

Ruomei raised an eyebrow. "I've worked to suppress everybody who stands in my way. You're just the only one too stubborn to take a hint and fall in line."

"So why did you relent so easily just now?" Xiulan said. At last, she could get to the heart of things. "If you see in me the threat of a competent alternative to which Father could look, why provide me with the opportunity to solidify my position?" But no sooner had she posed the question than she understood the answer: "You don't believe I can. You're giving me an opportunity to humiliate myself in the most public manner possible, so that Father will have no choice but to unequivocally extend you his favor."

"And if it took you that long to figure it out, it would appear I have little about which to be concerned." Ruomei dropped the cigarette on the sidewalk and didn't even bother grinding it out. It just lay there on the pavement, smoldering. "You've defined your whole life in opposition to me. I'm fine letting you stand unopposed now, because I know it'll show the whole world what's left when you take me away: nothing at all." And then she sauntered toward her waiting car.

Xiulan clenched her teeth and fists alike as she watched her eldest sister strut away. Today's victory should have been the sweetest broth she'd ever tasted. But she should have remembered: Any broth Ruomei served her would always come with mushrooms.

It would have been so comforting, to let the stony grip of anger squeeze everything else out of her heart. To act on her every vengeful fantasy in the pursuit of balancing the scales. Anger was not a complex emotion, and there was an overpowering appeal to letting it simplify matters, the way a glacier flattened and smoothed the earth beneath it.

And yet.

And yet.

Xiulan's exhale was long and painful. "What was that?" she said quietly.

"You heard me," Lee said, bristling a little now.

Xiulan shook her head. "I want to hear you again."

Lee gathered herself before answering: "I said, 'Nothing at all.'"

But this time, when Lee spoke, it wasn't Lee's voice Xiulan heard. It was Ruomei's.

It'll show the whole world what's left when you take me away.

The words came out of her before she quite realized she was saying them. "I forgive you," she said simply.

"You what?" said Lee.

Xiulan echoed her incredulity, but the longer the words hung in the air, the truer they sounded in her own ears. "I forgive you," she said again. "When the time came for you to be tested, you failed me as a partner, Lee Yeon-Ji, in every capacity in which I've enlisted you as one." She took a long, deep breath to steady her pounding heart. "And for that, I forgive you."

Lee blinked. Xiulan had the distinct impression that she'd probably never heard those words addressed to her before. Xiulan supposed it made sense; they generally only came in response to an apology, and from all appearances Lee was just as unfamiliar with those.

"But . . . I ran out on you," Lee said. "Right when you needed me most, I saved my own skin. I did the same shit I always do."

"And then," Xiulan said gently, "you came back for me. Which," she added with a gentle caress of Lee's midriff, "you've only done for one other." A tear glistened in her eye.

Lee's mouth hung open in disbelief. "What're you doing crying, you idiot?" she said. "You've got it backward."

"Perhaps," Xiulan said. "But I have you back, and I don't care about anything else."

For a moment, she saw a glimmer in Lee's own eyes before her partner closed them and leaned in for a kiss that made all Xiulan's hair stand on end. The frost in her chest thawed and ran. Without the anger to keep it at bay, she felt every single angle and contour of the hurt lodged there. But there was comfort to be found: in the soft lips on hers, the deft fingers slipping her shirt hem out from her trousers . . .

She sat up straighter and pulled herself back. "Forgiveness is a, ah, multi-stage process," she said carefully.

Lee turned the kind of bashful red Xiulan never would have expected from the thief. "Er, right, sorry," she muttered. "Old habits." She smoothed the front of her dress, then reached for the letter on the floor. "Guess you'll be wanting to read this?"

Xiulan eyed the letter. The seal on it was unmistakably that of the

Mountain Throne. For better or worse, Iron Prince Jimuro had ascended. Ruomei had failed. Strictly speaking, so had she. But her voracious consumption of the Bai Junjie canon had given her a keen eye for story structure, and one thing she knew was that failure did not necessarily mean the end.

She had so many questions she wanted to ask Lee, about how she'd come to be an envoy for the Steel Lord. Xiulan was certain it would be almost as interesting a story as the misadventure she herself had shared with Sergeant Tala.

But that misadventure had changed things. She was far more than just an agent of the Li-Quan now.

Somberly, she nodded for Lee to hand her the letter. "Let's see what His Brilliance has to say."

CHAPTER THIRTY-FIVE

JIMURO

He didn't hear the Copper Sages approach. One moment, he was alone in the family shrine; the next, he knew that to no longer be true.

"Your Brilliance," came a voice from behind him. An old man's.

Jimuro didn't rise, didn't even open his eyes. "Is it time?"

"We're sorry the moment must come now, of all moments." A different voice this time; younger, and a woman's.

He nodded, then rose and opened his eyes. His vision filled with a grand steel altar, big enough to take up the entire wall by itself. It had been sculpted centuries ago as a replica of the Palace of Steel, every detail lovingly rendered by the finest metalpacters of their age. The lanterns hanging from either side of the room cast distorted reflections in its gleaming surface, so that Jimuro looked as if he were surrounded by ghosts.

But the true haunting came from the three copper urns on display before the altar. The surface of each had been pacted to display the likeness of its contents. On the left: Steel Consort Soujiro. On the right: Iron Princess Fumiko. And there, in the center, her gaze somehow less stern when rendered in metal than in flesh, was Steel Lord Yoshiko. Before each stood a cluster of three incense sticks. All nine had burned down to smoldering stubs, though the remnants of their smoke still hung thick and sweet in the air.

He bowed again, touching his forehead to the wooden floor, and offered up one last prayer to the spirits of his family. Then he rose at last and turned to regard his company.

Two Sages had come to collect him. The first was indeed an old man, so stooped with age that his chin was practically buried in his thin chest. The second was a younger woman, though in this case "younger" meant perhaps fifty, her black hair just beginning to lose the civil war it waged on its gray insurrection. When he stood, they both knelt, their deep-blue robes pooling around them. They rose when he bade them.

"Do you feel ready, Your Brilliance?" asked the old man.

Jimuro's stomach turned from the question. He slapped his hands to his thighs to hide how much they wanted to tremble. "The wise king is the one who knows he isn't."

The Sages didn't smile, per se, but both looked vaguely pleased. As one, they nodded, then each took him by a hand and led him out of the shrine.

They took him to what had once been his mother's throne room, and would soon be his own. Normally blue banners of the mountain sigil hung from the walls, but they had all been rolled up to the ceiling, revealing the flat steel underneath. The long azure rug that normally ran like a stripe across the floor had disappeared as well, replaced by a large copper basin full of water. At the very far end of the room sat a raised pavilion of black steel chased with gold. Beneath its peaked golden roof sat the Mountain Throne, though at the moment Jimuro's view of it was obscured by thick white sheets of linen that hung from the pavilion's eaves.

He swallowed as he at last regarded his destiny.

Carefully, the Sages undressed him until he stood naked in the middle of the throne room. He felt foolish; after all, this was where he'd practiced his solemn face while attending court for the first time. It was where he and Fumiko would sneak and play after it was supposed to be closed. It was where his father had taught him wisdom, and his mother had taught him justice. Being so bare before their spirits almost felt disrespectful.

But he knew this was necessary. The Steel Lord, after all, was no ordinary king. He was a living god. And to be a god, the man had to be washed away.

He reached up and undid his topknot, so that his hair fell down past his shoulders in a blue-black sheet. Then he removed his glasses and handed them to the nearest Sage while he blinked to adjust to the blurry world.

Two more Sages stood at the basin. Each held a hand on one side of it, and between the two they made the copper generate enough heat so that the water gently steamed. He was led up to the lip of the basin, where all four Sages bowed in perfect unison as he climbed into the tub.

The water's heat grazed the very ceiling of what his skin could tolerate. He stared for a moment at his feet, distorted by the ripples of his bath. Then he knelt, so that the water came up to his chest. In perfect unison, the four Sages approached, each bearing a large copper cup. Muttering prayers, they dipped them into the water, and then as one poured them over Jimuro's head.

He closed his eyes as the water hit him, and he shaped his face into a mask of serenity. But inside, he panicked. He was running out of chances to leave this behind. If he did nothing, said nothing, he would remain a prisoner in this throne room for the rest of his life.

He tried to center himself as the second of six blessings of water washed over him. He told himself that he needed to be an empty steel vessel, and that the spirits would flow into him and give him courage: Those of Steel Lords past, and their families. Of the great heroes of Tomoda. Of the people of Tomoda, to whose service he would pledge his body and soul.

And most of all, he hoped for some touch of the spirit that lived within the sergeant who always frowned, whether it be bird or man.

But though he opened himself up for the spirits to flow into and through him, he felt no onrush to fill his empty vessel.

It was only his stoic Tomodanese upbringing that stopped fear from showing on his face as he rose to his feet and held out his arms. Two new Sages stepped forward, bearing pads of steel wool. With surprising gentleness, they ran the steel wool over his skin, its touch as gentle and rough as a cat's tongue. They murmured new prayers as they scrubbed away the shell of man from him, leaving behind the gleaming, clear skin of a living god.

But once again, panic wrapped itself around Jimuro's heart like a serpent. He didn't feel like any sort of god. He just felt like a very clean man.

He stepped out of the tub, feeling the throne room's draft on his bare, wet skin. Then five of the Sages dabbed his skin dry, while one handed him back his glasses before busying herself running a warm metal comb through his hair to dry it. He felt some small relief to see the world sharply again, but with that clarity came an even stronger vision of the throne he had just walked halfway toward.

Dexterous, practiced hands tied his now-dry hair back into a top-knot. Naked but otherwise whole, he walked forward. With every two steps he took, he stopped so that a Sage could add another piece of regalia to his body. He stared straight ahead, remembering what his mother had taught him as one Sage slipped a pure-white kosode over his bare shoulders. He stared straight ahead, remembering how the Sages had coached him as a boy, while one tied his hakama over his legs. With each robe slipped over his head, each sash tied around his waist, each smear of holy oil on his disappearing skin, he stared straight ahead.

And beneath the golden pavilion, behind the fluttering white veil, he knew the Mountain Throne stared back.

A new Sage had emerged to provide each piece of his regalia, and when he turned to regard them all, what had once been an empty throne room was now quite full of holy women and men in voluminous sapphire robes. As one, they all sank to their knees and pressed their foreheads to the floor. But for once, it was not for Jimuro that they bowed. It was for a fat middle-aged man whose temples were streaked with hair the color of storm clouds. He was First Sage Shuichi, and with two hands he offered forward the Mountain Crown.

It was tall and chimney-shaped, meant to slip neatly over one's topknot. The top was flat, square, and wide, and fine golden chains dangled from its edges. He was grateful it was only meant for special occasions like this one; he couldn't imagine wearing something so impractical for day-to-day governance the way his ancestors had.

He knelt, and felt the weight of the crown as it was placed atop his head. Gingerly, he rose, feeling the chains sway with every twitch of his neck. Without moving his head, he glanced down at his feet, and saw he had no floor left between himself and the throne. There were only the stairs, and the destiny that lay atop it.

He thought he would contemplate how he'd gotten here with each step. He thought that with each one, he would grapple with the uncertainty of what came next. But to his surprise, he suddenly found himself standing at the top of the stairs, with nothing left to separate him from the throne save for some clean white linen.

This was his last chance. He had prematurely convened the delegations as the Steel Lord, but nothing would stop him from meeting them as the Iron Prince and explaining that there would be a change of plans. He would not take the coward's way out, as he'd been considering so often these past few days, but he would relieve himself of the burden he was unworthy of bearing.

As soon as he thought that, he was stricken with . . . it wasn't quite a vision. Seeing was part of it, but it was the least part of it. More than anything, it was feeling: anguish, despair, and resignation, all sawing through him.

Through that haze he saw, clear as a photograph, Sergeant Tala. She looked hurt. Betrayed.

And perhaps most cruelly of all, unsurprised.

Once his mother had told him that in the old days of Tomoda, those who had disgraced themselves would offer up their life to their lord in penance. They would kneel, take up their sword, and plunge it straight into their own guts. And then they would kneel there, enduring the unbelievable pain of a slow death, until their lord deemed their suffering sufficient to grant them the mercy of a swift one by beheading.

Seeing that look on Tala's face, even only in his mind's eye, felt like kneeling there, a blade in his guts, as he waited for a second sword stroke that would never come.

He reached for the cloth that separated him from the throne. It was the final test. Woven into its surface was a single filament of metal thread. He had to find it, pact with it, and will it to draw back the rest of the curtain. If he did that and sat the Mountain Throne, it would be his until the day his bones were fed to the fire.

But that look he'd imagined on Tala's face had cut him like a blade, and it had bled away all his doubt.

The single thread called to him like a singer in a silent room. It was a small vessel, as small as any he'd ever pacted with, but he filled it with his spirit nonetheless.

The steel is empty, he reminded himself. *The steel is bone, and you are blood.*

And as he felt his soul stretch into the very last corners of that thread, he willed it to open.

The curtain parted as though it were bowing out of his way, one last polite courtier. Light fell across a surprisingly simple chair of pacted steel. The seatback bore the image of a mountaintop identical to the seal from his mother's desk.

His desk, he realized with a jolt.

He turned at last to face the assembled Sages, the Mountain Crown swaying atop his head. Through its dangling chains he saw them standing there, hands hidden inside their voluminous sleeves, watching intently. Along the edges of the room stood the Kobaruto in muted blue. They looked on solemnly, though none more so than Captain Sakura.

But all Jimuro could think as he surveyed his subjects was, *She should be here.*

And then at last, Jimuro sat the Mountain Throne, and was Iron Prince no more.

As one, the Sages and Kobaruto fell to their knees, a field reaped by an invisible scythe blade.

Only the First Sage remained standing. "For too long, that throne has been empty, Your Brilliance," he said in ringing tones. His voice echoed easily through the throne room. "But now, great Tomoda's heart beats again. Blood will flow to every corner of its body, and its strength will be renewed."

Captain Sakura had gotten to her feet while the First Sage was speaking. "How would you direct that strength, Your Brilliance?" she said, taking her place at the old man's side. "We live to serve."

Jimuro remembered how often he'd seen his mother drumming her fingertips on her armrest when she was in thought, and he was surprised to notice himself doing the same thing now. He pulled his hand away and let it fall into his lap.

Then he said, "I've summoned the foreign delegations here so I might address them in advance of tomorrow's talks. Please inform me when they all arrive, and have them gather here." And then he rose and descended back down the stairs, the folds of his robes swishing around him like water.

"Your Brilliance," said the First Sage in surprise. "Where are you going?"

"Back to my chambers," said Jimuro. "I can hardly face them looking like this."

Murmurs arose from the Sages, but the First Sage silenced them all with a reproachful look. Evenly, he regarded Jimuro. "You don't deem our nation's most sacred vestments—your birthright—suitable for greeting your guests? Your will is beyond reproach, but matters have changed. The first impression you make as Steel Lord will matter more than that of any Steel Lord that's ever come before you."

Jimuro nodded. "I'm not unaware of the long shadow my mother casts, even in death." He pointed to the wide, flat top of the Mountain Crown. "If you haven't noticed, she's literally casting it right now."

The First Sage's mouth thinned. He glanced over his shoulder, then nodded to the Sages to dismiss them all. Captain Sakura took the cue, albeit reluctantly, and the Kobaruto filed out as well. In seconds, the doors to the throne room had slid shut once more, leaving just the two of them at the foot of the throne.

"I appreciate you preserving my dignity by scolding me in private," Jimuro said mildly. He imagined that would be quite the sight: the Steel Lord himself, in full regalia, being whacked with a slipper by an irate priest.

The First Sage frowned. "This isn't a dressing-down, Your Brilliance. My predecessor simply told me that there might come a day to tell you something, the way he once had to tell it to Steel Lord Yoshiko when she was first crowned."

Jimuro raised an eyebrow. "And what would that be?"

"You're thinking of it, even as it sits upon your head, as your mother's crown," the First Sage said simply. "Don't do that, Your Brilliance. It does you and the office both a disservice to think that only one person could ever be its true owner. It was Steel Lord Yoshiko's, but before that it was Steel Lord Kenjiro's, and before that Steel Lord Fujiko's, and so on. Now the crown belongs to Steel Lord Jimuro. Wearing it is your right, and no one else's."

Jimuro blinked. He hadn't known what to expect, but it certainly hadn't been such bluntness. "First Sage Satoshi had to tell my mother this, you say?"

"Yes."

Jimuro coughed. "I hadn't realized my family was so predictable."

The First Sage chuckled. "There's a reason we're designated 'sage,' Your Brilliance." He nodded to the crown atop Jimuro's head. "Are you truly intent on meeting them without your regalia? As you take your first steps onto the gladiatorial sands to fight for our future, will you deny the Tomodanese people the sight of their champion, cloaked in his heritage and armored in his ancestors' legacy?"

"Quite the opposite," Jimuro said. "That's precisely what I intend to give them. Now I need to return to my chambers. I have remarks to prepare."

If the First Sage had any more misgivings, he was careful and tactful enough to betray none of them. He simply bowed. "I live to serve you, Your Brilliance," he said. "You are the Steel Lord now."

A thrill ran down his spine, one miraculously devoid of fear.

Well, no, he realized. There was a healthy amount of fear.

But with it, he felt a humbling awe. He'd just been vested with the spirit of his people: past, present, and future. He'd been gifted with the power to make possible whatever he wanted.

And as Captain Sakura reappeared to escort him from the throne room, his mind was already fixed upon the question—and answer—of what that was.

CHAPTER THIRTY-SIX

TALA

She hadn't been able to enjoy the view of Hagane at night as their motorcade sped through its streets. Nor was she able to properly delight in the splendor of the Palace of Steel, with its elegantly sloping tiled roofs. Blue banners bearing the mountain sigil hung at half-mast: a sign to the people that they would mourn, and continue to mourn, until the throne was once again filled.

"I appreciate Jimuro's restraint," General Erega said, eyeing them out the window of their car as it came to a stop. "Maybe he learned something during our chats after all."

But the general's voice felt distant and muted to Tala, as though she were on a phone call with a bad connection.

"Eyes forward, Lieutenant," the general said. It took Tala a moment to remember that that meant her now. Her tone lightened as she added, "I get sleepy after a good plate of longganisa, too."

"No, sir, I can eat longganisa with the best of them," Tala said. "I'm just remembering the last time I was here."

General Erega nodded. Something changed about the way the light caught her eye as she regarded Tala. "The Thirteen-Fifty-Two-Two wasn't assigned to the final assault on the palace."

"No, sir," Tala said. "We were cleanup."

The way Tala's memory worked, she always recalled smells more sharply than anything else. And what struck her about the Palace of Steel was that despite its lofty occupants, they smelled the same as the dead everywhere else. All their fineries—their linens, their perfumes, their glittering gold—had amounted to nothing, reduced by fire to carbon and slag.

The 13-52-2 was a marine unit that had no business doing battlefield cleanup. But old Colonel Chona, CO of the Thirteenth Regiment, was a petty man who'd felt his ambitions were threatened by the Fifty-Second Company's CO, Lieutenant Varna. Tala had heard this and that about what exactly they were spatting over, but the net effect was that while the officers up the food chain argued, the 13-52-2 had to wade into the ashes of the abattoir.

Her squad had wrapped rags soaked in vinegar around their faces to cut the smell, but these hadn't been very effective. So they grumbled in muffled voices about being put on this detail, and set about picking through the ruined jewel of Tomoda.

The bulk of the final assault had been courtesy of Shang, with long-range assistance from Dahal. Tala had largely been unimpressed with the Shang troops she'd served alongside—an attitude widely shared by the Sanbuna troops, who loved to gripe about mainlander softness. But they'd wreaked havoc upon the Palace of Steel with the force of a great typhoon: doors smashed, floors scorched, art and artifacts ripped off the walls, and bleeding bodies left where they lay.

"Shades take us," Private Kapona had said, taking in the carnage for the first time. "They really went for it, didn't they?" She was smiling, but Tala could see her expression carried sickliness around its edges.

Tala regarded it all with cold eyes and a set jaw. It didn't look as though anyone within the palace had died well, but as far as she was concerned, even the servants had Sanbuna blood on their hands. After all, couldn't one of them have ended this long ago with a dose of cyanide in the right cup of tea, or a knife in the dark?

It was remarkable, how thoroughly the palace had been repaired in the months since. The façade had been pocked with bullet holes when last Tala laid eyes on it. But now it looked as gleaming and immaculate as it always had in all the garbage Tomodanese propa-

ganda newsreels that used to play before movies. The front gates had
been huge chunks of twisted, misshapen metal by the time the 13-
52-2 had crossed their threshold. But the massive steel doors that
now slid open before her were fully formed, gleaming as if fresh
from the foundry.

Tala saw she wasn't the only member of the Sanbuna delegation
staring up at the palace. All ten members had their necks craned to
take in the sight of it. She wondered how many of them had fought
to secure it the first time around, and how many were just swooping
in to bask in the glory now that the hard work was done.

"Delegates," General Erega said, "summon."

The delegates muttered the names of their shades, and the creatures appeared in a cascade of light. It was a sign of respect among
the people of Sanbu: the idea that you were going into this meeting
with your soul literally laid bare for whatever came next. The general was one of the only few not to summon hers, but it was with
good reason: Here on dry land, a dolphin-shade would've had more
than a few difficulties.

Tala whispered Beaky's name, but it only underscored the bottomless absence she felt.

"Is that the legendary Typhoon General herself that I spy?" someone called out in accented Tomodanese. Into the light spilling out
from the palace strode the Dahali delegation. Most of them wore
beige silk, which contrasted starkly with their brown skin. But the
young woman at their head was wrapped in a flowing silk dress that
was the exact bright golden-orange of a perfectly ripe mango. Her
wrists clattered with shiny bangles and bracelets, while a brilliant
gold chain across her cheek connected the elaborate ring in her nose
to the collection of matching ones up and down the length of her ear.
But most noteworthy of all was the knife at her hip: its platinum hilt
sculpted in the image of a lithe naked man, with small sapphires for
eyes.

Tala had heard of her: High Treasurer Bhavna Devarajah, merchant among merchants and one of the only people permitted by
Dahali society to use personal pronouns. Unlike the merchants
who'd preceded her, she'd made her fortune in international bank-
ing, and rumor had it she might even be the single richest person in

the world. She'd been a major financial backer of both the Jasmine and the Peony revolutions, as well as her country's own Lotus Revolution. General Erega had told Tala on the way over that the high treasurer likely wanted to finance as much of the reconstruction of Tomoda as she could, so she would have the Mountain Throne in her debt forever.

Now General Erega smiled. "High Treasurer Devarajah. It's good to see you."

Devarajah marched right up to the general, then took the general's hand and pressed the back of it to her own forehead. Tala was surprised to see her do it; it was the pagmamano, a Sanbuna gesture of respect for one's elders. It'd never occurred to her that an outsider might know of the custom, but she guessed a woman like Devarajah couldn't have gotten to where she was without a good amount of savvy.

"How long have you been in Tomoda?" the general said conversationally.

"Longer than you," Devarajah said simply. "I'm told you and your fleet only arrived yesterday, after encountering some unexpected resistance on the seas."

General Erega's eye glinted. "Nothing more than pirates," she said carefully. "Ones without any affiliation, I'm sure."

Tala didn't know what exactly they were talking about, but she at least knew enough to know they were talking about something else.

"I was most surprised to learn that despite you being the Iron Prince's public jailer, he arrived two days in advance of yourself," Devarajah continued.

That, Tala understood perfectly.

General Erega looked neither abashed nor embarrassed. "It was a necessary precaution. His Brilliance isn't well liked."

An angry voice cut in, speaking fast and aggressive Shang. Into view swept the Shang delegation: by far the largest, with perhaps forty people in all. Half of them had summoned tiger-shades, like Tala had seen at the train station earlier that day. Their partners looked to be soldiers, from their dress and bearing. Another quarter looked more like politicians, and they marched in the company of all different sorts of monkey-shades. Still another quarter appeared to be clergy of some kind, marked by the snake-shades that slithered alongside them.

But at the head of the delegation was a white crane-shade with a long, elegant tail a peacock would've envied and a beak like a yellow sword. Its partner was a red-robed man: older, with a lined face, gray hair, and a double chin his high collar only served to emphasize, and which his short beard failed to effectively hide. Even if he hadn't been wearing a gold crown adorned with rubies and white crane feathers, Tala knew him, too: the Crane Emperor of Shang.

At his approach, the general and the high treasurer bowed, while Tala and everyone else of lesser station took a knee.

The Crane Emperor continued to rant in Shang, seemingly heedless of the people kneeling around him. He looked worked up enough to go on all night if he weren't stopped. So Tala was grateful when a familiar voice cut across him in Tomodanese:

"Apologies, most esteemed General and High Treasurer. His Most August Personage merely wishes to express his dismay that after such a strong and healthy alliance, you did not see fit to trust him with your plans for transporting the Iron Prince safely home where he belongs."

On her knees, Tala risked a glance up. Sure enough, she saw a white rat-shade and a familiar pair of boots. But the true tipoff was the scent of pipe smoke that wafted down to her nostrils.

Over her head, the Crane Emperor spoke again, still in Shang.

"Will he insist on speaking in Shang all night, while the rest of us converse?" said Devarajah mildly.

"My venerated father knows of my strong grasp of the language," said Xiulan. "As such, he has charged me with translating his words for him, so that I might, ah, lend them the poetic flair that would otherwise be lost were he to speak them himself."

Tala grinned.

"Oh," Xiulan added, as if only realizing herself that she was surrounded by kneeling people, "everyone may rise, of course."

When Tala rose, she was greeted by the sight of two faces: one familiar, one not. One, of course, was Xiulan, who had exchanged her dusty white three-piece suit and overcoat for brand-new ones that looked dazzlingly pristine and freshly tailored. Her white trilby, however, was the same one Tala had seen before. Her rat-shade, Kou, stood at obedient attention next to her, pink nose twitching curiously at their surroundings.

Next to Kou stood a huge dog-shade, its tails wagging excitedly as it stared up at the palace. And next to that dog-shade was a woman that Tala figured to be the Jeongsonese woman Xiulan had asked after so urgently. Her dress was slim and black, while her face was made up in shades of red—blush on her cheeks, scarlet on her lips, fuchsia shadow around her eyes—and a bright-red ribbon had been woven into her short black hair.

Xiulan caught Tala's eye and gave her the barest of smiles, though she was stuck translating as her father continued to grouse at both General Erega and Devarajah. But the Jeongsonese woman sidled up to her and said, "Xiulan told me about you." She gave Tala a quick look up and down. "I guess you clean up nice."

Tala wondered what Xiulan had said to prompt an observation like that. But she was too tired to take the compliment at anything but face value. "Thanks."

The woman smirked. "Not as nice as me, though."

The ambient discussion abruptly died around them. Everyone turned to see three people in simple blue robes standing in the doorway. In unison, they bowed low, from the waist. Their leader, a fat man with graying temples, smiled at all assembled and spoke to the Dahali delegation in their lilting tongue. From the impressed looks shared among the delegates behind Devarajah, apparently he did a pretty good job of it.

He turned next to the Crane Emperor and spoke once more, this time in Shang. The emperor listened with a scowl on his face, and interrupted midway through. Tala had no idea what he was saying, either, but she saw Xiulan's smile strain, while Lee just looked flat-out amused.

The man in the robe, however, merely bowed again and issued a polite response. It didn't seem satisfactory to the Crane Emperor or his ruffle-feathered companion, but Tala could hardly ignore the way the Jeongsonese woman's grin widened.

And then at last, the man turned to General Erega and said in perfect Sanbuna, "General Erega. I am First Sage Shuichi, of the order of the Copper Sages. We have of course corresponded. It is my greatest honor to meet you at last."

At this, the man and both his cohorts bowed again.

"Tomoda will forever be in your debt for ensuring the safe return of His Brilliance, in defiance of those who would have preferred he not make it here alive," First Sage Shuichi continued. "It's because of you that I'm able to issue the Steel Lord's official welcome. Given that Tomodanese is the sole language all four delegations share, I respectfully beg your permission to conduct the business of the evening in our own native tongue."

General Erega replied with a single deliberate nod.

"Then if you would please follow me to the throne room . . ."

As the Copper Sages led the delegations through the maze of corridors in the Palace of Steel, Tala marveled yet again at how well the palace had been repaired since she'd last walked its halls. She imagined they'd had artificers and carpenters working around the clock to undo the devastation wrought upon its halls by Shang.

Next to her, Beaky trundled along, his head pumping like a piston with every step he took. She felt his desire to spread his wings and take to the air, but it wouldn't be appropriate for her to let him loose in the halls. She wouldn't have necessarily cared about upsetting Jimuro, and really he should've been used to the sight of Beaky by now, anyway. But such close proximity to General Erega made her all the more aware of how even the tiniest action she took now would reflect on her country.

To her left, she heard the Jeongsonese woman mutter something to Xiulan. It was in Shang, and therefore not for her ears, but something about the surprise on her face was just enough to stoke Tala's curiosity. She hung back a step, then drifted toward them. "What'd you say just now?"

Lee raised an eyebrow. "Just an old Jeongsonese saying about how eavesdroppers can go fuck themselves."

Tala scowled, but she supposed she deserved that. Life generally worked out better for her when she kept her nose where it belonged. She shrugged, then lengthened her stride to reclaim her original place in the procession. But before she got far enough, the woman sighed. "I said, it looks just like the drawings." She gestured to the halls around them. "At Kohoyama, he had books and books full of sketches. Lots of them were of this place."

Tala frowned. Kohoyama? Sketchbooks? "Who?" she said.

"Who d'you figure?" she said. "Jimuro."

"Lee," Xiulan said gently, "he is now a ruling sovereign. That warrants him a certain measure of formality and respect."

Lee grinned. "He can get those once I start giving them to you."

But as the two slipped into their banter, Tala found herself taking on a new appreciation of the palace in which she found herself. This wasn't just a seat of government and a symbol of Tomoda's power; it was Jimuro's childhood home.

Suddenly it was as though her memories of the Palace of Steel had a filter laid over them. The dead servants she'd cleared away, she now imagined alive and cleaning up toys left behind by a pint-sized Jimuro. She considered the burned-out mess of a library she'd found. How many hours might Jimuro have spent in there, to require those glasses of his?

She hadn't even known that he liked to draw.

She eyed the blank walls. She doubted the prince's art would've hung on them, but surely family portraits and priceless tapestries had. The Shang had burned all those, too, in a fit of long-simmering spite. But in their absence, would this place feel like home to Jimuro anymore? Would it feel that way without his family? She'd lost all hers in the worst way possible, but at least the bomb had destroyed their house with it. The palace, on the other hand, was an enduring monument to everything Jimuro had lost, and he had no choice but to live in it. It would be like sleeping in a pile of his family's ashes.

She staggered a step. She hadn't realized it, but the farther she'd walked down that mental path, the harder the throbbing in the back of her head had become. It felt as if it were crushing her entire brain to the front of her skull.

Next to her, Beaky croaked with concern. She waved him off, and gritted her teeth. She had to hold it together. Until she found the splintersoul and took back what was hers, this was going to be her life. She couldn't give in to the pain after barely a day.

It took a seemingly endless array of twists and turns to reach the throne room. As Xiulan explained on the walk, that was actually by design, to intimidate those seeking an audience with the Steel Lord. Tala sniffed at that. The republic had no such palaces. Congress convened in what had once been the mansion of the daito of Lisan, while General Erega had converted her personal residence into a government building, to be inherited by the next head of the republic. And yet she found herself staring contemplatively at the high ceilings and long, wide floors, and wondered if its architecture wasn't doing its job after all.

The throne room was perhaps the least changed from how she remembered it, if only because it was, in typical Tomodanese fashion, so sparse. The walls were gray-polished steel, adorned with fluttering banners of mountains and Tomodanese characters. The floor was a wide expanse of dark polished oak, with a streak of blue rug that led directly to the elevated throne. Along the left side of the rug stood a line of sapphire-robed Copper Sages, while along the right stood the sapphire-clad members of the Kobaruto.

And sitting upon the throne, in full military dress, was the man she now had to think of as Steel Lord Jimuro.

Though she'd thought of him as the enemy, it occurred to her just now that she'd never seen him in uniform. This one traced his body much the way his clothes from the Kinzokita safe house had: emphasizing the length of his limbs and the width of his shoulders. It was deep blue, with gold epaulets and a bright-blue sash running diagonally across his chest. The steel buttons on his coat gleamed even from this distance, as did the collection of medals pinned to his chest. He wore white gloves: one of which rested upon his leg, and the other of which toyed with the golden hilt of a sheathed sword standing next to him.

Murmurs arose from every delegation at the sight of him. Some seemed upset that he'd chosen to greet them in military regalia, sword in hand. Some seemed upset that he was there to greet them at all.

Tala, on the other hand, was silent. She was awed to see how strikingly at home he looked up there. She'd seen him at his lowest, at his least flattering, at his objectively terrible. But up there, sitting that throne, he looked undeniably regal.

Lee smirked. "I fucking *knew* he had a fancy chair."

"It is my honor to present to you," First Sage Shuichi said, "His Brilliance, the divine vessel of the spirits and beating heart of the Tomodanese people . . . Steel Lord Jimuro."

When he rose, the entire room knelt. Tala hesitated half a heartbeat. But then she felt her legs bending as if her will weren't her own. She wasn't sure if it was the room, or the throne, or the regalia, but something about Jimuro now encouraged . . . if not deference, at least respect.

She knelt.

He stepped out from beneath the pavilion, so his face was in full view. Tala felt her pulse race as she saw, to her immense relief, that he was still whole. Still unharmed. Still Jimuro.

He took a moment to survey those assembled in his throne room. He did an admirable job of evoking regality, but she could see his eyes searching . . . until at last, they met hers.

The corners of his mouth turned up in the barest, smallest smile.

Slowly, her scowl softened, until she smiled back in turn.

For one heartbeat, two, three, Tala and Jimuro shared a private moment in a crowded room.

And then, on the fourth heartbeat, the moment passed, like a cloud over the moon. Jimuro disappeared. In his place, wearing his body and face, there was only the Steel Lord.

"Hello," said the Steel Lord. "And thank you for coming."

CHAPTER THIRTY-SEVEN

JIMURO

Including the shades present, there were more than a hundred souls in Jimuro's throne room. And yet when he stared down at them, it was as if the collective gaze of the entire world stared back, fixed and unblinking. He felt like an ice sculpture, trying in vain not to melt under the sun.

But melting was no option at all. Not for him, not for his country, and not for his people. Steel did not melt.

Of course it does, he reminded himself. *Don't be stupid.* And then, after a moment: *But don't melt, either.*

His knees trembled within the folds of his pants. He hoped it wouldn't be visible. At the very least, he was glad of the gloves on his hands to keep them dry. For what came next, the last thing he needed was to drop his sword.

Scanning the room, he saw familiar faces: Erega, of course, who looked quietly pleased to see him standing there. Shang Xiulan, who looked significantly less pleased, though nowhere near so much as her sour-faced father. Lee Yeon-Ji, who seemed vaguely amused by everything around her. Kohaku, whose canine eyes had brightened up at the sight of him.

And Tala.

As fine a figure as he cut in military dress, she took to it in a way that made him feel like he was playing dress-up. He saw a new rank insignia adorning her jade uniform, and felt a swelling of pride, despite the fact that she wore what had so recently been the uniform of the enemy. Whatever promotion she'd received—lieutenant, if his memory of Sanbuna designations served—had been richly earned for everything she'd done.

Now it was up to him to show his own gratitude.

"Hello," he said. "And thank you for coming. I apologize for the short notice, but I felt it to be of vital importance that I address you all at the outset of my reign. In these fraught times, I feel the need to set the tone properly. And there are even more important matters to discuss than those of state."

He remembered what his elocution tutors had taught him growing up. He was careful to fully enunciate his words, and to take his time. He kept his breathing slow and steady, so that his tone would betray neither nerves nor haste. In this regard, the throne room helped him; it had been specifically designed so that any who stood where he did could be clearly heard even in its farthest corners.

"The Sages wished for me to meet you in the traditional regalia of the Steel Lord: The Mountain Crown. The twenty sokutai of the prefectures. The flawless mirror of Steel Lord Sanjuro. But I told them the only treasure I intended to display tonight was the ever-keen blade of Setsuko, the first Steel Lord."

He held the weapon aloft, still in its sheath. It was surprisingly plain: a black wooden sheath capped with gold, and a simple hilt of unwrapped steel with a gold pommel. It was so unassuming, one would never have imagined it was the single most important sword in all of Tomoda, if not the world.

But then, Jimuro reminded himself, it had been forged humbly to begin with. It had been the hand of Steel Lord Setsuko that had made it remarkable.

So, too, he prayed, would his own hand make it worth something.

It took him a moment to remember what came next in the remarks he'd prepared. He hoped his pause would be interpreted as regal gravitas, rather than uncertainty. But at last, he continued, "I've already had a great many of my subjects weigh in on how best to use this blade. Some wish for me to brandish it in defiance. Some want me to keep it tucked away in the depths of our archive. And still others," he added, thinking of Kosuke, "wish for me to turn its edge on you—either right now, or after I've taken the time to hone it to its finest."

"Spare us your posturing, boy," came a grating voice that spoke in Shang. Of course, it was the Crane Emperor himself. Why couldn't it have been a lower courtier, whom Jimuro wouldn't have thought twice about rebuking?

He glanced for a moment at General Erega, but hopefully tore himself away before she noticed. This was his throne room, he reminded himself. It would be up to him to set the tone. His mother wasn't there to save him, and neither was Erega nor the lieutenant by her side, whose gaze Jimuro had been studiously avoiding since he began speaking.

"We are in my house, in my country, Most August Personage of the Crane," Jimuro answered in his best Shang. He was certain the delegates were judging his accent, but it was the prerogative of kings to not care. "I will tolerate interruptions as well as I will tolerate the way you blithely refer to me as 'boy.' And," he added, switching back to Tomodanese, "it is a great sign of disrespect to your fellow delegates to refuse to speak our agreed-upon common language as you have. I'm certain the Most August Personage of the Crane will understand."

Stunned silence greeted him, and he derived a delirious sort of satisfaction in it. He saw Xiulan immediately look stricken, while Lee couldn't stop herself from grinning. Devarajah had tactfully hidden her mouth behind the folds of her dress, though the faint crinkles in the corner of her eyes betrayed the presence of her own smile. Erega kept her expression diplomatically impassive, but Jimuro knew her and her moods well enough to know what it looked like when she was impressed with someone.

He forced his eyes to slip over Tala. He couldn't look at her, not yet.

At long last, the Crane Emperor grunted and nodded. Jimuro supposed it was the closest he'd get to an apology from the old goat, and opted to continue. He had a lot to get through.

"For those of you who don't speak Shang," he continued, "the Most August Personage of the Crane just accused me of empty posturing. But with this sword, I intend to make a very real gesture."

He took a step down toward the floor. "I appear before you today in military dress because for a century and a half, this is the Tomoda you've known. When we beached our ships on your shores, when we pulled your ore from the earth, when we filled those holes with the bodies of your dead . . . this is the Tomoda that did that to you."

He took another step down. His mouth felt dry, but he could hardly stop for a glass of water now. "My ancestors had their reasons for colonizing your homes. But I am not my ancestors, and in this moment I tell you those reasons were wrong. For me, the future is a clear and open road, and I have the freedom to take it along any path I so choose. I choose to travel a path previous Steel Lords have not."

A third step. Only two more remained. "Yet, I dress this way to say I won't forget what my ancestors did to you. What I have been complicit in doing to you," he added, with a quick glance toward Lee. "If my people run from the horror of what we've done, in time we would forget. And if we forget, we might one day do it again. Your peoples do not have the luxury of forgetting how you've suffered. And so I intend to deny my people that same luxury."

A fourth step. His voice took on a more rehearsed cadence as he said, "In the old days of Tomoda, a warrior who had disgraced themselves would offer up their life to their lord."

A ripple of alarm passed through the Sages and the Kobaruto alike. Jimuro supposed that made sense enough; after all, it wasn't as if he'd cleared this with any of them. The delegates, on the other hand, were still too confused to understand what he was doing. But soon enough, they would.

"The disgraced warrior would kneel, and then impale themselves upon their own sword and hold it there. A sideways slash would cause them to bleed out quickly, but they were not allowed to grant themselves the release of an easy death. They were to kneel before their lord in excruciating pain, waiting for their lord to decide that they had suffered commensurately to their crime so that they could be relieved with a beheading."

The fifth step. The final step. "According to legends, a great warrior named Mitsuha once disgraced her liege lord by bedding his husband. Incensed, the lord demanded her life for the crime. So she knelt at his feet, impaled herself upon her sword, and waited for her lord to end her suffering. Except he didn't. So bent on vengeance was this lord that he intended to wait until Mitsuha clung to life by a single thread, so that she could suffer as much as possible before he granted her mercy.

"For three days, Mitsuha knelt, transfixed upon her own blade, demanding neither food nor water. She spoke no words, not even to demand the mercy she was due. Each day, the lord would wait at her side, saying nothing himself, and each night he would leave, so that she could continue to suffer while he slept. But on the third day, her strength finally failed her and she died while the lord ate his breakfast."

The legend of Mitsuha was one of the most famous in Tomodanese folklore, so there were many different versions Jimuro had heard over the years. Some said that when she died, her lord choked on a mouthful of rice himself, so that their two spirits intersected in the afterlife. Some said that the lord's husband came in the night and granted Mitsuha the release his cruel spouse wouldn't. Still others said that the spirits themselves took pity on her and, to punish the lord for his vanity, gave her the strength to kneel there for fifty years, so that the lord died before she did.

But the version he'd just told had been his mother's favorite, and she'd insisted it was the true version of the story.

"We've forgotten the lord's name and remembered Mitsuha's because the lord was a fool," Jimuro said simply. "Mitsuha was the greatest warrior of her age. He was lucky to have her in his service, but he forced her to use her sword to enact vengeance when he could have used its might to make himself Steel Lord, if he wanted. Nonetheless, that's the choice I offer you now."

He took his step onto the floor. This was the most important one, symbolically speaking. Royal protocol dictated that the Steel Lord should always be the highest in his own throne room. For those who understood that about his culture, they would understand the significance of the gesture he'd just made. Certainly, he saw Xiulan's eye light up in surprise.

"You all have ample reason to make me plunge this sword into my guts, then walk away without ever finishing the matter. I don't deny that. But even with the sins that hang over Tomoda's past . . . and present," he added, with a lingering look around the throne room, "I'm here to argue that Tomoda offers more to the world alive than dead, or as some shriveled-up vassal state.

"I called you here so I could offer you three things," Jimuro said. He swallowed. There wasn't much more to his speech, but what was left would be the hardest to say. "The first is a warning: that there's a greater threat in the world than Tomoda, and it will require our collective might to effectively deal with him."

That certainly evoked some reactions. The Dahali delegates muttered among themselves, though Devarajah remained separate from them, her curious gaze fixed on him. The Crane Emperor puffed up like an angry bird. Of the three leaders present, only General Erega seemed to have even the faintest inkling of what he was talking about. But even her reaction was nothing compared with the grim expressions of knowing that flitted across Xiulan's, Lee's, and Tala's faces.

"The next," Jimuro pressed on, "is to offer up an apology. And it comes hand in hand with the third thing I offer you."

And then he unsheathed the sword of Steel Lord Setsuko.

Even with the lights overhead taken into account, it was the most brilliant thing in the room, like a shaft of sunlight in his hand. Despite the centuries, careful pacting and maintenance had left the steel gleaming and flawless. There wasn't so much as a notch on the blade's edge. It was as if it had never bitten into flesh, had never split sinew, had never spilled blood.

He knelt, placed the sheath at his side, and held aloft the sword with both hands.

Xiulan's mouth hung open. Lee glared at him in warning. Tala frowned, the way she always did, but he could see how her whole body tightened.

First Sage Shuichi and Captain Sakura rounded on him at the same moment. *"Your Brilliance—!"* they chorused.

"Mitsuha's lord was a fool," Jimuro repeated, ignoring them. "Mitsuha could never have bled enough to satisfy his thirst. To those of you who come here with vengeance in your heart: I submit to you, neither can Tomoda. You can strip us of our resources, feed my people to your shades, and plant your seeds in our land, but especially if you divide the spoils among the three of you, it will never feel like appropriate recompense for what you've lost.

"But if you accept my apology and give Tomoda a chance to earn your forgiveness, I pledge to use the might and resources of my country to rebuild yours. I will share the secrets of our engineering and industry, so you can use them as you see fit to help your people. All this and more, I promise in the pact that I would make with you."

Once again, he elicited murmurs of surprise, but this time there were no strings attached to the satisfaction he found there. After all, he'd chosen the word *pact* very carefully.

At last, he brought himself to look at Tala directly again. He'd let his sight glide over her, but now he lingered and caught her eye. She was, as ever, the picture of soldierly discipline: stiff-backed and stiff-lipped. His most tireless servant, and the one he'd thrown away most carelessly.

"I'm sorry," he said. "Tomoda was selfish, and greedy, and short-sighted. No matter Tomoda's intent, even one innocent person harmed in the pursuit of good intentions is enough to taint them. I wish there were a stronger word in any of our languages to communicate the depths of my regret, but I'll spend the rest of my life using the one we have."

He sensed the world's eye on him again, but now he could shut it out. Now he had eyes only for Tala.

"I'm not about to disembowel myself," he said, and saw the First Sage and Lee both breathe tiny sighs of relief. "But nonetheless, I leave the future of my people in your hands, delegates. The choice is yours to accept, or not, but I will live with the decision of the triumvirate all the same."

A ringing silence fell over the chamber, one that felt even louder than his voice had just been. Though people looked at one another, none dared speak.

Until Bhavna Devarajah said, "Before Tomoda so foolishly violated Great Dahal's borders, she was always a valuable trading partner. I know her funds are depleted, but she has both the location and the infrastructure to become an economic asset once more. The Merchants Council would be foolish to bypass such a lucrative opportunity . . . pending some negotiations and concessions."

Jimuro had expected as much from Devarajah. Dahal's priorities were reliably mercantile, and they had suffered by far the least of the three nations present.

The Crane Emperor spoke next. "Your theater does not impress me," he said. "In your children's children's lifetimes, you will still owe Shang a debt for what you've taken. Abasing yourself does not earn you credit with me."

For the first time, Jimuro's temper truly rose in the back of his throat. What did the fool expect him to do, exactly? It wasn't like he could just unravel the past centuries with a snap of his fingers. "Gestures are meaningless without follow-through, it's true," he said. He heard his mother's voice in the back of his head, counseling restraint.

But he also heard Tala's voice in his head, counseling an ass-kicking.

"For instance," he continued in a theatrically mild tone, "a formal declaration of peace means nothing if the daughter of a head of state attempted to assassinate another head of state while he was traveling home, don't you think? If such a sovereign conducted himself that way, don't you think everyone would agree that his word was meaningless, and that he was perhaps unfit to sit his own throne?"

Lee let out a cackle that she hastily disguised as a cough.

Xiulan remained impassive, but Kou's nose twitched excitedly.

The Crane Emperor glared at Jimuro with wide eyes. He looked like a lightbulb that had suddenly blown out. Clearly, he hadn't expected his daughter's subterfuge to be so widely known. But when he glanced around to Devarajah and Erega looking for support, he received stony glances in reply.

"Tonight is the gesture," Jimuro said. "Everything from this point will be my follow-through, to lend it actual meaning. But for me to follow through, Most August Personage of the Crane, you need to accept the gesture."

He couldn't believe he was mouthing off to the Crane Emperor himself. He supposed his throne room was the one place in the world where he could do so safely, and even then he still couldn't believe his own audacity. He was grateful a lifetime of Tomodanese upbringing had taught him how to keep a straight face. The last thing he needed was for everyone to see precisely how terrified he was.

At last, the Crane Emperor scowled and nodded. He couldn't have given a less enthusiastic nod if it had been coaxed out of him at gunpoint, but it was a nod nonetheless, and it would have to do. And besides, Jimuro reminded himself, the Crane Emperor was an old man. As long as Tomoda could secure the backing of Xiulan and her siblings, then the old man wouldn't matter all that much.

Last of all, General Erega grinned. "The Sanbuna Republic was forged out of its ten islands' need to unite in our fight for freedom," she said. "So I think there's plenty of virtue in what you say, Your Brilliance. Especially if there's something else on the horizon . . ."

At last, Jimuro felt like he could get to his feet again. "I don't know his name," he said simply. "But what I can say is that he wears a purple coat, he can summon a seemingly limitless number of shades by himself . . ."

He noticed a ripple pass over the Shang and Sanbuna delegations as they caught his second use of the word *shade.*

". . . and where he goes, death follows."

"And he's a threat to us, why?" said Devarajah.

"Because," Jimuro said, then swallowed. "More than anything else in the world, he wants me dead." By now, he knew that not to be true. But he'd deduced the only other common factor in their every encounter thus far.

"I wonder why that would be," Devarajah said, smirking.

"I know it seems outlandish," said Jimuro, "but I'm not the only one who's seen him in action."

"I can certify the veracity of his statements," Xiulan called out.

"I've . . . heard of him," General Erega said. "Do you really think he's that severe of a threat?"

"In such a fraught political climate, I think the danger of any unbalancing factor is multiplied tenfold," Jimuro said. "And even in peacetime, I'd still think of him as the most dangerous man alive. For better or for worse, I'm the fulcrum on which our future peace rests. Without me, there's no sovereign Tomoda. And despite your warranted feelings on the subject, I'll stress again: That's nothing to hope for."

"So what do you propose?" said Xiulan. Her father gave her a reproachful look, but she seemed to pay him no heed.

He nodded gratefully to her. "Given the gutted state of the former Tomodanese military, I will require the aid of your nations' strongest warriors, so that we may bait him into the open to take him down. And to lead this special force, General Erega, I humbly request the services of my escort, Lieutenant Tala."

This was the penance he hoped to offer her: a full army of the world's best, so that she would no longer have this monster stalking her footsteps. With the man in the purple coat gone from the world, she would be free to live her life however she wanted. Wherever she wanted.

With whomever she wanted.

But as he turned his attention to the spot beside General Erega, to gauge Tala's reaction himself, he blanched. Where before his faithful bodyguard had stood, there was now only a single long, black crow feather.

Tala was gone.

PART SEVEN

$\cdot\ \cdot\ \cdot$

VENGEANCE IN VIOLET

CHAPTER THIRTY-EIGHT

TALA

Her heart had become a howling black cloud of hunger, and it beckoned her to his side.

She'd been living with the throbbing since last night, following the ways it changed and fluctuated. For most of the day, she'd chalked it up to her general unfamiliarity with having one's soul reaved, and tried not to think about it. But while Jimuro was speaking, she'd felt it grow stronger and stronger, until it was so overwhelming she could hardly see.

That was when she'd understood why, as the night had gone on, the hunger she felt had gone from background noise to a constant roar. Why that hunger had risen up within her, sick and caustic as vomit in her throat, and urged her to tear apart General Erega herself. It was a thread that tied one half of her soul to the other, like the last sinew that kept a severed head lolling on its neck.

It was a thread she could follow.

And it had just stretched itself taut.

She had no idea what would happen next, but she knew that she'd barely had a day with this pain in her and already found it unbearable. This man had been living with it for years. She had to believe that they would both want to end this quickly.

Though she didn't know the twists and turns of the Palace of Steel well, the throbbing in the back of her head guided her feet. With inexorable certainty, she made her way through the corridors, sliding doors aside and skulking away from unaware servants and guards when they neared. Avoiding their notice was easy; they were soft palace pets, while she was a beast who had sharpened her teeth jungle-running. She donned the shadows as easily as she did her uniform, and shed them like a snake did its skin.

Beaky hopped along behind her, his dark plumage hiding him even more easily than she. She wished she could've allowed him to fly free, with the moonlight on his back. The whole time they'd been in Tomoda, flying free was all he'd wanted, and for one reason or another she hadn't been able to give him that freedom. She just had to hope that would change soon.

No matter what happened next.

She could tell Beaky was grateful for the sentiment. But she couldn't ignore the mounting trepidation he felt with each step they took toward their target.

She projected a mix of feelings into him: Reassurance. Gratitude. Understanding. Sympathy. But it felt like trying to bring light to a dark hole by chucking down a single lit match at a time.

She stopped and knelt. "Hoy," she said to Beaky, who cocked his head to get a better look at her. She patted his beak. "We don't have to do this." The words felt hollow in her throat, but she meant them nonetheless. What she was about to do involved asking everything of Beaky. She'd pledged to be a better partner, and that had to start here.

She could feel the crow-shade considering her offer. A small part of her feared what she would do if he decided to decline. She wanted to believe she could trust herself to do what was right for her partner. But when the hunger was so overwhelming, the pain so impossible to escape . . .

At long last, Beaky offered up a feeling that was vaguely shaped like assent, and which solidified more with each passing moment. The relief Tala felt herself was like balm on a bullet wound. That aura of fear was still there, but Beaky's crest stood tall, his breast feathers fluffed, and a certain reluctant certainty shone in the one eye she could see.

She swallowed, then gave him a gentle kiss at the base of his beak. "Thank you," she whispered. "I'm sorry."

Beaky projected feelings to her that her brain roughly translated as an eye roll. Tala smiled anyway, and felt the inside of her chest grow tight. She swallowed hard. It wasn't fair. For someone who'd lost so much, she was still so bad at saying goodbye.

She'd understood right away what Jimuro was trying to do, the moment he'd started talking about the splintersoul. If he convened a multinational effort to take the splintersoul down, and insisted Tala be kept close, it would insulate her against further attacks from him. She got it; he was trying to make up for dismissing her. And she appreciated it.

But she couldn't stomach the thought of any more innocent people dying for her sin. She knew the only thing that could make her feel whole again was having Mang back. If she had to fight her way through a palace full of soldiers with just Beaky at her side, that was what she would do. Even though the man in the purple coat had far more than a single bird at his disposal, that didn't matter. Many years ago, she and this bird had made a pact with each other that they would keep fighting. There was no one she would've preferred to have at her back for what came next.

And besides, Jimuro didn't know that Mang had been taken from her at all. If the man so much as caught a lucky stray bullet before she had a chance to lay hands on him . . .

She shuddered, then stepped away from the thought. She couldn't even allow herself to consider going on without Mang. No matter what happened next, no matter if she even walked away from this, she would get him back.

Beaky clacked his beak in approval. She hadn't realized she'd been broadcasting her feelings to him, but she welcomed his support. He was more than she deserved.

She offered up a silent thanks to him, and then another to Jimuro. After all, she'd gotten this idea from him.

In time, she came upon one final door: paper stretched over dark wood, illuminated by the moonlight that lay beyond. And etched into the paper from somewhere beyond it was the distant silhouette of a single man in a billowing coat.

When she slid it aside, a warm summer breeze and the song of cicadas welcomed her to the remains of the imperial garden. The Palace of Steel had been repaired to an impressive degree, considering the amount of punishment it had taken during the final assault. But while wood beams could be replaced and steel could be pacted, there was no rushing a garden.

She imagined there had once been mighty trees, but now there stood only saplings. The grass had mostly grown back, though there were patches where it lay thin enough for Tala to glimpse bare soil. Three ponds lay evenly spaced across the courtyard, ringed by carefully arrayed stones. Their waters were still, save for the ripples created by the koi swimming beneath each one's surface.

In the far corner stood a fountain with a bamboo tube slowly filling with water. Just as Tala glanced at it, it filled enough to tip over, pouring the water back into the pool at its feet. And as it rotated back into a standing position, the bottom of the tube struck a nearby rock with a loud, hollow-sounding *thunk* that she could hear even over the cicada song.

The way she'd had it told to her, the Tomodanese kept gardens in their homes as a place for wandering spirits to take refuge and bless the house. And as the country had become more industrial, it had become more important than ever for the spirits to have a place where they could commune with the land as it once was.

Given how much the Tomodanese cared about these gardens, it made perfect sense that the Shang had put this one to the torch.

But the man waiting for her amid a patch of hydrangeas was capable of doing far worse.

In the day since she'd last seen him, he seemed to have degraded even more. His long black hair was thickly matted and a scraggly beard infested his face, patchy as the grass underfoot. One hand hung at his side, while the handless stump of his wrist was in his pocket. His purple coat was even filthier somehow, splotched with blood and pocked with cuts and tears. But the real difference was the mad sheen of hunger in his bloodshot eyes. He was a wolf, and he stared at her like she was an exposed throat.

"I've been told this is where the war ended," he said without greeting. "That this was where the Steel Lord breathed her last. Is that true?"

She was taken aback by the calm in his voice. In their previous two encounters, he'd been a bloodthirsty lunatic. Nonetheless, she nodded. "Shang troops found her here. She fought hard, but she was one woman against a dozen shades."

Within the depths of his thin black beard, she caught the yellow glint of his teeth.

"I fought at the beginning of the war," he said, glancing around the garden with unhurried calm. "The blood I shed then . . . it all flowed here, like a stream feeding into a great river and following it all the way to the sea." Something subtle shifted in his gaze, and it took on a harsh, appraising feel. "But it didn't stop flowing, did it, Tala?"

Her name sounded like an obscenity in his mouth. "I don't know what you're talking about."

"The war," he said. "It didn't really end. With every beat of your heart, every breath you've drawn since Steel Lord Yoshiko died, you've kept it alive."

Tala narrowed her eyes. "I fought for the freedom of my people. I fought for peace."

His voice was like a blade scraping across a throat. "You fought to hurt the bad people who took Mommy and Daddy away," he hissed. "You can't lie to me, soldier. I knew you were vicious for what you'd done to me . . . I had no idea how vicious you'd become since."

Tala scowled at him. She hadn't come to hear him out. "What I did to you, you returned. I'm here to settle accounts. You return Dimangan to me . . . and I'll make you whole, too."

She stepped aside to reveal Beaky standing there. His anxiety spiked in her head, but she could feel him resisting the urge to fly away. She sent back a wave of gratitude, in the hope that it might calm him even a little.

When the man's eyes fell upon Beaky, all the flintiness in them vanished immediately. He gave a strangled sob and surged forward a step, tears already flowing freely down his eyes.

But he stopped when Tala brought her gun to bear on him. "That's far enough."

He lurched forward, then caught himself. "I bear your brother's soul," he said. "End my life, and you end his."

"My firing instructor always said someone with good aim can kill. Someone with great aim doesn't have to. And besides: You know I can metalpact now. I won't miss."

She didn't actually know how to pact with a gun or a bullet to improve its accuracy. Nonetheless, the man growled and clutched at his stump of an arm.

She adjusted her sight so it was parked right over his kneecap. She'd seen him in action. He was fast, but not fast enough to stop her from turning his knee to powder and pulp with a twitch of her finger. "We're going to do this civilly," Tala said. "An even, equivalent exchange, and then we both walk away. Understood?"

The man in the purple coat shook his head. "There's nothing equivalent about what you're proposing," he said in a low, hollow voice. "You doomed me to years of agony. I gave you a rough night."

"He's my brother," Tala said. She felt the strength in her burnt hand starting to leave her already, and she steadied her gun with her other hand.

"Did you care who Beaky was to me before you took him?" His voice shook as it rose. *"Did you?"* Fear pulsed through her, and she didn't know how much of it was her, how much of it was Beaky, and how much the difference even mattered.

"I'm here to make that right," Tala said. "And with the aim I've got, you should be glad that's the only score I'm looking to settle."

The man's eyes narrowed. "The platoon."

Their faces swam before her eyes, one by one. *"My* platoon," she said. "And however many people you killed before them and after."

He shook his head. "Those aren't yours to avenge," he said. "And besides . . ." He took a step toward her. "Would I have killed them all if you hadn't torn me in two?" He took another step. "Have you yet stopped to ask yourself: If you hadn't committed your sin, how many people would still be alive?"

She gritted her teeth and fought to stop her hands from shaking. But each thing he said felt as if it were gouging away more of the earth beneath her feet. "I didn't kill those people. You did."

"When a person dies from a gunshot," the man whispered, "you don't blame the bullet. You blame the shooter." And then he took another step. Whatever hesitation he'd had in approaching her before had completely evaporated. He was starting to get that mad gleam back in his eye, the one he'd had during his rampage aboard the *Crow's Flight*.

When he'd slaughtered his way through the 13-52-2.

When he'd fought his way through Maki.

Tala exhaled, then leaned her pistol back so it rested under her chin, angled perfectly to blow her own brains out. Panic surged through her from Beaky: *This wasn't the plan!*

"For the sake of my brother's soul, I won't end your life," she said. Though she'd never been more terrified in her life than she was in this moment, she fought to keep her voice steady, her eyes cold and focused. "But take another step, and I'll end mine."

"You'd orphan your own brother?" said the man. The madness was still there, but wariness undercut its menace.

"If I leave him with you long enough, he'll figure out a way to kill you himself," Tala said. "I'm not worried about him. But if I'm going to die without him either way, I'll do it in a way that makes sure you spend the rest of your life hollow." She paused, silently offering up Jimuro a preemptive apology for spilling blood on his freshly rebuilt garden. "So what'll it be, then?"

The man glared at her. He clenched his hand into a shaking fist.

Beaky cocked his head. More panic and unease ran through Tala: *You can't be serious.*

But the moment Tala had said it, she'd known she was.

Her eyes met his. Where madness glinted in his eyes, she knew focus and discipline shone in her own, hard and bright as steel.

They stood deathly still, while all around them the world moved: The summer breeze. The koi in the pond. The singing cicadas. The bamboo fountain, striking its stone base again with another hollow *thunk*.

Then something new moved in the corner of her eye, in the upper reaches of her vision. She spared a momentary glance toward it, just in time to see a white-furred, three-tailed monkey-shade leap from the roof where it had been lurking, its hands outstretched and its fanged mouth wide open.

In the heartbeat it took her to notice Sunny, the splintersoul darted sideways. Too late, she tried to squeeze off a shot and stop him. The bullet gouged a hole in the grass as Sunny tackled her to the ground.

As her world became a tangle of white fur, limbs, and teeth, she willed Beaky to take to the air, where he'd be safe. And as she did, she looped her gun around and emptied its remaining five chambers into Sunny's hide. The tight cluster of wounds immediately sparked with magical energy as they healed up, but it stunned the monkey-shade just long enough for Tala to shove him off. Unsteadily, she climbed to her feet—

—only for a familiar hand to envelop her entire face.

Her body seized with panic as her world went dark.

She arched her back with agony as she felt her soul beginning to tear, his grip tightening over her skull—

The report of another gun shattered the stillness of the night. The hand fell from her face, and she staggered back, gasping for air and blinking to readjust her sight.

One of the rocks in the garden had shifted itself aside, revealing a tunnel beneath. And surging out of that tunnel: Shang Xiulan. Lee . . . whatever her name was. Their shades appeared beside them in twin flashes of light, then charged for Sunny, who had almost recovered from his gunshot wounds.

But the one holding the smoking gun was Steel Lord Jimuro, his glasses glaring pure white in the moonlight.

"Jimuro!" Tala shouted. "No! Stay back!"

"Wow," Lee said. "Guess we can go fuck ourselves, eh, Princess?"

"Remember me?" Jimuro called to the splintersoul. "You didn't know who I was then." Loudly, he chambered a round. "I bet you do now."

The splintersoul roared as blood oozed from his shoulder, where Jimuro's shot had sunk in. He gave an angry sweep of his arms, shouting names the whole way, and in reply streams of light surged through the air, solidifying into a small army of shades.

"Ah," said Xiulan. "The proverbial army at your fingertips. Perhaps, sir, it would surprise you to know that we, too, are in possession of armies . . ."

All around the courtyard, walls turned into doors, sliding aside to reveal what must have been every able-bodied fighter in the palace: the delegation of the Republic of Sanbu, General Erega at their head, their ranks rippling with fear and surprise as they beheld a splinter-soul for the first time. The delegation of Great Dahal, led by Bhavna Devarajah with hands that glowed deadly white. The Kobaruto, their steel cables dragging behind them as they charged into the garden in disciplined silence.

General Erega limped forward. "I know you, son," she called to the splintersoul. "You were one of mine, back in the early days."

Surprise pierced the man's wild, desperate air. "I was, sir." He reached up with his good hand and tapped his left eye. "You had both of these."

"And you had both of those," General Erega replied, holding up a hand. "We fought together, son. No need for us to fight each other. Stand down, and we can talk all this out."

The man leveled a surprisingly clear stare at the general. "You didn't really think that'd work, did you, sir?"

The general shook her head sadly. "I wanted it to."

Above, Beaky circled and circled. Tala could tell more than anything else that he wanted to help her, but he couldn't bring himself to. She wished she had his backing; it had gotten her through some of the worst battles of the war. But now that she understood the truth, asking him to fight the other half of himself was too cruel.

But she had Shang Xiulan, and Kou's flashing teeth. She had Lee, and her dog-shade's huge paws. She had the blades of the Kobaruto, the hexes of Dahal, the shades of Sanbu.

And her heart soared to see that she would be fighting alongside Jimuro once more, even if she couldn't believe he'd been stupid enough to come after her.

She pointed a finger at the man, surrounded by his myriad stolen shades.

"*You killed my platoon,*" she shouted in clear, ringing tones. "*And you have my brother.*"

He snarled at her, his hatred wordless but clear.

She snarled back. "Give him to me."

CHAPTER THIRTY-NINE

XIULAN

In the twenty-seven novels, eight novellas, and nineteen short stories that made up the Bai Junjie canon, the few battle scenes that existed were all tidy affairs. They were inevitably between honorable, noble Shang on one side and brutish Tomodanese on the other. Archenemies would find each other amid all the chaos and clash, steel against shade. And inevitably, it would all come to a halt when Bai's bullet or Kou's claws found their way into the heart of the enemy commander.

This battle was not like that.

In the past three days since she'd landed in Tomoda, she had run afoul of Dahali garrisons. They had been aware of her status as a member of the Shang royal family, and been eager to collect on a bounty that stipulated she be brought in alive. So they had attacked her and Lee with hexbolts—disruptive, but ultimately non-lethal.

This battle was not like that, either.

"So we can't even shoot the bastard?" Lee had grumbled as they'd readied for battle. "It's too late to change our minds about this one?"

"We three are the only ones who know the truth about what he did to Tala," the Steel Lord had whispered, with a grateful nod Xiulan's way. "We can't kill him before she gets a chance to get her brother back."

"Then why not tell everyone not to shoot him?" said Lee.

The Steel Lord had frowned at that. "I want to give Tala every chance I can to rescue Dimangan. But I'm the Steel Lord now. Nothing I do is about just me anymore. I can't send my people to face that monster with orders that might get them killed. We just have to hope that one of us four gets to him first."

"Well, that's just great for everyone else," Lee had muttered.

Despite her own burning desire to avenge the massacred Shang troops she'd seen in the woods, Xiulan had just smiled at Lee. When Tala had gone missing, Lee had been the one to summon up Bootstrap and immediately lock onto the lieutenant's scent. It had been a fleeting moment, but it had opened a tiny spring of hope in Xiulan's heart.

Now, amid this maelstrom of mayhem, hope seemed like something only other people could feel.

All around her, the battle raged like a fire. People shouted war cries, and inhuman throats lifted up howls and roars, either in echo or in reply. Xiulan found herself confronted by shades of all sizes and shapes: a lumbering, inexorable snapping turtle. A snub-nosed crocodile-shade that charged into battle on two legs instead of four. A red-fox-shade with a writhing mass of tails. She didn't even know which shades belonged to which side.

The only thing she knew was that one of them, a spider the size of a child, was bearing down on her and Kou.

Droplets of venom fell from the spider-shade's fangs and wilted everything they touched, leaving twin trails of dead grass in their wake. But against such a fearsome foe, Xiulan stood her ground, though every instinct in her screamed to run for her life. Instead, she urged Kou to take this foul creature down, and in response her white rat leapt into action.

His tail whipped around like a snapped cable, hammering the spider-shade right between its fangs. It hissed in fury and staggered back a few steps before surging forward and sinking its fangs right into Kou's exposed flank. Kou squealed in pain, and the emotional feedback ripped through Xiulan's mind like a knife in her skull. *"Kou!"* she cried out. Her eye fell on a rock near her feet, and she picked it up in both hands without a second thought. With a shout, she brought it down on one of the spider's fangs and was rewarded with the sound of shattering chitin. It hissed again, but released its hold on Kou.

Kou limped away, and even though his wounds crackled with magical energy, Xiulan saw the spider's venom slowing the process significantly. She turned her attention back to the spider-shade, only to see that it had reared up again, its abdomen pointed at her like a gun. A thin tendril of webbing shot out, grabbed her by the ankle, and hauled her off her feet with the strength of a grown man. Before she knew it, she was being dragged straight toward its poisonous fangs, her coat bunching up beneath her as she slid along the ground—

From her coat, she yanked the only weapon she had: her pipe. And as the foul creature's jaws neared her, she sat right up and jabbed forward with all her might, stabbing the shade right in one of its bulbous eyes.

She let go of the pipe, leaving it in so that the wound couldn't close. Magic sparked and crackled around the wound, but couldn't heal it shut. The spider-shade tried to scratch it away with its forelegs, but by then Kou had rejoined the fray.

The white rat snapped the cord of web with a flash of his teeth, and Xiulan scrambled away from the spider-shade. "Finish him!" she shouted to her shade, who chittered in agreement. He dove for the panicking spider, already reared up, and headbutted it right in the underside of its own head. When the spider fell hard onto its back, Kou pounced on it, a blur of claw and fang and white fur. The spider's legs spasmed as it tried in vain to dislodge Kou, but it was too late. In moments, the shade discorporated, leaving behind only a flash of light and a pipe half melted by acid.

Xiulan grimaced. She was going to miss that pipe.

"Are you well?" she said to Kou.

His nose twitched. *Yes.*

"Can you keep fighting?" For all his ferocity, Kou wasn't a creature built for battle. He'd won her fights before, but everything around them was making her keenly aware of his limitations.

Nonetheless, Kou's nose twitched again.

She grinned, heartened. "Then let us fight together to secure peace in our time."

She remembered when Kou had been barely larger than her hand, a small warm spot in her covers at night. It was hard to believe that this was where life had taken them both.

A shout directed her attention to the Kobaruto, whose steel cables flashed like bolts of crimson lightning. They hunted shades like wolves after deer, tackling them in twos and threes. When they chose one to attack, cables would wrap themselves around the shade's legs and force it to the ground. And while the creature tried in vain to free itself, another Kobaruto would bring their red-hot cable down on the shade's neck like the blade of an ax, or else wrap the steel around its throat and tighten until its sharp sides sliced straight through.

The Sanbunas fought, too: some with guns, some with their long machetes, and some with the aid of their own shades. They worked as a unit, soldier and shade operating with an efficiency Xiulan had to admit she'd never thought she could reach with Kou. But then she considered how many battles each soldier must have survived to make it here tonight.

The Dahali lent to the barrage as well, their delegation's women laying down a thick hail of white hexbolts while the men shouldered their rifles and loosed shot after shot. But for all their fire, the man in the purple coat moved with the fluid grace of violet mercury. And he seemed to have a truly limitless number of shades to conjure and hide behind, and the hexbolts barely disrupted the magic that bound him to them. The Dahali delegates held on with admirable discipline, but they had yet to get in a good shot.

The crocodile-shade Xiulan had seen earlier charged through the din, jaws snapping with deadly force. It roared, its voice low and foreboding as distant thunder. But no sooner had it arrived than a tight trio of bullet wounds appeared in its chest, staggering it in its tracks. Xiulan's head whipped in the direction of the fire, just in time to see Tala give her a curt nod.

Steel cables shot out from the darkness as a pair of Kobaruto bound the crocodile-shade's beefy limbs. And then, fast as a bullet himself, Steel Lord Jimuro stepped inside the shade's guard, the sword of Steel Lord Setsuko glowing in his hands as though it were alive. His blade flashed once, twice, thrice, too fast for Xiulan's eye to follow. Long gashes seemed to carve themselves through the shade's thick, scaly hide, and the crocodile-shade burst apart in a flash of blue magical light.

For a moment Xiulan dared to feel a thrill. Already, she knew the battlefield was no place for her, but she couldn't help savoring this moment: *They were winning.*

And then she caught sight of the owl-shade above going into a dive, talons-first—

—right for Lee.

Xiulan was close, but not close enough to close the distance on foot. Even Kou, fleet as he was, wouldn't get there in time. And Bootstrap was currently locked in combat with a horse-shade whose mane burned like silvery flame in the moonlight.

She looked down at the rock in her hand.

Her fingers tightened around it.

And without even thinking, she cast back her arm and hurled the rock with all her might.

It sailed through the air, straight as an arrow flies, and smacked the owl-shade straight across its beak. The bird's whole body jolted with the impact—more from its suddenness than from any force she'd just exerted. Still, she stood there in disbelief.

She'd just thrown something.

"Don't just stand there, you idiot!" Lee shouted. She darted out of the owl's trajectory as it made a clumsy attempt at renewing its attack. But before it could lift back off the ground, Kou darted forward like a white shadow, leaping onto the shade's back. The owl screeched as Kou drove his fangs into it.

Xiulan's stomach turned as the owl-shade's head twisted all the way around, as if its neck were on a free swivel. Its beak flashed, and with a squeal Kou fell away from it, a fresh wound on his snout.

But before the owl-shade could fly away, huge jaws closed around its outstretched leg. With a toss of her head, Bootstrap slammed the owl-shade hard to the ground. Its wing folded beneath it with a snap that made Xiulan cringe as a whole-body reflex.

As Kou and Bootstrap made short work of the owl-shade, Lee looked her up and down. "Looking awful pleased with yourself," she said, but she was smiling.

Xiulan returned the smile with one of her own. "That's a long walk to 'thank you,' don't you think?"

Lee's grin stretched wider.

Xiulan nodded to the man in the center of the maelstrom, the man in the purple coat, who lurched this way and that like a cornered, wounded beast. He'd mostly kept out of the fight himself, save to summon more and more shades to replace the ones who fell. And of course, doing so meant falling right into line with Steel Lord Jimuro's plan.

"So long as he can call a shade, he's a threat," the Steel Lord had reminded her and Lee as they'd geared up for the fight. "The only way we're sure to take him in safely is if he runs out of them before we do."

The man in the purple coat was putting up as fierce a fight as he could. For all their discipline and teamwork, the ad hoc team of delegations and palace guards was taking more casualties the longer the fight dragged on. But while Xiulan had no idea how deep the well ran, she was confident if they just kept fighting, they would see it to its very bottom.

A chill of excitement ran down her spine. Her heart swelled from the mere thought that she, fighting alongside all these good people, would bring an end to this evil in the world.

But then the man threw a hand up into the sky. At the top of his ragged lungs, he shouted a name: *"Tivron!*

A jet of gray light shot into the sky, gathering and expanding like a storm cloud as it took the shape of an immense hammerhead shark, its jaws wide enough to swallow someone whole.

For one moment, the magnificent beast hung in the air, its forked tail thrashing wildly.

And then it plummeted straight for the garden.

Xiulan and Lee were well past the impact zone. Thankfully, so were Steel Lord Jimuro and Lieutenant Tala. But the same could not be said for the Dahali delegation and a large swath of the Kobaruto.

The impact was deafening. The shock wave nearly threw Xiulan off her feet. Lee staggered back, and Xiulan's hand shot out just in time to catch her by the wrist. Her other hand jammed her hat back onto her head just before it flew off, but her long hair whipped around her face as the cloud of soil and dust began to settle.

As the scene became clearer, Xiulan's heart climbed into her throat. The Dahali had been the easiest way to subdue the man in the purple coat without lethal force. But while some of them had gotten clear, others had been completely crushed beneath the hammerhead-shade's writhing bulk. The Kobaruto hadn't fared much better; while they were more spread out, several of their number had been caught in the impact before they could use their cables to zip away.

A strange lull settled over the battlefield as the Steel Lord's ragtag coalition reeled from the shock of a huge hole being blown in their battle line.

But the man in the purple coat wasn't taking any such reprieve. Once again, his voice rose up over the din of battle.

And that voice shouted, *"Dimangan!"*

CHAPTER FORTY

DIMANGAN

Dimangan heard his name and came when he was called.

He fell into existence like a bombshell. As he solidified, he saw horrified stares in every direction: Shock from the Sanbunas. Disgust from the Tomodanese.

Horror from Lala.

No, he thought, and tried to will his muscles to remain still. But his will was no longer his own. He belonged to Mayon, and Mayon wanted him to kill everyone.

He pounced forward, his huge hand grabbing a nearby cat-shade and slamming it face-first into the ground as though it were a mallet. With a roar, he brought its body back up, then snapped it in two over his knee. It dissolved into pure magic in his hands, then streamed straight back to its Sanbuna partner, who recoiled in terror and revulsion at the sight.

Since Lala had pacted with him, she'd been the only Sanbuna face he'd ever seen. While he was almost always glad to see his sister, he'd often yearned to be able to walk among his countrymen again. He missed being able to walk up to a shop and press his nose against the window, or to buy some puto from a cart by the side of the road, or to sidle up to a handsome boy and tell him exactly how handsome Dimangan thought he was . . .

But the look that soldier gave him now made him strongly desire never to look upon another Sanbuna face as long as he lived.

The shades he fought were all in a tangle, but the ones that belonged to Mayon shone brightly in Dimangan's vision. It was easy enough to step out of the way of that snapping turtle as it bit a woman's leg off. To shove a lizard-shade out of the way of a charging stag beetle, grab it by the horns, and hurl it into a cluster of blue-robed Tomodanese. To step over a snake-shade so he could envelop a man's head inside his entire hand and crush it to bone and pulp.

Bolts of white energy crashed into his broad back, one, two, three. With each impact, his body popped with small spasms of pain. These had to be Dahali hexbolts, devastatingly effective against human targets. But Dimangan hadn't been human for a very long time.

So he shrugged off the hexbolts. They felt like little more than wasp stings, tiny interruptions of the signal that kept his form cohesive, and nothing more. The pain mounted as the Dahali poured more fire into him, but it wasn't enough to stop him from picking up Mayon's snapping-turtle-shade and flinging it straight at the clustered Dahali. The foremost Dahali soldier was reduced to a red smear by the impact. The rest were scattered and dazed, but Dimangan didn't spare them a further thought. Mayon's other shades could take care of them, because he had already moved on to his next target.

He was disgusted by how methodically he moved. It wasn't as if he'd never used his strength to kill before, but that had always been in times of desperation and war, and Lala had always trusted him to hold back as he saw fit. Mayon had no such restrictions. And as long as he didn't, Dimangan didn't, either.

A guiding pulse of will appeared in his mind, and suddenly he felt as if the only thing that mattered in the world was slaughtering the blue-robed Tomodanese warriors who tried in vain to restrain him with chains that moved on their own like serpents. Dimangan recognized them by their blue-and-white kimonos. He'd even seen one of them before on a streetcar in Lisan City, on his very last day as a human. They were the legendary order known as the Kobaruto, holy guards of the Steel Lord, who trained from childhood to be unparalleled combatants. But even the best warrior couldn't move faster than someone whose legs were strong enough to carry him for hours without tiring. Not when that someone decided to really move.

He tore huge holes in the turf with every footfall, but it only took one to close the gap between him and the nearest Kobaruto. His body moved so fast, his own eyes could barely keep up with him as he threw a full-power punch that sent a man's head flying from his shoulders. One of his sisters-in-arms, a tall woman with gray hair and a hard face, shouted in fury and swung a red-hot cable straight through his wrist to retaliate, neatly slicing his hand off. But she didn't get a chance to issue a follow-up attack; before the cable could snake away, Dimangan grabbed it with his remaining hand and yanked with all his might.

The woman was pulled off her feet, tumbling end over end toward him. He jerked the cable again, spinning himself with all his formidable strength. The woman whipped with him as he let go, and she careened headfirst into a nearby wall with a spray of crimson and a scream cut short.

Three more Kobaruto stepped up. The old woman must've been important to them, because they fought against him with redoubled fury. With cruel nonchalance, he dispatched them all.

By the time they all lay dead, his hand had grown back, and the new wounds they'd managed to score had already begun to seal up. He felt his grip on his own form slip a little from the aggregate damage, and he prayed to the shades themselves that they might be enough to discorporate him, so Mayon could be taken down once and for all. But the world was not that merciful.

And under Mayon's control, neither was he.

He turned his sight next to the Sanbunas, whose numbers were already dwindling from the sheer pressure of Mayon's shades. The soldiers left behind fought valiantly, bolo knives flashing while their shades kept Mayon's pinned down as best they could.

But Dimangan knew with horrifying certainty that the moment he intervened, it would be over for them all.

From the minute he'd been in the world, he'd fought hard to take back control of his body. But Mayon's will was stronger. And though he could feel the man's hold on him slip every now and then, it was only for brief heartbeats, and never long enough for Dimangan to do anything.

He hoped his struggles were having some effect. That he was making Mayon pull punches, so that those he struck who did not get back up were merely unconscious, despite their crushed rib cages and twisted necks. He had to believe that was true, because he had to believe that if he could take back an inch of himself, then he could take back every foot.

He no longer had the tear ducts necessary to cry, but he could feel his body wanting to as badly as he wanted to stop altogether. His vision misted red as he tore his way through the Sanbuna delegation. Most tried valiantly to fight him. Two or three attempted to flee. None of it mattered. He felled one with each blow he struck, while behind him Mayon's shades tore into anyone he couldn't reach.

And then there was General Erega. He'd never formally met her, but he knew Lala had. He knew the deep-seated admiration his sister held for the general. Hell, he even remembered it himself from growing up with her, the way she'd fixate on every new report of the daring revolutionary's latest exploits. Now her latest exploit was standing against the inhuman monster he'd become, bolo in hand.

And, Dimangan thought helplessly as his fist careened toward her, her last.

Stop.

Dimangan felt all his muscles tighten. His fist halted a mere inch from the general's face with perfect precision. For a moment, hope blossomed in his chest: Had he managed to throw off Mayon's thrall at last? Was he clawing his way back to freedom?

But then he realized that it was Mayon himself who'd given the order. He didn't get any words, just feelings: Respect. History.

And, with a brief flashing image of a hospital bed, a debt being paid.

The general looked dumbfounded. Clearly, she'd expected to face her death in that moment. But before she could capitalize on Dimangan's hesitation, he found himself pivoting away from her.

He saw them next: the Shang, and their paired shades. The dog-shade came at him first, all teeth and paws, but Dimangan laced his fingers together and swung his hands like a club, and the dog-shade's whole body gave way beneath the impact, violently erupting into a cloud of white light.

"*Kohaku!*" Jimuro screamed.

As the Steel Lord's voice drew Dimangan's attention, something white flashed in the corner of his eye, moving so fast he almost didn't catch it.

Almost.

He snagged the white rat's tail. It'd nearly made it past him, no doubt ready to slip through the shades that stood between it and Mayon.

But Dimangan whipped the rat-shade right back at the two Shang. The impact sent both of them skidding across the turf, where they lay very still as the rat disappeared with a gasp of black light.

A gunshot rang out through the air. "*Mang!*"

With horrible slowness, he felt himself turn to face the only person in the world who called him by that name.

She stood there in a crisp new uniform, gun in hand. She had on her "sergeant's face," even though her rank insignia suggested she'd moved up in the world. It was the kind of look meant to scare all the insubordination out of a recruit by freezing their blood. But it wasn't quite right. There was something new in the way the moonlight caught her eyes. After a moment, he saw it for what it was.

Fear.

His own sister was afraid of him.

No, he thought desperately, reaching for every mental brake he had, every lever he could possibly pull. He couldn't hurt his own sister. He'd thought hurting his own fellow Sanbunas was impossible, but this was something else entirely. This was—

He felt the blade bite him just below the kneecap and shear clean through his leg. He collapsed to the ground and it shook beneath him. He barely rolled aside in time as Jimuro drove a sword into the ground Dimangan had just been lying on.

Dimangan swiped at him. In the depths of the prison his body had become, he noted that there was a time not too long ago when he'd have gladly swiped at Jimuro of his own free will. But the two had fought side by side now. And for whatever faults the man had, Dimangan had no doubt that he was at least loyal to Lala.

To Dimangan's relief, Jimuro danced just out of his reach. He rapped Dimangan's fist with the flat of his sword. He darted back in, sword flashing, and this time he scored a long, vertical cut down the length of Dimangan's torso. Dimangan was compelled to reach for him again, but Jimuro kept just to the edge of his vision, discouraging any attempts at grabbing him with a swipe of his blade. Each dodge led Jimuro to score a fresh wound on Dimangan, and with each one Dimangan prayed it would be enough to discorporate him and spare him what came next.

But though Dimangan felt himself losing shape as he bled magic, his leg had begun to knit itself back together and regrow. And the moment he had any flesh at all past the knee, he braced it against the ground and surged forward with a lunging punch.

The prince was fast; he whipped up his sword to parry it, even as he tried to dodge away from the impact. But fast as he was, Dimangan was faster. His hit made the prince tumble and slam hard into the roots of a nearby sapling, fracturing it at its thickest part and showering him with screeching cicadas. He slumped forward.

"*Jimuro!*" Lala shouted.

And then silence settled over the blood-soaked garden. The ground was covered in the broken bodies of the dead and the dying. Mayon's shades regrouped, while the only one left to resist him was the crow-shade flying high overhead. A few human fighters yet stood, including General Erega.

But at Mayon's direction, Dimangan had eyes for only one.

He begged his hands to stay open. He could've sworn he felt his fingers heeding him even, if only for a second . . .

But then his fingers curled closed.

He brandished a bloody fist at the woman who'd held his hand as he'd mooned over a boy.

She leveled her gun at the only person who'd lived long enough to watch her grow up.

Inside his head, Dimangan screamed for his body to freeze where it stood, trying in vain to hear himself over Mayon's murderous drone.

Outside his head, there was only silence, save for the singing of cicadas.

And then, from the corner of the garden, the hollow *thunk* of bamboo striking rock.

He took his first step.

And Lala opened fire.

CHAPTER FORTY-ONE

JIMURO

The Steel Lord blinked, and his eyes wanted nothing more than to stay closed.

Fumiko sat by the pond, giggling with her friends who had come to court for the Festival of Platinum: Akabayashi Akane, Ishikawa Ikumi, and Kurihara Kosuke, all in yukata. When they caught sight of him peering around bushes, Fumiko, Akane, and Ikumi giggled, while Kosuke's whole face went strawberry red, and he shouted to his friends that they were idiots who didn't know what they were—

His eyes opened.

All around him, bodies lay bent and broken. The ground was pocked with craters, its soil soaked in blood. It was as though a storm had ripped through his garden.

And that storm stood just over there, moonlight splashing across his broad, muscled back and jagged spines of bone.

As he saw Tala raise her gun at her own brother, Jimuro's eyes closed.

. . .

He was in uniform, ready to ship out tomorrow to quash these dam-
nable rebels once and for all. He would miss Hagane, but he was
leaving it to ensure its safety. And once he and his troops had given
the savages and slavers what for, it would be right here, waiting for
him still.

As he sat out there praying, one by one his family joined him. First
Fumiko. Then his father. And shortly after, his mother.

It was the last time they were all together in one place.

The last time he ever saw any of them alive.

His eyes opened.

A gun flashed, and Dimangan's hand whipped out to the side, absorbing both bullets with a spark of magical light.

Tala gritted her teeth. Jimuro could see: She'd been trying to shoot around him, trying to hit the man in the purple coat even once.

He tried to sit himself up, but his muscles felt like they had been mashed to paste. Briefly, panic surged through him. But then he felt his toes frantically wiggling in his boots. There was no telling what else Dimangan may have broken, but at least he could get on his feet again. And if he could get on his feet, then he could fight.

Then he saw the glittering shards scattered around him.

His heart leapt to his mouth.

The fabled sword of the first Steel Lord, Setsuko, a legendary national legacy of Tomoda's might and his family's brilliance, lay in pieces.

He could have it remade. Skilled pacters would be able to collect the shards and reforge it into something newer. Maybe even better, though he doubted that.

But he needed to fight now, and the only weapon he'd had left had been taken from him.

He glanced over to see if there was anyone else to assist Tala: Xiulan and Lee, both down for the count. The few remaining Dahali, fighting ineffectually against the man's other shades. General Erega, dragging one of her subordinates away from danger even as he screamed at the bloody stump where his leg had been a moment ago . . .

Tala was on her own.

His eyes closed.

He sat near a pond in the garden, as springtime winds carried the pink cherry blossoms past his face in a gentle cascade.

He didn't recognize this memory; the garden had never once contained a cherry tree. Nonetheless, he peered into the depths of the pond as small pink leaves landed on the water with a gentle ripple and floated just above the glittering koi beneath the surface.

He caught sight of his reflection in the water and did a double take. He wasn't an old man, but he was older: his face more lined, his temples graying, a trim beard adorning his jaw.

And the woman standing next to him, with her beautiful dark skin and blue-black hair, with hawklike eyes and a smile as rare and precious as a jewel—

His eyes opened.

No, he told himself. Tala wasn't alone. As long as he drew breath, she couldn't be. If they were going to lose this fight, Tala was going to lose it with Jimuro by her side, whether she liked it or not.

The man in the purple coat was saying something, though Jimuro could hardly hear it through the pain and the wailing of cicadas all around him. He tried his best to block it all out. Past Steel Lords had shown their worth by making impossible decisions to protect their people, and now he had to—

A possibility settled in his mind.

He looked down at his hands, and saw that they were bloody and shaking. What he was contemplating, he didn't even know if he'd be capable of pulling off.

And if you succeed, he told himself, *your ancestors will never forgive you. The spirits will never forgive you.*

But if he didn't do it, he realized, then he would never forgive himself, either.

The trembling in his fingers slowed, then stopped.

He closed his eyes and laid his hands palms-down on his thighs. He pushed away everything but the song of the cicadas, the unofficial anthem of Tomoda. He thought over and over again about what he would do, what he would endure, what he would force himself to live with, if only he could just survive.

And he prayed that after this was done, he would deserve to.

CHAPTER FORTY-TWO

TALA

Her aim was good as ever, but Mang threw his hands out to catch the bullets she fired at the splintersoul. The wounds crackled and closed, and the newly regenerated hand dropped to Mang's side.

She gritted her teeth. The 13-52-2 had been in its share of scrapes, and she with them, but this was as bad as it got. As long as the splintersoul had Mang, there were no conditions of victory that could be feasibly met. She couldn't take her own brother out, not with the amount of ammo she had left. And unless she figured out how to metalpact with a gun right this second, she couldn't take him out anyway. She had her gun leveled, but it was all just for show. She couldn't shoot him if she tried.

"Mang!" she shouted. "I carried you ten years, and I never made you do anything you didn't want to! Neither can this lilac son-of-a-bitch! Shake it off!"

The man in the purple coat strode up, careful to remain in Dimangan's shadow. "When a creature bonds its soul to yours, it becomes an extension of you," he said. "Right now, I'm Dimangan, and Dimangan is me." He didn't look particularly mirthful as he said it, and his expression grew even colder as he pointed up at Beaky circling overhead. Through crooked yellow teeth, he snarled: "Give him to me."

Tala's grip tightened on her gun. "I offered him up. You didn't like my terms."

"Your terms were merely fair," spat the man. "I. Want. *Justice*."

Tala put on her bravest face, but it was all she could do to stop herself from sliding into despair. There would be no reasoning with this man.

And there would be no stopping him, either.

Desperately, she searched her brother's face for any indication that he'd heard her—not that his ears had taken in what she'd said, but that *he*, Mang, was still alive in there. And she could have sworn she saw the barest hint of it in his eyes, for moments at a time, in a way that was too obvious to be just a trick of the moonlight.

"You can't make him hurt me," Tala said to the man. "No more than I can make Beaky hurt y—"

There was a rush of wind as Mang charged for her even faster than her finger could pull the trigger. She barely had time to comprehend his shadow falling over her before an inhumanly strong hand wrapped itself around her gun arm and squeezed.

Her vision went white as every nerve and neuron in her arm lit itself ablaze. She heard the sickening snap of every bone shattering, felt the muscles tearing and the tendons snapping. Her gun clattered to the ground as her hand surrendered all the strength it had left.

"Drop her."

Obediently, Mang's hand opened. Tala realized she'd been lifted off the ground only a heartbeat before she crumpled back to it.

"You can do anything if you hate someone enough," the man said quietly. "Think about that as I take back what's mine. Every part of me burned with a hatred for you, Tala, and I was able to resonate with your brother well enough to steal him from you. If you ask me . . . it all speaks for itself."

General Erega was shouting something, but Tala couldn't understand it. The throbbing pain in her ears drowned out everything else. She looked up into the face of her brother. Was there truly hatred there? Had there always been hatred there, buried just below where she could see it?

Or worse, in plain sight where she refused to?

She screwed her eyes shut. Maybe Mang had always hated her, no matter what he'd said to her over the years. But that didn't change the fact that she loved him with everything she had left.

She opened her eyes. "Mang," she whispered through bloody lips. "Mang, please . . . We're all we have left, Mang, please . . ."

The man finally stepped out from behind her brother. There was no triumph in his expression: just disgusting, bottomless hunger. "I'm going to have him take your limbs, one by one," he whispered. "I want you to lie there, helpless, as I take everything from you." He flexed his fingers. "And then I'll take you with me, Tala. And I will take my time visiting upon you every shred of agony that you—"

"*Fumiko!*" cried a voice, and a green blast of energy arced through the air, straight for Dimangan. In midair, it took its final shape, revealing a gigantic cicada-shade. Its eyes were wide-set and red, its carapace a gleaming shade of emerald. Its gossamer wings carried a hard edge to them, as did its swollen, jagged forelegs. On its right foreleg, it bore a deep-green pactmark in the shape of a triangle with a separated peak. A mountain.

And an identical mark blazed like a verdant flame on the back of Jimuro's fist as he thrust it forward and shouted, "*Now, Fumiko! Attack!*"

Despite her size, Fumiko moved with incredible speed, wings becoming a blur as she darted around Dimangan's face, attacking with slash after slash of her sharp forelegs. Dimangan swatted, but even with his formidable speed he was too slow to catch her.

Tala and the splintersoul sported looks of disbelief at what they were seeing: the Steel Lord himself, shadepacting. For the splintersoul, his disbelief was tinged with disgust and surprise. But for Tala, that disbelief rapidly gave way to the only thing she had left: hope. Because if Jimuro could find it in himself to split his soul with another, then Tala knew she could do anything.

Please, Tala thought, as Fumiko slashed a bright line directly across Dimangan's eyes. *Everything depends on you. Please. I can't do this without you.*

The splintersoul dropped to a knee and wrapped his hand around the side of her face. His breath was heavy and foul, and it felt as if he was trying to crush her skull between his fingers. "You delayed justice," he rasped. "But your mongrel friend can't stop—"

A streak of black unfolded from the sky, zipping past the man and bowling him onto his feet. His grip on Tala's face slipped, and Tala tried in vain to squirm away from him.

The man in the purple coat sat up, bewildered. A fresh cut had been gouged across his cheek, bleeding freely onto his coat. "What?" he said. "How—?" But then his eyes widened. *"No."*

Beaky landed on the ground between him and Tala. He spread his wings wide, clacked his beak, and issued a loud, throaty caw.

Tala could have cried at the sight of him. *Thank you,* she thought.

In reply, she received a wave of annoyance and fear . . . but also the kind of resignation Tala knew she could depend on.

This, more than anything else that happened, seemed to send the man in the purple coat reeling. "But . . . you . . . you're part of me," he said. His voice was quiet. Even heartbroken.

Tala's right arm hung at her side, useful as an empty sleeve. She had to push herself up with only her left arm and whatever wreckage remained of her core muscles. "Not anymore," Tala said.

Beaky flew forward, beak flashing like a machete blade. The man in the purple coat was flat-footed, and barely managed to parry it with a swipe of his handless arm. But Beaky was right there, relentlessly raining peck after peck down on his former partner.

Something emerald tumbled through the air: Fumiko. She crashed through a nearby wall, her bladed limbs and wings shredding its paper like spreadshot through flesh.

His massive shoulders heaving, Mang returned his attention to Tala once more. All across his body, laceration wounds were shutting themselves, but slowly, so slowly. All the damage Mang had taken was adding up, and whatever grip he had on his solid form was probably tenuous at best.

She had to hope his own grip wasn't the only one that had weakened.

"Mang!" she shouted. "I know you can hear me! I still don't know much about shades, but I know everything about you. And if there're two things I know about you, it's that you're listening, and you're fighting!"

Mang lumbered forward another few steps. But Tala refused to allow herself to fear him anymore. He wasn't some monster; he was Mang. He was her brother. He was the only thing she had left.

"A pact works two ways!" she shouted. "You're not a slave, and you don't need to be one! You're my brother, and I'll always love you, no matter how many people he makes you hurt! Even if it's me!"

Another step that made the earth shake. Though Tala's fear rose like a flame, she held steady, looked him in the eye, and said the one thing she hadn't already, the only thing she had left to say: "I'm sorry."

It was as if a curtain behind his eyes had lifted. Suddenly her brother's gaze seemed sharper, surer.

His own.

He vanished from her sight and reappeared just behind the man in the purple coat and enveloped him in his huge arms. The man roared at the top of his lungs, froth forming at the corners of his mouth as he ranted and raved. He struggled in vain, but he was too weak to break Mang's grip.

Beaky retreated, flapping his wings and cawing with triumph. Shouts of surprise rose up all around her: some voices Tala recognized, some not. But all of them were thinking the same thing Tala was: This was her chance.

But as she began to climb to her feet, Mang called: *"Stay back!"*

She froze. "I need to touch him!" she shouted. "I need to get you back!"

Mang shook his huge head. "I can't hold him for long! He's fighting me, Lala, and I'm not gonna beat him! You have to end it!"

The words hit her like the lash of a whip, and tears instantly formed in the corners of her eyes. "Mang—"

"It's the only way!" Mang shouted. "I'd have snapped his neck myself, but—" As if on cue, his hand wrenched itself away from the man's body, then clamped back down on it before he could escape. "Lala, you've got to do it! If he gets free, he'll kill you all! You have to take him out!"

Tala blew right past all the screaming rage and inconsolable howling she wanted to feel, and landed hard in disbelief and despair.

She'd carried Mang in her soul for ten years. In the war, on the days she'd wanted to roll over and stop fighting, she'd kept on surviving because she owed it to him. So to end it all now . . . did that mean it had all been for nothing? That by saving her brother, she'd only set herself up to lose him in the cruelest way possible?

"*Lala—!*" Mang shouted through gritted teeth.

She looked down at the gun next to her. She had only one arm left, and it was her bad one. With distant horror, as if she were watching someone else do it, she reached for the pistol.

A hand laid itself over hers. "Let me do it." Prince Jimuro had dragged himself across the courtyard to her side. His topknot was undone, long hair hanging loosely around his handsome face. His deep-brown eyes bored into her own through cracked lenses.

"Jimuro . . ." She blinked through her tears. "You shadepacted."

The Steel Lord forced a weary smile. "You can do anything if you love someone enough."

She thought of breaking the most basic law of shadepacting. She thought of the secrets she'd kept, of the lives she'd taken, of the lies she'd told, all just to keep Dimangan alive. She thought of why she'd done it.

Her fingers curled around the grip of the pistol, and she lifted it with a shaking hand.

She breathed in. She breathed out. Breathed in. Breathed out.

Her finger tightened over the trigger . . .

. . . and froze.

The more she focused on the sight, the more violently her hand shook. Her sure aim had all been in her right hand. Her left was just a hand: good enough on her best days, and this was far from her best. She only had one shot to do this, and using her left hand left too much to chance. Even when her spirit had found the resolve to do it, her body was ready to fail her.

But then she felt Jimuro's breath on her cheek, his voice in her ear. "The steel is empty," he said. "The steel is bone, and you are blood."

Her hand wouldn't stop shaking. She tried to extend herself into the steel, to fill it like the empty vessel Jimuro said it was, but all she was doing was gripping the gun harder, which made her hand shake more.

The splintersoul shrugged out of his purple coat, and it came away in Dimangan's hands. With a roar, he charged forward.

The gunshot rent the night air, silencing the cicadas.

Her hand shook, but the bullet flew straight and true.

The man's entire body jerked back as the bullet sank into his chest and erupted out his back in a spray of blood. The anger bled from his face, erasing hard-worn lines as he pitched forward to the ground and lay there, dead.

She didn't hold back her tears. She recognized them like an old friend.

They were the tears she cried when she'd done something unforgivable.

As the man keeled over, Mang's eyes widened in—surprise? Relief? "Lala!" he shouted. "Lala, I—"

He blew away like smoke from a candle.

PART EIGHT

· · ·

THE PEACEFUL PATH

CHAPTER FORTY-THREE

JIMURO

A day later, the throne room sat empty. The Steel Lord had set up court elsewhere.

He hadn't seen the servants take Tala into the east wing. He'd wanted to follow them, but there were too many pressing matters he'd had to take in hand immediately following the attack. There were heads of state to assuage. Media to address. Bodies to bury.

But after an exhausting night, he'd declared that he would be retiring: not to his chambers, but to the hallway in the east wing outside the room where Tala was in recovery. The First Sage had objected, on the grounds that such conduct was unbecoming of a reigning Steel Lord. The newly elevated Captain Tamaki had objected, citing how difficult it would be for their guards to secure him in such an exposed place. But Jimuro knew that in the coming peace talks, he was due to make many, many compromises. On this, he would accept none.

With Bhavna Devarajah, he bargained for the use of her finest healers. It hadn't felt like a bargain at the time; she'd smiled and offered them up freely. But he knew enough of Dahal's mercantile ways to know that he had not been given a gift, merely purchased a service on a deep line of credit.

As he stared at the shut door across the hall, he reminded himself that it had been a worthwhile trade.

The Crane Emperor, predictably, had been inconsolable. He'd insisted that everything had been an elaborate ploy by the Tomodanese working in concert with the Sanbunas, and that Shang was outraged by the deceitful conduct of everyone present . . . except, of course, for the noble delegation of Shang. In the newspapers that his servants had brought Jimuro with his morning tea, the Crane Emperor was already on the record claiming that last night's terror attack had been an inside job orchestrated by some vast international conspiracy. It was a charge that would be easy enough to brush away over time. This morning, though, it was the last thing Jimuro needed.

Across the hall, the door slid open. A Dahali healer in cream-colored robes exited. Jimuro sat up straighter. "How is she?"

"Her condition is stable," said the woman. "And this one is doing everything she can to improve upon that. But healing is not a process enacted by sorcery alone. The patient must fight at least as hard as the physician, if not much harder."

Jimuro's mouth thinned. "I know of no better fighter than she," he said.

Shortly after the healer departed, the door opened again. This time, the one to exit was none other than the venerable General Erega. Despite Jimuro's somber mood, she chuckled when she saw him kneeling on his mat, anxious as a father-to-be. "You can go in, you know," said Erega. "For one thing, it's your room."

Jimuro shook his head. "I'm certain she doesn't wish to see me. I know I've done nothing to earn the right to see her."

Erega rolled her eye.

"I'm serious," Jimuro said. He'd thought it was a very earnest, honest thing to say, which was why he was surprised to hear Erega chuckle in response. He felt color rise in his face. "What?"

She just chuckled more. "Shades take me, you're so young."

"General . . ." he said warningly.

"What, Your Brilliance? It's a fact: If you were a cherry tree and I chopped you down, there wouldn't be enough rings there to decorate all my fingers." She sighed as her laughter subsided. "I was in your position only recently, you know. I didn't have a throne room, or a palace. But I had a country to rebuild and a people who needed me. That kind of thing weighs on a person. More like than not, it'll end up crushing you."

"Not if you're strong enough," Jimuro said fiercely. "Not if you're true steel."

That got Erega chuckling again. "Fine, so you're true steel. A single beam, impervious to the elements. But you're still a single beam." Her eye glinted with the wiliness Jimuro had seen back when he'd asked her to let him try bistek. "You can hold anything up with a single beam, but only if you balance it just right. Tilt it too far one way or the other, it all falls down. Even if you balance it just right, shades forbid you get an unlucky breeze . . ."

Jimuro looked away. "I believe I take your meaning."

"Well, forgive me if I continue to elaborate on it anyway," said Erega. "I think it's pretty clever, and besides that, I'm old." She gestured to the hall around them. "The Palace of Steel isn't held up by a single beam, Your Brilliance. And most of the beams that hold it up aren't even steel. So how do you expect to support a whole country with only one beam when that's not even enough to support your house?"

He sighed. "As I said, I take your meaning. But the mutual endeavor of support doesn't come without trust. The good lieutenant has no reason left to trust me."

Erega's eye fell to his hand. "Doesn't she?"

Jimuro followed the general's gaze down to the white glove he wore, but he knew they were both thinking of the green pactmark on his skin. He still hadn't grown used to the sight of it. For his entire life, he'd thought of marks like it as a surefire sign of savagery. Now the Steel Lord himself bore one, in as prominent a place as any, save for his face. He intended to wear gloves in public to avoid too many questions, but this was the age of radio news. Sooner or later, people were going to find out.

"Eventually, I'm going to have questions," Erega said mildly. "About how you came to shadepact. About what relationship Mayon had to all this." A cloud passed over the general's face. "About what Tala . . . did."

"As I understand it, General," Jimuro said evenly, "the only thing Lieutenant Tala ever did was what she had to."

General Erega opened her mouth to reply, but she was interrupted by loud footsteps. From around the corner, Shang Xiulan appeared, arms clasped behind her back.

At once, Captain Tamaki materialized from the shadows, stepping smoothly into Xiulan's path. "No closer," they said sternly.

Princess Xiulan shot Jimuro an imploring look.

Jimuro sighed. "She can approach, Captain."

They leveled a lingering stare at Xiulan before stepping out of the way.

Gratefully, Xiulan tipped her trilby, then bowed low as she approached. "Your Brilliance," she said. "General Erega, sir. I'd hoped to call upon our esteemed guest and pay her my respects. Is she currently of a suitable condition or temperament to receive such a visitation?"

"And I thought you were bad," General Erega muttered to Jimuro in Sanbuna.

"Tala and I both said—"

But the general had already switched to Tomodanese. "The healers say Lieutenant Tala's arm is coming along as well as can be expected. The bones and nerves and muscle will need time to realign, and in some places regrow. Even with all their best healing, she probably won't shoot straight again. Not with that hand, anyway."

Jimuro thought of her violently shaking hand in the courtyard.

"During my brief travels with the good lieutenant, I became aware of how much value she placed in her talent of marksmanship," Xiulan said. "I can only imagine how devastating it must be . . . to lose such a key part of one's identity."

Jimuro noted the careful pause in her speech. So, too, did Erega, because she raised a thick eyebrow at the princess.

"You're welcome to go in and see her," Erega said eventually. "In fact, it'd probably be good for her. Just ignore her when she tries to get you to leave." She nodded to Jimuro. "Consider having dinner with me tonight, Your Brilliance. There are a few things we have to discuss." She bowed gently to Xiulan. "Your Majesty." When Xiulan bowed in return, she took her leave.

Xiulan sighed in her wake. "It's so rare to meet a person who actually lives up to their reputation."

Jimuro could hardly disagree. Even Captain Tamaki gave the general a nod of respect as she passed them. But he suspected the princess wasn't there to extol General Erega's virtues. "Where's Lee?" he said.

Xiulan tried to hide the way her smile faltered at the woman's name, but she wasn't entirely successful. "Occupied with other important matters," she said. "Surely by now you know as well as I that she's not one for standing still. I fear you will have to make do with the pleasure of my humble company."

Jimuro wasn't even slightly buying it, but he opted to let the princess keep her dignity intact. "To what do I owe that pleasure?" He indicated the iron teakettle before him. When Xiulan nodded, he began pacing with it to reheat its contents.

"First, I believe I owe you an apology for our unfortunate encounter aboard the *Crow's Flight*," said Xiulan.

Jimuro shook his head. "When I had need of you last night, you and Lee came to my aid without hesitation. However the scales were imbalanced before, I consider them level now."

"To be fair, I've also traveled briefly with Lieutenant Tala. I owed her a debt as well." She reached into her coat. "I also wished to thank you for your gift," she said, and produced a glossy wooden pipe that she nonchalantly began to fill with leaf. "I was surprised to discover it already waiting for me on my desk when I returned to the consulate this morning to collect my things."

Jimuro frowned. "I didn't have a pipe sent over."

It was Xiulan's turn to frown. "Well, I suppose the gratitude doesn't hurt matters . . ." She lit the pipe, filling the air with a thick, rich smell that reminded Jimuro, for whatever reason, of an old library.

"If you collected your things," Jimuro said, "I imagine your father sacked you?"

Xiulan nodded. "He wanted Shang to take no part in last night's battle. My very presence in it undercuts his preferred narrative. He won't disown me outright because he owes my uncle quite a good deal of jian, but he intends to take every step he can to marginalize me, I'm afraid."

Jimuro wished he could've done something to help her, but he had no credit with the Crane Emperor, and likely would never earn any. "I'm sorry," was all he could offer up, along with a cup of steaming hot tea.

The princess accepted it gratefully, and at last sat with him to drink it. "I know my country is far from the paragon our state media claims it to be, Your Brilliance," she said. "In another world, these peace accords would be happening in the ashes of a Shang Empire that had come and gone, rather than a Tomodanese one. And there are those within my country who, in the ensuing vacuum created by your country's downfall, would love nothing more than to slot my kingdom into your place."

Jimuro sipped his tea politely and nodded. He'd heard as much from his many chats with Erega.

"I truly wished to use my elevated position to chart a change in course for Shang. But with the throne now permanently denied me, I fear you will be on your own."

"You're still an agent of the Li-Quan," said Jimuro. "You have options."

Xiulan chuckled ruefully. "Your estimation of my father's character isn't as strong as you would believe it to be, if you think he intends to let me do anything but sit idly in court and collect dust until he dies."

Jimuro sighed. Truly, he could think of nothing meaningful he could do to help her, and that frustrated him. With Tala lying in bed on the other side of that door, he needed to feel like there was some way he could effect positive change. He had to prove that the spirits hadn't made a mistake in leaving him alive.

"We Tomodanese have an old and famous saying," he said eventually, "about the karmic nature of good deeds."

"I fear I don't know that one."

Well, he'd tried. "I know this is a stupid question before I ask it, but is there anything I *can* do to help?"

"I fear not," Xiulan said. "Though the tea is welcome. I confess, while your presence here isn't unpleasant, my chief aim was to attend Lieutenant Tala. Might I inquire as to why you've not seen her yourself?"

Jimuro's grip on his teacup tightened. For a moment he considered omitting the truth. But as Xiulan herself had just pointed out, she had been a traveling companion of Tala's. "I don't know," he said at last. "I haven't been able to bring myself to go inside and look her in the eye. Pardon the expression."

"I'm used to it."

Jimuro sighed. And then he remembered: In the panic after Tala had disappeared, it had been Xiulan who had informed him that the man in the purple coat had stolen Dimangan. The spirits had shuffled the tiles of fate so that of all the hundreds of souls in the Palace of Steel, the one he could speak to most openly was the one who'd been trying to arrest him two nights prior.

"Dimangan was everything to her," Jimuro said. "It's because of me that she was ever put into a position to lose him. If I'd just listened to her, trusted her more . . ."

"My understanding of the matter is that the man in the purple coat was some sort of Sanbuna revenant that would have stalked the good lieutenant to the ends of the earth and back before resting," Xiulan said. "With my deepest respects, Your Brilliance, I find the notion that you could have stopped him to be, ah, dubious at best. And besides," she added, her eye straying to his hand, "I don't believe she considers you to have sacrificed insufficiently in the pursuit of making things right."

Jimuro's gaze followed hers until it fell on the cloth of his right glove. Self-consciously, he slipped his other hand over it.

Xiulan rolled her eye. "Pardon me if my sympathy is limited." She pulled back her bang, and Jimuro couldn't help recoiling in surprise as she stared at him with the pactmark on her eyeball.

Shame welled up in him for reacting so childishly. "That was unworthy of me," he said.

Xiulan's acceptance of his apology was chilly, but it was acceptance nonetheless. She took another drag of her pipe, then set it down and exchanged it for her teacup. "You and the lieutenant might find you have more common ground than at first glance," she said eventually. "For one thing, you two are the only ones in known history who are capable of both shadepacting and metalpacting."

Jimuro nearly spat out his tea. "What?" he said, then self-consciously lowered his voice. "Tala can metalpact?" How many more secrets could the lieutenant possibly have?

"How do you suppose the man in the purple coat was relieved of a hand?" Xiulan said. "How do you suppose the lieutenant was able to make such a perfect shot last night, while in a weakened state and relying on her non-dominant hand?"

Jimuro had been kneeling upright, but at this revelation he sat back hard. Tala could metalpact. He could shadepact. It was incredible. Unprecedented. Surely, there had to be some meaning to it.

Xiulan seemed to be able to read his mind. "Perhaps there's some larger significance at play," she said. "Perhaps you two were simply thrust into the sorts of circumstances stressful enough to produce new branches to climb."

"Branches?"

"A favored metaphor of mine when discussing mystical matters. Forgive me."

Jimuro refilled his cup. "I need you to understand: I have no secret here. I did what I had to do to save Tala."

"And I don't blame you for it," Xiulan said, shrugging. "You may recall, my own culture does not hold shadepacting in so low an estimation as yours does."

"I've been thinking about it a lot," he said. "I was so worried about what kind of Steel Lord I'd be. At least this way, I've gone and done something that guarantees they'll hate me. Uncertainty's no fun. I don't even know how I did it, honestly. I just . . . knew I had to."

"And now your soul's split," said Xiulan. "How are you adjusting to that, incidentally?"

"I've been made to understand that's a personal question in shadepacting cultures."

Xiulan beamed. "Hence my curiosity."

In truth, he hadn't spent any time with Fumiko so far. Posting himself outside Tala's room had put him squarely in everyone's line of sight for every hour he'd held vigil. He'd been aware of the extra consciousness within his own, though: curious and friendly, but untroubled by her dormancy. That made sense, he supposed. If there was any creature comfortable with being buried for long periods of time, it was the cicada.

"I wonder if I haven't engineered circumstances so I won't have to face her until I'm ready," Jimuro sighed. "It's exactly the sort of needlessly convoluted thing I would do in lieu of growing as a person."

Xiulan nodded knowingly. "Kou and I were great friends before we pacted," she said. "For us, pacting was simply the next logical step. But you . . . you truly believe you subjugated that cicada's soul to make it a part of your own, don't you?"

He was surprised by how stricken her blunt summation had made him feel. "I don't know what I believe right now."

"Of course you don't." She relit her pipe, which had apparently gone out. "But I would point out that we only ever found you because Lee's shade wanted to find you, thanks to the past you share."

That had been true enough. "Hn," he grunted in acknowledgment, then caught himself.

"And last night, was it not the case that Tala's shade chose to fight its former partner of its own volition? That the human-shade . . ."

"His name was Dimangan," Jimuro said quietly.

"Dimangan," Xiulan agreed. "He ultimately proved to be no slave, correct?"

Jimuro nodded.

"And most crucially of all . . . did the cicada not ask something of you in the formation of your pact? Something by which you agreed to abide?"

Jimuro nodded again.

"Then perhaps you should consider the possibility that if you yourself have not in fact taken in a slave, then you are no slaver."

The logic followed smoothly enough, but it flew too much in the face of everything Jimuro understood to be true.

Xiulan seemed to sense what was going through his mind. "The notion is one that deserves to be thoroughly chewed before swallowing," she said. "And one you may ultimately opt to spit out . . . though, if I might belabor the metaphor just a bit more, I have sufficient confidence in my culinary abilities that you won't."

Jimuro nodded mutely. He was still trying to work his way around it. But he couldn't just let go of this guilt. What kind of unfeeling monster could just shrug off that weight as if it were nothing? And if he were that kind of monster who could, what was he doing anywhere near the Mountain Throne?

Xiulan sighed. "It's the nature of life to gift us with clarity on the lives of others, while clouding our perception of our own." She slid her pipe back into her coat. "I'll come to call on Lieutenant Tala another day, I think."

"There's no reason you can't see her."

"I'm aware," Xiulan said. "But I think you should first. You've clearly left much unsaid between you, and I believe some of it to be what the good lieutenant might need to hear in this dark teatime of her soul." She rose, bowed low, tipped her trilby, and took her leave as well.

In the silence that followed Xiulan's departure, Jimuro had no choice but to turn once more to the door across the hallway. He knew there were Kobaruto stationed near enough to come to his assistance should he need it, but for now he tried to enjoy the illusion of solitude.

He longed to cross the hall, slide the door open, and . . . he wasn't sure what. What words could he say that could encompass everything he was feeling? What course of action could he possibly take that would assuage the pain she was in?

What could he do to make her whole?

Steel Lord Jimuro was a smart man: well educated, widely read, versed in wisdom both current and classic. But in the face of these questions, he had no choice but to stare down at his own hands and admit: He didn't know.

CHAPTER FORTY-FOUR

XIULAN

Since she'd been a little girl, Xiulan had been keenly aware of abundance. She understood that even as part of a government-in-exile for a country under Tomodanese rule, she still had greater luxuries than any citizen of Shang. Though her own personal wealth was highly conditional and subject to change, she still had access to formidable resources. Whatever access her name alone hadn't been able to buy her, her Li-Quan badge had. But the true abundance Xiulan had inherited, and the one she'd tried hardest to reject, was time.

At first, Xiulan had filled her leisure time with books. When she'd exhausted those as an outlet, she'd turned to law enforcement, spending a year and a half attempting to reestablish order and justice as the Snow-Feather Throne reclaimed vast swaths of the land that Tomoda had taken from it. She'd been particularly proud of the job she'd done there; she'd set the tone straightaway that Shang would no longer be a land where bureaucrats and functionaries could luxuriate and prosper at the peoples' expense. But now she had no badge. No throne to strive for. And perhaps most cruelly of all, she didn't even have a book.

When she'd woken up that morning, she'd known she was finished in Shang politics. Coming to Tala's, and by extension the Steel Lord's, aid had been the end of her career. It had been the cashew too sweet to ignore, even though it sat behind the snapping jaws of a rattrap. And of course Xiulan had taken it, exactly as Ruomei had predicted.

She tried to tell herself that she'd done the right thing: not just for Shang Xiulan, but for the world. She tried to tell herself that in her position, it was precisely the choice that Bai Junjie would have made. She told herself that history would vindicate her, and one day there would be stories about the nobility and selflessness of the Twenty-Eighth Princess's sacrifice. But all those assurances together weren't nearly enough to fill the empty hours before her.

Because her father was a spiteful man, she'd been barred from attending the peace proceedings, even as a nonspeaking delegate of Shang. He couldn't stop her from going to the palace, so she'd been free to check in on Lieutenant Tala and confer with Steel Lord Jimuro. But after that, her docket seemed depressingly wide open. She'd been strongly encouraged by her father and Ruomei alike to put herself on the next boat back to Shang, but the one bittersweet victory in all of this was that neither her father nor her sister had any leverage on her anymore.

So she walked the streets of Hagane, the way Bai Junjie would prowl his home city of Sanjiang. She kept her hands thrust in her deep coat pockets, her trilby angled down and a jazzy song in her head, mournful and shapeless as smoke. There was a time when she might've been daunted to stalk the streets of the old enemy capital, but after last night she didn't think she feared much of anything anymore.

She wished it could have been raining, just to reinforce the mood. Instead, the sun shone jubilantly in the sky. And why shouldn't it? Xiulan thought. That was always what was supposed to happen after the battle was over and the good guys stood triumphant. The clouds parted, Bai said something pithy (or at least witty) to sum up the last three hundred pages, and then it was on to the promise of a new great adventure just around the corner.

She removed the pipe from her coat again and looked at it. She'd been so certain that it was a gift from Steel Lord Jimuro. She couldn't think of anyone else in Hagane who would have thought to give it to her except for Lee, and Lee hardly had the resources to acquire one on such short notice.

She corrected herself. Lee didn't need resources to acquire things. But Xiulan now had significant doubts that Lee would have ever bothered to do something so thoughtful.

She'd retired in the penthouse office last night, bone-tired and knowing full well it would be her last night in such accommodations. And knowing that, she'd invited Lee to join her, brazen as Shang Xiulan had ever been. Wearily, they'd peeled off their blood-stained clothes and collapsed together onto the waiting bed of red-lacquered wood. Xiulan didn't even remember falling asleep; she just remembered the softness of Lee's body as she held it in her arms, and the warmth of her breath as the world faded away around her.

And then this morning, she'd woken cold and alone.

She'd tried to tell herself that Lee had just gone for tea or something, as the words of Lee's self-proclaimed one law rang through her head like a cruel song. When she'd discovered the pipe waiting there, she'd assumed at first, however irrationally, that it had been a gift from her partner. But when she'd begun asking the staff on duty, none of them seemed to remember seeing Lee Yeon-Ji that morning at all. Her name didn't appear on any of the consulate's visitor logs. She'd taken to the palace to keep her mind off things, but now Xiulan was truly out of distractions, and all she had left was the truth: Lee was gone. Again.

It didn't make sense. Lee had been the first person to volunteer her services to find Tala. In the garden, the two had fought side by side. Xiulan had truly believed that Lee had turned a corner, that Xiulan had managed to get through to her. That was what was supposed to happen when the good guys triumphed, too, wasn't it?

But Lee was never a "good guy," she thought bitterly. *That was what you liked about her in the first place. Remember, stupid White Rat?*

She realized that she'd stopped walking. She wasn't sure how long she'd been standing there. Next to her stood a simple metal trash can, a little over waist-high.

Before she knew what she was doing, she was kicking it again and again, her boot gouging a larger and larger dent into it with each impact. The jazzy horns in her head screeched to an abrupt halt, drowned out by the frantic *thunk-thunk-thunk* of her boot's reinforced toe striking aluminum.

She didn't know how many times she kicked the trash can. When she staggered back, she was breathing hard, her face flushed with color and her bangs limp with sweat. She'd been in no shape to do that. Stupid, stupid White Rat. She had nothing, and thanks to her little tantrum, all she'd gained was the scorn of everyone around her and a left foot that could no longer bear her body's weight. Instead of the smooth, driven gait of a detective on the prowl, she had to hobble away like a beaten dog.

"*Kou,*" she whispered, and the rat-shade materialized at her side. The Shang nearby gave her looks; Kou was well known, as far as individual shades went. The Tomodanese gave her looks, too, but those she expected.

She didn't care about either of them, she decided as she went on her way, one white rat alongside another.

When she and Kou wandered back into the consulate, the staff greeted her warmly, but carefully. Theirs, Xiulan knew, was a delicate balance to strike. They had to show her respect, because even with his disfavor she was still a daughter of the Crane Emperor. But they also couldn't be too personable, for fear of crossing societal boundaries and risking the Crane Emperor's personal displeasure. Xiulan had been careful to keep herself isolated, but she knew if word got around that any functionary had helped her, that person would more than likely find themselves conveniently reassigned by Ruomei . . . all in the interests of efficiency, of course.

So she drifted through the lobby without speaking to any of them, thinking idly that clad as she was in all her whites, she and Kou must have looked something like ghosts. She supposed it was melodramatic to demand the comparison, but that was how she felt: like an echo that had begun to linger too long in the ears of everyone around her. Idly, she scratched Kou on his forehead.

She couldn't let herself be set back by this, she thought as the elevator doors closed behind them. She was without rank or privilege, but she was not without allies. She still had Lieutenant Tala—

A freak of nature doomed to be cast out by her own people before long.

—Steel Lord Jimuro—

The one person in your father's court more despised than you.

—her other sisters and brothers—

Who've always made it clear, given the choice, which sister they would pick.

She hung her head. She wanted to tell herself that she wasn't thinking straight. That she was too emotional right now, and that with time she would be able to utilize her formidable intelligence to improve her station once again. She just had to find a different platform. Perhaps, she thought desperately, she could become a champion of the people. The Shang dynasty only held sway in the country it had named for itself because the people allowed it to. Before Shang, the land had been called Zhou, and Qizhong in the era before that, depending on the dynasty that sat the Snow-Feather Throne. Who was to say Shang couldn't enter a new chapter in Xiulan's lifetime?

Who was to say Ruomei truly had to be the next Crane Empress?

As quickly as she entertained the thought, she dismissed it. For all the pain Lee Yeon-Ji had caused her, at least she'd given Xiulan a hard lesson: She could never be a champion of the people. She was the least favorite princess, perhaps, but the least favorite princess was still a princess.

She shrugged off her overcoat and folded it neatly over one arm as she fiddled with her room's lock and slid the door open.

The room was much smaller than her previous accommodations. And it felt smaller still, because it was currently occupied by a tall, angular woman in a sleek black dress.

Xiulan froze in the doorway.

Lee waved sheepishly. "Afternoon, Princess."

Xiulan's entire body tensed. She wanted to hurl her pipe right in Lee's face, or order Kou to bound forward and attack.

Instead, her arm fell limp at her side as she turned on her heel and left.

"*Wait! Xiulan, wait up, you brat!*" A hand placed itself firmly on Xiulan's shoulder and spun her back around so they were face-to-face. Xiulan's nostrils filled with an aroma: smoky, earthy, intoxicating. "I can explain—"

"Remove your hand from my person this instant, or Kou will remove it from yours," Xiulan snarled.

Lee's hand withdrew. "Sorry. I know this looks bad. But I need you to hear me out here. You're the cleverest woman I know. Think it through: If I was really looking to get away from you for good, why would I ever come back?"

"Because you missed the comforts of royal company," Xiulan jeered. "Because a new angle occurred to you, one you hadn't yet seen fit to work with regard to me. Because you remembered I owe you money. Those all seem like perfectly tempting reasons to break your vaunted 'one law' . . . not that law has ever amounted to much for you to begin with."

She had honored her promise never to lay a hand on Lee again, but the thief looked as if she'd been slapped anyway. She swallowed hard. "Look. I get it. It's not like I've got a clean record with you. But I've got a good reason for it, and I just need five minutes to explain myself. When I'm done, if you're still pissed, I'll leave for good and never look back. Thieves' honor."

Leave for good and never look back. How could such a thing be so appealing, but also the opposite of everything she'd ever wanted?

Xiulan nodded to Kou, dismissing him. As he disappeared, she swept past Lee into the room. "I forgave you, Lee," she said. "I forgave you because I believed we wouldn't have reason to revisit this conversation. And *certainly*," she added, raising her voice, "*not a mere day later.*"

"I know, I know," Lee said, shutting the door. "But I had to go. It was the only way I could get your badge back."

Xiulan had been ready to do a bit more shouting, but that brought her up short. "You . . . you what?"

Lee reached into the front of her dress, producing a shiny bronze pentagon that she tossed to Xiulan. Without adrenaline to steady them, her clumsy fingers failed to close around it, and it clattered to the floor.

Lee chuckled. "Guess we've still got some work to do on catch-ing."

Xiulan ignored the jibe. She knelt and plucked it off the floor. Her jaw dropped. It was no mere badge. The exact dents and scratches were present in its face. This was Xiulan's specific badge, which she'd been issued the day she'd been recruited into the Li-Quan.

"How did you get this?" she said quietly. Then, after a moment's thought: "And where were you hiding it?"

Lee's grin was fleeting and foxlike. "Tricks of the trade, Princess. As for the how . . ."

Fear gripped Xiulan's heart as she considered the worst-case sce-nario. "Please tell me you didn't simply steal it back," she said. "You do understand that this is an affecting keepsake, but on its own . . ."

"You really trying to explain how cops work to a thief?" Lee said. "Yeah, I get it. What you've got there is the real deal, with all the fun rights and privileges and all that, guaranteed. I . . ." For the first time, she looked furtive. "I went to see Ruomei."

The bottom of Xiulan's stomach fell away. "You *what*?"

"Yeah," Lee said. "I had to. It was the only way. That's why I didn't tell you I was doing it. You'd have tried to stop me."

Xiulan's entire mouth went dry. Lee had taken on Ruomei by herself. Unthinkable. Unimaginable.

And yet here she stood.

She didn't know how to feel. Never had Xiulan been brave enough to directly defy her sister. For her, it had been all about embodying the white rat: skittering between walls, gnawing on the wiring and pipes, so that one day Ruomei's house would all come crashing down. So there was a small undercurrent of bitterness that Lee had turned out to be the kind of woman born lucky enough to stand against Ruomei openly and walk away unscathed.

But that bitterness was swept away by the overwhelming burst of affection that she felt for her partner now.

"Do I want to know?" Xiulan said at last, her voice soft with disbelief.

Lee shook her head. "Best not. But you can know this much," she added with a gleam in her eye. "I fought her. And I won."

CHAPTER FORTY-FIVE

LEE

HOURS AGO

Lee's eyes snapped open, and she knew in her bones that she had two minutes before the fighting would start.

She blinked once to adjust to the darkness of the room, but she already felt all the way awake. You could never sleep too deeply, leading a life like hers, unless you wanted it to be a short one.

The door wasn't visible from the bed, so she sat up and listened carefully. As she strained to hear even the slightest creak that would have been out of place, she glanced back at Xiulan's sleeping form. Her breath caught as she took in the princess's tousled and tangled hair, and the sight of her petite body at ease. With her eyes closed, her face had an appealing symmetry, but that only made Lee appreciate all the more how much the asymmetry made her heart race.

She reached over and shook Xiulan. "Princess," she whispered. "On your feet. We've gotta move."

Xiulan's head lolled every which way, but she showed no signs of waking up. The brawl in the garden had taken everything out of her, apparently.

Normally, Lee would've tried again, but she felt that tightness in her gut again and she knew she was out of time. Like a knife from its sheath she slid out of the bed, snatching her dress off the floor and tossing it over herself as she crept to the door.

She felt another anxiousness inside, something separate from her own. Bootstrap. Lee wanted to call her, but she knew that doing it now would tip her hand, and surprise was the only advantage she currently had.

Gingerly, she eased the door open, and to her relief didn't come face-to-face with a glittering gun barrel. Instead, she saw an empty hallway. The sight seemed inviting enough, but Lee was convinced it wasn't about to be empty for long.

The only cover she had was the three elevators at the far end of the hall. She darted for them, a shadow within a shadow, and threw herself flat against the doors of the farthest elevator. She reached for the button to summon it, thinking she could set up an ambush from inside it whenever their company arrived.

But before she could hit the button, she heard a car arrive in the shaft just behind the closed doors at her back.

She bit her tongue to stop a curse from escaping and dove to the side, pressing herself against the middlemost elevator just as she heard the far one open with a soft *ding*. She heard two soldiers—who else would have such a measured step, even when sneaking?—step out, and a moment later the first one walked right by her. His coat was black and bore no rank or unit insignia, but the cut of it could only have come from a Shang clothier.

So, Lee thought as she took note of his black-masked face. This was Ruomei.

When the second soldier, a similarly masked woman, stepped into Lee's field of vision, the thief swung herself into view. With an outstretched arm, she hammered at the woman's throat. The woman clutched at her neck, gasping and rasping, but by then Lee had grabbed her by the shoulders and shoved her toward her startled comrade. The man bunched his shoulders and blocked with his forearms, so his partner bounced off him and into a wall. But Lee took advantage of his wide, rooted stance to close the distance and bring a shin straight up between his legs. Even though she wore no boots, he collapsed with satisfying suddenness.

You'd think someone would armor that bit, Lee thought.

"Knives, not guns, eh?" she said as her downed foes fumbled for the blades sheathed on their belts. "Ruomei wanted you to do this nice and quiet, then. She should've warned you that I'm a contrarian shit." She raised her voice. *"Bootstr—"*

From behind, a knife appeared at her throat. She felt the keenness of its blade as it pricked a tiny wound.

The knife's wielder spoke in accented Shang. "Stop this nonsense immediately. Our orders were to refrain from killing you if necessary, but you *are* an acceptable casualty, Lee Yeon-Ji. Call your slave or alert Her Majesty in any way, and I'll invoke those orders. Nod if you understand; don't speak."

Lee swallowed carefully, then nodded. This was hardly the first time her life had balanced on a literal knife's edge. This was a game where she knew how to play her cards. If she kept saying yes, eventually she'd get an opportunity to turn the tables.

And when that time came, every Tomodanese son-of-a-bitch here—she hadn't missed that word *slave*—would be grateful they'd worn a mask tonight.

The soldier seemed to accept her nod. "Blind her," he said.

The bag swallowed her head, turning her world inky and black. And as she felt him prod her toward the elevator, she spared one last thought for her Lady of Moonlight, tangled in the sheets as the mattress next to her grew cold.

I'll come back to you, she promised as she heard the elevator doors shut.

By her estimation, she spent about an hour with the bag on her head. She felt herself being led down hallways, down stairs, down other hallways, before she was eventually stuffed into the backseat of a car. Honestly, it wouldn't have been that bad. They were brusque but not terribly rough, which meant she could at least rest easy knowing her life was safe.

The real problem was that the bag smelled like someone had washed it with sour goat's milk instead of water.

That, she promised, would be the first thing she said when they yanked the bag off her head. Something quick and pithy that would immediately put her kidnappers on the defensive. There was no point in making them feel bad about kidnapping her, but she could make them feel stupid for not knowing how to launder a bag.

The car glided to a halt, and she was herded into the chilly morning. The cicadas had just begun to sing, as had the birds, but the sound echoed strangely in her ears. Then she felt the texture of the ground beneath her feet. It was concrete. So she was still in the city. And based on the kinds of birds she was hearing, probably somewhere near the Hagane waterfront. The question was: Why?

When the bag finally came off, she saw she'd been seated in a chair in that old classic, an empty warehouse. But she was surprised to see that her hands were free. She was more surprised still to see that instead of some kind of torture device or something, there was a table set in the Jeongsonese style: with a hot metal grill in the center, bowls of raw meat and vegetables carefully arranged around it in a circle, and smaller bowls with rice and soup at each place setting.

Sitting on the other side of that table, smoking a long, thin cigarette, was a plump, beautiful woman who had all of Xiulan's beauty and none of her warmth. This, Lee knew, had to be Shang Ruomei. But the man at her side was far more surprising: a short, handsome Tomodanese man with close-cropped hair and slanted eyebrows. They'd never met, but Lee had seen him from afar. He was easy to recognize as Kurihara Kosuke.

Pieces slotted into place, and Lee gave a slow nod. "Right," she said without preamble. "You and your Cicadas give the princess here some deniability. Anyone catches you trying to break into the Twenty-Eighth Princess's rooms, it'll be easy to pin it on you being a well-known lunatic."

Kurihara bristled. "I'm a warrior fighting for the survival of his people," he said. "I would've thought I'd have the sympathy of a daughter of Jeongson, at least."

Lee snorted. "You're not gonna get far with me, comparing our history with whatever bill Heaven's about to make you people settle."

Her dismissal seemed to only incense him further, but when he opened his mouth to retort, Ruomei raised a hand to silence him.

"We're not here for one of your fiery speeches, Lord Kurihara," the Second Princess said in flawless Tomodanese. "We're here for breakfast. A breakfast for two."

For a moment, Kurihara's outrage persisted. But then Lee saw the man visibly swallow his pride, before bowing deeply and respectfully from the waist. "Your Majesty," he said with an admirable lack of venom in his voice, then turned to leave.

"Hang on," Lee called after him, and he stopped. "You say you fight for your people, but you're doing Shang's dirty work. How's that square away, exactly?"

Slowly, Kurihara turned around and drew himself up proudly. "Once, Tomoda was the steel that suspended the weight of the world. In my pride, I fought to recapture those days. Now I understand there's a more important fight to be had . . . one that can't be won without allies." He was talking to her, but for the first time he met her eyes, and Lee was struck by how resolute he looked. "I'll crawl through whatever mud I have to if it means the Tomodanese people remain clean."

Ruomei's cigarette glowed orange as she inhaled. "Comparing an ally to a mud pit doesn't say much for your diplomatic acumen, Lord Kurihara . . ." She exhaled a silver-blue cloud. ". . . but I appreciate the sentiment. Now, I believe you were going . . . ?"

"Not far, Your Majesty." He gave Lee a small nod. "Thief."

The bastard almost made it sound like a compliment.

Once he'd gone, the half smile slid from Ruomei's face like rain off a window. "Your entanglement with my sister is an embarrassment to my family. I know you're for sale, Lee Yeon-Ji. What price will buy your disappearance?"

Though she completely believed Ruomei was capable of offering up a blank check, Lee folded her arms over her chest and said nothing.

Ruomei studied her a long moment, then nodded. "Good. You're not susceptible to the obvious." She nodded to a nearby servant. "Now, I don't have time for further displays of defiance, so let's get down to the real business."

The servant took up a pair of tongs and began laying thin slices of meat on the griddle, where they sizzled and curled. Their smoke

mingled with the thin tendrils of it emanating from Ruomei's cigarette. When Ruomei caught Lee eyeing it, she said: "I went to great
expense to have this food imported and properly prepared, so you're
going to eat it, Lee Yeon-Ji."

Lee blinked. Then she said: "If your spread's anything like your
bag, I won't be impressed."

Ruomei rolled her eyes and took another drag.

Disappointed she hadn't gotten more of a reaction, Lee turned her
attention to the spread in question. She had to admit, it was pretty
impressive. The kimchi smelled right. The beef looked like it'd been
properly marinated. Even the chopsticks were pointy and metal, in
contrast with the long, blunt bamboo ones typical of Shang dining.
The familiar smells twisted her tired stomach into knots, and she
reached for her soup spoon. "Bit early in the morning for a full grill-
up."

"I've yet to encounter a bad time of day for bulgogi."

Lee quirked an eyebrow. "How long've you been eating Jeongsonese food, Princess?"

"Long enough," said Ruomei, resting her cigarette in an ashtray
and sampling some of her soup with a spoon. Lee followed suit. The
spicy, salty warmth of the broth was almost enough to make her
forget the predicament she was in.

Almost.

"I figure you've got to like it quite a bit, to have it brought all the
way to Hagane just so you can keep on eating it."

Ruomei shrugged, then nodded to her servant gratefully as he
peeled strips of pork belly away from the grill and laid them atop a
bed of rice on Ruomei's plate. As the servant moved to tend to Lee's
plate, Lee watched the princess casually roll the rice and pork into a
lettuce leaf with some kimchi and eat it.

Lee raised an eyebrow. "You eat like a proper daughter of Jeongson."

Ruomei frowned. "You've now found three ways to state what
are essentially the same single fact," she said impatiently. "I'd
thought you were supposed to be astute, Lee Yeon-Ji. Yes, I enjoy
Jeongsonese food. You'd be surprised to learn that I have a great appreciation for the rest of Jeongsonese culture, too."

Lee's spoon clattered back to the table. Smoothly, mid-sentence, Ruomei had just switched from Shang to Jeongsonese. Her accent was thick, but her grammar and tone were impeccable.

Even Xiulan couldn't speak Jeongsonese.

"What is this?" Lee said, switching to Jeongsonese herself. Being able to speak it felt like stretching her legs after a long, cramped car ride.

Ruomei reached beneath the table and produced a familiar bronze badge. She slid it across, so it was within Lee's reach, then let it lie there. Lee stared at it.

"His Most August Personage revoked my sister's powers of office this morning. I'm giving them back to her, but I don't want her to know that they were given. I want it to come from you."

Lee blinked, then picked up the badge. It wasn't some cheap tin copy, nor a cleverly disguised bomb. She placed it back down, then met the Second Princess's eyes. "Why?"

"Because you love her," Ruomei said simply. "That tells me that, as well as anyone can, you know my sister's heart. Would you say that's true?"

Lee nodded.

"Then tell me honestly—"

"You're asking a thief to be honest?"

"I'm asking the woman of my sister's heart," Ruomei said impatiently. "Do you believe Xiulan would be a good Crane Empress?"

Lee hesitated, but only for a moment.

Then she said, "Today? No. Probably not tomorrow, either. But someday, Xiulan's going to be the kind of woman Shang's always needed to sit the throne." And to her own surprise, she added: "I'll make sure of it myself."

She'd thought it was a pretty impressive thing to say, but Ruomei just shrugged. "That's nice, but the world doesn't have time to wait for her to find herself." She folded up another sangchu-ssam. "I want to make something clear: To my dear meimei, the world will always be a story, and she will always be its hero. Did she paint her crusade to you as a noble endeavor, meant to deny an unworthy, villainous heir the Snow-Feather Throne?"

Lee rolled up a sangchu-ssam of her own and took a big bite to give herself time to answer. "The way she said it, you're a blood-thirsty nationalist who'd drag the whole world right back into a war if you thought Shang stood a chance of coming out on top."

Ruomei rolled her eyes, then leaned back so she could be served some fresh bulgogi. "She sees what she wants to see. You saw our father in action last night. Do you think he would cede his throne to any other kind of person?"

Lee grinned. "Look at you, Your Majesty," she said. "Playing a long game."

"Yes, Lee Yeon-Ji. In the face of an obstacle between myself and what I want, I've opted to advance myself by playing the roles I need to play. I'm sure an upstanding citizen such as yourself is scandalized."

Lee just grunted, taking a bite of her bulgogi next. She wanted to say something snide about its quality or authenticity, but there was no getting around it: The stuff was damn good. "So you give your sister her badge back. How's that line up with being Daddy's girl?"

"I'll tell my father that Xiulan is far too clever to be left unoccupied and unsupervised, and that keeping her old job will be a good way to neutralize any threat she'd pose. And by making her think she's doing it as a way to defy me, that means she'll actually do it, instead of hurling it back in my face." She seemed almost bored as she tapped away some ash from the end of her cigarette. "It's a useful thing when my lies happen to be true."

Lee had let her guard down once before, and had promised herself not to do it again. So she continued to dine on exquisite Jeongsonese food with a calm, even light demeanor, while on the inside she screamed because the dogs take her, Ruomei had her partner's number down.

"What if she uses her badge against you?" Lee said eventually. "Even if she's not going to be the heir, she's still got decent juice as an agent of the Li-Quan."

"If Xiulan's really devoted to maintaining order in our country, then she can be against me all she wants," Ruomei said. "If she roots out some actual wrongdoing, then she'll be doing Shang a favor. And if she doesn't . . . well." She smirked. "She's been against me her whole life, and she hasn't won yet."

. . .

It hurt her to lie to Xiulan again. That was an honor only the princess could claim: that in Lee's book, she alone deserved the truth, triple-distilled of all its murk.

But Ruomei had poured her a glass of that same truth. Her princess was a stubborn one. Maybe someday, she'd be able to hear the truth Lee was hiding from her now. But forgiveness was a journey, not a choice. When it came to Lee, Xiulan's journey had been quick. With Ruomei, it would be a long walk . . . if she ever decided to take the first step at all.

"You're certain there are no details you wish to disclose?" Xiulan said carefully.

Lee opted to play on the side of enigmatic. "There's a reason I smell like a bonfire," she said quietly. "I was sending a message, and your big sis got the point." Eager to take control of the moment again, she pushed forward. "There's a catch, though." A mischievous quality crept into her face, one she didn't have to fake. "I was able to get your badge back. But I wasn't able to restore you just yet."

Xiulan's face fell. "But you just said—"

"You see," Lee went on, "at this moment, there's only one active agent of the Li-Quan in this room. Recently recruited, so she's a bit behind on her paperwork, but still one with all the privileges that come with being a cop. Including," she added with a sly smirk, "the power to deputize."

Comprehension dawned in Xiulan's eye. "Inspector Lee . . ."

"Should you kneel?" Lee said. "I feel like I should make you kneel . . ."

She'd only been joking, but to her surprise, Xiulan very deliberately sank to one knee. "What else would you like me to do . . ." She reached for the bottom hem of Lee's dress and began to slide it up her bare leg. ". . . Inspector?"

A cool, electric thrill spread through Lee's body when she heard Xiulan call her that word, in that tone, with that hungry look on her face. She had been on wanted posters before, but this was the first time in a long time she felt truly desired.

"I never thought I'd like being on the right side of the law this much," Lee said.

Xiulan planted a kiss on her inner thigh, just above her knee.

Another shiver ran through Lee. She backed herself toward the bed and sat down on the edge of the mattress. She plucked Xiulan's hat off her head and casually tossed it onto the corner of a nearby chair. She reached down with a finger and angled Xiulan's chin up, so her bang fell away. And then with a smile, she leaned in close and whispered, "What you're doing right now isn't in accordance with official Li-Quan *hey!*"

Xiulan shoved her back onto the bed where she collapsed, laughing. She looked up to see her partner frantically shedding one layer of white after another, until her last stitch of underclothes came away, leaving her bare before Lee at last.

"I could've helped you with that," Lee said. "All those buttons . . ."

Xiulan crawled up her body, undoing. "Be quiet, Lee," she said, then kissed her.

She shed her black dress, letting Xiulan's fingers and tongue roam her bare skin. As she lay back and sighed up to the ceiling, she found words crystallizing in her head, growing more solid and heavy and real with each passing moment:

I love you, Princess.

She opened her mouth to finally give those words voice, but they were lost in a moan as Xiulan did something with her fingers that made Lee's eyes go half-mast.

Her toes curled.

Her breaths grew short and sharp.

Her back arched off the mattress.

And in the throes of love, Lee Yeon-Ji thought: *I'll tell her later.*

CHAPTER FORTY-SIX

TALA

By the end of the second day, her arm was strong enough to use, if not particularly well. The regrown muscles were significantly weaker than they had been, so that even the effort of bringing a cup to her lips made them tremble and splash her. The Dahali healers told her she likely wouldn't be able to shoot straight with that hand again, but as far as Tala was concerned, they'd gotten it wrong. She'd go to her grave an old woman who could shoot straight. But the desire to shoot at all had been carved out of her.

It wasn't just shooting. Food, which she'd delighted in, tasted sour and sickly on her tongue, its flavors lingering seconds too long after each bite. The general had sent her a carafe of Sanbu's finest coffee, but she'd only had half of one cup before the bitterness had made her sick to her empty stomach. She'd thought that at least sleep could be a refuge from everything else, but while she had no trouble falling asleep, deriving any rest from it was a different matter entirely.

She cried a lot. That was the only thing that seemed to help at all, but even that wasn't enough.

The healers came every two hours to lay hands on her wounds and undo more of the damage. She'd wanted to just grit her teeth and get it all over with in a single sitting, but she'd been assured that tough as she was, even her system wouldn't be able to withstand that kind of strain. She'd pressed for it nonetheless, only relenting when General Erega had specifically ordered her to take her rest. Her military career was over, but she would always be a soldier. When the general ordered, she obeyed.

Still, she tried not to stay confined to her bed. She'd get up and exercise as best she could. She'd walk in circles around the room, trying to remember the streets of Lisan City and pretending she was there instead. She'd open her window and watch Beaky take long flights over the palace, trying and failing to enjoy the feel of the summer breeze on her skin and the song of cicadas in her ears.

But despite all that, she couldn't bring herself to cross the threshold and leave the room, no matter how badly she wanted to. Letting Beaky out was one thing, but if she stepped out into the world herself, it would mean her life was no longer on pause. It would mean she would have to go on without Mang, and she just wasn't ready to face that yet.

Two days after the fact, her feelings still waged as furious a war on one another as she'd ever waged on the Tomodanese. Some part of her desperately tried to rationalize it: to remind her that what she and Mang had was untenable in the long run. That the release from pain had been a mercy. That his very existence had been an imbalance the man in the purple coat had arisen to correct, in a roundabout way. That someday, she might be able to live the sort of normal life that always would've been impossible as long as she was carrying him in the back of her head. But on the other side of things, there was the simple fact that her brother was gone, her brother whom she'd loved with everything and who had loved her back, and that alone outweighed everything else.

More than anything, she found herself regretting how little time she'd made for him. He'd always been there, and she'd always been grateful to have him so close at hand. But he'd always been there, which meant it was so easy to fall into the trap of thinking he always would be.

It'd never been a good time, of course. Military life didn't lend itself to much privacy during peacetime. During war, all bets were

off. But she thought of the times when she had managed to steal a
minute to herself, and hadn't summoned him. Should she have risked
it, just to see him? If they'd been caught, would it have been worth
whatever scrutiny or confinement came next? Right now, she wanted
to say yes, if only because it would've meant more time with him,
but how clearly was she really thinking?

The amount of things she knew was now vastly outweighed by
the amount of things she didn't. But she now feared the certainty
she'd once craved. If she went out into the world, she was terrified
that the facts she'd learn there would all point to a single conclusion:
that this horrible dark feeling eating her alive from the inside out
was nothing more than what she'd earned, and that it would gnaw
and gnaw at her until there was nothing left.

She was standing at the window, letting some air in and Beaky
out, when the door behind her slid open. She glanced at the clock. It
was an off-hour, which meant this had to be one of the palace staff,
trying to feed her. Without turning around, Tala waved the attendant off. "I'm not hungry today."

There was no verbal response, nor the sound of shuffling feet or a
sliding door. There was, however, the sharp, familiar aroma of fresh
adobo on the air. Tala whirled around. "I don't care what orders
you've been given," she snapped. "I'm still a lieutenant, so unless
you're a colonel in a waiter's jacket, I—"

Jimuro stood there, clad in a simple blue kimono with a mountain
pattern woven into its fabric. He had a book and a long, narrow
copper box tucked beneath his arm. Just behind him, a servant
wheeled in a steel cart with two bowls, a pot of rice, and a pot of
adobo, bubbling and rich brown. But when she caught sight of Tala's
face, she froze in her tracks and averted her eyes.

Jimuro was a good deal more composed. "Lieutenant," he said
smoothly. Shades take her, he even sounded kingly. "It's good to see
you on your feet."

Tala's discipline took over. She bowed deeply. "Thank you, Your
Brilliance."

Jimuro coughed. ". . . May I come in?"

"Of course, Your Brilliance," Tala said, bowing again. It felt
strange to be so stiff with him, but she felt like she had to keep a

handle on things at least while there was someone else with them. "It's your room."

Jimuro chuckled. "Erega said that, too." He nodded to his servant. "Thank you, Anji. You can just leave that here." The woman squeaked out a grateful reply, then hurried from the room.

Jimuro's gaze lingered on the newly shut door. "I still haven't gotten used to how they treat me now," he said. "Some of them have known me since I was in diapers, but the way they've looked at me since I took up the throne . . ." He shook his head. "I didn't come here to talk about me. Sorry. And I'm sorry for not coming sooner. I had . . . matters of state to attend to."

Tala nodded. "Of course, Your Brilliance." She'd heard the opposite: that he'd been camped outside her room for two days now, save for the meals he was required to take with the other heads of state.

Right, she thought. *A head of state is talking to me.* But he didn't feel as if he were on some elevated plane above her, the way General Erega did. He was just . . . Jimuro.

A stiff silence fell between them.

". . . So, how are you?" Jimuro said eventually.

Tala snapped back into the moment. "Right," she said. "I mean, all right. I mean . . ." She nodded down to her bandaged, emaciated arm dangling from her shoulder. "I'm on the mend, Your Brill—Jimuro."

He smiled softly when she dispensed with the honorifics. "I'm glad to hear it. And I trust your accommodations have been suitable?"

She glanced around at her low-slung furniture. At her futon, lying flat on the planks. No matter how much she puzzled it out, she still didn't really understand Tomoda's fascination with its own floors. But that wasn't something a gracious guest said, so instead she merely bowed and said again: "Of course."

"Good," said Jimuro. "Good, good, good."

Another stiff silence fell over them, like rust on iron.

Gamely, she supposed it was her turn to try breaking it. "How have you—?"

"I'm sorry," Jimuro said.

She blinked. "What?"

"I know I just said that, but it bears repeating: I'm sorry," Jimuro said again. "For not visiting sooner, for leaving you behind in Shinku, for not being able to save—" He stopped himself and hung his head. "I've done a lot of terrible things to you, Tala, and I want to spend the rest of my life making them up to you."

She was prepared to laugh him off: to tell him that he was worrying over nothing, that this was nothing she couldn't handle, that it would just take time for her soul to heal up, same as her body.

Then she realized that sometime before he'd stopped talking, she'd begun to cry again.

Jimuro's eyes widened, so they looked even bigger than his glasses. "Oh no," he said, carefully setting his things down next to the adobo and crossing to her. He was blinking fast, and she saw tears forming on his long lashes. Shades take her, she'd grown contagious.

She made no effort to wipe her tears away. "It's not just you," she said. "I've been holding on to him for so long. He was the only thing keeping me together. Do you know what that's even like, to lose that?"

But even as the question left her lips, she knew the answer.

"I do," he said quietly.

"I'm sorry," Tala said. "I didn't think that through."

Jimuro shook his head. "For your entire life, my family was the enemy. That's not lost on me, Tala. To me, my mother was everything I wanted to be someday, and she was everything you hated and feared . . . not without good reason, I might add. We took everything from you."

He gave her a furtive look. She took it in. Saw the way his hands were awkwardly frozen at his sides, half risen.

She nodded, and with visible relief he put a hand on her good shoulder.

"I don't know what it's like to carry around that kind of hurt as long as you have," Jimuro said quietly, "or for it to lodge itself so deeply in your soul. And I don't believe I quite know how to move on from it, not yet. But I do know how to live with it. And . . ." He hesitated, then said: "I've found that the ones you lose have a way of coming back to you." He pointed his finger at the ceiling. "*Fumiko.*"

In a flash of emerald light, his cicada-shade appeared, hanging upside down from a wooden beam.

Tala stared in wonder at the creature. A son of Tomoda, shade-pacting. Even a week ago, the thought would have been impossible to consider.

Said the metalpacting Sanbuna, she thought.

"She's magnificent, isn't she?" Jimuro said. "Do you know what she asked of me, when we made our pact?" He thought a moment. "Right, dumb question. What I meant was, would you like to know?"

"Your Brilliance, you don't have to—"

"She asked me to survive, Tala." He smiled fondly up at Fumiko. "My second guardian in green."

Tala sat with this for a long moment. "Fumiko saved my life, too," she said eventually.

Jimuro shrugged. "Your brother saved mine, several times over. It was the least my sister could do in return." He waved his hand at her. "She's not literally my sister, of course, but when the time came to seal the pact, it was the only name that made sense."

Tala remembered the newsreels about the late Iron Princess. "She was killed trying to rescue you from us, wasn't she?" When he nodded, she went on: "You named your shade after her, and used her to save a Sanbuna?"

Jimuro nodded. "I couldn't hate your people forever. I still have to share the world with you, after all. And you, specifically, I could never hate."

A rustle of feathers heralded the return of Beaky. When he caught sight of Jimuro, he cawed in recognition. But when he saw Fumiko crawling along the ceiling, his chest feathers puffed out.

"Quit being dramatic," Tala muttered. "You saw her in the garden the other night."

He clacked his beak, but cocked his head at the cicada-shade nonetheless.

"In the garden," Tala said, remembering suddenly. "That thing you said to me—"

"'You can do anything if you love someone enough,'" Jimuro said with a small, sad smile. "I understand if you don't return the feeling. I'm the enemy, and I've done little to change your stance on that topic."

Tala balked. "You can't be serious, Your Brilliance," she said. "You stopped being the enemy once the war ended. I'm the one who didn't stop fighting. That man . . . Mayon . . . he was right about me." The words looped between her ears like a catchy song: *I knew you were vicious for what you'd done to me . . . I had no idea how vicious you'd become since.* She looked down at her hands: one still, one shaking. "I killed that woman. Harada. Murdered her."

"She tried to murder *you*," Jimuro said gently. "And I might remind you, everything that came after I abandoned you rests on my shoulders: Your injuries. Dimangan's abduction. His . . ." He trailed off.

Tala shook her head. "The more I think about it, the more tangled it gets."

"It is," Jimuro said. "Which is why I'd like to propose a radical solution: I forgive you."

She blinked. "What?"

"For the crime of killing Harada Hanae," he said. "Lala, I for—"

Her head snapped to him. "What?" she said. "What did you just say?"

He looked at her furtively. "'Tala, I forgive you'? Did I cause some offense?"

She blinked again. She could've sworn she'd heard . . .

She looked to Beaky for confirmation. The crow-shade clacked his beak. Jimuro had been telling the truth.

"Sorry," Tala said after a moment. "I just . . . something about the way you said it, I thought I heard his voice again."

He smiled, small and understanding. On any other face Tala would've mistaken it for pity, but him she understood as well as if he were her own shade. "Then I will forgive you that, as well. Which," he added quickly, "brings me to the reason why I came."

He let his hand slip from her, and she felt a tiny pang of disappointment as he went back to fetch his book and box. "The truth is, Tala, I didn't have matters of state to attend to. Or that is, I did, but I neglected them in favor of—"

"I know."

"You do?" he said, surprised.

She rolled her eyes. "Paper walls aren't good for anything, but especially not privacy."

"The one thing my ancestors never accounted for . . ." Jimuro said, casting an eye at the walls in question.

Up above, Fumiko clicked her forelegs against each other. It was hard to interpret the expression and body language of an insect, even a giant one, but Tala took it to be a sign of agreement. Her thoughts were confirmed when Jimuro shot a look up at her, smirked, and said, "Oh, be quiet." He looked around, as if seeing the room for the first time. "It feels like our conversation is pulling me in many directions at once. What was I . . . ?"

"Why you came," Tala said. Her tears had almost completely stopped now. She even found the corners of her mouth twitching upward, if only a little.

Recognition flitted across the Steel Lord's face. "Right!" he said, suddenly remembering the things on the cart. He retrieved them, then knelt on the floor and bid her to do the same. Her discomfort with kneeling aside, she obliged as he opened the book to reveal a detailed sketch of the façade of the Palace of Steel. "In times of peace, this was my greatest passion and pursuit. I'd sit in the garden, drawing flowers and trees and insects for hours . . . until Fumiko and her friends found me, anyway."

Tala blinked at the drawing. "It's . . . very good," she said, not sure where this was going.

"I know it is," Jimuro said with a proud huffiness she couldn't help laughing at. "But it wasn't just flowers and buildings, you know." He flipped the page to reveal a drawing of a bright-eyed dog, her tongue lolling happily out of her wide-open mouth. Eyeing the familiar patterning, Tala did a double take.

"That Jeongsonese woman . . . ?" Tala began, but Jimuro waved her off.

"It's a long story that's neither here nor there. But yes." He flipped the page again, revealing a familiar face. The shape of it and the hairstyle told Tala it was Steel Lord Yoshiko. But this was not the snarling, ugly woman on the propaganda posters, or the crone played by grotesque actresses in the movies screened to raise troop morale. His brush had captured her mid-laugh, her face lit up by her smile, eyes closed and crinkled around their corners.

Tala's breath caught at the sight of her. She didn't look like Steel Lord Yoshiko, the butcher-queen of Tomoda. She looked like somebody's mother.

Jimuro caught sight of her reaction, pleased. He flipped the page again to reveal a new face: a man's. He was plumper than Jimuro, but there was something familiar in the knowing shine Jimuro had managed to bring to his eyes. This had to be his late father, Steel Consort Soujiro.

And then he flipped the page one more time to reveal a third portrait: just a simple head-on drawing of a young woman with a vibrancy that sprang off the page. Though she was only visible from the neck up, Jimuro had managed to create the impression that she was one who moved through her life springy and loose.

"This was my sister, Fumiko," he said quietly. "At night, while I would draw, she would read from her favorite books and have me illustrate scenes for her. She was always so picky; she'd have me redraw a scene two or three times, until it looked precisely the way it did in her head. I tried to teach her how to draw so she could do it herself, but she always told me since I was going to be the Steel Lord someday, it was my duty to serve my subjects. So . . . I would draw."

Vaguely, Tala was aware of her tears regaining their strength. She found herself thrown back to memories of her own: Of herself and Mang at the market, him letting her carry more mangoes than she could handle because he trusted her to do it anyway. Of him stroking her hair and telling her things would be okay after their mother lost her temper and yelled again.

Of him the way he'd been, not the way she'd made him.

"It took me a very long time, but eventually I forgave Sanbu for taking her from me," Jimuro said. "Now I want the chance to earn forgiveness from you." He turned the page again . . . to reveal a blank one.

And at last, Tala understood what he meant to do.

"What do you need?" she said, her heart swelling in her chest.

"Just . . . tell me about him. Every little detail you can think of, no matter how insignificant. Let me understand what you've lost, so I can bring him back . . . in one way or another."

He smoothed the page out, then rose and began ladling rice and adobo into a bowl. "And this won't be the last, either, Lieutenant. Each day, as long as you choose to stay beneath my roof, I'll come find you. And each day, you'll tell me more about Dimangan, and I'll draw what you tell me." His eyes shone even brighter than the glasses he wore. "I would give the world to you, if I thought it would do some small thing to ease your pain. But all I can offer you is this pact, so if you want it . . ." He held the bowl of adobo out to her. ". . . it's yours."

Slowly, stunned, Tala took the adobo. For a long moment, she stared into its glossy brown depths, counting the sauce-glazed mushroom caps she saw there. The familiar scent wafted up to her face, and for the first time in days she found she wanted to eat.

At long last, she set it down and looked at him again. "What if I already forgive you?"

His concern broke into a wobbly smile. He blinked three times very fast, then said, "It's unbecoming of a Steel Lord to cry, you know." He thought a moment. "Again."

She laughed, and he laughed, too, as if the sound were a fire that had leapt from one house to the next. Their voices mingled, and though the room was large and airy, they filled it effortlessly. And as they laughed, they fell into each other, her head pressed against his chest and his arms wrapped around her back. She closed her eyes, feeling the strength of his grip and the fluttering of his heart, and she laughed until she found herself at the edge of tears again.

Long after their laughter subsided, they held each other, enveloped in a warm, soft silence.

But eventually, Jimuro stepped back and tapped his long metal box. It sprang open to reveal a brush and a pot of black ink.

Tala frowned thoughtfully. "Jimuro . . . what you said in the garden . . ."

Jimuro didn't look up from the prep work he was doing, and

when he spoke it was with a passable attempt at nonchalance. "It's
as I said: I understand if you don't return the feeling. More than
understand, really. It's—"

"No, it's not that," Tala said, and Jimuro looked up, face shimmering with hope. "It's just . . . with everything else happening right
now, I don't know if I have room for you . . . yet."

To her surprise, his hope didn't dim even the slightest degree.
"You have all the time in the world now to make room, or not," he
said simply. "The war's over, isn't it?"

She nodded only once, but once was enough.

She closed her eyes for a moment, to gather all her memories.
Shades take her, she had so many. But when her eyes opened again,
her recall was clear, and it came to her tongue easily and freely.

"Do you remember visiting Lisan City when you were a boy,
Jimuro?" She hadn't meant to start with this memory, but now that
she'd given it voice it felt right.

Jimuro blinked in surprise. "Yes," he said. "A state visit, to show
me the subjects I would serve one day. Jungle-runners actually attacked us while we were touring the city."

"I know," Tala said quietly. "I was there."

He started. "You were?"

"Yes," she said. "With Mang."

He dipped his brush into the ink, then sat straight-backed and
ready. "Why don't you tell me about it?"

She smiled softly. She knew just where to begin.

"Dimangan would hear his name," Tala said, "and come when he
was called."

And as she told Dimangan's story, Jimuro's brush began to flow
across the page.

ACKNOWLEDGMENTS

My agent is DongWon Song. Thank you, my friend, for making room: for this book on your shelf and for me on your team. My editor is Tricia Narwani. Thank you, my friend, for your generosity: in your notes, and in your supply of cat pics. And thank you, my friends, for reading this book and getting it.

My publisher is Del Rey. Thank you, fine folks who work there, for bringing this book out of my hard drive and into readers' hands.

My alpha readers are Calder CaDavid and Leslie Wishnevski. Thank you both for being this book's first and fiercest champions, and for knowing what I want to say even when I don't.

My beta readers are Katherine Locke, Nilah Magruder, Ashley Poston, Tess Sharpe, and Andrea Zevallos. Thank you for helping me dig down and level up.

My support network is Holly Aitchison, Matt Brauer, Conor Colasurdo, Grace Fong, JJ Jones, Sarah Kuhn, CB Lee, Dustin Martin, Connor McCrate, Cara McGee, Alan Mills, Omar Najam, Trung Le Nguyen, Annette Nowacki, Morgan Perry, Dan Reed, Mia Resella, Kristy Staky, Christina Strain, Sam Sykes, Katie Tolle, Matt Willems, Alyssa Wong, and Cassie Zwart. Thank you all for your friendship, and for the times you didn't even know how much you were helping me with this book.

My parents are Cecilia and Kurt, but to me they're Mom and Dad. Thank you both for getting me hooked on this whole book thing early. My brother is Timm. Thank you for generously letting me be the second-coolest brother.

My cat is Wrigley, and my stepcat is Mira. Thank you both for reminding me of what really matters in life, by way of sitting on my keyboard while I tried to write this book.

My hero is the programming executive at Cartoon Network who many years ago decided to slate anime on its Toonami block. Thank you for genuinely changing my life.

My previous book was about an Asian-American recession victim millennial from Chicago who finds meaning in food service. I tell you all this so you can take my full meaning when I say that *Steel Crow Saga* is the most personal, autobiographical thing I've ever written.

So thank you, my dear readers, for letting me show you who I am.

PAUL KRUEGER
stranded overnight in a North
Carolina baggage claim
October 15, 2018

PAUL KRUEGER is a Filipino-American author. His first novel was the urban fantasy *Last Call at the Nightshade Lounge*. A lapsed Chicagoan, he may now be found literally herding cats in Los Angeles.

Twitter: @NotLikeFreddy